SPARK

PAT DAILY

HOUSTON, TX

This book is recommended for mature audiences (over 18 years old).

Cover Design: Verstandt
Copyediting: Ashley Conner
Development Editing: Steph Matthiesen
Formatting: Manon Lavoie

ISBN: 978-1-944428-63-1 (Print)
978-1-944428-64-8 (e-book)

Dedication

This book is dedicated to Ethan, Laine, and any future siblings they may have. I hope that you grow to love reading as much as I do.

And to their mothers and fathers, cousins, aunts, and uncles.

Most of all, to my beloved wife, Ardith, who saved my life and soul.

ACKNOWLEDGEMENTS

Whatever success this book may have is directly attributable to those who were willing to give me honest feedback on earlier versions—even when it bordered on caustic. You gave hours of your lives to reading drafts and rewrites. Thank you!

Ardith, Shannon, and Christy

Cindy

Mack and Fern

Hecker (I still have one of his critiques on my board.)

Alex, author of *Pighearted*, and leader of my writing group.

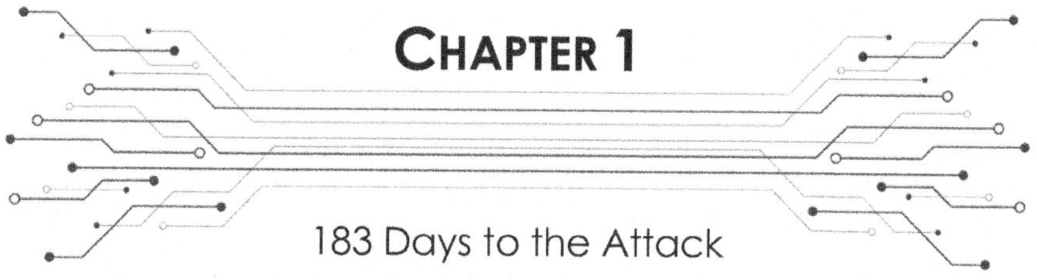

Chapter 1

183 Days to the Attack

Run first. You can figure out that stuff about "Are you running toward something or away from something" later. If you wait, you may not be able to run at all.
—Name withheld, #fleeingfostercare

They came for him at night, in his sleep. They always did.

The dream started happy. Will played catch with his dad in the front yard of the old house. A beautiful spring day in Houston. Then, without transition, it became dark, and he was in the house. He stumbled over layers of trash. His foot slipped on an old pizza box and he fell. He tried to recoil from the familiar fetid smell of spoiled food and cat urine. He couldn't move.

"Mom? Mom!" he called.

No answer but for the noise coming from the walls—a skittering scratching sound that stopped and started but always drew closer.

His arms and legs didn't work, but he managed to roll over onto his stomach and began to inch worm-like toward the kitchen. He *had* to make it to the kitchen. A million miles of worming through newspapers that had once been neatly stacked, but toppled, cascading old headlines across the room. Milk cartons meant for recycling that never made it out the door, their caps coming off, and the last few drops slowly congealing and adding to the general stench of the house. If he could just make it to the kitchen, he could get a butcher knife to protect himself.

He butted aside a Clean Cuisine tray with his head. Almost there! He needed to stand to reach the knife drawer.

Will forced himself upright in his dream but was unable to find the drawer as the counter transformed into a featureless slab stretching endlessly before him.

In the darkness, the eyes appeared, red and glowing. First one set. Then dozens.

He whipped his head around.

"Mom!"

– 1 1 0 1 0 0 1 0 –

Will Kwan bolted upright in bed. His heart pounded in his chest, and he was coated in sweat.

Where am I? He looked around and took a few deep breaths. *Just the foster place.*

Will snaked his arm between the mattress and springs, groping for the knife he'd stashed there. *Crud. I thought this time might be different. I slept okay a few nights. Two nights without the nightmares. Dang it!*

He rubbed his eyes with his palm and clutched the knife in his other hand. At this point, he might as well go pee.

Will pulled on his jeans. *Too soon to be walking around the foster house in my boxers.*

He'd been there a couple months.

"This house is safe. I'm safe," he whispered the mantra, fervently wanting to believe it.

Still, the nightmare gnawed away at that certainty, and he picked up the knife again as he stepped into the darkened hallway.

"Will, are you okay?"

He turned and saw his foster mom coming down the hall in her faded pink house robe.

"I heard…" Her hand flew to her mouth. "What are…" She began backing away, staring wide-eyed at the nine-inch butcher knife in his hand.

"No, it's okay. It's not what it seems—"

"Burt! Burt!" she screamed for her husband.

Will turned and bolted down the hall, not even stopping to pick up his shoes. He spun the deadbolt on the front door and was sprinting down the sidewalk as lights came on and raised voices trailed after him. A hundred yards later, he was at the entrance to the cul-de-sac. He stopped. What now? Where was he going?

He turned left, toward the bayou. *I must look like a criminal, running down the street in the middle of the night with this big-ass knife.*

A weapon he had picked up for protection was now a liability.

Don't think I'm going to be sleeping anymore tonight.

He ducked into a yard and buried the knife in the mulch of an azalea bed. As he brushed the slivers of bark from his hands, he heard the first sirens.

I need to keep moving.

He'd stick out on the deserted suburban streets.

Don't run. You'll look suspicious.

Will settled into a brisk walk and rubbed his hands on his jeans. The sirens were getting closer.

"Nothing to see here, Officer," he whispered. "Not the droids you're looking for."

Will glanced over his shoulder and saw the red and blue lights reflecting off the oak trees that lined the street leading to the subdivision. Another twenty yards and he'd be able to cut into the bayou.

Fear overcame caution. He bolted, turned left again at the end of the street, and was cloaked by the gloom that surrounded the bayou. The darkness that haunted his sleep was now his ally. But the grass and dirt footpath were slick from the afternoon's rain, and he slipped and landed on his right elbow and hip.

"Dang it," he whispered.

Electric pain reverberated up and down his arm.

The sirens stopped. *Must be at the house.* He wanted to peek around the corner. *No. Don't blow it now.* He stood and carefully trod down the inky path, his bare feet occasionally squishing into a muddy spot on the trail. *I'm leaving footprints. Nobody walks out here barefoot. Except for runaway kids whose foster parents think they're going to murder them in the night.*

A few hundred yards later, he crept down the bank toward the water, easing down the concrete culvert where two branches of Houston's primary drainage system came together on their meandering path to the Gulf of Mexico.

In movies, escaping prisoners always walked in the stream to break their trail, so Will did that until he remembered about water moccasins. Then he scrambled up the bank on the opposite side of his neighborhood and ducked into the woods. He picked his way deeper until he was out of site of the bayou. Twigs and rocks stabbed at feet tenderized by running down the sidewalk.

He sat on a log to wait. For three hours, he swatted at mosquitoes and other bugs with a taste for human flesh.

By the time it was light enough to distinguish colors, he'd decided to go back.

— 1 1 0 1 0 0 1 0 —

The rumble and squeak of school buses broke through the incessant whine of mosquitoes. *That'll be the high school bus. I'll gut this out for two more cycles, until the middle schoolers and elementary kids are gone. Then all the Karens and Chads will have fled suburbia for work.*

Nobody would be left to see him return except the occasional retiree and a rare stay-at-home parent.

I just need to make it two years. He continued to walk. *Then I'll be eighteen and out of the system. I can apologize to the fosters, but I can't take another two years in a group home.*

His head echoed with the whispered slurs of "Kimmy," and gut punches when no counselors could see.

If nothing else, I need to get my stuff. If I'd paid attention to Remo, I'd've stashed anything that mattered outside the house.

The small, wiry kid with the weird accent had been a source of wisdom: "Keep all important stuff—money, passport, phone, keys—with you at all times, or someplace you can get, even if you get locked out and have to run."

Will hadn't paid attention then, thinking that he'd never have to run, and he didn't have a passport to worry about.

Shoes and socks would drastically improve his situation. A change of clothes. Maybe a towel. Definitely some bug spray. The coins and the letter were critical. The gold coins he'd hidden from CPS when he cleared his stuff out of the old house. His dad started buying them when COVID-19 hit, and he was worried about the econopocalypse. Mom sold them off, slowly, after Dad died, keeping her and her son afloat. There were two left. That, and the letter. The only thing he had left connecting him to his dead parents.

He had a plan: write a note of apology to his fosters, get his stuff, and leave. Call that evening to see if they'd take him back. Explain about the knife. Life could be okay again.

Just make it two more years.

– 1 1 0 1 0 0 1 0 –

He turned the corner into his cul-de-sac and froze. There was a car in their driveway. A nondescript four-door sedan that might as well have had CPS painted on the side. He turned around and cut down the street behind theirs. He walked up Mrs. Derr's driveway. She was a nice old lady with painful arthritis that made her movements slow and lopsided. She often paid him to walk her obese Corgi, Hannibal.

He didn't see Mrs. Derr through the kitchen window, and when he peeked through the gate, she wasn't in the backyard. Hannibal gave a single muffled pre-bark, then recognized him and trundled over to the gate. Will reached through the wrought iron bars and scratched the Corgi's ears.

"Who's a good boy?" he whispered to the dog, and pulled open the latch, making sure to keep Hannibal in the yard.

The dog had a rep as an escape artist.

Will walked bent-over to the back fence and peered between the pickets. *Nobody in sight. I've got to get my stuff.* His pulse pounded in his ears. *If I get caught...*

Climbing up and over the cedar fence earned him two new splinters in his tattered feet. The back door to the garage was locked, but the key still hung behind the barbecue grill. He carefully pushed it into the lock and turned. The door swung open and Will was in. He quietly wheeled his bike into the backyard and dropped it over the fence into Mrs. Derr's yard. He tossed his helmet after it. Back into the garage. Wiped his feet on the welcome mat, leaving two smears of mud. Unlocked the kitchen door and stepped silently in. He could hear voices coming from the living room.

Will crawled behind the island, straining his ears, but couldn't make out the words.

Up the stairs, avoiding the creaky third step. He tiptoed into his room. *Coins and letter first.* He stretched his arm behind the dresser to where he had taped the coins and peeled them free. They went into his front jeans pocket. He slowly pulled open the top drawer, mentally willing it to silence. The letter was under his socks. He stuffed the letter into his back pocket and pulled on the socks. The soft fabric snagged his abused feet and he grimaced. Will slid on his trainers and stood, feeling nominally more human. Then he caught sight of himself in the mirror.

He looked like a wild man. His ginger hair was tangled and disheveled. He had streaks of mud on his face and arms where he had slapped and scratched at the man-eating mosquitoes of the bayou.

Glancing down, he saw his shirt had been torn diagonally across his chest. He peeled it off and tried to wipe his face. Better. He pulled on the Quaranteens T-shirt he'd dropped on the floor yesterday and reached for his phone.

It was gone. Should have been on his nightstand, charging. Even the charger was gone.

With a sinking feeling, Will turned toward his closet. His backpack was gone, too, along with some of his clothes. *They've already decided. They're sending me back to the group home. They're already packing up my stuff. It wasn't my fault! Maybe the CPS lady will listen to me.*

Will crept down the steps and stopped when he heard the voices again. This time, he could make out words.

"...find him, he'll go straight to Harris County Juvenile Detention."

Juvey? What the heck? He felt a twinge of panic. *That has to be the CPS lady. Why juvey?*

Foster mom said something he couldn't quite understand. She habitually mumbled.

"Well, since he's sixteen now, he may be tried as an adult."

Tried? What is she talking about? Every hair on his body was standing on end. His mouth went dry, and a chunk of ice formed in his stomach.

More mumbling.

"Yes, assault with a knife would be a third-degree felony, at least. Maybe even second degree. There would be mandatory jail time."

He couldn't stand it anymore. *There's no way I'm going to juvey. If group homes are bad, how much worse would juvey be? Gotta sneak back out.*

Will crept downward, trying to hear more. The third step groaned loudly as he weight settled on it. The conversation in the living room stopped.

"Will?"

He ran down the last two steps.

"I didn't do anything!" he yelled over his shoulder, as he headed for the back door. "I never would have hurt you!"

"I'm calling 911." The CPS lady's voice followed him into the back yard.

Frantic, he yanked his bike out of Mrs. Derr's azaleas and grabbed his helmet. Hannibal was initiating a rove alert. Neighboring dogs picked up the call. Will was through the gate when he heard his name.

Mrs. Derr stood beside her open garage door. She peered at Will through thick glasses framed by curly gray hair. She wore a coral muumuu and slippers.

"Running away?"

"Yes." He nodded and glanced back over his shoulder.

She stared at him for a moment, then pointed a key fob at her vintage minivan. It chirped and the side door slid open.

"Get in."

"No, Missus Derr—"

"Go on, boy. This may be my last opportunity to help a fugitive escape injustice." She chuckled with glee.

Will hesitated, then pushed his bike through the side door and climbed in behind.

"Oops. Forgot my purse. I'll be right back." She limped into her house, pausing long enough to let the Corgi lead the way.

Sirens sounded in the distance, and Will whispered, "Hurry. Please hurry."

He crouched down behind the driver's seat and began to sweat in the still air.

Mrs. Derr toddled back out and settled in. The van clicked once as she turned the key.

"I really should drive it more."

She tried again and it clicked, paused as if weighing the merits of aiding Will's escape, and started.

"There we go." Mrs. Derr patted the steering wheel and dug into her purse, then handed Will a pack of wipes. "You look a fright, dear. Try to clean up a bit."

She put the van in reverse and slowly backed out of the driveway.

As they passed the entrance to Will's street, she said, "Oh my. Two police cars today. Last night, you only warranted one."

"You saw what happened last night?"

"The whole neighborhood must have. Flashing lights, sirens, people standing in the street, gawking. I walked around the corner to get a better view. Want to tell me what happened? The police car drove around the subdivision, shining their spotlight into everyone's yard."

Will filled her in.

When he had finished, she said, "Well, I never did think her elevator went all the way to the top. When I heard they were taking on a foster child, I thought, *God save that little boy or girl*. Did you ever hear about the exchange student they had? Kicked him out for standing too near a window during a thunderstorm."

"No. When was this?"

"Couple years back. Listen, Will, I'm only driving you as far as Katy. That gets you out of the county and into a different jurisdiction. Should I drop you off at the mall?"

He thought for a minute. It was only 8:30. The mall wouldn't be open yet.

"How about the Bullseye store? I need to buy some stuff."

"Have you thought about where you're going?"

As much as this whole disaster had caught him off-guard, Will did know.

"I'm going to SPARK."

"All the way out in California?

"That's the one."

Mrs. Derr was quiet for a minute.

"Will, you're a smart young man. You should finish school. Go to college. Not spend your whole life playing games."

"It's more than that. I mean, I'm going to get a job and work there. I have to figure out the school thing, though. I don't know if they'll let me enroll after this." He waved his hand vaguely toward their neighborhood.

Once they were on the freeway, Will moved up into the front seat and buckled in.

"Hmm," she said softly. "Oh. Oh. I just had an idea." Mrs. Derr was speaking quickly now, leaning forward as she drove. "I don't know the geography precisely, but is SPARK in SCAZ?"

"The Southern California Autonomous Zone? I don't know…"

"It should at least be close. Will, if things don't work out at SPARK, or if this mess doesn't blow over…well, you might want to try SCAZ. I don't think they'd care that your foster mom got her panties in an uproar."

Will laughed. "Missus Derr!" He feigned shock.

She settled back in her seat and concentrated on changing lanes.

"It's settled, then. You'll have to send me a postcard." She reached over and patted his arm.

"You bet." He paused a moment, staring out the windshield as if he could already see SPARK in the distance. "I went there—SPARK—with my parents once. We had fun…"

Mrs. Derr drove for a few moments in silence.

"Almost there, dear."

They pulled up in front of the store, and Will unloaded his bike and helmet. Mrs. Derr got out and gave him a hug.

"Will, you have two things going against you right now. The first is that you're Korean—"

"Half."

She shook her head. "Most people aren't going to care either way. But some can't understand the difference between the South and the North. You know how it is."

"Kimmy," he muttered the slur.

Mrs. Derr's gray curls bobbed as she nodded. She pushed her glasses back up on her nose.

"You said two things," Will said. "What's the other?"

She tousled his hair. "You might want to do something about that. It's rather distinctive."

He grinned. "Will do, Missus D. And thanks. Really. Thanks."

He felt a lump in his throat as he rolled his bike away from the van. *Why can't everybody be as nice as Missus Derr?*

As she pulled away, Mrs. Derr rolled down a window and gave him one last bit of advice.

"It's a long way. Wear sunscreen."

Will rolled his eyes but gave her a parting smile and wave. He stashed his bike behind a display of prefab picnic tables and entered the store.

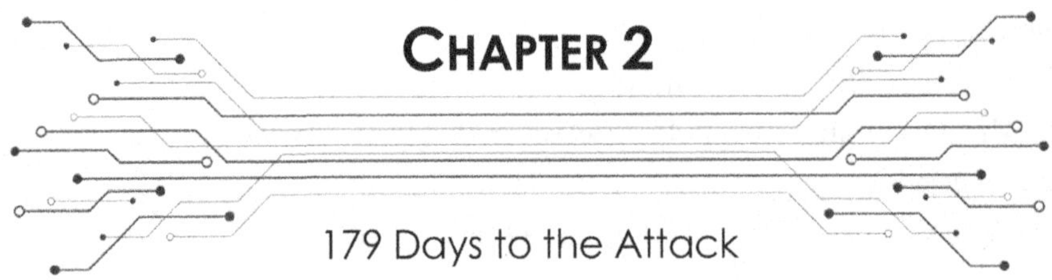

CHAPTER 2

179 Days to the Attack

"War scars a nation."
—Remo to Will

It took him three days of riding to make it to San Antonio. Slow, he knew. *Probably too paranoid.*

He stuck to back roads and slept in small-town baseball parks. It took him a while to find a place to sell the gold coins, and when he came out, his bike was gone. *Knew I shoulda bought a lock.*

– 1 1 0 1 0 0 1 0 –

"Hey, would you buy me a ticket to Barstow? You can keep the change." Will held out three hundred-dollar bills.

The man smiled as he turned around. And Will knew he had made a mistake.

From behind, the guy in the bus station looked normal when Will approached him in the restroom. He had shoulder-length hair the color of straw. The right side of his face was unblemished, but as he completed his turn, Will's blood ran cold. On its left side, the man's face was tragically disfigured. Melt, they called it. The horrible result of close contact with a chemical bioweapon the North Koreans deployed when they realized they were going to lose Seoul. It attacked the flesh, and the neurotoxin killed the nerves. Victims that survived ended up with patches of flesh that looked like melting pudding.

The man's smile disappeared the same time Will's did. The guy gut-punched him and plucked the money from his hand.

"You freakin Kimmys are always looking for help, aren't you? It's not enough two hundred thousand of us died on that godforsaken peninsula, saving you from Uncle Kim. And thousands more ended up like me." He pointed a scarred left hand at his face. "We should have killed you all."

He seemed ready to strike Will again, but then turned and walked out.

Will's eyes watered, and he thought he might vomit. He refused to cry but had to take several shaky breaths before he could stand back up. Kids in group homes had punched him before. But melt-guy had been to war and punched at an entirely new level.

A tall black man walked into the restroom. His jeans were faded colorless. He wore a tattered US Army jacket, its digitized camouflage pattern coated in dust. He gave Will a glance, then went about his business. As he put his hand on the door to leave, he looked back at Will.

"You okay?"

Will nodded, still trying to draw a full breath.

"Just trying to get to Barstow."

The man kept his hand on the door a moment, then let the door close and moved closer to Will. He smelled of diesel fuel and had a week's growth of stubble on his face.

The vet nodded to the door. "That guy hit you?"

"No. It's okay. I…I shouldn't have asked him…I didn't see the—"

"Melt?"

Again, Will nodded.

The vet's eyes focused at infinity for a moment.

"The lucky ones died." He shook his head. "No call to hit a kid. What's keeping you from buying a ticket? Money? ID problem?"

"I've got the money, but yeah, ID problem."

"Been there. C'mon." The vet turned and walked out of the restroom.

Will followed him. He tried to give the veteran the sixty-dollar change from the ticket, but the man refused.

"Little man, you're gonna need it more than me." The man looked at the digital clock high on the wall of a bus station that had seen better days. "But I wouldn't say no to a burger. You got a couple hours."

"Sure," Will said, a little too enthusiastically.

They sat at the counter in the rundown bus station diner and ordered. As they waited, Will looked around. The place was filled with the destitute, the down-on-their-luck, and those that couldn't, or wouldn't, fly across the country. A couple drivers in their Rabbit Bus Lines uniforms ate in a booth across the checkered-floor diner. As depressing as the cramped space was, the food was surprisingly good.

"Why Barstow?" the vet said. "SPARK?"

Will nodded and swallowed a bite of the burger he had to hold with both hands.

"Yeah. My parents took me there the first year it opened. We all loved it and planned on going back. Then…" He shrugged. "Stuff changed. I planned on going out there when I turned eighteen, but…well, more stuff. So I'm going now. Maybe get a job working one of the quests. They seem to be ahead of everyone with AI, and I'm pretty good with computers."

"Heard that helps," the vet said. "Me? Not so much. Heard good things about SPARK, though. Guy that runs the place, HVH, he's got a rep for liking vets. Hires a lot. Thought about heading out there myself."

That piqued Will's interest. Maybe he'd have a friend for the trip.

"Why not?" he said. "You got something going on here in San Antone? Or are you on the way somewhere?"

"I was all set to go. Then a buddy hooked me up with their website, and I started reading 'bout that Underground City below the park." He turned to look at Will. "Know what I'm talking about?"

Will shook his head.

"It's supposed to be huge—nearly as big as SPARK itself. Full of offices and people and machines. All to run what happens topside. That's what changed my mind. I don't do underground. Not since Seoul."

"You fought in Seoul? So did my dad…" Will stared at his fries, lost in memories of his father.

He felt the vet tap his shoulder.

"Little dude, you still with me?"

Will blushed and mumbled, "Sometimes I kind of zone out. Get lost in my own head."

"It's okay. It just kind of freaked me out. You were gone five minutes."

"Really? I lose track of time, too."

The vet pointed to his empty plate. Will still had half his burger and fries left.

"Who'd he fight for? Your dad." There was a coolness to the man's tone now.

"Both, kinda," Will said. "I mean, he was a citizen of both the South and the US, and he'd been in the ROK Army before he came to the US. So when it started, he went back into the ROK Army, but was *seconded* or something, to a US Marine unit as a translator and interrogator."

The older man relaxed a bit and rubbed his forehead.

Eyes closed, he said, "Seoul was bad news, man. You know about the tunnels? The sewers?"

"Yeah, I knew that the North built infiltration tunnels. Is that what you mean by *the sewers*?"

The vet rubbed the stubble on his chin and shook his head.

"Everybody knew about the tunnels up by the DMZ. Nobody knew that they'd tunneled all the way to Seoul, tapped into the sewers. Middle of the damn night, up they come." He gestured with rising hands, like a geyser erupting. "They were everywhere. *The Front* doesn't mean a thing when suddenly the enemy is boiling out of the ground like fire ants all around you. We were shooting in all directions. People screaming. People dropping. We ran out of ammo. Had to pick it off corpses. Come morning, there were bodies everywhere. North, South, Army, Marines." He nodded to Will. "Men, women, kids, even little babies. It was a real sh—" He cleared his throat. "It was a mess."

Will remembered hearing from his dad almost every day. Then nothing. Lots of stuff on the news about the huge battle in Seoul. The North had taken the city. His mom cried every night. Three months with no word. Then an email that had started with, *We regret to inform you...*

He forced the thoughts from his mind.

"Did you..." A vague gesture at his face, where the guy who punched him in the bathroom was disfigured.

"Get the Melt? Nah. I was the only one left from my unit. Took me most of the day to find any sort of US command and control."

The vet buried his face in his hands and shook his head. Will waited, returning the favor.

When the man finally pulled his hands away and turned on his stool to face him, Will could see that his eyes were moist.

"They were all gone, see? Everyone I'd trained with. Guys I ate with. Bunked with." He sniffed and dug the palms of his hands into his eyes, regaining some of his composure. "Turns out, if that happens, they send you home. Try to fix you." He tapped his temple. "Can't unscramble an egg." He shook his head.

Will nodded, realizing the depths of the man's pain, but uncertain what to do. He reached out a hand and placed it on the vet's shoulder and said nothing.

"Anyway," the vet continued, "that's why I need to be someplace with nothing but solid earth under me. No tunnels, no big city with sewers, no Underground City."

– 1 1 0 1 0 0 1 0 –

"You're gonna be okay," the vet told Will, as they stood by the door of the bus Will was about to board.

He offered Will a dry and calloused hand. "Maybe I'll make it out to SPARK someday, and you can hook me up."

"Count on it." Will boarded the bus.

Would it have been weird to have hugged him?

– 1 1 0 1 0 0 1 0 –

Passing through Tucson, Will saw a sign at a bank claiming the temperature was 121 degrees. *Getting my bike stolen might have saved my life.*

When they changed busses in Phoenix, Will forgot his aluminum water bottle in the seat back. *That's okay. Plastic ones are lighter.*

The bus station in Barstow was seedy but was next to a place claiming to be the world's largest Micky D's. He ate and wandered the town until dusk, when the lights of a softball park showed him the way. When he got there, he arbitrarily picked a team to root for and climbed into the aluminum bleachers, worked his way to the top. He let the game, the smell of fresh mown grass, the slap of ball into glove, and the ping of the bats wash over him.

Tomorrow, SPARK!

In the glare of the lights illuminating the field, Will pulled out the letter and reread it for the hundredth time. The envelope was smudged with age and handling. It was a pearlescent gray and matched the letter within. *That's Mom's touch. Dad would have just pulled a sheet of paper off the printer. Mom had a sense of import.*

Billy was written in his dad's hand. Below it was *Billy* again. This time, in his mom's handwriting. Will pulled the letter out of the envelope and carefully unfolded it.

> *Hey Sport,*
>
> *This is one of those "Just in case" letters. I'm heading off to Korea tomorrow, and I want you to understand why I thought it was important to go. I'm a citizen of both the US and the ROK. Some things are worth fighting for, and freedom is at the top of the list. Both of my countries are in this war, and I can't stay on the sidelines in Houston. This is my fight.*

At some point, everyone has to make tough decisions. We have to choose what path we're on. I made a decision to choose this one. I hope you understand.

Take care of your mom. She's not always the tough Shield Maiden she seems to be. If all else fails, remember SPARK and how much fun we had.

Love,

Dad

Below was a note his mom had written. It was dated the night she died. For the hundredth time, Will wondered if she had known she was dying.

Billy,

I should have given this to you years ago, but I couldn't part with it. It was the last thing your dad wrote. I'm sorry for keeping it to myself. I guess I thought he wasn't really gone, that it was all a mistake. Giving you the letter would make it real. I'm sorry for so much...I know things aren't right. I know I'm not right anymore. I'm broken, and that's hurting you, too. I've fallen into an abyss. I'm lost and can't find my way home. I love you, Billy. Dad was right. Remember SPARK and how much fun we had.

Find me. Save me.

I love you,

Mom

What did that even mean? *Find me. Save me.*

Commotion in the stands pulled him back to the present. The game was over. He'd missed the last two innings, lost in his memories. Now, parents and players were filing away. Words of congratulations and commiseration filtered through the cooling night air.

Will tucked the letter into its envelope and returned it to his backpack. He walked away from the baseball diamond. *I'll wait until they kill the lights, and then come back to sleep in the dugout.* He'd made it to San Antonio this way, watching games and then sleeping in darkened ball parks, reconnecting to memories of his dad and their love of the game.

When the last car left and the field was dark, Will returned. Cicadas thrummed loudly in the dim moonlight. He walked around the fence and down the first-base line to the dugout. The bench was smooth, polished by the butts of a thousand little leaguers. He pulled out the butcher knife and made sure the duct-tape-coated cardboard sheath was secure. It was the first thing he'd bought after Mrs. Derr dropped him off. There were a couple scars on his legs and left arm from where he nicked himself during one of *those* dreams. Nightmares of before. Of scratching sounds in the wall and red eyes following him in the night. *The Thing in the Wall.*

He stretched out on the bench, clasping the knife to his chest. Slowly, unwillingly, he closed his eyes.

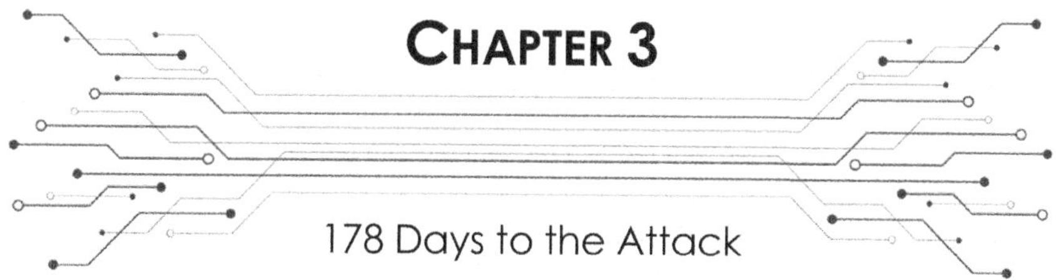

CHAPTER 3

178 Days to the Attack

Comparatively, Black Grass was the easy part. Figuring out how to control it and use it on a large scale, that was tough. That's where AI came in. Functional AI allowed us to create Solar Prime and produce electricity in commercial quantities. SPARK? That's just for fun.
—Hecker Van Horne

In the Security office of the SPARK bus station in Barstow, the voice in the Security supervisor's headset was surprisingly calm.

"Weapon detected."

The calm female voice of the aural alert shocked Destardi Hollingsworth. She silenced the alarm before it could sound again. *I must have been daydreaming. Thank God for automated systems!*

Mostly, Destardi just saw happy families entering the SPARK terminal in Barstow. That made her a complacent. So when the aural alert sounded in her earpiece, "Weapon detected," she was shocked into hypervigilance.

She zoomed her camera in on the kid that set off the alert. *Asian. Maybe Asian-Anglo. Something off about his hair.* She saw some smudges of black on the shoulders of his shirt. *Bad dye job?* Her finger hovered over the call button. The kid was just standing there.

The millimeter wave scan built into the terminal's doorway clearly showed the outline of a huge knife in the kid's backpack. He was on SPARK property, and Destardi was completely within her rights to detain him, but he wasn't doing anything yet. Just watching people board the buses. *What the heck. I'll give him a few minutes. See what he does.*

Nothing. The kid did nothing. He just stood there. *Why?* She tapped her console. *The weapon gives me justification to run FaceRec. The hair hanging in his face isn't going to help.*

Nothing came back on him, but law enforcement databases didn't always play well with private sector security. They only screened for criminal records and histories of violence.

She checked the kid. Still motionless, just inside the entry portal.

A couple of low-probability matches, including one for a previous guest, six years prior. That file was tagged for special monitoring. She checked the tag: Summary of SPARK activities to be sent to HVH.

Destardi sat bolt upright in her chair. *The* HVH? She didn't know another one.

HVH was Hecker Van Horne himself. Chairman and CEO of Solar Prime, Solar Prime Augmented Reality Park, and a few affiliated companies.

She'd never seen that before. Why would the Big Boss want to know what a kid was doing?

She checked him again—still standing there.

She compared the file pic to what she saw on the monitor. The kid in the file was ten at the time, so he'd be fifteen or sixteen now. File-kid had short red hair bordering on orange. Knife Boy's hair looked black and hung down into his face, covering half of it. *Probably another runaway. They burn through their cash and then just fade back into the real world.*

She expanded the millimeter-wave view of the knife in his backpack. *Clearly a butcher knife. Who carries a butcher knife around in a backpack?*

The kid turned around and left. *Okay.* She let the tension drain from her shoulders. *No longer my problem.*

Destardi forgot about him until the next day.

– 1 1 0 1 0 0 1 0 –

She was more vigilant this morning. The automated alert of the day before was a professional embarrassment. Today, she silenced it before it could even begin.

Knife Boy was back. Same clothes, same backpack, same weird hair. Today, though, he studied the signs in the terminal. He stood in front of the sign where Sparky, Solar Prime Augmented Reality Park's mascot, read the park rules aloud, in whatever language you selected. She noted the kid seemed content with the English default.

Destardi knew the words by heart, but they boiled down to: No weapons. No backpacks or large purses. No liquids. Pretty much just the clothes you were wearing and a way to pay.

The kid still had the backpack and the knife. *Until he tries to get on a bus, or do something stupid, I'll leave him be.*

He left after studying the sign but was back again the next day. Same clothes, but the backpack was gone. He walked straight to the boarding line. Destardi Hollingsworth tapped her manicured nails on her desk twice as she checked her roster. She hit the comm button.

"Bull?" she broadcast to the earpieces of the Security personnel working the terminal.

"Yeah, boss?" Earl Bullard answered.

"There's a kid in line two. Teenager. Stocky. Greasy blackish hair."

She watched Bull on her monitor as he scanned the crowd. At six-foot-six and a solid 250 pounds, he stood out. Blond hair cut close in a hairstyle unchanged since his time in the Marine Corps.

"Got him," he replied. "That's Knife Boy, right?"

They had talked about him in the morning briefing.

"Trouble?" he said.

"Yeah, it's him," Destardi said. "No knives today. I want you on the bus with him. He doesn't have any history, but I just want somebody near him. Just in case. Somebody that doesn't—"

"Doesn't think every Korean is evil?"

She smiled in her solitary office, surrounded by monitors.

"Exactly."

"You want me to follow him into the park?" Bull said.

"Nah, just get him through the gate. Then Janne and the internal guys can take over."

"On it."

"Hey, Bull?"

"Yeah?"

"Take lunch while you're out there. The cafeteria in the Underground City beats the hell out of anything around here."

"Thanks, boss. And it's free!"

She could hear the smile in his voice. Bull had done two tours. He'd seen his share of action in Korea II before a landmine sprayed shrapnel into his knee. He still limped.

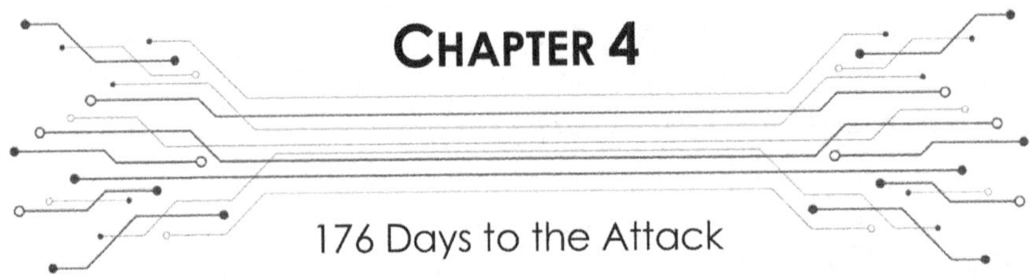

CHAPTER 4

176 Days to the Attack

Silent men, like still waters, are deep and dangerous.
—Proverb

Ragnar Sarnak was in Dubrovnik. He was here to send a message. Sarnak was excellent at sending this kind of message.

He sipped a coffee in a sidewalk café along the main road of Old Town, and rubbed the dark stubble on his chin. He kept a three- to five-day growth when work permitted. That way, he could trim his hair and beard with the same blade. *Efficient.*

Lately, he noted there was some gray coming in. He shrugged philosophically and watched the family leave their apartment.

Standing, he stretched and casually checked for anyone paying attention to him. *Clear.* When they were out of sight, he walked to the door and examined the lock. It was nearly as old as the building itself.

Sarnak sighed. Digital locks were easier to hack. Codes simpler to guess or bribe from someone. Only in Old Europe could you still find a lock like this.

He pulled his tools from his pocket and looked around. Still clear. The lock took him more than a minute. Standing at a door increased his exposure, and Sarnak did not like being noticed.

Finally, the lock clicked, and he entered. He caught his reflection in the hall mirror.

Just over six-feet tall, Sarnak preferred tighter-fitting shirts that showed off his muscular arms. Eyes the color of unpolished iron. A non-descript eastern European male. Easy to miss in a crowd when he was off the job. When he was working, however, people gave him more room, stepped off the sidewalk to avoid bumping into him.

He smiled at himself in the mirror. People could sense he was dangerous. He had a chipped incisor on the top left—damage from a job in Bosnia. *I'll have to get that fixed next time I'm in Romania.* The tooth was dying and starting to fade to an ugly gray. *Good women, cheap dental care in Romania.*

He looked around. *Holiday rental. Nice. Well-appointed.* It even had air conditioning, which was pricy here in Old Town. He'd try not to leave too much of a mess, but four bodies can leak a lot of blood.

He explored the apartment and appreciated the Bukovac reproduction over the couch. *Velika Iza,* he remembered. *Nice quality.* He'd seen the original in the Dubrovnik Museum of Modern Art just this afternoon. *Only Croatia would consider something painted in 1882 as modern.*

He smiled and continued to look around. Finally settled in to wait in a darkened alcove deep in the apartment. There would be no chance his victims could flee before he killed them.

When the primary target and his family returned home that evening, Sarnak was waiting. He heard them close and lock the door, chattering happily in English. *American accent.*

He emerged from the alcove and shot them, starting with the mother and daughter. Females, in his experience, were more likely to scream.

Next, he shot the son, leaving the father for last. Those were his orders: give the primary target enough time to understand what his traitorous actions cost.

When realization settled into the father's eyes, Sarnak shot him. Once in the heart to kill him. The second two shots—one to the forehead and one to the groin—sent the message: Even Eastern Europe is not out of reach.

Sarnak assumed it was a cartel. They specified all four members of the family had to die. In Sarnak's experience, only the cartels killed the children. Sarnak didn't mind the boy but regretted the girl. He'd had a girl himself, once upon a time. Still, it was a contract, and it paid well.

He collected his spent brass and saw himself out, careful not to step in the pools of blood. He disposed of the gun in the Adriatic, dropping it casually off a wall and into the sea along a stretch of the walls out of sight of any obvious drones, then wandered the tourist-laden areas before finding a spot to enjoy a cognac and the satisfaction of a job well-done.

Tomorrow, it's off to Budapest. Should be another easy job.

Sarnak checked his watch, left a generous tip, and headed back to his hotel. He had an online meeting with a client.

After the call, he ordered room service and reviewed his notes of what he now called The SPARK Job. It would be bigger, splashier than normal. Two client groups were jointly funding this. One wanted a big body count and lots of fire. *People burning to death always gets media attention.* The second group wanted to take SPARK and HVH down a notch. They told Sarnak they also wanted a certain piece of tech—an AI's data core. They were coordinating with an inside asset they recently turned. But for the other part, the money was good, and Sarnak wouldn't have to recruit fighters. The client—ISIS, or Daesh, as they called themselves—would provide those. Supplies were trickier.

Guns were no problem. They were widely available in the US, but he wanted everyone to carry the same type and ammo. *Makes for easier training.*

Incendiaries were trickier. He'd have to source the materials in the US. He had a chemist contact who could make the napalm. What about a delivery mechanism? Ignitors? How would he get the weapons into the park? America had grown touchy after Korea II and the Mall of America episode.

When the Budapest job was over—two weeks, a month at the most—Sarnak would fly to California and scout SPARK himself. *Maybe I'll retire after this one. There will be enough money.* Then he smiled. *Who am I kidding? I'm never going to retire. I love this too much. Makes me feel alive.*

– 1 1 0 1 0 0 1 0 –

Will sat on the bus and let the buzz of excited families wash over him.

The blurred darkness that was the thousands of acres of Black Grass at Solar Prime caught Will's attention. He was fascinated by the stuff.

He listened to a dad in the row behind him, obviously an engineer, entertain his son with details about the Black Grass, just as Will's own father had done. His throat constricted at the memory.

"Every blade is individually controlled. They compare the sunlight—really, the whole EM spectrum—at every edge of the blade and then twist the blade for maximum absorption, using a microscopic current differential. Once every second for millions—maybe billions—of blades of grass, and turn it into electricity to sell to the grid. It's so much more efficient than the old solar panels were. That's where Van Horne makes his money—the Black Grass, not the park. He created an AI to control it. Even gave it a name: Janne, but with a double N. No idea what the second N is for. Sounds just like *Jane*."

Will remembered his dad saying it, smiling at him. *It was all good then. Before the war, before Mom broke.*

Will returned to the present and looked at the Black Grass fields. Twenty-five square miles, according to the pamphlet he picked up at the bus station.

There were a few wisps of fog. He remembered his dad calling it a micro-climate. The infrared absorption of the Black Grass caused the borders to be cooler than the surrounding desert. If the humidity was high enough, you got ground level clouds—fog.

"I know they have a demo in SPARK," his dad had said, "but I hope we have time to go out to the fields themselves. Maybe we can see the blades moving."

Sure, Dad. I'll try to do it this time.

The fields faded from sight as the bus rolled into the parking lot of SPARK and up to the entrance. The gates of SPARK were familiar. This was the last place he remembered being happy. The last time things had been good.

Will had enough left from selling the gold coins to cover three days at full price. Then he'd have to get a job. *I'll play the park today, and then apply for work.*

Everything that had happened in the intervening years led him to hedge his bets. *The park is probably going to be stupid. Full of stuff for little kids.*

He was next in line.

At least Dad died quickly. Mom took years. Quick is better.

But slow kept him out of foster care. *Thirty months, three families, three group homes.*

Will knew it was his own fault. *It's the dreams.*

He shook his head and returned to reality.

The light turned green, and he pushed the door open and entered alone. A holographic avatar appeared behind an old-fashioned ticket booth. *Something you'd see in an old black and white vid in a train station in Tombstone.*

Janne was waiting. At least, he assumed it was Janne. *She looks the same as before.*

"Welcome back!" the avatar said. "We're glad to see you again, Billy."

"Hi, Janne. It's *Will* now."

She didn't correct him.

Dad was right. The avatar is run by Janne. How does she know it's me? Is she going turn me in as a runaway?

Will slouched into one of the chairs and felt a slight tug as the entry trolley began its trek to the Hub. For reasons unknown, he felt better than a moment before.

"Of course, Will," the avatar replied in a smooth tone.

He remembered her face and voice. For Billy and his family, Janne manifested as a twenty-something woman of indeterminant race. Black hair flowed over her shoulders, and a minute fold to her inner eyes gave a suggestion of Asia. Her voice was animated and soothing.

A lump formed in Will's throat as he realized he was finally here. But this time, he was alone.

"Do you want to make any other changes?" Janne said.

After his father died, Will had retreated into SPARK Online and played avidly until the contrast between fantasy and reality became too stark. Fear, rejection, and anger put him on a different path. He hadn't played a SPARK game in nearly three years.

"Can you show me my profile?" he said.

"Certainly," Janne replied in a smooth tone.

She seemed better at dealing with guests than before. Billy remembered his mom calling Janne *brusque*.

An image of ten-year-old Billy Kwan appeared next to Janne and slowly rotated. *WonderBoy* floated beneath the image. White pinstriped baseball uniform. Old school. A Little League version of Roy Hobbs, with Billy's face. Will aged his avatar's appearance and kept the blond hair. He didn't really like the ginger locks genetics had granted him. He kept the number 9 on his back, and the general styling of his persona, but lengthened the pants so they looked more like regular ones than the knee-length uniform version.

Will was about to change his avatar name—WonderBoy might be okay at ten, but felt a little childlike at sixteen. When he opened his mouth to speak, he choked up. Janne waited silently.

"Could you…" he rasped out. "Could you just abbreviate it to *WB*? For public viewing?"

"Of course," she said. "Do you want to make any changes to skills or weaponry?"

"No." He sniffed. "Leave all that the same."

He wiped his nose on the sleeve of his hoodie. *Can't believe I'm crying.*

"Do you want to use one of your free days today?" Janne said.

"Huh? What free days?"

"According to our records, your family made an agreement to keep a certain Easter Egg quiet, in exchange for one free entry per year. In your case, you have," the avatar made of show of consulting a data pad, "six free days available."

"Hey, I remember that!" His face lit up. "We—"

Janne put a finger to her lips. "Not speaking of it is the best way to maintain a habit of not speaking of it," she intoned. "Ready for your gear?"

Will nodded, and augmented reality glasses, ARGs, appeared in a drawer below Janne's image, along with his wristband and a pair of gloves. He put the wristband on and strapped the ARGs to his head, but pushed them up out of the way, for now. He inserted the earbuds.

"What's with the gloves?" he said. "I don't remember any gloves."

"They're a new haptic interface we introduced last year," Janne said. "They give you a better sense of virtual objects. Now, when you pick up or use your bat, blaster, or a sword, you'll feel like you actually have something in your hands. The gloves give you tactile feedback. They provide resistance to movement, and a sense of impact during combat. They're not perfect, but most players consider them a significant improvement."

Will donned the gloves and eyed Janne dubiously.

"I don't feel anything."

"Try grabbing your bat or your blaster," she said.

He reached over his shoulder to access his bat, and grinned as he felt his hand close around something. He let go and dropped his ARGs into place and reached back again. This time, he pulled the virtual baseball bat in front of him. *Graphics have definitely improved.*

The lightning bolt and WonderBoy name were clear and crisp. Instead of making a fist, as he had years ago, his fingers seemed to wrap around the bat's handle and stop. Curious, he squeezed harder and noticed he could overwhelm the haptic interface and close his hand. He relaxed his grip again until it felt like he was holding the handle. He took a few swings.

"This. Is. Awesome!" he yelled. "God, my folks would have gone nuts over this."

He felt another pang in his chest at the thought, but powered through. The haptics provided a sense of resistance and momentum as he swung the bat.

The memory of his parents invoked grief more than anger now. Will teared up again and sat back down. Janne shuttled the entry trolley into a holding area and waited as Will's shoulders shook silently.

When he stopped and could take a ragged, controlled breath, he said, “They would have loved this. Thanks.”

Janne resumed their trip and whispered, “We’re almost to the Hub. There have been changes to the park since your last visit. Do you want me to summarize them for you?”

“No.” Will blurted. Then in a more measured tone, “No, I think I want to discover it all myself.”

“Have a great stay!”

The doors opened, and Will entered the Hub as WB.

He wanted to hit the park hard, do all the quests solo, and beat it in the six free days.

Am I going to be hauled back to Houston? They could have stopped me here or at the bus station. Will California extradite me?

For the time being, Will was going to be cautious, but assume he was in the clear.

He grinned. He wasn’t just going to beat the park. He was going to dissect it, peer into its guts and learn all of its secrets. *If finding one Easter Egg is worth a free day every year, what do you get if you find them all?*

The Hub was overwhelming. Everywhere Will looked, something caught his eye. People—at least, he assumed they were people—walked past. His own avatar—a baseball player with a bat slung across his back, and a red and blue blaster on his hip—was benign, by comparison. From where he stood, he saw fearsome frost giants, slender elves with upswept ears, delicate pixies and fairies with shimmering wings, barely dressed barbarians, and aliens. Some were familiar. He saw what had to be a Klingon, a Barsoomian, and possibly a Wookie.

He raised his ARGs, and the fantastic disappeared, replaced by normal-looking people of all varieties.

“I remember the interface was good,” he whispered, “but it’s definitely leveled up.”

He picked someone nearby—a short, portly balding man in cargo shorts and a T-shirt proclaiming, *Remember MoA*. Will lowered his ARGs back into position. The man disappeared, and a towering barbarian took his place—six-and-a-half feet of gleaming muscle, with a wild mane of black hair tied back with a headband, and an enormous war hammer strapped to his back.

Will smiled. *Impressive.*

For a few moments, he simply gawked, becoming a human roadblock impeding the flow of other guests—some hurried and intent, others content to wander from shop to shop. The Hub itself was a rough circle at least a hundred yards in diameter, and mostly dedicated to commerce, both real and virtual. There was a shop for avatar design, money changers where you could convert real currency into SPARK gold, outfitters, and an impressive array of souvenir shops.

Will had emerged from the center. The people mover where he met Janne traveled below ground from the park gates. Then you climbed a ramp to SPARK itself. Behind him, other guests poured out of the entrances that formed the center of the circle.

Nearby, he saw a tall yellow spark with oversized shoes and three-fingered white gloves. *Gotta be Sparky.* The park's mascot.

Sparky had a halo of children around him, waiting for a chance to have their picture taken. Will vaguely remembered doing the same thing.

He raised his ARGs. No change. *So it's a real person in a costume.*

When he was ten, he'd just followed his parents around. Now, he realized he had no idea where he was going.

A holographic map glowed nearby, next to an exhibit titled *The Miracle of Black Grass.* Will walked over, stood on the comically large yellow footprints, and looked at the map. SPARK was laid out like a wagon wheel. The spokes were called *arcades.* Seven of them radiated out from the Hub.

Will raised his ARGs again and saw that reality matched the map. From where he stood, he could see four of the roads—*arcades*, he corrected himself—leading out from the Hub. The remaining three were blocked from sight by the physical structure of the entrance.

He lowered his ARGs, and the map reappeared.

The arcades led to SPARK's seven major quests. Will zoomed in on the map and saw that the arcades loosely followed the theme of the quests housed in the large plazas on the rim of the wheel. He tried to get a sense of scale, and realized that the diameter of the wheel was around a mile.

He looked through the semi-transparent map. *KT Crossing must be dead ahead.*

That's where he needed to go first. It's where they had started as a family. Chronologically, in the fictional timeline of SPARK, KT Crossing was the first major quest.

Ignoring all the stores, exhibits, rides, and minor quests along the Pre-History Arcade— at least, that's what the signpost called it—Will kept his head down and tried to make sense of his feelings. *Maybe this will fix things, change my path.*

Finally, he stood before KT Crossing, but didn't get in line. He just looked at it from the outside. Graphics flooded his ARGs: towering megaflora, glimpses of raptors, the fearsome mouth of the T-Rex visible over the entrance to the quest.

He looked up. Even in the daylight sky, the comet that had killed the dinosaurs was visible. *Will we see our end coming?*

The pavement beneath his feet now appeared as a well-packed earthen path through a primordial jungle. The smell of humus tickled his nose. He stood there and relived his memories of the day he and his family found the Easter Egg.

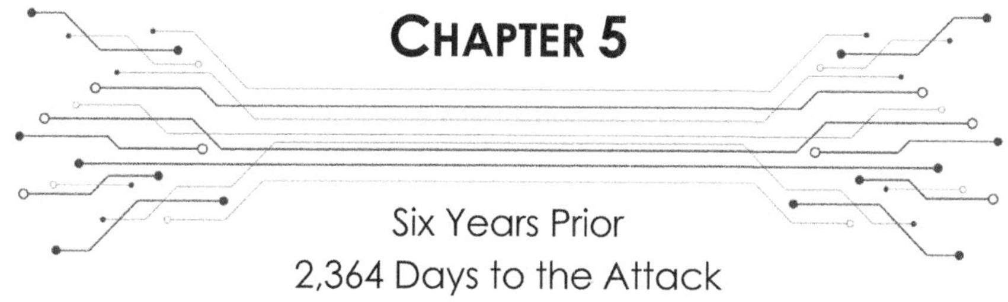

Chapter 5

Six Years Prior
2,364 Days to the Attack

The creation of something new is not accomplished by the intellect, but by the play instinct acting from inner necessity.
—Carl Jung

The baby dies. Get over it.
—SparkLord312 blogging at sparkinsider.com

Billy and his family were next. The SPARK guide was dressed in safari gear.

"Remember, you are about to enter a wormhole that will transport you to the Cretaceous Tertiary—KT boundary. It will be very loud, with a lot of flashing lights. Nobody's photosensitive, right?"

They all nodded and stepped through the entrance. The door closed behind them and they seemed to be surrounded by a metal grid, silver against a black background. A mechanical voice sounded in their earbuds.

"Ten seconds to wormhole insertion."

Billy squeezed his mom's hand, nervous and excited.

Bam! The room and grid vibrated. A kaleidoscope of color erupted and wheeled around them, flashing and pulsing to painfully distorted music.

As quickly as it started, it stopped.

Sound returned first. The wormhole had temporarily blinded Billy. He couldn't see more than vague shapes, but he heard the sounds of the jungle.

Then the noises stopped. They were in trouble. Billy felt it—a slight, rhythmic thumping vibrating up his feet and legs.

"Mom? Dad?" he whispered.

He knew some of the predators used sound to help locate their prey.

"Yeah, Sport. I'm here," came the strained reply from Yul.

"Oh my gosh," whispered Kathy, his mom.

Billy's vision was returning. He could make out the shape of his father. He was bent over with his hands on his thighs. Billy's mom had fallen to her hands and knees. Her blonde hair hid her face.

The thumping was stronger now. Nearer and louder.

"Mom!" Billy said. "You've got to get up!"

He grabbed one of her arms as his dad stumbled closer. His vision was completely recovered, and he could see the trees behind them moving, as something enormous pushed them out of the way

Yul Kwan grabbed Kathy's other arm and helped Billy pull her upright.

She brushed her hair back with one hand. "That was—"

The deafening trumpeting of a T-Rex blasted their ears. It was hunting. Hunting them.

"Run, Mom! Run!" Billy tugged at her arm.

His dad seemed to be back to normal now, and he helped Billy pull Mom along.

"Which way?" Yul asked his son.

"Over here!" yelled Billy.

It was too late to worry about being quiet.

They raced through a primordial jungle. *There's no path!* Ferns towered over them, and plants with leaves the size of an elephant's ears tugged at them as they fought their way through. Mom seemed to have recovered and was running on her own now, but Billy could hear her gasping for air in the damp atmosphere. The ground itself fought them by shaking more violently with every footfall of the Rex.

Mom said, "Where—"

Billy was leading and still held her hand. A flash of vibrant blue caught his attention. Two small primates were ahead of them, also fleeing the deadly flesheater.

"There! Follow them!" Billy pointed with his free hand.

He heard the ripping of trees and leaves behind them as the Rex drew closer. They were getting closer to the blue primates. Billy could see that one carried a baby, staring at Billy over the shoulder of its mother with its large opal eyes, as now human and primate raced for their lives.

The mother stumbled. Time seemed to slow for Billy. He saw the mother primate trip. Her arms flew out to break her fall. She let go of the baby. *She let go of the baby!* The cyan-colored child flew out of her arms, mewling in terror. The mother tried to follow the baby but was pulled away by the father.

Billy let go of his mom's hand.

"Follow them," he repeated to his parents.

Now that he wasn't pulling his mom along, he could run faster. He traced the trajectory of the child, saw it bounce off the ground and then roll to a stop against the base of a giant fern. He sped toward the child.

"Billy!" his own mother yelled.

"Son!" from Dad.

"Just go," he called over his shoulder.

That second of inattention caused Billy to trip over the same root that had tripped the infant's mother. He sprawled face first to the ground, landing hard on his chest and hands.

Billy scrambled up and grabbed the blue infant. He ran, carrying the little Cyanite like a football, its fuzzy head tucked in the crook of his elbow. Everyone was screaming. His mom was yelling at him to come back. His dad was yelling at his mom to hurry, and at Billy to *come on.*

The two Cyanite adults were yelling at each other. The Cyanite infant was crying so loud it hurt Billy's ears. Even the T-Rex was screaming. Billy could hardly hear himself think, and was running so hard he didn't have any breath left over for yelling. Leaves and vines slapped at his face and arms. Roots tried to slow him and tackle him.

He glanced back over his shoulder. The Rex had decided to chase him, and was close enough now that Billy could see it crashing through the vegetation behind him, head down, shredding the jungle as it ran. It focused on him and opened its mouth and bellowed again, loud and close enough that Billy felt it in his chest. It was closing in.

I can't outrun him! Got to do something different. He passed a tree and cut to his right, fighting through the vegetation. *Maybe I can outmaneuver him. Like playing tag. You don't have to be faster if you're more agile.*

The first turn earned him a couple steps before the Rex rounded the tree and spied him again. It altered course, eyes on the prize again. Another tree, another turn. Again. Again. Adrenaline blasted through Billy's veins as every tree let him open the distance just a bit, and every straight path cost him.

Billy ran and ran. Sweat poured down his face and stung his eyes. He felt like he'd been running forever. The heat and humidity of the jungle was sapping his strength. He felt himself slowing down. His legs ached and were threatening to cramp. *I can't stop!*

A root snagged his foot, and Billy slammed to the jungle floor, cradling the tiny Cyanite in his arms and twisting to take the impact.

He scrambled to stand up. His legs were on fire and his chest heaved, trying to capture enough oxygen to let him run again. The Rex had slowed. It was close now. Billy could see saliva dripping from its enormous teeth, and smell its rancid breath. *Spoiled meat.* The Cyanite infant was quiet now, as if it, too, sensed that the end was near.

The tyrant lizard reared its head back and drove its open maw toward Billy, who dove forward, tripped again and rolled as the giant mouth slammed into the ground just behind him.

Billy stood and froze. He was between the legs of the Rex.

The dinosaur seemed confused, turning this way and that. Billy shuffled to stay beneath the beast's pale belly. Its front claws, disproportionately tiny for the creature, opened and closed repeatedly. An angry roar erupted from the Rex, deafening Billy. *What now?*

Billy glanced behind him. No room to squeeze between the giant thunderous legs. He couldn't sneak away in that direction.

The Rex took a step. Billy moved with it and looked down at the baby Cyanite, who looked back with wide eyes. For the first time, he got a good look at the alien child. Short blue fur framed a face the color of antique oak. Human-ish features, like a baby chimpanzee.

The Rex stepped again. Billy followed, as if in a dance. A dance for survival. *When he moves, we move.*

Slowly, the deadly beast began to walk back the way it had come. Beneath its enormous belly, Will and the Cyanite crouched and played silent shadow, creeping along between its powerful legs. An eternity seemed to pass as they danced this way.

The Rex chuffed and paused. Billy heard voices in the distance. *Mom? Dad?* The trio turned toward the sound.

"Billy?"

He could make out his mom's voice now.

"Billy!"

That was Dad.

I'm here. He kept dancing. Step by step, in the shadow of death incarnate.

They drew closer to the voices. The Rex sped up to a thundering trot. Billy had to zigzag to avoid getting crushed by the enormous feet, claws as long as his arm.

A small clearing appeared in front of them, and Billy saw his parents in the mouth of a cave.

"Billy!" His mom was jubilant, then clearly realized his predicament.

The Rex bellowed again and charged the cave. Billy's parents backed deeper in. Billy and his cargo skidded to a halt as the dinosaur's mouth battered the cave entrance, chewing ineffectually at the rock. It reared back for another attempt, and Billy risked everything on one more dive. Three quick steps, then a jump and a roll into the cave.

His father's strong arms hauled him up and deeper into the cave. Mom wrapped her arms around him.

"What were you thinking?"

Her complaints about his behavior were motivated by concern for him more than anything. He knew that. His dad frequently said that parents overreact when they get scared.

Billy was about to tell the story, when they were interrupted by a gentle, cyan-furred hand reaching up and tugging at his arm. He turned to see the Cyanite mother holding her arms out. Billy was a little shorter than most boys his age, and the Cyanites were both smaller than him and slender.

Billy transferred the baby to maternal care. After a thorough examination by both mother and father, the Cyanite family came over to where Billy was telling his tale and stood patiently outside the Kwan family circle. Yul noticed them and broke their triangular conference to admit the smaller primates into the discussion. The slightly larger of the two chattered musically, his voiced pitched like a six-year-old human. He embellished his story with gestures and pantomime. Billy recognized the T-Rex when the Cyanite hunched over and stomped with accompanying roars, and thought he saw himself portrayed carrying the baby. The smaller one held the child until the larger one had finished, then handed Billy the infant.

Billy cradled the child as he had seen the mother do but was unsure what to do next. *Are they giving me this baby?*

The infant itself solved the confusion. He reached out with his small blue-furred hand and placed it palm first on Billy's chest. Then things got weird.

The cave was illuminated with aqua light bright enough to cause Billy to squint. Both adult Cyanite's heads tilted upward, and their normally opalescent eyes turned cyan as well. They each placed a hand on Billy's shoulders. A swell of voices sang in an unknown tongue and reached a crescendo when a woman's voice said, in clear English, "Receive the Mark of Cyan."

Things rapidly scrolled through Billy's ARGs, until three lines remained in his field of view:

Dino Whisperer (L15 required)

Mark of Cyan

Level up!

The light faded, and the eyes of the adult Cyanites returned to normal. The mother reclaimed her child from Billy.

"What the heck was that?" Dad said.

"They sounded like angels," said Mom.

Billy said, "Did you guys see…"

"Yeah," Dad replied. "My ARGs went nuts. We're going to have to review our inventories."

"What's *Dino Whisperer*?" Mom said.

"And what's *The Mark of Cyan*?" said Billy.

"What are you talking about?" Dad said.

"It's the last line I can read in my ARGs before *Level Up*," Billy replied. "Isn't it what that lady said? *Receive the Mark of Cyan*?"

Dad said, "I think so—"

"Billy, look at your armor," Mom said.

Billy had fashioned his armor to look like an old-school baseball uniform. Now, over his heart, where the infant had placed its hand, was a glowing cyan handprint.

"That's weird," he said.

"You've got them on your shoulders, too," Mom said.

Billy pivoted his head left and right, confirming it for himself. He checked his parents— no handprints on their more traditional leather armor. Whatever the marks meant, they were his alone to bear.

"Kwans against the world?" he said to his parents.

It was a family tradition. They played together, they quested together, they stuck together. Billy felt vindicated for having left his parents behind to go chase the baby Cyanite, but still knew he had committed a family foul.

"Kwans against the world," they echoed, putting the incident behind them.

Together, the two families huddled in the back of the cave until the T-Rex set off after easier prey. Yul was scrolling through his ARG inventory, the wraparound goggles invisible through Billy's own ARGs, but the light they cast reflected in Dad's eyes, Billy noticed.

A melodious voice interrupted his thoughts. He turned to see the Cyanites gathered near the door. The eldest was gesturing to follow him.

"Dad, I think the blue crew is leaving."

"Yeah. Wait, what?" Billy's dad turned and looked. "I think we should go with them. Allies never hurt."

Billy nodded and looked over at Mom. She stood and brushed some dirt off of her Viking-style armor and equipped her spiked shield. Her hand rested on the pommel of her short sword.

"Ready," she said.

Yul equipped his matched swords. Billy considered his options and then drew his blaster. *It's only a Level 1—no, make that a Level 2—weapon.* He smiled. *It leveled up with me, but it's the only ranged weapon we have.*

Mom normally led in quests. She had better vision IRL, and generally carried higher Brains points, which allowed her to better sense danger and traps. Billy waited for her to follow the Cyanites. Standard order was Mom, Billy, Dad. Even in quests, they protected their ginger-haired son.

Mom bowed elaborately, the leather and iron straps of her armor rustling softly.

"After you, oh Cyan Marked One," she intoned, with a smile.

Billy shot a look at his dad, who grinned and pointed toward the Cyanites with his off-hand sword.

With a false gruffness, he said, "It is best to follow the commands of She-Who-Must-Be-Obeyed."

Grinning himself, Billy followed the Cyanites out of the cave. As he passed the entrance, he looked up. The comet was clearly visible. He pointed up.

"I see it," his mom said. "I think it's bigger than when we started."

"Definitely." Yul was looking up. "We've already been here an hour. I'm not sure how much time they'll give us to cross the river to the post-impact zone."

"Four hours max, I think," whispered Kathy.

"I thought we were staying off spoiler websites," Yul replied.

"Purely accidental," she said. "Couldn't be helped."

Before they exited the clearing, the largest Cyanite paused and pointedly looked behind a boulder. He reached back and drew out a first aid kit, which he ceremonially handed to Billy.

"We should have looked around," Kathy hissed to Yul. "What a noob mistake."

They exited the clearing and followed a path that Billy wouldn't have found on his own. From time to time, the baby Cyanite peeked over his mother's shoulder and granted Billy a dimpled smile.

They had a few minor encounters, took some damage, but managed to slay the variety of predators that attacked, including a gigantic Venus Man Trap. All of the Kwans now had blood stains on their armor. They wore those stains proudly—marks of experience within SPARK.

It felt to Billy as though another hour had passed. The heat was oppressive, and they had run out of water.

The Cyanites entered a small dusty clearing with a fire pit charred in the center. Yul checked it and reported no smoke or heat. The Cyanites looked concerned as they scanned the nearby trees. Billy thought he could see some sort of nests higher up, but nothing moved. The air was still.

Kathy adjusted her grip on her sword and whispered, "I've got a bad feeling about this. Eyes out!"

They formed a rough circle with the fire pit at the center, the Cyanite mother and baby inside the perimeter formed by the Kwans and Daddy Cyanite. At first, Billy thought it was an overreaction. Then he noticed thousands of three-toed footprints in the dust where they now stood.

He said, "I think—"

The circle of vegetation around them erupted with small dinosaurs. They looked like miniature velociraptors, and were wickedly fast.

Billy shot first and kept shooting. They weren't invincible. They weren't even tough, Billy realized. But they made up for those weaknesses in speed, size, and numbers. *They're hard to hit.*

Billy squeezed the trigger as fast as he could, missing more often than he hit, but still killing several. They began to give him a wider berth, concentrating on the Cyanites and his parents. Billy turned to his right and took out a couple that had made it close to his mom. Then he did the same for his dad.

"Billy," Dad called, "The Cyanites!"

Billy turned and looked behind him. Daddy Cyanite had only a club to use for protection and was flailing it about him, taking out one or two on each swing. The problem for all of them was not that the dinosaurs were tough to kill, but that it was impossible to kill them all.

Billy heard his mom scream in pain.

"Oh God. Spitters!"

Venomous lizards with debilitating saliva. Mom was trying to wipe some poison off her bicep.

As Billy turned, he got hit full in the face. Three times. *Splat. Splat. Splat.* His vision blanked, and he could see his health indicator begin to decrease as small green numbers were subtracted from his total.

He tried to remember which direction he was facing—he couldn't afford to fire blindly and take out a member of his party.

"Point me, Dad!"

"Straight ahead. You're good." His dad's voice was strained.

Behind him, Billy heard a ululating cry, loud but melodic. In the distance, it was echoed. He began to hear whistling sounds—high-speed projectiles—piercing the air. They ended with a wet impact.

"Cease fire. Cease fire," Dad said.

Billy stopped pulling the trigger but continued to point his blaster down range. He checked his health. He was at 30 percent and dropping.

"Mom, Dad." He tried to sound calm. "I need some help here." *I don't want to get killed out.*

"Hang on, hang on," his mom said.

Twenty percent and falling. At 11 percent, he heard the pneumatic hiss of a first aid hypo.

10%. 9%. 8%. 8%. 8%.

He would make it but couldn't afford any more damage.

His vision began to clear—only enough to make out shapes. The world remained monochromatic, gray, and fuzzy.

"How you doing, Sport?" His dad sounded tired but relieved.

"Holding at eight percent. Still kinda blind."

Billy could make out a number of shapes moving in his direction. He raised his blaster.

"No. No. Hold your fire," his dad said. "They're friendlies."

Billy began to hear several quiet, sing-song voices. Small hands touched his arms and chest. He heard the hiss of first aid hypos, and his health climbed rapidly.

When his vision cleared, he was surrounded by a dozen or so Cyanites. His mom and dad were both standing, but he heard the singing behind him turn mournful. Daddy Cyanite was dead. Mommy held the baby and knelt next to her mate's body, crying her sorrow. Billy felt a lump in his throat.

Around the fire pit were at least thirty dead Spitters. The Cyanites were ignoring them, but Billy's dad was checking the bodies, occasionally making approving noises as he found something to add to their inventory.

Billy walked over to the dead Cyanite and squatted down next to the mother and child.

"I'm sorry, guys."

They looked at him and nodded, then stood.

A pair of Cyanites had started a fire. Another pair lifted the dead father and placed him on the fire. Electric blue flames shot into the sky, and the fire quickly died out. The body was gone. In its place was a flawless blue sapphire. Baby and mother presented the gem to Billy and his family, singing a solemn tune tinged with gratitude.

As Billy was adding this to his inventory, a disagreement broke out between two of the larger Cyanites. They were speaking in low, urgent tones, first pointing to the sky, and then pointing in two directions. While this went on, Kathy pulled Yul and Billy aside.

"Okay, true confessions time. I may have seen more on that spoiler site than I should have."

Yul rolled his eyes.

The Kwans tried to avoid spoilers because they did just that—spoiled a quest.

"Well, do you want to know or not?"

Billy and his dad looked at each other.

Billy shrugged. "Don't tell us anything major."

Yul nodded his agreement.

"Okay," Kathy said. "Two things—really, just two is all I know. How many Cyanites do you see?"

Yul looked around. "Maybe twelve. Fourteen?"

Kathy nodded. "Weird thing number one: there are only three mentioned. Mommy, Daddy, and Baby. Nobody said anything about an entire tribe."

"Maybe they did an update," Billy said.

Kathy shook her head, blonde hair tangling with her ARGs until she brushed it out of the way.

"The revision numbers for the major quests were all the same when we checked in. No major updates since SPARK opened a year ago."

"Huh," Yul said. "What's the second thing?"

"The baby always dies during the T-Rex battle."

The two Cyanites in disagreement walked over to them and began talking. They pointed up.

Above the group, the comet had gotten visibly larger. Billy thought he could see jets of gas billowing off a solid rocky core.

"It's way closer," he said.

Yul tapped the side of his ARGs. "We've been in here over three hours. We need to get moving."

"Yeah," Kathy said. "The Kwans aren't going to be taken out by some stupid space rock."

Billy nodded.

"We understand," Yul told the argumentative pair. "We need to go."

They both gave him very human nods and gestured for the Kwans to follow. They did so, with Billy leading again. Within ten minutes, they were on the bank of a river so wide, Billy couldn't see the far side. Spray leapt up where the strong current slammed against a couple rock formations.

"How do we get across?" Billy said.

"Good news, bad news, Sport," Dad replied. "The good news is that if we make it across the river, we're in the post-impact zone and won't be killed off by *a stupid space rock*."

"Hey!" Mom said in good nature.

"Bad news is that I don't know how."

"Maybe the Cyanites do," Billy said.

The two that had disagreed in the clearing joined them. The first pointed west, then pantomimed something falling—possibly a tree, Billy thought—by holding one arm straight up and then lowering it to horizontal with plenty of crashing sound effects. He then used his other hand to walk two fingers across the fallen tree. The second interrupted and pointed east. His pantomime was less clear but seemed to involve a large lumbering beast. In his version, he walked his fingers up on to the back of the beast.

"That's the brontosaurus we saw in line while we were waiting," Dad said. "It had people on its back. That's how we can cross!"

"I wish we had some way to ask which is closer," Mom said.

"Let's do the brontosaurus," said Billy.

Both Cyanites were looking at the sky and chattering with excitement. Apparently, they came to an agreement, as all of the Cyanites began pushing the Kwans west, urging them to run.

"I thought the brontosaurus was the other way," Billy yelled to be heard, as they crashed through the jungle, speed now prioritized over stealth.

The Cyanites just pushed them to run faster.

Within minutes, they were at the fallen tree. Billy had to admit, the Cyanite had done a decent job of conveying the concept. It must have rivaled a giant redwood in size. Had it been flat instead of round, you could have driven a car across. Had it been clean, dry, and equipped with a handrail, crossing it on foot would have been a cakewalk.

Spray from the river flumed over the tree bridge. Moss coated it like a slimy blanket, except where the bark had stripped off and left behind a slick, shiny core of wood. The flow of the river seemed erratic and nearly random, occasionally shooting spouts of water against, or just above, the tree.

Billy peered over the riverbank. Icy water ricocheted off the craggy boulders below stinging his face. *Wouldn't be the fall that would kill you. It's not that far. No, it would be the current slamming you against the rocks.*

With one Cyanite leading them, and the rest of them urging the Kwans onward, Billy and his dad agreed that Mom should go first.

"No, no, I'll take the rear," she said.

Yul gently pushed her forward. "You'll go faster knowing we're behind you."

"Don't rush me! I like to be sure of my footing."

Billy looked up at the comet. "Mom, I can see it getting closer. We don't have much time. Please!"

She cast him a withering look that promised a later discussion, and stepped onto the tree. Several steps in, she seemed to have gained confidence.

"It's not so bad—" Her feet flew out from under her and she landed with a grunt on her side.

She slowly began sliding off the tree.

"Mom!" Billy yelled.

Cyanites skittered over and around Billy. They swarmed Kathy. Clearly, their bare feet and prehensile toes gave them better traction. They stopped her slide and pulled her back to the top of the tree bridge. She elected to crawl from that point on.

On the far side of the river, the Cyanites bade them farewell and gifted them with a few spare first aid kits and one of the slings they used to bring down the Spitters.

"Come with us," Kathy pleaded. "You'll die if you go back across!" She pointed upward to where the comet now outshone the sun.

They simply waved and trotted nimbly across the tree.

Just as they were about to disappear from sight, the sky lit up. Incandescent crimson and ambers made it through Billy's tightly shut eyes. The shockwave knocked them off their feet. The river vaporized and hit them with a wave of steam.

When they could stand, the south side of the river was blanketed in ashy gray and black clouds. The tree bridge was gone. Shattered remnants scattered the jungle floor around them.

"Whoa," Yul whispered. "That was way too close."

The Kwans stood looking at the devastation for a few moments.

Using her Mom voice, Kathy said, "I'm tired and thirsty and hungry. Let's take a break."

Billy and Yul nodded.

She tapped her ARGs. "Show me the nearest exit."

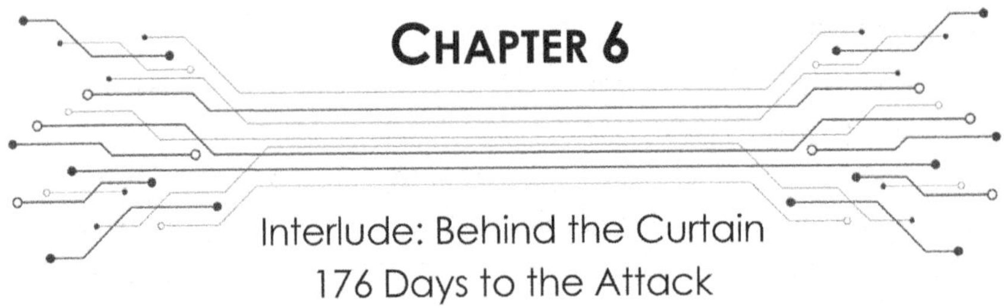

CHAPTER 6

Interlude: Behind the Curtain
176 Days to the Attack

"Pay no attention to that man behind the curtain!"
—The Great and Powerful Oz

"Let's keep it magic. No guests should ever see behind the curtain."
—HVH

"Kid's messed up," Taggert said from his wheelchair, scrolling the camera and zooming in on WB's face.

"True." Bull squinted at the screen.

He'd decided to swing by Security before getting chow. The kid's face was slack, like there was nobody home.

Bull had been in Korea II with Taggert. Both were nearly killed by the same land mine. Bull ended up with a permanent limp, but Taggert lost both legs from just above the knee down. He never adapted to prosthetics, and rode through life in a wheelchair. Old style. Manually pumping the rims of the wheels to propel himself along. Claimed it was the only way he could stay in shape. Now, his fingerless gloves sat on his desk as he patrolled SPARK virtually.

"What do we know about him?" Taggert said. "I mean, besides the whole knife thing?"

He didn't take his eyes off the screen, where Knife Boy stood motionless in the middle of PreHistory Plaza—the large open area at the end of the arcade, on the rim end. It was home to the quest itself, plus a bunch of smaller quests—independent of KT Crossing, but with similar, prehistoric themes.

"I checked with Hodgins before I came down," Bull replied, also staring at Taggert's main screen. *The kid's like a rock in a river. People are just flowing around him.* "Janne gave us a positive ID. Name's Will Kwan. He's been here before, but not for six years. Came with his parents then."

"Well, he's definitely alone now. Right?" Taggert directed his flinty eyes sharply at Bull.

"Relax. He's definitely solo. He came to the bus terminal in Barstow two days in a row before today. Nobody was with him or really paid any attention to him either day."

Bull understood Taggert's sudden concern. One of the big fears in Security was people that entered separately and looked innocent but were working together for some ill intent.

"He do this at the terminal, too?" Taggert pointed a calloused finger at the screen. "Freeze?"

"Yeah," Bull replied. "First time kinda freaked Destardi out, but he just stood there. Had a backpack with him then. That's where the knife was."

"What kind of knife are we talking about? Pocket knife? Bowie?"

"Big ass butcher knife. Millimeter-wave scan pegged it at a nine-inch blade."

"Huh. Not really a weapon, then. Although, you could do some serious slicing and dicing on someone, I guess."

"Yeah," Bull said. "I mean, if you were going to fight with a knife, you'd want something with a guard on it, right? And a solid pommel to crack heads if you needed to? Like a KA-BAR."

"Exactly like a KA-BAR," Taggert said. "'Cept I'd want a knuckle guard on it, too."

Bullard rolled his eyes—they'd had the whole optimal combat knife design conversation before—and bit his lip to avoid re-starting the argument. *A knuckle guard just makes it too hard to change your grip.*

"Anyway, kid's avatar name was WonderBoy back in the day," Bull said. "Just changed it to WB. Check out his avatar design."

He reached out to change the view on the monitor so that they'd see what guests saw, but Taggert swatted his hand away.

"Don't touch." He made the change himself.

Knife Boy, with his greasy blackish hair, cargo shorts, and T-shirt, disappeared. In his place stood a player with Knife Boy's face, but now with blond hair and dressed in an old-style baseball uniform. Taggert toggled camera views so he could get a 360-degree look at the kid. He had a baseball bat strapped to his back, and a blaster on his hip. The number 9 was visible on the back of the uniform.

"Well, that's not something you see every day," Taggert said. "Armor styled to look like a baseball uniform."

"Hodgins says to check out a movie called *The Natural*. Says the kid's avatar is styled after some fictional baseball player named Hobbs." Bull shrugged. "Says it's a decent vid."

"And what's up with his hair?" Taggert switched back to raw video.

"I'm not sure," Bull said. "I sat behind him on the bus. Looks like he tried to color it, but the red or orange is burning its way back out. Looks like crap. Greasy as hell."

They watched silently for a few seconds as Knife Boy remained motionless on the screen.

"Thousand-yard stare," said Taggert. "That's what he looks like. Remember Creegan after Seoul? Guy just checked out. Sat there looking into the distance, but not focused on anything. Kid looks like that."

"Yeah, you're right," Bull said. *What has the kid been through?* "Hey, I'm going to get some chow. Want to come along?"

"Nah." Taggert shook head, graying stubble catching the light. "I've got to monitor this *threat* external Security decided belonged in our park." He pointed at the screen and the image of WB.

"Can I bring you back something?" Bull stood upright.

"Yeah, but none of those damn cookies." Taggert patted his flat stomach. "Trying to stay in fighting shape."

"All right." Bull shook his head.

Even without legs, Taggert was one of the fittest guys he knew.

He started to walk away.

"Hey, Bull!" Taggert called out. "Whatever happened to Creegan?"

Bull didn't like the topic but answered truthfully.

"Came back and stayed in a VA hospital stateside for a while. Then, the day he got out, he punched his own ticket." Bull mimed a gun to his own head, his thumb dropping like the hammer of the weapon.

"Too many." Taggert shook his head.

"Too many," Bull said.

– 1 1 0 1 0 0 1 0 –

Will stood still, eyes not quite focused on KT Crossing, lost in the memory of six years ago.

Billy and his parents emerged from KT Crossing, back into the sunlight of midday in the High Desert. Their ARGs darkened quickly and gave them respite from the glare.

They were trying to decide where to eat, when Billy said, "Mom, Dad…"

Kathy and Yul looked up to see a tall, bald, stocky black man with a goatee, walking toward them. He stood out because, in a sea of barbarians, elves, and knights in armor, he was wearing khakis and a blue long-sleeved, pinstriped button-down—and no ARGs.

"I'm Jeffrey Hodgins," he said. "I work here at SPARK and would love to talk to you about your visit so far. I don't want to cut into your questing time. Could I buy you lunch so we can eat and talk at the same time?"

Billy's dad seemed skeptical, but his mom overrode him.

"We'll be happy to let you buy us lunch."

They let Hodgins lead them to the Cretaceous Cocina. Along the way, a tall skinny man joined them.

"This is Fitz Flaherty," said Hodgins. "We call him Double F. He's the head referee for KT Crossing. Do you mind if he joins us?"

Kathy and Yul exchanged glances and micro-shrugs.

"It's okay with us," Yul said.

The five of them entered a quiet booth.

Billy halted and backed away from the table, frowning. Near the table, it was silent. Eerily so. Away from the table, he could hear the normal conversation and clatter of people eating lunch.

He stepped up to the table again. Silence. Stepped back, sounds of the restaurant returned. He repeated this a couple times, until his dad grabbed him by the arm and pulled him into the booth.

"It's a sound curtain," he whispered to Billy. "They're using noise-cancelling tech to make the booth quieter." He looked over at Hodgins. "Two-way?"

Hodgins nodded, and Yul turned back to Billy.

"It works both ways. People on the other side won't be able to hear us, either. What's this about?"

"Can we just order first, please?" Kathy was polite, but hungry.

After tapping in their orders on the tabletop touch screen, Hodgins asked them to recap their morning.

Billy was somber. “Are we in trouble?”

He looked at his parents and then at the referee, who gave him a big smile. Like Billy, Fitz Flaherty was a ginger. Billy’s hair was cropped short, where the referee wore his longer, in a not-quite-contained ponytail that bobbed as he talked to Billy.

“Absolutely not, little dude!”

Hodgins said, “It’s just, no one has done it before. When you did what you did, you discovered an Easter Egg.”

The family looked at each other.

“Did what?” Billy’s dad said.

“Generally, the encounter with the T-Rex results in guests meeting the Cyanite family and sheltering together in the cave. Normally,” Hodgins lowered his voice, “the baby doesn’t make it.”

Double F held up a hand. “Hodge, let’s limit the spoilers, okay?”

Hodgins nodded, then gestured for Double F to continue.

“You saved the baby Cyanite. That earned you a thing called the Mark of Cyan.” Flaherty was hunched over the table, whispering, in spite of the sound curtain. “Then you went on to battle the Spitters, meet the entire Cyanite tribe, and were the first guests ever to cross the tree bridge. Saving the baby opened up an entirely new branch of the quest.”

“Woo-hoo!” Billy said. “We found an Egg.”

The family high-fived around the table.

Hodgins tone became somber. “What happens when Eggs show up on the fan sites?”

“They lose their specialness, Mister Hodgins,” said Billy’s mom.

“Please, call me Jeffrey. So what happens?”

“Everybody knows where and how to find the eggs,” said Yul, “and goes after them, if they’ve got good loot or perks.”

Both Flaherty and Hodgins nodded.

“It took your family almost four hours to cross the river,” the ref said. “You were very close to being killed out, based on time—four hours is our max to cross the river.”

“Yeah,” Billy said, “but we’re almost at Level 3 already!”

They liked playing this way, exploring all the nooks and crannies of a good game. It was the Kwan way. They were completionists.

Hodgins leaned back and nodded, hands chest-high, palms forward.

"No argument here," he said. "But let's talk about the Egg. Keeping Easter Eggs hidden makes discovering them a joyful, momentous experience."

"So you're buying us lunch to keep us quiet?" Yul said.

Billy's dad was giving the man the kind of look he sometimes gave Billy. It meant, *Think about your answer.* His black hair and dark eyes gave him an intense air.

"There's more," Hodgins replied. "If every group followed your path, we'd overload KT Crossing—too many people taking too much time to complete it."

Kathy's blue eyes lit up. "There's nothing wrong with taking your time in a quest!"

Hodgins held up his hands again.

"You're absolutely right. But SPARK is still a business, and we want it to run smoothly."

Kathy visibly calmed, and Hodgins continued.

"We're offering some perks to sweeten the deal. Free days, comped room, things like that. Think of it as loot attached to the Egg."

"Well…" Yul said.

"Throw in free meals at resort restaurants," said Billy's mom.

Hodgins looked thoughtful.

"We might be able to do that." He nodded.

"Deal." Kathy looked at Yul. "We're not made of money." She turned back to Hodgins. "And all we have to do is keep our mouths shut about this Easter Egg?"

Both of the SPARK employees nodded.

Yul and Kathy looked at each other and at Billy, who was giving them his best wide-eyed puppy stare. They all nodded to each other and then solemnly shook hands with Fitz Flaherty and Hodgins.

Double F looked at Hodgins. "Business over?"

Hodgins nodded.

"Great." Double F turned to the family. "Let's talk about where you are on the quest, and why you took the path you did."

Billy took over the conversation and acted out a few encounters. By the time the Kwan family hit the re-entry point for KT Crossing, they'd spent a full hour at lunch, but were refreshed and eager to get back at it.

Following lunch, the Kwans could skip the line and re-enter the quest just past the river. Feeling vindicated in their strategy, they took a tedious approach to finishing KT Crossing. When they finally exited, they were tired, and it was too late to try another major quest. They'd been in SPARK over ten hours.

"I'm kinda hungry," Billy said, when they exited.

"We don't have time to hit another major quest," his dad said. "Want to just churro-up, and then do some of the small quests along the PreHistory Arcade?"

They spent another hour doing that. Each arcade's theme matched the major quest at its rim end. For PreHistory, it was megaflora and megafauna. Deep greens, vivid blues, and the sounds of a jungle.

Billy's mom finally called a stop. As they rode to their hotel, they talked about the KT Crossing launch.

"It was so cool!" Billy exclaimed. "First, just darkness. Then, right when I start thinking something's gone wrong—*bam!*"

Yul smiled and nodded. "It was as if a rainbow exploded. Colors swirling everywhere."

Kathy laughed. "Then we're suddenly in the jungle. I don't know what scared me more—the roar of the T-Rex, or you screaming *Run!* at me." She smiled at her son.

"Maybe next time, we'll be Leveled-up enough to take on the Rex!" Even after a long day, Billy was animated.

His dad reached over and tousled Billy's hair. "Maybe, Sport."

Kathy frowned. "Weird that they had a Princess Quest in the middle of the PreHistory stuff."

"I'm just glad it was a short quest," Yul said. "Tough riddle. I think we can safely skip it from now on." He glanced at Billy.

"Yeah." Kathy was quiet for a moment. "She seemed so sad, though. What was that about?"

The day after they got home, Kim Jung Un and North Korea followed through on a long-standing threat and nuked Guam, a territory of the United States. One month later, Yul Kwan, a citizen of both South Korea and the United States of America, left to fight in the war.

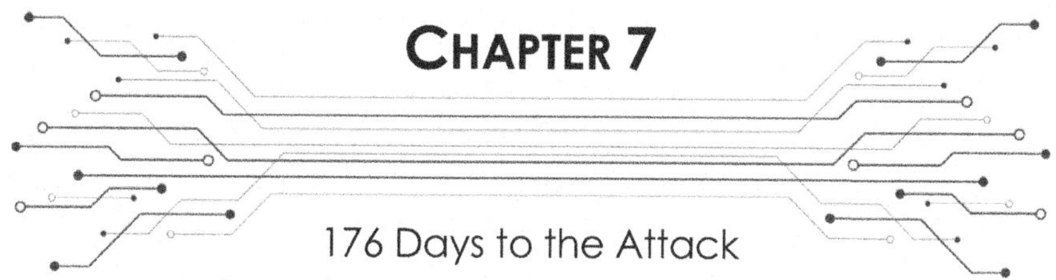

Chapter 7

176 Days to the Attack

Someone has justly remarked, that "eternal vigilance is the price of liberty." Let the sentinels on the watch-tower sleep not, and slumber not.
—The Virginia Free Press and Farmers' Repository, May 2, 1833

Sitting in his office, Hodgins ran a hand over his bare scalp. His concern about Knife Boy was mostly gone—mostly. Something was familiar about the kid. The knife still bugged him, but when the kid's palm print was covertly read as he pushed the entry door open, the security system ID'd him as Billy Kwan. Hodge relaxed and sent Janne the data.

William Arthur Kwan aka Billy, aged 16. Last park entry: six years ago. Status: orphaned. Listed as a ward of the state. Houston PD lists him as a runaway from foster care, but no extradition request. No history of trouble or violence. Ref: Cyanite Savior/Egg. Admit.

It would have been nice to be able to turn it all over to Janne. They couldn't. Connecting the AI to the net was too risky. Hodge insisted and Hecker Van Horne agreed: Keep the Jannes isolated. It meant having a human in the loop sometimes—another weakness—but less so than a door that was always open.

The kid's ID brought its own problems. California law required notification regarding runaways. Theoretically, SPARK had a duty to inform law enforcement about Will's presence. Failing to do so put SPARK at risk. This wasn't SCAZ—as much as some people thought it was.

Within the first year of opening, they'd ID'd a guest as a runaway. Hodgins went directly to HVH. They'd argued.

"Boss, it's the law!"

"Just because a bunch of morons got elected and passed a law, doesn't make it smart!" Van Horne retorted, his gravelly voice gaining a hard edge. "Look, Hodge." Van Horne's tone softened, and he stood and tugged down his loose black T-shirt as he walked around the desk to stand closer to the head of Security. "I would rather SPARK police itself. *We* keep our guests safe. As good as local law enforcement is, they'll never be here in time to stop something bad from happening. It's on us. That's why we put so much covert surveillance in place to begin with. *We* need to know. If a kid reported missing shows up at our gates with an unrelated adult, we'll turn them over to Barstow PD before they make it to the Hub. But a kid runs away from a bad situation and manages to make it here? We're going to welcome them with open arms and wish them a great day in the park."

Hodgins got the point, but it went against his core to ignore the law.

Van Horne ran his hands through his dark, wavy hair, with streaks of gray near his temples, and continued.

"Besides…eventually, someone's going to ask how we ID'd the kid, and how we even knew he was missing. I mean, it's not like Iowa sends us specs on every kid who runs away. Those questions are going to get asked, and that means revealing how much data we gather, how closely we watch our guests. Every time a guest's palm hits the entry door, we grab their prints. Every time they sit in the trolley, we scan their retinas. We do it because we know it's important to keep people safe. And knowing who is in our park gets us ninety percent of the way there."

In time, Hodgins came to see the wisdom of this approach. He spec'd the systems SPARK installed. They *did* make the park safer. It was proven by the number of attacks they'd prevented over the years—everything from notorious pedophiles to international terrorists got stopped before they ever hit the Hub. So Hodgins agreed they would ignore runaways. Since Korea II and the associated terror attacks, there were too many orphaned and abandoned kids for the system to handle. *At least here, we can keep them safe.*

That decision consequently led to tolerating the Pod—a small group of kids, all in their teens, who figured out how to beat the system and stay overnight in SPARK. Now, they lived there. Hodgins could accept that, but he wasn't going to make it easy on them.

What scared him was stuff like the email he'd just gotten from the Department of State.

Hodgins re-read the email. Today's was the second he'd gotten from State this month:

From: Greyman@us.state.gov

To: Jeff.Hodgins@SPAugRealityPark.com

Subj: Specific Mention

Mr. Hodgins,

It is the policy of the US State Department to alert individuals and organizations when they or their organization is specifically mentioned in a post by a known threat group. You are receiving this email because you are listed as the point of contact for:

Solar Prime Augmented Reality Park (SPARK)

Hecker Van Horne (HVH)

The above entity/entities were mentioned on social media by Daesh (formerly ISIS/Islamic State of Iraq and Syria).

Translation follows.

"...and HVH attack the Prophet. Death to the infidel! Death to SPARK!"

The screed went on, but the message was the same. Hodgins noted wryly that even Daesh had picked up on the American media's habit of referring to the boss as HVH. *Hecker Van Horne* apparently took too long to write in a terrorist blog.

This is in response to HVH's answer in an interview for PlayMax. Hodge recalled the segment.

"Mister Van Horne, would you please describe your perfect woman?"

"Happily. I think the ideal woman, and life partner, is smart, well-educated, and lethal."

Daesh is probably okay with lethal, but not so much with smart or well-educated women. Or it could be in response to SPARK's adults-only area. Some truly bizarre stuff happened there—but all between consenting adults. There's no crossing that line.

I'll let Hecker know in the afternoon staff meeting.

Hodge was about to click on to his next email, when SPARK's head of non-Janne IT knocked on his open door. A thin young woman with a dark complexion and short hair. Perennially in jeans and a sci-fi T-shirt. Today's read, *Han shot first.*

"Got a minute?" said Connie.

"Anything to get me up from behind this desk," Hodgins replied. "Can we walk and talk? I'm thinking of wandering down to the cafeteria for one of those cookies they put out around now."

"I'm training for the SCAZ triathlon," she said. "Maybe just one."

Hodgins pushed away from his desk, and the two made their way together.

"So what's up?" he said.

"I wanted to give you an update on those cyberattacks we've seen in the past month," she said. "It's a good news-bad news-worse news thing."

"Huh," Hodge grunted. "Okay, let's go from good to terrible."

"Here goes," Connie said. "We've had four in the past month. The good news is we stopped them all. One was a simple denial-of-service spam attack on our public-facing network. Easily handled, but surprisingly quick and precisely timed. They hit us during peak traffic. Still, we slapped them down without any problem. Now, for the bad. The other three were way more subtle and ingenious attempts to access our intranet." She made a wiggling gesture with one hand, emulating a worm or snake. "The first two were probes that looked legit but were quickly caught by the mini-Jannes. The last was the scariest. It was simultaneous with the spam attack, and was from a legitimate vendor sending back delivery information on an order. We talked with the vendor, and they never knew they'd been hacked. They've checked all their traffic. Hodge." she took him by the arm and turned him to face her. "None of their other customers or contacts were touched. Somebody hacked them specifically to get to us."

They reached the cafeteria. Hodge grabbed a chocolate chip cookie, and Connie went for an oatmeal raisin.

"Raisins don't belong in cookies," Hodgins muttered around a mouthful of chewy, chocolatey goodness as they headed back to Security. "Any idea where the hacks might be coming from?"

"Yeah, it's kind of weird," Connie said. "All four were eventually traced to either what's left of North Korea, or Mozambique. North Korea, I figure that's just a degree of separation from China. But I had to google Mozambique. What's up with that?"

Hodgins knew he was going to be hitting the antacid as soon as he got back to his desk.

"Mozambique used to be very close buddies with North Korea," he replied. "They were the conduit for skirting UN sanctions. North Korean troops trained Mozambique forces." He sighed. "Thanks for the update. Keep me in the loop."

He bumped fists with Connie as they separated.

Four attacks in the last month, and they are getting more sophisticated. It made his gut churn. Elite attacks meant two things: big money and big brains. He worried it wasn't just a group. It might be a government. When a tech-savvy country with lots of cash decided they wanted to get into your system, they were almost guaranteed to be successful. *Maybe these four are just the ones we've stopped. Maybe we're already compromised.*

Hodgins scowled at the thought and popped a couple more Tums into his mouth, chasing the cookie.

– 1 1 0 1 0 0 1 0 –

A smaller kid bumped into Will, pulling him out of his reverie. Will checked the chrono corner of his ARGs. *Crap!* He'd been standing in front of KT Crossing for nearly a half-hour. *Why do I do that?* Time was wasting.

He turned and headed back to the Hub. He would work his way back up one side and back down the other.

Will knew online trolls called these arcades *Aisles of misfit quests*—minor, fairly easy, and potentially time-consuming, generally skipped by park-goers. Even those who didn't mock them seemed to feel time was better spent elsewhere, and a common refrain was, "C'mon, shouldn't everything in the arcade leading to or from KT Crossing somehow pertain to PreHistory? Does there *really* need to be a Princess in every arcade?"

In a methodical manner that would have made his parents proud, WB turned back up the PreHistory Arcade and began doing every quest and attraction on the right-hand side. He spent two hours doing minor quests all related to PreHistory: The Big Bang, Inflationary Universes, Aggregation of Matter, and Birth of Stars. Some were first-person shooters. Some puzzle or experimentation based. All immersed him in their own virtual universes and challenged him physically or mentally. Often both. He'd earned some XP and enjoyed the experience. *This is actually pretty fun. These quests aren't misfits.*

Along the way, he gained some fundamental insights into light, gravitation, and electricity. He was learning an impressive amount of physics.

I don't need any plush Sparkys. I can skip the shops.

He was almost back to KT Crossing Plaza when he ran headlong into what people griped about most: the Princesses. The theme of the arcade was jarringly interrupted by his first Princess encounter.

He was at the top, or rim end, of the PreHistory Arcade. He could see the entrance to KT Crossing in the distance, the line already long. Will had progressed up the right side of the arcade, doing each of the small quests in order. Now, he got to a doorway that wasn't even labeled. It was just next in line.

He entered a small hall. In it stood a young virtual Princess. She was wearing a pale gown the color of ballet slippers, and a cone-shaped hat with a veil attached to its apex. Eyes that, at first glance, were wrongly assumed to be brown. Only greater scrutiny revealed them as deep violet shot through with flecks of gray.

"Good." She looked right at him. "You're here."

Will looked around.

Not only was he *here*, he was the only actual human in the room. It seemed to be a chamber in a castle, complete with stone walls, flickering torches in sconces, and a couple tapestries hanging from the wall. He popped his ARGs up and saw the blandest room in SPARK: lightly textured beige walls, and a polished concrete floor.

Will lowered his ARGs. The far wall showed a number of doors. The Princess hurried toward one and looked back over her shoulder at Will.

"Come along," she told him. "We don't have much time."

A door slid aside as they approached. In the next room, she knelt down on the floor and began explaining.

"You've got to help me. The points of the star will guide you. Our first challenge is this." She began to sketch on the floor.

The diagram showed up and persisted in Will's ARGs as if she were writing on the floor with chalk.

"The attraction of bodies warps the heavens and confounds people everywhere," she said. "Why are some more strongly attracted than others? Why are some weak and some strong?"

She seemed to be drawing dots on the floor, and then stick-figure people emerged as she connected some of the dots. She put long hair on one of the stick figures—the universal manner to differentiate stick-figure men from stick-figure women.

"Does absence truly make the heart grow fonder?" she continued. "If so, why do bodies closer together seem to exert a stronger pull on each other? What's the relationship?"

She paused and looked at Will. The Princess looked to be younger than him. *Maybe nine or ten.*

She gazed earnestly into his eyes and repeated her question.

"I don't know..." he replied.

"Please," she implored. We haven't much time." She pointed to the half-drained hourglass she carried. "They'll know I've gone. What's the relationship?"

Will racked his brain. Clearly, this was a puzzle-based quest, but he had no idea what she was asking.

"Husband and wife?" he said tentatively.

The Princess lost some of her solid appearance.

"No, that can't be it." She seemed to have a touch of a Scottish accent. "What's the relationship?" Another glance at the hourglass.

The Princess said something about stars and the heavens when he first entered this room. Were her dots supposed to be stars? Were the figures constellations? Was there even a constellation with a man and a woman? Hadn't he just seen something in one of the other exhibits?

"They're twins!" he blurted, thinking of Castor and Pollux. *Aren't they both guys?*

His hopes were dashed as she faded.

"Find me. Save me..." She grew more and more transparent.

When she was gone, a door opened and WB's ARGs showed, *Exit now, please.*

Every hair on Will's body stood on end. *Find me, save me?* Those were the exact words his mom used in her letter.

Will felt a sudden urgency to solve the riddle as he stood and walked out.

That was a clear failure. What was the point? What did it have to do with anything else in PreHistory, or even in SPARK?

He still didn't have an answer to the riddle. *Maybe I should go back and hear it again.* He couldn't remember the exact wording.

He decided it was worth the ten minutes it would take him.

Once again, he was the only one in line, and walked right in.

"Good." The Princess looked right at him. "You're here."

Will tried to take in more of the virtual décor this time. *Sometimes game designers put clues in the environment.*

The tapestries on the wall showed stock medieval themes: a couple in a glade with a dog; two girls playing near a well, a picnic lunch laid out nearby; a battle scene with a coat of arms in the corner. The coat of arms was pitch black on one half. The other half had a sky-blue background with a multipoint star in the center. Will assumed it was a stylized rendition of Sparky that caused a single synapse in his brain to fire. Enough to feel important, but not enough to resurrect a thought or memory.

This star, or Sparky, had no facial features. *Maybe that's why it seems a little off.*

The Princess was trying to lead him to the door.

"Come along," she said. "We don't have much time."

She repeated this line when he didn't immediately follow her.

Once they entered the room, she didn't kneel down and start drawing, although she used the same introduction:

"You've got to help me. The points of the star will guide you. Our first challenge is this: *It lies to our eyes. It lies to my eyes. I see the key dimly in the glass, but when I reach through the opening, I can no longer see the glass and what I reach for is not where it should be. How does it move? Why does it move?*"

Throughout this, she was miming looking for something and then reaching for it as if having to turn away to put her arm through an opening.

"It's not the same riddle!" Will said.

The Princess lost some of her solid appearance.

"No, that can't be it. How does it move? Why does it move?" She glanced at the hourglass.

"How many different riddles do you ask?" Will said, irked.

His hope for a relevant response faded as she did.

"Find me. Save me."

There it is again! Could it just be coincidence?

His ARGs repeated the annoying display, *Exit now, please.*

"No wonder people hate this part," he muttered, as he left.

It was aggravating. He got two guesses. Period. From the urgency the Princess expressed, Will figured it was both time-based and guess-based. As soon as you ran out of either, she would fade, and you'd be shown the exit.

At least it was mercifully quick. How do they expect you to solve a riddle that changes every time?

Most games gave you a menu of choices. Most would repeat the riddle as many times as you needed to hear it, and certainly none of them changed the riddle.

He needed to blow off some steam. He remembered seeing a shooting gallery across from KT Crossing. He'd head there. Along the way, he looked at other players.

So many beautiful women. It's hard not to stare. He barked out a laugh when the realization hit. *Of course all the women are beautiful. All the men are handsome. Who creates an ugly avatar?*

There were some skeletons, orcish halflings and whatnot, but they were the exception.

– 1 1 0 1 0 0 1 0 –

Turn and fire! Turn and fire!

WB was a ball turret gunner on an orbital defense platform. His cockpit buffeted as he blasted meteoroids out of existence to keep Earth's sky clear. The plasma cannon sizzled and boomed with each shot. *Am I actually smelling ozone?* The pungent thunderstorm odor seemed to accompany each blast.

Plan the shots. These things follow orbital trajectories, not straight lines. Big swooping arcs that tightened and accelerated near gravity wells. Even with the wait, WB loved it, played three times and finished soaked in sweat.

His ARGs displayed a *Level Up!* message during the third game.

Will found a quiet spot and tapped his way through the ARG menu. *Where's the Help button? Tutorial?* Scroll and click. He was in.

WB skimmed the rules. *Fairly consistent with other game universes.*

Every player started at Level 1, with one point in each of six attributes: Brains, Brawn, Likability, Vigor, Agility, and Aptitude. Players got an additional four points to allocate as they desired. When you leveled up, you gained another point. Since the system wasn't in place when WonderBoy first built his profile, SPARK's systems—in other words, Janne—spread his points evenly across the six attributes. The tutorial said, in this case, players could rebalance once at no cost. As a newly minted Level 15, WB had twenty-five points to allocate.

Something's wrong. The numbers don't add up. If you start with ten points and then gain a point for each level, I should have twenty-four, not twenty-five. Did I somehow earn an extra point when we were here before?

He shook his head and tried to set them all to zero. *Can't get Likability to zero. It's stuck at one. Huh. I'll just go with it, figure it out later.*

As a kid, he always went heavy on Brawn and Vigor. Brawn allowed you to hit harder and carry more gear. A brawny character could also wear heavy armor, which offered more protection from damage. Vigor dictated how much damage you could take, and how soon you would get tired if you were doing a virtual activity such as climbing, fighting, or swimming.

How do they balance actual physical strength with virtual strength? He found no answers in the FAQ and jumped back to his profile.

Agility was a measure of how nimble you were in the game. It also governed how successful you might be doing certain activities like picking a lock, shooting a bow, or dodging an attack.

Brains could actually be a multiplier. *Smarter players perceive clues easier and learn more from any experience.*

Aptitude players cast more effective spells, got more benefit out of potions, and were sometimes able to intuit danger or solutions. Likability impacted prices for in-quest trades or purchases, and success in persuasion.

"Likable players," one of his game-playing friends had sagely intoned, "have way more success with virtual babes."

As much as it may have appeared inane to novices, allocation of attributes was a big deal.

Will was at the park alone. He wanted to play alone. *I haven't quested with anybody in three years. Not even online. Stuff 'em. I'm better alone.*

Will—and by extension, WB—was a loner at heart. Maybe not six years ago, but definitely now.

In the end, WB's profile looked very close to what his parents would have advised:

Brawn: 2	Brains: 9
Vigor: 3	Aptitude: 7
Agility: 3	Likability: 1

His ARGs gave him a cautionary, *Are you sure? This cannot be easily undone*, message. He clicked Yes, and WB was reborn as a smarter, wiser, but weaker, player who in-quest characters might not like much. *My character is a lot like me*, he thought with a touch of sadness.

He took a few more minutes to peruse his inventory. He remembered the Dino Whisperer perk but wasn't sure what it did. A quick check of the Help and FAQ sections proved to be of zero actual help. There was no mention of such a perk.

Huh. Maybe it's not legit anymore. Sometimes game engineers pulled perks if they gave players too much of an advantage. Sometimes they added a perk or some easily found first aid kits or weapons if challenges were too difficult. At SPARK, most encounters in the major quests scaled.

The scaling of opponents wasn't universal. The T-Rex never scaled back in difficulty. He was always a bad-ass.

Will gave up on trying to figure out the Dino Whisperer perk. *I'll just have to try whispering to a dinosaur.*

Understanding the nuances of the game could pay off big. So could experimentation—if it didn't kill you.

His path seemed to be inexorably leading him back to KT Crossing. He stood looking at it again for a few minutes, before turning away for the second time today. The Princess encounter was bugging him. His mind was picking at it, scratching around the edges, looking for handles. He just couldn't let it go. Was there some sort of pattern?

He headed back. Still no line, but he saw a family disappearing through the door he went through earlier.

The Princess greeted him in the same way as before and presented him with yet a different riddle he couldn't solve. He tried to get her to repeat the riddle to him, and was met again with a frustrating, "No, that can't be right," and her image faded.

Dang! How many riddles does this witch of a Princess have?

It made him pause. *There's an AI involved. How many riddles could an AI come up with?*

He decided it would be a ton. How did they expect anyone to beat the Princess? If there wasn't a way, it was just cruel—an irritating hoax.

He walked out dejected and decided to check out the other side of the PreHistory Arcade.

They couldn't. They wouldn't *just make this a frustrating time waster. There has to be a point and a way to beat it.*

He stopped to grab a churro, and decided he'd finish this arcade and then go in search of some dinner.

Will took his time, doing every minor quest and attraction until he reached the Hub again. He found a place to eat, grabbed a Sparky burger, a Sparky soda, some Sparky fries, and settled down to eat and think. The food was probably decent, but he was just pushing it through his pie hole. His mind was on the Princess. What had he learned? Was there a consistent underlying thread in the fabric of each arcade?

The first riddle was about attraction. Will hadn't cared about girls when he visited SPARK before. Now, he couldn't turn around without seeing attractive avatars everywhere he looked. It was distracting. He'd developed the habit of slipping his ARGs up every time he saw an enticing avatar. That usually quashed any further curiosity. Virtual appearances couldn't be trusted.

If the first riddle was about attraction, and the second about having your eyes lied to, were they trying to make the point that avatars are false?

He tried to remember the third. It was something about curves and trajectories. Was that somehow related? Did it tie into the false avatar theory? *Sure, I've seen false curves on a good number of avatars today.*

He munched more of his fries and slipped into his memories of his parents and the games they played together. They were playing a MMORPG, and his dad wanted to divert from their current quest to go help some voluptuous avatar in a side quest. His mom slammed her controller down and yelled at his dad about thinking with the wrong part of his anatomy.

Will hadn't understood what she meant then. But now the epiphany was immediate. Was that what his mom meant? His dad was letting sexual attraction interfere with real cognition? Had Will been guilty of that today?

Snap! Maybe the Princess hadn't been talking about attraction between the bodies of people at all. He started thinking so hard he stopped chewing.

He remembered his dad saying that sometimes clues are hidden in plain sight. *Maybe the answers are in the arcades.*

All along the arcade, guests were bombarded with stuff about comets and asteroids, orbits and dark matter disk intersections. He'd let a bunch of it just wash over him. He knew the basic story. A meteoroid, or some sort of cometary chunk, was displaced from a stable orbit. This changed its path, so it hit Earth and killed off most of the dinosaurs. That whole event was the premise behind KT. That's why you had to cross the river within the given time. Flash fires drove dinosaurs toward the river. The river was both a fire break and a barrier some of the dinosaurs couldn't cross. Once you got to the far side of the river, you were safe.

Will sat in the diner, thinking about it. *Okay, that's not realistic, but it's a way to make you keep moving.* Like a timed challenge where you only had thirty seconds to pull the lever, race through the fiery hallway, and jump over the pit before the door closed again.

Every stop along the PreHistory Arcade talked about gravity, gravitational disruptions, impact energy, and the problems with observing things in space from earth. Something about gravity lenses. Some stuff about light.

He started chewing again, feeling like an idiot for freezing with a mouthful of Sparky Burger. *Maybe there's something there.*

He sorted his trash and headed back to the arcade.

– 1 1 0 1 0 0 1 0 –

"The kid's going back to the arcade," Taggert told the referee.

"For real? He's got more patience than I expected."

"Yeah," Taggert replied. "He was sitting there eating with his ARGs up, and then he just froze for like five minutes."

"Third time today he's gone motionless. Think he has, you know, a problem upstairs?" The referee pointed toward his own head.

"Dunno. Doesn't look like he's seizing or going catatonic or something. Just looks like he's mentally somewhere else. Stuck in his head, maybe."

"Think we need someone to get closer to him in the park?" said the ref.

"Not yet," Taggert said. "I'm all over him."

Over the course of the morning, he'd been getting less and less concerned about Will. *It's weird—borderline stupid—to go back to the Princess three times.* With park time as expensive as it was, why waste it on frustrating riddles? The day was nearly gone, and the kid hadn't been on a major quest or ride yet.

– 1 1 0 1 0 0 1 0 –

What did I miss? Will plowed through the same side of the arcade he'd visited earlier. This time, he paid attention. It wasn't obvious, but his rebalanced Brains allowed him to see more than before.

When you looked at it in the right light, the arcade had a clear theme: gravity—how it worked; its impact over long periods; and the threat of what could happen again if we couldn't identify, track, and destroy or deflect an incoming massive body.

KT Crossing was no longer a cool dinosaur-based adventure. It was a cautionary tale.

– 1 1 0 1 0 0 1 0 –

"He's back at the Princess!" Taggert yelled out to the referee for the second time.

As the referee for PreHistory wandered over, he asked Janne, "How often do we see someone go back to the same Princess four times in a day?"

"On average," the sentient AI said, "this behavior happens once every one hundred eighty-seven days. It is rare, but not unknown. It is, however, a common trait for those who eventually beat the Arcade Princesses."

"How many people have beaten all seven?" the ref said.

"Since SPARK opened," Janne replied, "we have had over thirty-seven million unique visitors. Of those, just over forty-four thousand have successfully completed seven Princess Quests. Three-quarters have done it in groups, and just over three thousand employed subject matter experts to help them."

"Hang on," Taggert called. "Looks like maybe he froze again."

– 1 1 0 1 0 0 1 0 –

Will had been hurrying back to the Princess with the kind of excitement he hadn't experienced in years. He wished his parents were back with him. His dad always got the science stuff before anyone else. Will was sure his dad would have figured out the Princess's riddle the first time around.

For a moment, in his enthusiasm, he became Billy again and saw again with Billy's eyes. He looked around the arcade and saw with a fresh perspective. He no longer saw the advertising and hype Will saw, but the amazing scenery and graphics of the coolest place he'd ever been.

"There is wonder everywhere you look," his dad said during their first trip.

Billy stopped dead and thought hard again. *Could it be? Could clues be hidden in plain sight, just like hidden Sparkys?*

– 1 1 0 1 0 0 1 0 –

By this time, the ref was looking over Taggert's shoulder. Curious, Taggert called up a view of what WB was seeing through his ARGs. WonderBoy was staring at some of the graphics. His head snapped, and another graphic centered in his view.

"Go, kid, go!" the ref whispered.

Taggert turned around and looked at him.

"What are you talking about?" Taggert said. "The kid's just staring at the scenery."

"No," the ref said, "he's looking for, and at, clues."

"For real?"

The ref nodded.

For the next hour, they watched WonderBoy race around PreHistory, simply looking.

Taggert said, "Seems to me like this kid is just squandering his entry fee."

The ref shook his head "No…no…this could pay off. He's…well, he's learning."

Then he shut up. He wasn't about to assume Taggert was cleared to know anything about Princess Quests—the game within the game. A game even the players kept secret. It wasn't nefarious. Just that those who found it and played it, learned along the way that it wasn't for everybody. Riddles and solutions were not posted about online.

WB was about to take his first step into a deeper layer of SPARK without having played all of the major quests.

– 1 1 0 1 0 0 1 0 –

With thirty minutes of park time left, WB returned to the Princess. His brain was afire with a much deepened understanding of orbital mechanics. He knew how gravity boosts worked, and understood the angular momentum exchange they required. He got why you couldn't just park a satellite over someplace like Seattle—even in a geosynchronous orbit. He had a feel for the dark matter disk and its period, and how, just maybe, it perturbed the Oort cloud enough to send the comet toward Earth, and created the Yucatan Crater, resulting in mass extinctions. He didn't yet have the math to calculate or prove any of these. Nor could he prove any of the other topics. But he understood different materials had different indices of refraction, and how that could fool your eyes. Even gravitational lensing seemed to make sense.

He'd had none of this understanding when he entered SPARK this morning. The quests, attractions, and graphics had done their job.

– 1 1 0 1 0 0 1 0 –

Taggert didn't leave when his shift ended. He wanted to see this play out. In a world of routine, this was different and made it interesting. So when WB headed back for a fourth attempt, he spread the word. Several other quest monitors and referees wandered over to watch.

– 1 1 0 1 0 0 1 0 –

It was nearing the end of the SPARK day, and the arcade was crowded. People heading back to the Hub perused the shops and played the smaller quests in the hope of grabbing a few more XP before having to leave. The Princesses normally had a run of customers at this time of day, and there was a short line.

Will waited impatiently. Finally, it was his turn.

"Good." She looked right at him. "You're here."

Will looked around. This time, the chamber seemed rich with what he hoped were clues. He tried to take them all in. *How had he missed them before?*

The Princess hurried toward a door and looked back over her shoulder at Will.

"Come along," she told him. "We don't have much time."

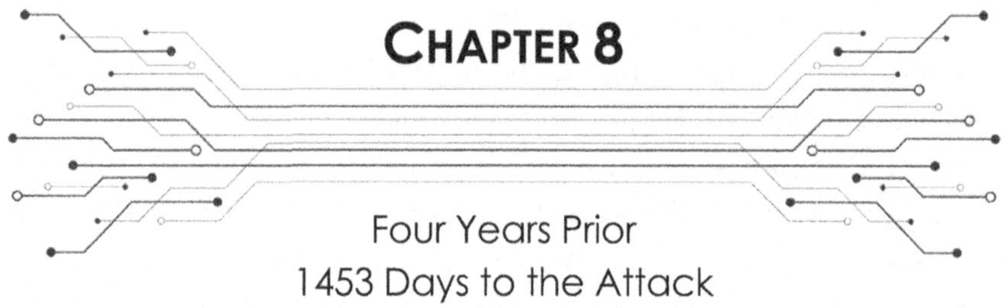

CHAPTER 8

Four Years Prior
1453 Days to the Attack

Kill them all and let God sort them out.
—Originally attributed to the French monk Arnaud Amalric, 1209

"Intense," Ardi said to her sister-in-law. "Your little ShaChri is an *intense* child. Santosh was the same way as a boy. I normally don't believe in this nonsense about giving in to your children, but in this case, it may save us all."

Ardi had the same piercing eyes as her niece, and a reputation for being intense herself.

ShaChri's mother, Puja, remained placid. She was from a calmer family, but Santosh's intensity led her to agree to the marriage. Their daughter inherited that preternatural focus.

At ten, ShaChri Patel announced she no longer wanted to take dance lessons with her peer group. She wanted her parents to enroll her in martial arts. Her parents gave in after the ballet instructor complained: "Every arabesque is tortured into some sort of mutated karate thing. Her hands are clenched fists. Her toes are not pointed, because she says it's inappropriate for a heel strike."

Puja and Santosh Patel caved then, and they would cave now.

ShaChri progressed from martial arts to mixed martial arts to kendo, because she wanted "to learn to fight with a sword." When ShaChri's friends posted videos of themselves in their latest ballet recitals, ShaChri posted a video of her making a boy two years older tap out during an MMA tournament. Santosh began referring to ShaChri as his *feral daughter*. Lovingly. Jokingly. Mostly.

When she turned twelve, her parents acquiesced to ShaChri's incessant nagging about going to SPARK. Finally, after the conversation with Ardi, they decided taking ShaChri to SPARK might expose her to more serious fighters and gamers, and possibly, hopefully, redirect her toward a more peaceful life.

At twelve, she was petite, surprisingly muscular, with dark eyes so intense they seemed able to bore a hole through steel plate. A perennial ponytail was lopped off in five-centimeter chunks when it annoyed her.

Her strategy for all games was simple: kill everything not clearly friendly. Her *almost* anti-social nature, willingness to go against conventions—particularly those of her parents' native India—and overall prickliness, justified her nickname. She was a handful, with an apparent desire to follow life's most difficult path.

When ShaChri built her SPARK profile, Feral Daughter became her avatar's name. When her family donned their ARGs as they entered SPARK, they saw ShaChri's floral-print bike shorts and pink top disappear, and Feral Daughter emerge, garbed in black tactical gear, only her eyes visible.

Mom was horrified. Dad was philosophical.

"We run a much lower than average risk of having a daughter who will ever be taken advantage of," he said, looking for a silver lining.

The Patels had a disastrous outing at SPARK. ShaChri was the only experienced gamer in her family. Her mother played as a pixie—like Tinkerbell—and her father played as a wizard. Neither had gamed before. Bowing to ShaChri's experience, they let her decide their agenda. She chose KT Crossing as their first major quest.

"We'll have to do a little running at first," she cautioned her parents as they stood in line for the quest.

They nodded but seemed too busy looking at other avatars to really pay attention to their daughter's guidance. Then it was their turn, and they launched into the wormhole.

"Run!" ShaChri screamed, and pushed her mother along.

They felt the thuds of the T-Rex's footfalls as he pursued them.

ShaChri stopped pushing when her mother tripped and fell. She stumbled a few steps before she caught her balance and turned around in time to see her mother become T-Rex Snack #1. ShaChri saw her father a few steps away, staring in horror, and yelled at him to begin moving.

The Cyanites flashed by. ShaChri's father failed to heed her advice, and became T-Rex Snack #2. Suddenly on her own, she turned and chased the Cyanites. When Mommy Cyanite dropped the baby, ShaChri didn't think she had time to save it, but managed to punt it soccer-style into the cave. She dove through the opening just behind the rolling, squalling baby. The cave was in an uproar: Baby crying, Daddy and Mommy Cyanite torn between anger and gratitude, both yelling at ShaChri and each other.

ShaChri had had enough. The squabbling was driving her nuts. She drew her katana just as Dino Whisperer scrolled through her ARGs.

The first strike decapitated Daddy Cyanite. Mommy followed him into death. The cave became quiet.

"Stupid NPCs," ShaChri muttered.

Azure blood dripped from her sword. She raised the katana to kill Baby but relented and left the NPC child behind in the cave. Neither parent seemed to have anything of value.

ShaChri pondered her options: no teammates, no allies, and a hungry Rex stomping around outside the cave.

"Ah, the heck with it." She walked out to do battle. "Might as well try. It's not like they can knock me down lower than a Level 1."

ShaChri managed one good strike before the Rex ate her.

Their total time in KT Crossing was less than three minutes, and ShaChri's parents refused to play the quest again.

For the rest of their visit, they played enough quests to keep their daughter's behavior somewhat in check, rode all the rides, and departed as Level 4s. Her parents vowed never to return. ShaChri couldn't wait to go back.

Reality intruded in its brutal, heartless fashion, and it was three years before ShaChri would return. She vowed never to leave.

– 1 1 0 1 0 0 1 0 –

One Year Ago: 544 Days to the Attack

Feral Daughter—*FD* to her friends, *Fully Dysfunctional* to her detractors—now lived in SPARK. She paid for entry. Then she worked odd jobs in town, saving up for admission. She applied to work at SPARK but was refused because of her age.

At first, she worried her Aunt Ardi might have reported her as a runaway. She had not. Ardi decided an intelligent, capable, fifteen-year-old girl could make her own decisions and live with the consequences. Once ShaChri figured that out, she purchased a phone and checked in with her family every few months. The discussions were short:

"Aunt Ardi, it's me, ShaChri."

"Of course it is. Are you well? Can I send you money?"

Ardi Gupta managed the estate of ShaChri's parents. It wasn't huge, but with ShaChri not taking anything out, it was slowly growing.

"No, Aunty," ShaChri said, with a hint of exasperation. "I'm fine. How are you and the family?"

"We are all well. Here, talk to Sanjay."

It wasn't always Sanjay. It was whichever cousin was closest. On average, every couple months, ShaChri and her aunt had identical conversations of twenty words or less.

Even as hardboiled as Feral Daughter was, she knew her aunt and cousins weren't jerks. They just didn't understand her.

I might be feral, but I don't have to be a complete bitch.

Eventually, ShaChri became an unofficial guide.

UGs, as they called themselves and each other, were park veterans who hung around outside the entrances and offered to help groups find their way around the park. UGs helped guests figure out the best times to hit the attractions, and generally made guests' lives easier. In exchange, the guests who hired them paid for park-entry fee, lunch, and promised the UGs at least an hour on their own, with no guide duties. HVH and SPARK saw this as a value-added service and condoned it.

Sometimes UGs even babysat as parents went on quests too physical for their kids, or while they snuck away for some Mommy and Daddy time in the adult-only area, or grabbed a quick beer.

ShaChri considered this behavior completely irresponsible. *Who trusts their kids to a complete stranger? How messed up is that?*

Still, she took the job seriously. No kids in the care of Feral Daughter were ever at risk. She never left them alone, and glared away anyone who got too close to her charges. She got great reviews and built a following.

Living in town was slow going, and the commute wasted a lot of her time. ShaChri noticed, even when she took the first bus, there were always a couple UGs already at the gates looking for work. Eventually, she approached a guy she saw repeatedly. He called himself Fantom. Skinny and sallow, with a mane of oily black hair.

"How do you get here so early?" she asked him.

"That's the secret to being a good UG," he said, as he approached another family. "See SPARK with the guidance of a Level 50 expert!" he called out.

The family just shook their heads and walked past.

There was a lull between bus arrivals.

"Seriously," ShaChri said. "How do you get here?"

Now that she was closer, she could see his hair wasn't really black. It was simply so greasy it looked black. *Probably a decent brown, if he would ever wash it.*

Fantom looked at the girl whose eyes were such a dark brown it was hard to distinguish pupil from iris, and relented.

"Look, meet me an hour before closing at Cluesades. You any good at puzzles?"

"Yeah," she said, "but I'm much better at combat."

"Tough. I want to hit Cluesades today. New puzzles dropped last night. We'll play for an hour, and then I'll show you how to skip the bus trip."

– 1 1 0 1 0 0 1 0 –

Fantom had figured it out. He wasn't the first to spend the night in SPARK. He was just the first to do it consistently.

"You have to ditch your wristband. It's how they track you. Dump it, your gloves, and your ARGs in somebody's bag as they exit."

He taught Feral to saw the wristband off using the corner of a building or a landscaping paver. She followed him to one of the unmarked maintenance doors that led to the Underground City. After ten minutes of twists and turns, she met the Pod. The Pod was a group of teenage stowaways. Fantom explained their technique.

"Find someplace quiet and secluded to sleep. When the night shift leaves, blend in with them as they go out the employee exit to the parking lot. Walk around to the main entrance. Find work. Do it all over."

"What about food?" she said. "Clothes? Staying clean?"

"Employee cafeteria's free and has food out twenty-four-seven. Lost and found for clothes. Employee gym has showers. Stay away from all of them during peak times for the night shift. You'll learn."

Feral was dubious, but the Pod was a small group—almost always less than ten kids—and it seemed to work.

She stayed. By the time Feral Daughter joined the Pod, Fantom had lived in the outskirts of the Underground City for two years.

Janne, of course, knew they were there.

– 1 1 0 1 0 0 1 0 –

SPARK was mocked as *the most surveilled place on earth*. It was not an exaggeration. Only in the medical treatment areas and restrooms was Janne truly blind. And in those, she watched who came and went. HVH told her to let the kids enjoy their fantasy—keep track of them, and then rat them out to security if their families came looking for them, if they damaged property, if their health was at risk, or if they became a danger to anyone.

"How long do I let them stay if they do not meet any of those criteria?" she said.

"Interesting question. Let them stay as long as they want. Treat it as a social experiment."

Janne pondered the ethics of the experiment, and decided that as long as she stuck to HVH's criteria, it was ethical. Thus, the Pod was unmolested.

As the Pod grew and endured, HVH gave Janne some guidance.

"This is a little like watching Peter Pan play out in real time. A social order is emerging. Please include updates of their activities in my daily summary."

"Sure, boss. I'll begin now. Pod size is currently seven. Fantom remains the unofficial mayor. They are tidy squatters."

In the morning, Pod members slipped out in twos and threes, split up, and approached groups that looked like potential customers. Parents with young kids, and anyone looking like they were pressed for time, were prime targets. Some just wanted help and guidance, but some groups wanted the win. They wanted to be able to say they beat the park—successfully completed all the major quests. And they wanted it to be easy.

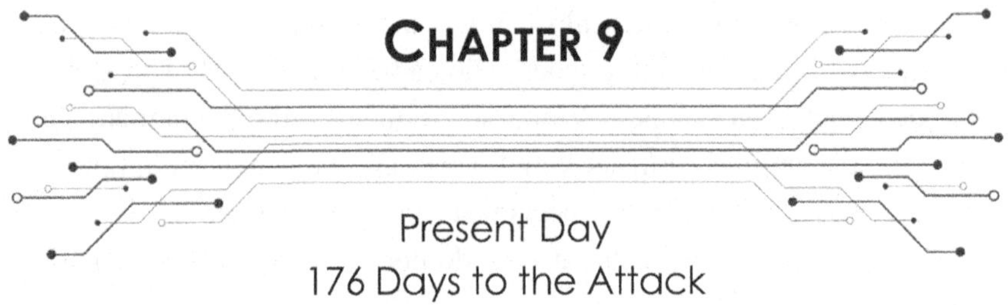

CHAPTER 9

Present Day
176 Days to the Attack

People who think they know everything are very annoying to those of us who do.
—Isaac Asimov

Today, Feral was guiding two young couples. They had gamed some. The guys were more experienced gamers and booked Feral in advance. Their email to Feral said they wanted two things: a pleasant and successful questing experience for their dates, and the chance to show those dates that the world of SPARK was not just for kids and overgrown boys. They wanted the women to see a kick-ass Top 100 player in action.

ShaChri had been an UG for a year, and just cracked double digits on the leaderboard. She had started taking bookings online, and got decent reviews.

Now, she was wearing the agreed-upon Sparky T-shirt and standing in the right spot at the right time, and still her clients walked past her.

Wasn't the first time. It was an ongoing issue for her when it came to guiding. She was short, but not tiny—around five-feet two-inches—and surprisingly muscular to people who didn't know her background. She had skin the color of an umber scarf lain over shining gold—unique and beautiful.

When she was eleven, her friends and relatives all used the same refrain: "Yeah, she's skinny now, but wait until she turns fifteen. You'll have to keep a shotgun handy to keep the boys away."

That hadn't happened. At fifteen, she still looked like she was twelve, except now she had acne. It wasn't terrible like some kids, but it was terribly annoying. Just this morning, a new zit had taken up residence on the side of her nose. She popped it, but it still left a red lump, one of several, on her face.

"Excuse me," she called out to the foursome as they passed. "Are you looking for me?"

The group stopped and looked at her.

"*You're* Feral Daughter?" one of the women said.

ShaChri already hated the women. They were staring at her zits, and they weren't dressed for questing. Short skirts—cute, but not practical for some of the more physically active quests. Too revealing when you were doing something like climbing a tree or scaling a wall. As long as everyone wore their ARGs, their avatar image would provide some privacy, but she saw more than one guest flip up their ARGs to watch someone dressed like these women climb a wall. *Pigs.*

They were also wearing flat, boat-style shoes—again, cute, but not the best choice. ShaChri recommended high-top trainers, T-shirts, and shorts to her clients. *Why pay me to guide you if you won't follow my instructions?*

"I am." She stared the women down.

The women looked at each other.

One of the men said, "I thought you'd be—"

"Older?"

"Bigger, actually. I've watched some of your open melees online. You certainly fight bigger."

That calmed her a bit. Of all the events and quests in SPARK, only open melees were routinely streamed. Major tournaments were held every month. They would have seen Feral Daughter in her black tactical gear. Not the acne-plagued girl standing before them in a ridiculous Sparky T-shirt, compression shorts, and trainers.

The clients didn't seem convinced.

"Who'd you fight in the first round of the open last month?" said the taller of the two men.

Feral figured him for early twenties. Semi-athletic build, with curly blond hair. The slightly shorter guy was an obvious gym rat—hypertrophic and physically imposing. Darker hair gelled back, and blue eyes Feral found distracting.

ShaChri searched her memory. It was only a couple of weeks ago, so she remembered the fight. It was short, but she couldn't remember the other player's profile name.

"Don't remember his name. Big guy in blue plate armor. Might have been his first tourney, since he thought a two-handed broadsword was a good choice. He didn't have the constitution to last."

The client still wasn't convinced.

"How'd it end?"

She sighed. *Is it going to be like this all day?*

"I waited for him to swing his oversized sword, ducked under it and drove my blade up through his unprotected armpit and into his head. Game over."

"Yes!" the client shouted. "Quick and merciless." He held out a hand for a high-five.

She accommodated him. *Well, that turned around quickly.* The women seemed unconvinced but went along as they entered the line.

As they waited, Feral coached them.

"Look, we're called UGs—unofficial guides. We're not SPARK employees, and I can't get you anywhere you couldn't go on your own. You're paying me for my knowledge and ability. I can help you hit the right quests at the right time to minimize lines, and I'll help you avoid catastrophic mistakes in the quests, and defend you as best I can. I guide for a living. I love gaming and fighting in the tourneys. I'm very, very good at all of them. If you follow my advice, you'll have a great visit."

The blond guy pushed open the door, and Janne welcomed them and acknowledged ShaChri with a nod and a quick, "Feral." She watched them go through their avatar setup. Both of the guys had established profiles and had been here before. Level 18s. The women were entering as Level 2s. They had likely been badgered into doing some of the online training and profile building.

The men had military-looking avatars—one human, one alien humanoid ShaChri didn't immediately recognize. The gym rat now had pointed ears and a greenish tinge to his skin.

"Elf?" she said.

He shook his head. "Vulcan."

His avatar wore a blue uniform shirt, with black trousers tucked into the tops of his boots. The lighter-haired man now wore a similar shirt, but gold. Both men wore blasters at their hips and swords over their backs. The blonde woman looked like an elf in a curve-hugging green frock. The one with ebony hair and extensions weaved in was playing as a sorceress.

ShaChri noted, sardonically, that the sorceress avatar seemed more voluptuous than the real-life woman beneath.

Their avatars seemed to fit. The blonde was lithe and seemed playful. The sorceress had a more serious air.

Well, could be worse. They could have just gone with a stock character. Mentally, she slotted them into the *still dating, and wanting to look enticing* category of player. Older, married, and more experienced gamers tended to go with more demure looks.

ShaChri chose Flighty Damsel from her list of possible profiles.

The Vulcan noticed immediately. "Wait. You're not going to play as Feral Daughter?" All four of them were looking at her now through their ARGs. What they saw was a raven-haired young human wearing pink robes of the princess variety, but with leggings and boots underneath. She sported a single sword over her back.

"Not unless you insist," she replied. "Feral's currently a Level Fifty-Two. SPARK could introduce opponents up to Level 54. Even if the party remains balanced, Level Fifty-Four bad guys can be a whole lot of trouble, and there's no promise I could keep all four of you alive. If I play this avatar," she did a spin to show off the rainbow cascades of her gown, "I'm playing as a Level Twenty—strong enough to deal with anything we face, because they'll be capped at throwing nothing higher than a Level Twenty-Two at us. It makes us more balanced and more likely to all survive. Even when I play as Flighty Damsel, I'm capped at gear and skills she can use, but I've got the knowledge and cunning of a Level Fifty-Two—not in terms of my profile attributes, but in here." She pointed to her head. "If you want, we can add a quick arena battle to our agenda. If the lines aren't long, it shouldn't take us more than forty-five minutes, and I could fight as Feral alongside any of you that want to join." She grinned. "It would give you a chance to go face-to-face against some amazing baddies."

"Aren't you locked in to whatever profile you enter the park with?" said the blue-shirted Vulcan.

"Nope," replied ShaChri. "The only restriction on changing profiles is within a quest. Once you start a quest, you're locked into a profile until you complete the quest or get killed out."

The client seemed dubious and glanced over at Janne's avatar, which remained active and alert behind her virtual ticket window.

Janne nodded. "Feral Daughter is correct."

"What if we don't like it, and just want to quit?" the elf said, with a hint of whine.

"Quitting is always allowed," Janne replied. "Once you say the words, *I quit*, your avatar disappears from the virtual world of the quest, and your ARGs display directions to the nearest exit. However, quitting is treated the same as being killed out, and you drop a level."

"That doesn't seem fair," said the sorceress.

"Having something at risk incentivizes players to put out a higher effort," Janne said. "It makes them play a bit harder."

"Huh." The elf rubbed her chin.

They arrived at the Hub and entered the park. Feral led them off at a fast walk, looking every bit a cute princess while emanating an unmistakable aura that let you know she might just kick your butt if you got out of line.

When they got to the arena, Feral coached the women first. She turned to Sorceress.

"There are lots of interesting and tempting spells to buy and to learn. You're only here for one day, so I advise you to just pick two: Heal and Fireball. Heal will help the entire party—even during combat. You can cast whenever needed, even if someone looks like they're out of the fight. Every single opponent you face is susceptible to fire. Some more than others. Stick with getting better with these two."

Feral moved on to Elf.

"Your main weapon is going to be your bow. Ever shoot a real bow?"

"Yeah, at summer camp a long time ago."

"Okay, great! Ever shoot at anything moving?" Elf shook her head.

"It's a little different," Feral said. "All of the basics are the same: full draw, relaxed shoulders, good posture, same release. I suggest you keep your eyes open for aiming. It'll help you stay aware of the whole battle, and make aiming and leading your targets easier."

Feral led them to the edge of the arena and worked with them all as they practiced for a few minutes. Then it was her turn to demo her own skill.

ShaChri switched profiles and become Feral Daughter. She chose a one-versus-X encounter. The park spawned her opponents. Since it was in the melee arena, there were no environmental conditions to worry about. Hard-packed floors made of recycled tires were covered with a thin layer of sand.

Footing was solid, but you could slide as well. If you chose to anchor yourself to a position, you had to dig in a bit—like a player in the batter's box.

Today, she faced two Level 40 Orcs carrying swords and wearing armor, and two unarmored Level 30 elves with long bows. It was a good fight.

Feral immediately closed with the elves. They stunk at close-in combat, but their bows were vicious from a distance. She'd taken some damage from one as she dispatched the other.

Meanwhile, the Orcs moved in, while the second elf backed up. Feral took a risk and did a running slide on her knees between the Orcs to get to the elf. The Orcs, perennially stupid brutes, tried to hack at her with their swords, but ended up hitting each other and inflicting a fair amount of damage. They growled at each other in Orcish and gave her time to take out the second elf. Then it was a maneuver and agility game. She circled to keep one orc between her and the second orc at all times, and hit the closer with whatever cuts she could get into the gaps in their armor. She hamstrung one and left him nearly immobile while she dealt with the second. Feral Daughter killed the second quickly, and then returned to the first and offered him the chance to yield.

Orcs never yielded, but some opponents would, and Feral thought it important to stay in the habit of offering. Sometimes it paid off in the quests, and you could turn an enemy into an ally.

The orc refused, and she decapitated it with a single swing of her katana. The gathered crowd cheered her victory. It was a good warm-up for Feral.

She switched back to Flighty Damsel and led her group off to their first major quest. The group had a newfound respect for their guide.

"Let's start with The Keep. It's a cool quest with a Middle Ages theme, and shouldn't be too crowded yet. No fetch quests. Do you guys want to defend the castle, or attack it? Either is fun…"

They debated the pros and cons of their options as they walked to the quest.

At the end of the day, her clients were chattering and animated as they headed Hubward for a little shopping before calling it quits. ShaChri smiled. She'd successfully led them through two major quests. They followed her basic rule: only fight when you have a good chance of winning, or have no other choice. Otherwise, run.

They were going to leave the park feeling successful. Both guys were now Level 21s, and the women were respectable Level 6s. Most important to ShaChri was they were leaving as happy customers. Maybe they'd come back tomorrow, maybe next week. But when they came back, they were sure to book her. They'd also tell friends. *References from wealthy people are even better than tips.*

Her clients had just beaten KT Crossing. They were talking about their favorite parts. Predictably, Elf and Sorceress both loved the Cyanite encounter and crossing the river on the back of the brontosaurus. The guys were reliving their battle with the velociraptors.

They entered the arcade and were heading toward the Hub for a little shopping when Feral heard a rare sound and halted.

The elf almost ran into her. "What's up? Is something wrong?"

"Did you just hear trumpets?" Feral said.

Chapter 10

Master your anger. When you act out of anger, the consequences live far longer than the anger itself; longer still for the victim.
—Lesson from Miss Sparkle's Charm School

WB followed the Princess through the door. The room beyond was the same. The Princess now held a torch illuminating the wall. As she moved closer to the wall, she repeated her standard line: "You've got to help me. The points of the star will guide you. Our first challenge is this." She gestured to the wall where words appeared to have been burned into the rock.

Will looked at the wall and immediately wanted to punch whoever selected the font. Couldn't they ever use something easy to read, like Arial? Will was already feeling pressed for time, and an archaic script didn't help.

Then he refocused his thoughts. *Wait. What did she just say? Was it the same as before?*

He thought it was. But since he was paying closer attention this time, he worried he might have missed something.

How are the points of a star related to the riddle?

The jewel on each ring,
Sparkles high, Sparkles bright.
Some jewels are not seen
Lest the sky is just right.
Rings within rings,
Tho the rings aren't quite round.
How can one jewel track
A lone spot on the ground?

Any ring that isn't round, would be an oval or an ellipse. Rings within rings could be a two-dimensional representation of orbital tracks around the sun. That would make the jewels planets. *In orbital mechanics, there's only one way to stay over a spot on the ground.*

"Please," she implored. "We haven't much time." She pointed to the half-drained hourglass. "They'll know I've gone. How can one jewel track a lone spot on the ground?"

"It's an orbit," Will said to the Princess.

She looked expectantly at him but didn't fade and didn't tell him he was wrong. Clearly, she wanted more of an answer.

"A geosynchronous orbit can track a spot on the ground," Will said.

Again, the Princess didn't respond verbally, but she looked pointedly at the hourglass. It was nearly empty.

Will racked his brain. It was mostly new knowledge about this stuff rattling around in his head. There was something about orbital tracks and geosynchronous orbits.

He closed his eyes and tried to visualize what he had seen, heard, and learned over the day. Grains of sand trickled through the virtual hour glass.

His eyes snapped open. He looked at the Princess.

"An equatorial geosynchronous orbit can track a single spot on the ground," he blurted out.

The Princess smiled, her face glowing with an inner light.

"Of course!" she said. "I should have seen that myself. Thank you, WB. You are a true knight."

A fanfare of trumpets played as Will exited.

– 1 1 0 1 0 0 1 0 –

"Did you just hear those trumpets?" Feral said.

"Yeah, I guess," her clients replied.

"That means someone has just solved one of those stupid riddles the Princesses ask. It doesn't happen often. I want to see who it is." She turned and backtracked to where the players would exit.

ShaChri wasn't sure what she expected. In general, groups had better luck than solos. Highly educated people also tended to do better. *Maybe it was stuff they learned in college. Or maybe just better verbal skills.*

Feral had only beaten one Princess, and she knew her victory was sketchy. Fantom claimed to have beaten six Princess Quests, and said he would leave the Pod once he beat the seventh. *The problem with that claim is, even though Fantom's a Level 60 in SPARK, he's a Level 80 in BS.*

Unless someone shared their profile with you, all you could see was their avatar image, their avatar name, and their level. He wasn't lying about being a Level 60, and his level alone got him customers, but his attitude rarely got him repeat business.

They stopped a respectful distance from the exit and waited. Feral was expecting to see a party of mages emerge. In real life, they would be ubergeeks in their twenties, with skin that never saw the sun. What she saw was some kid in an old baseball uniform, wearing the biggest grin imaginable and pumping his fists in the air.

"Hey, dude, congrats!" Feral called out.

The rest of her party gave him a round of applause and a few well-dones.

"First Princess?" she said.

"Yeah!" Will was still grinning.

"How many times did it take you to beat her?" Feral said.

In her experience, people either nailed it first time, or it took them ten times or more. It was the equivalent of spending an entire day at SPARK, doing nothing but visiting a Princess. ShaChri couldn't imagine a more tedious way to blow $200.

"Uh, four, I guess," Will replied. "Yeah, four."

"All in the same day?" Feral said.

The kid showed as a Level 15. She was trying to figure out how he played. He had a red and blue entry-level blaster at his hip, and a baseball bat slung over his shoulder.

Is he a fighter? A mage? A wizard? Some sort of blend? He's a little taller than me. Maybe he's some kind of Halfling. She looked closely for elven features and saw none. If he was playing as a Dwarf, she would have expected to see bare hairy feet, and the requisite ax or hammer. *Nope.*

"Yeah!" The kid, who appeared in Feral's ARGs as *WB*, was still clearly jacked from his victory and still smiling.

"Any recommendations for someone who hasn't beaten this Princess Quest?" Feral said.

She was walking a fine line here. Park protocol dictated details of Princess encounters and riddles were to be kept a secret. As a professional unofficial guide, and Pod member, she knew she was kinda-sorta asking this kid to break protocol.

He balked. “Uh…”

He seemed to be searching for something to say. He obviously knew the rules.

“Um…do your homework?”

“Thanks, jerk.” Then she turned and said to her clients. “Let’s hit the shops.”

ShaChri looked back and was going to apologize. There was no need to blast the kid for playing by the rules. Then she saw his ARGs were up.

She knew the move. Pod members called it the SPARK 10 phenomenon. Nobody—well, almost nobody—created an ugly avatar. You could make your avatar as beautiful as you wanted. Fantom once observed you could “tailor your avatar to emit butterflies from your rectum if you wanted. But ugly is out.”

The SPARK 10 phenomenon: in SPARK, everyone was a ten. Serious suitors hoping for IRL relationships knew this was a problem. They minimized enhancements—whiter teeth, bigger muscles and breasts—and generally remained recognizable when ARGs were raised.

Cautious gamers quickly developed what became known as the Park Peek. A guest would lift his or her ARGs to get a look at someone they were interested in. Ideally, this would be done subtly, when the other party wasn’t looking. Advocates called it a safety measure—you had a right to know what you were getting into. Detractors decried the move as *realist* and unnecessary. True appearance, they proclaimed, shouldn’t matter.

So when Feral saw the kid WB doing a Park Peek, she got angry. Any overt gesture would get her banned, but she knew SPARK. She turned her body so her back blocked surveillance from one side of the arcade, and then shielded one hand with the other and flipped WB off. Her mouth clearly formed a single-word, two-syllable vulgarity. Then she turned and stormed after her party.

She forgot she’d called him a jerk, and dismissed the whole encounter by the end of the day.

As she bade farewell to her group of clients, one of the girls, the elf, hugged her and slipped her a fifty-dollar tip. It brought her total tips for the day to nearly a single-day entry fee. Her goal this year was to earn enough to be able to pay for her own all-access pass, so she could have as many days to herself as she wanted. No clients, no problem.

As the elf released her from the hug, she said, "Check out Accutane for that acne. Worked great for me."

ShaChri Patel had no idea what Accutane was. She appreciated the suggestion but was irked that someone had brought up the acne to begin with. *Like I have health insurance*. She huffed.

Now, for the tricky part: getting safely underground. Feral looked around. The Hub was crowded. *Perfect.*

She squatted down next to one of the floral displays, pretending to be tying her shoes. She pulled the slack out of her wristband and began sawing it on a landscaping paver. It took a couple minutes, and she began sweating, thinking she was being too obvious.

Finally, she managed to cut through. Still squatting, she pulled off her haptic gloves and stood. *Almost done*. She pulled off her ARGs and removed their attached earbuds. Around her, the world became mundane. Amazing avatars were replaced by ordinary people in ordinary clothes, doing ordinary things. Every time she did this, she felt a touch of melancholy at the disappearance of the virtual.

Covertly, she scanned the exiting crowd. *There!*

A large group was exiting with plenty of bags. The mom was collecting gear from the kids and stowing it in the top of a bag. ShaChri made her way over. When the mom turned away, ShaChri added her gear to the group's pile and watched them exit. She felt smug. *As far as SPARK knows, Feral Daughter has left the park.*

Now, to get underground.

She stayed away from the obvious doors. Her heart pounded faster. This was real now, and getting caught meant getting kicked out of the park. The stakes, for her, were critical.

She scanned the area—anything marked *Employees Only* usually led to busy areas. ShaChri was going against the general flow, but the plaza around Cluesades was still busy.

She checked the crowd, then slipped through an unmarked door leading to a mechanical support area. It was clear, but she could hear voices. A few quick steps down a hall, down some steps, and into an HVAC room. *Safe!*

From here, as long as she stuck to the rim of the Underground City, there was little chance of being caught, and less chance of getting lost. The closer you got to the center—around the Hub and the Druid's Castle—the more labyrinthine and congested the Underground City became. Full of employees. Under the rim, it was quieter, more straight-forward.

She dialed back her vigilance and headed toward KT Crossing. She squeezed between a pipe and the outer wall, and was home.

The Pod was sleeping in the maintenance area between KT Crossing and the central part of the Underground City. *Danger close.* But people rarely came here, and the main entrance—a metal door—was normally locked, and sounded like a wailing banshee when it was pushed open. It gave the Pod enough warning to let them scamper away, leaving no trace.

"Good day?" Fantom said, when she squeezed her way into the open space.

"Yeah," she replied. "Good tips, decent clients. Paid for all my meals."

Fantom nodded. Those were the Big Three.

She squatted down next to him and offered him some of the leftover carrots from lunch. You shared food when you had it. The employee cafeteria was always there, and free, but you never knew when you were going to find it occupied. Minimize detection, minimize risk. It was Pod Code.

"I'm thinking about buying an All-Access," she said to Fantom.

He crunched carrots and nodded.

Fantom had stringy, oily hair he wore too long, and didn't shampoo often enough. Sallow complexion. Narrow, ferret-like, face.

"Where are you going to eat and sleep?" he said.

There was the problem. Pod life only worked because you ditched your wristband, became invisible, and had a safe, dry place to sleep. Free food, and gym/locker access. All-Access meant having to actually leave SPARK at the end of the day. You couldn't saw that wristband off. It would void the pass. All-Access let you play all day, every day, but it ended the squatter's life. Pod members usually just bought a day pass when they wanted to play without clients.

But ShaChri felt like she had stagnated. As Feral Daughter, she had been Level 52 for a while. Every ten levels, the required XP to level up increased by another thousand. At fifty, it jumped to five thousand. It was hard to build that kind of experience playing only an hour each day on your own. Feral Daughter knew she could open up a whole new path by tackling the Princesses, but she found them *so* annoying. She much preferred fighting.

"Thinking about camping in Barstow, riding buses," she replied.

"Lot of lost time," Fantom said. "Lots of food cost. Hard to stay clean."

He had an indifferent relationship with cleanliness, but knew it was important to Feral.

"Yeah," she replied.

The conversation died, and they munched carrots for a few minutes, pondering her options.

"I'm almost sixteen now," she said. "I could get a legit job."

"Mmph," Fantom grunted. "Not here."

SPARK required all employees to be eighteen and have a legal right to work. They also did background checks. ShaChri thought she was clean there. Fantom knew he was not. That was why, at nineteen, he was still working as a UG.

"Yeah." She paused. "Maybe in Barstow."

"Suck City," was Fantom's only response.

Going All-Access would allow Feral to level up faster, do a bunch of challenging high-level stuff solo, but would burn through cash quickly. It was the Pod conundrum.

It had been two hours since shift change. The gym and locker rooms would be empty.

"Gonna go get sweaty and clean," she told Fantom.

He just grunted.

She walked off. *Maybe I should hit the Lost and Found again. These shorts are getting kinda rank, and the Lost and Found might have something that fits me.*

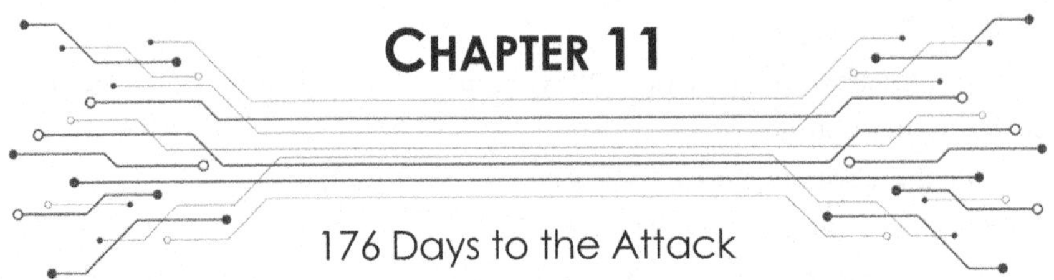

Chapter 11

176 Days to the Attack

In the desert, the line between life and death is sharp and quick.
—Brian Herbert

Will felt as if he had been slapped. What had he done? He had pushed his ARGs up because he wanted to apologize for whatever insult he might have given. What he saw was a girl around the same age as him, maybe older, but skinny enough to be younger. Just a girl in bike shorts and a Sparky T-shirt. A girl who gave him the finger and followed it with a crude insult.

He trudged toward the exit with his head down, trying to understand what he had done, and ran smack into a man carrying an armload of souvenirs.

The man dropped his packages. Will heard something break and started to apologize, but the man cut him off.

"Hey, moron! Watch where you're going."

Will scurried away, burning in shame.

Since his dad's death, Will struggled with rejection and conflict. When a teacher scolded him, or he got into a fight with a friend, it haunted him. He replayed the scenes over and over in his mind, each replay feeling as fresh and strong as the initial encounter.

"*Just let it go,*" was his mom's advice. "*If it's something you can fix with actions or an apology, then do it. If you didn't do anything wrong, then just let it go. Maybe they were just having a bad day.*"

He tried. But then later, when he was alone, and it was quiet, the embarrassment returned and set up camp in his brain. He ran hundreds of scenarios for things he should have said, things he could have done differently, apologies he ought to make. He learned to apologize, but continued to struggle with the past.

His elation at beating the Princess Quest was overwhelmed by his embarrassing encounters with Flighty Damsel and the man. He left the park feeling hurt and dejected.

He rode the bus back to town and recovered his backpack and knife from where he stashed them at the softball park. As he fell asleep under the bleachers, he replayed the two scenes over and over. First, with the girl.

What did I do wrong? We were just talking. Was it the *do your homework* comment? What was so bad about that? Was she bad at homework? At school? What triggered her reaction?

Then he thought about the man. *I should have apologized. Offered to replace whatever broke.*

He tried to decide what was worse—being called a moron, a jerk, or a Kimmy.

Moron or jerk, he decided. *Kimmy is their problem.*

What made me a jerk? The loop in his brain restarted.

He squeezed the handle of the knife as he dozed off. The knife would keep him safe. It always did.

– 1 1 0 1 0 0 1 0 –

In the morning, he decided to skip the park for the day. *Sometimes it helps to put a day or two behind me. I'll camp here another night. Today I'll walk out to the Black Grass fields. Dad said we'd do it the next time we came out here. It's only a couple miles. I'll take my pack, bring some water. And Missus Derr's sunscreen.* He smiled.

Will filled his thin plastic water bottle at the ballpark's drinking fountain, threw it in his pack, and headed to the mom-and-pop diner by the SPARK bus terminal.

As he stuffed himself with pancakes as large as the plate, Will reviewed his cash situation. He was down to less than $200. *I need to get a job or find someplace free to eat and sleep. Sleeping's not that big of a problem. I can camp at the ballpark indefinitely. But I'm getting pretty grungy, and sprinkler showers aren't cutting it.*

Will decided to hit the restroom before he left. He looked in the mirror over the sink as he washed his hands. *Jeez, I look like crap.* He turned his head side to side. *Pants aren't bad. Kinda dirty. T-shirt's shot. Really, it's the hair.*

The shoe-polish dye job he'd attempted in the Bullseye store's restroom in Katy, where Mrs. Derr dropped him off, had been effective but was wearing off. His shirt now had permanent black-gray smudges on the shoulder and collar where the shoe polish had migrated from hair to neck.

He looked around. He was the only one in the restroom.

Why not? Will soaped up his hands and started scrubbing his hair. Its natural ginger was already reasserting itself, and the soap helped.

The door opened behind him. A large man wearing a nametag proclaiming him to be both Josh and the manager, entered the restroom and stopped, staring daggers at Will.

"What the hell are you doing?" He advanced toward Will. "You think this is your own personal bathroom? Come in here and wash your hair in our sink? Mess up our restroom? Restroom I get to clean up?"

He grabbed Will by the shoulder and propelled him out of the restroom and out of the diner. Will tried to explain, but the manager wasn't interested in hearing it.

As he pushed Will out the door, he said, "I don't care if you are a Kimmy. Have some damn dignity."

The soap and embarrassment stung his eyes. Will wiped his hands on his shorts, then wiped his eyes. The shame remained.

He resettled his pack and headed back to the ballpark, thinking that, this early, he could blast the soap out of his hair and eyes by following one of the sprinklers around.

It worked somewhat. He dried off with his T-shirt, put it back on and vowed to replace it with something clean. Cheap, but clean. There was a Good Salvation store close to the Rabbit Bus Lines terminal. He headed there. Not the best part of town, but okay in daylight.

The terminal, the Good Salvation store, and their mission kitchen—*Prayers and Three Squares a Day*, according to the sign in the window—were in the same block. Across the street was the public library. Will loved to read, but all his books were either on his phone or in his former room—both far away in Houston.

After I get a clean shirt. He pushed open the door of the resale shop.

Two dollars later, he had a shirt declaring him a finisher of the High Desert 10K from five years ago. The pale blue wasn't really his color, but it was clean and it fit.

He caught sight of himself in a mirror and realized his hair wasn't completely shoe-polish free. It now looked like he had orange-and-black striped hair, like some genetically cursed zebra. *Wonderful.*

He dropped his Quaranteens T-shirt in the trash on the way out. *Mediocre band, anyway.*

Will diverted to the library. *Need to get online and apply for work at SPARK.* The librarians inside were nice, so he smiled patiently as they explained how to get online. *Do they really think I can't figure out how to get on the web?*

His first search pointed him to SPARKInsider—a fan guide to all things SPARK. He clicked on a button labeled *SPARK Faux Pas.* The first thing listed was something called *The Park Peek.* It showed a graphic of a man lifting up his ARGs, and then explained: *Everybody's curious. We get it. Remember how much time you spent building your avatar? They did, too. SPARK-goers want to be seen as their avatars, not the flawed humans beneath. When you're in the park, keeps your ARGs on. Peeking is an insult. Don't do it. But if you must, be extremely subtle. A blatant Peek is as insulting as an obnoxious comment, inappropriate gesture, or staring.*

Will sat back in his chair. *Was that what it had been about?* He'd lifted his ARGs, but it hadn't been an intentional Peek.

Will could hear his dad quoting that Covey guy: "*Remember, sport. We judge ourselves by our intentions and others by their behavior.*"

Actions have consequences, even if intentions didn't.

I never intended to Peek that girl, but I did. It was a jerk move. No wonder she was mad.

He was embarrassed all over again. He'd Peeked more than a couple avatars yesterday, before deciding that the virtual was more fun to look at. *Probably wasn't all that subtle, either. Jeez.*

He kept searching the site but kept away from the spoilers. The Underground City interested him.

He scrolled through the sites but found scant descriptions: Some rumors that HVH's office was in the Druid's Castle, just off the Hub. Alleged banks of supercomputers to power the AI necessary for the quests. A lady on SnapGram, claiming that she was the voice of Janne. SparkLord312 said that the Underground City was just an office complex below ground—"like where your dad works, but more boring."

Then there were walkthroughs of all the major quests, which Will avoided, and arguments that the walkthroughs were invalid since the quests changed based on the questing party that entered.

Spitters were replaced with velociraptors. A single Orc could become an army of them, or a random party of elves. First aid kits and swag moved. Fetch quests within the major quests changed quest giver and goals.

Very little about the Princesses, other than the standard troll gripes: Waste of park space/time/energy. Stories of people reciting random words and getting credit for solving a riddle. But about the Princesses themselves, what their role was, and why they even existed, there was nothing worthwhile.

Before he realized it, hours had passed. He had intentionally skipped lunch to save money.

He went to the SPARK home page and clicked on *Careers at SPARK*. His hopes were dashed quickly.

In Houston, when he thought about coming out here, he always saw himself as a high school graduate, eighteen years old, and not in trouble with the police, CPS, and his former foster parents. He also assumed he'd have his ID. None of that was true now.

SPARK didn't hire minors—not even to sell Sparky burgers or churros. You had to be eighteen to work at SPARK. Period.

Will also realized that getting a legit job was going to mean filling out paperwork with his name, social security number, and other stuff. *That's going to be a big red flag pointing the cops my way. Crap.*

Disheartened, he decided to think about his options while he hiked out to look at the Black Grass. He logged out, put on his pack, and walked out into the hot afternoon sun.

Will tried to follow the path the SPARK bus had taken yesterday. He'd seen a turn-off for Solar Prime—the control center for the twenty-five square miles of Black Grass. At least, according to the net. *Probably an hour's walk. No sweat.*

He was cutting through a strip mall and passing a bar called The Stumble Inn, when the door burst open with enough force to knock him backward. He tripped off the curb and ended up on his rear end, as a red-faced man with spider webs of blood vessels spread over his nose stumbled out. Will gaped at the man and slowly picked himself up.

"What the hell are you looking at?" the drunk yelled, as he closed the distance with Will and shoved him hard.

Will backed up a few steps. The drunk pursued, cursing.

"Why don't you go back to where you came from?"

Flecks of spittle flew from the man's mouth as he continued to stagger towards Will.

The racism was implicit, but Will couldn't stop himself from responding. "Houston?"

The drunk was now in a rage. "We should have nuked the whole damned peninsula. Wiped all you Kimmys out!"

Will watched the drunk's hand form a fist.

This is stupid. He turned to run.

The punch hit him in the back, but was hard enough to make Will stumble a few steps.

The bartender and a couple patrons heard the ranting and came outside to investigate. They grabbed the drunk, who continued to rant until the bartender threatened to shut him up.

Will took another look at the drunk before turning his back and walking away.

It was Juneteenth, he realized as he passed a time and temperature sign that proclaimed it to be ninety-seven degrees. Almost six years to the day since he'd been here with his parents. *In another week, it'll be Guam Remembrance Day.* The day set aside to commemorate the nuking of Guam by North Korea. And the day that turned Will's life upside down.

He grew melancholy and walked on, lost in thought.

A mile past the bar, Will detected a flaw in his plan. The bus took the interstate. He couldn't. *That's a quick way to end up roadkill.* He stuck to side roads.

When he saw the dark smudge of the Black Grass fields in the distance, Will decided to cut through the desert. It was harder going—the sand and dirt soft in places—and occasionally, he had to detour around rock formations or scrub brush.

Okay, I'm working harder, but cutting off distance. That should make up for it. Thought I'd sweat more. He rubbed his temples. *Getting a headache.*

– 1 1 0 1 0 0 1 0 –

This is farther than I thought. The dry wind peppered his legs with sand, and his arms felt gritty. *How long have I been walking? Hour and a half? Two?*

He looked toward the Black Grass fields. *Definitely closer, but still can't see the fence. Thought I'd be there by now. I'll take a break, drink some of my water.*

Will squatted in the shade of a weird-shaped cactus-looking tree and shrugged off his pack. When he reached in for his water bottle, it crinkled under his touch. *Uh-oh.*

He pulled the split and empty bottle out of the pack.

"Dang it!" He slammed the broken plastic bottle to the ground. *Must have happened when that drunk hit me. Crap.*

Will stood and looked again at the Black Grass fields. They carpeted the low hills in the distance. Off to his right, he saw some buildings shimmering in the heat radiating off the sand. *They've got to have a visitor center or something, where I can get water.*

Okay. He picked up the bottle, stuffed it in his pack, and put the pack on. His lips were dry, and the knowledge that he had no water made him feel parched. He headed toward the buildings, hoping that they were not a mirage.

Within a hundred yards, he felt the first twinge of a cramp in his right quadricep. He stopped and squatted to stretch it out. It abated somewhat but didn't go away.

Gotta keep going. This whole idea was stupid.

Will walked another couple minutes, before the cramp came back with a screaming vengeance. His entire right leg locked up so hard that he stumbled and fell to the ground, scraping both palms when he hit.

The agony was debilitating. He rolled onto his back and tried to massage the cramp away. He used words that would have embarrassed his mother, and managed to bend the leg enough to stand again. That action caused his left leg to threaten to get in on the act.

He hobbled on, grimacing with every stiff-legged step. *If I die out here, they should put* Here lies Will Kwan. Too stupid to live, *on my headstone.*

He started counting steps. Life reduced to one hundred wobbly steps at a time. Walk. Count. Stop. Try to stretch out his legs. Repeat. He fell again. Got up. Continued. Walked. Counted. Fell. This time, he couldn't get up. *I am truly screwed.* He was scared now.

He heard a single chirp of a siren and craned his neck to look toward where it came from. From where he was on the ground, all he could see was sand, rocks, and some scrub brush.

"Come on. Come on," he whispered to himself, as he massaged his thighs.

His eyes shut against the sun and the pain.

He heard the soft crunch of footsteps.

"Nope. He's alive. Pay up."

Will opened his eyes, squinted, and saw two silhouettes standing over him, hands on their hips, looking down at him. They were wearing helmets.

"Later." The second man squatted down next to Will. "Having a spot of trouble, mate?"

The voice had a Scottish or Irish accent—Will wasn't certain he could tell them apart.

"Yeah," he grunted. "Legs are cramping up. Can you help me get up?"

Will tried to get into a sitting position. The man gently, but firmly, pushed Will back down.

"What are you doing out here?" said the one who was still standing.

He seemed to be scanning the area, looking for something.

"Came to see the Black Grass."

"Uh-huh. Well, you're on private property now. No trespassing."

The squatting man said, "Do ye have any weapons on ye, lad?"

Friendly words, but a serious tone.

"No," Will said. Then, "Wait. Yes. I've got a knife in my backpack."

The man that Will had decided was Scottish said, "All right, then. We'll take that."

He slid the backpack off Will and handed it up to his partner.

Both men were armed, Will could now see, and wore some sort of uniform with *Security* emblazoned across their chests. They had sunglasses on that reminded Will of the ARGs in SPARK—wraparound style with no visible frames. ARGs were clear. These were dark and mirrored.

"What's your name, kid?" His voice sounded American.

Just enough of a drawl to remind Will of Houston.

"Will Kwan."

Then the man began speaking to someone else that Will couldn't see.

"Prime? This is Olsen. Kid says his name is Will Kwan. Minor medical emergency. Says his legs are cramping."

Will watched Olsen rummage through his backpack and pull out the knife.

"He's got a pretty big pig sticker with him. No other weapons?"

This last was directed at the Scot, who now frisked Will.

"No."

"No other weapons." A pause. "No, he doesn't seem to have any water on him. There's an empty water bottle in his pack." Another pause. "Okay, Prime, we'll bring him in."

“She confirmed his identity and says the doc wants a look at him,” the Texan told his partner, then grabbed Will under one arm while the Scot took the other.

They helped him to his feet.

The security guards’ demeanor had changed, Will realized. They were polite but firm before. Now, they were friendly as they loaded him into the front passenger seat of the open-air Jeep. The Texan climbed in behind him as the Scot took the wheel. Will could now see that they had nametags. The Texan was Olsen. The Scot was McIntosh.

Olsen passed Will a water bottle over his shoulder.

“Here.”

“Thanks.” Will spun open the cap and raised the bottle to his lips and began guzzling the water.

“You might want to take it easy on that for a while,” said Olsen.

Will couldn’t. His need for water was pathological. He chugged the bottle.

“Or not…” Olsen said.

The sudden influx of cold water hit Will’s empty stomach like a tsunami and was promptly regurgitated. Will hung his head over the side and vomited.

“Sorry,” he said, as McIntosh began driving.

Another bottle of water appeared over his shoulder.

“Just a few sips at a time, kid.”

As they drove in toward the buildings, McIntosh said, “Why the knife?”

“Protection. I’m on my own.” *True, but not complete.*

The Scot scoffed. “Wi’ that? Sure’n it’ll work against a coyote or stray dog, but it’s hardly a weapon, lad. You’re as like to slice your own fingers off. That thing yew’ve got…well, it’s dandy in the kitchen, not in the field.”

“Man’s got a point,” Olsen said from behind him.

Will turned around to face him, and saw a distorted view of his own face reflected in Olsen’s goggles.

“Any decent combat knife should have a guard to protect your fingers, a solid pommel for skull cracking, and a handle that won’t get slippery when it’s wet.”

“Or bloody.” McIntosh nodded sagely.

A moment later, Olsen said, “What’s up with your hair?”

“Bad decision on trying to change the color,” Will said.

“No kidding. You kinda look like a striped pumpkin from behind.” Olsen chuckled.

They pulled up in front of a building and escorted Will inside. A man in a white coat met them and escorted Will to an examining room.

Ten minutes later, he'd been put into a set of scrubs and hooked up to an IV.

The doc said, "You'll survive. Could have been much worse if Olsen and McIntosh hadn't found you. You might not have lasted the night. Desert's no joke, Mister Kwan. Stay hydrated, and you'll stay alive. It's as simple as that." He stood and indicated the bag that held Will's clothes. "We'll get these washed. After you finish that bag of Ringer's, I'll have another look at you. If you're okay, I'll show you to the shower. Then we'll get you some chow and a ride into town. Meanwhile, drink this—slowly." He handed Will a glass of something faintly yellow.

"Thanks, Doctor."

As the doctor walked out, Olsen walked in. Without the nametag, Will wouldn't have recognized him. *The helmets and goggles they wore in the desert make them almost anonymous.*

He gauged the man at thirty-something, with a short halo of blond hair on his head and chin, and a disconcerting tat of a knife on his forearm.

"Sounds like you're going to make it," Olsen said.

McIntosh joined them. He was more slender than Olsen, with dark hair and eyes.

"Ye know they've got a Black Grass display over at SPARK. Way safer. Way less stupid." His accent made it sound like *stew-pid.*

Yeah, but that's not what my dad and I were going to do.

"I wanted to see the fields. Is it really twenty-five square miles?"

"Maybe a bit more," McIntosh said. "Feels like more when you're driving the perimeter, checking the fence. Lots of twists and turns around rock formations and areas that don't get good sun. At night, especially when there's no moon, the wee little blades o' grass twist and track you if you get close enough. Ye can hear 'em rustling a bit as they turn."

"Kinda creepy," Olsen said. "You think you're being quiet and stealthy, but you're emitting all that heat. Sometimes I think they want to suck the life out of me."

McIntosh laughed. "It's just tech, ye daft cowboy. Not Baobhan Sith come to drink your blood."

After the doc was satisfied with Will's condition, he disconnected the IV and led him to the shower.

"Your clothes should be dry by the time you get out."

"Thanks again, Doctor."

In the shower, Will was surprised how much dirt he saw flowing down the drain. He scrubbed his hair three times. When he checked the mirror, most of the shoe polish was gone, and the flaming orange was back.

Olsen met him when he emerged from the locker room. The guard raised his hand as if to shield his eyes.

"Dang, Will. Is that natural?"

Will knew what he meant. All his life, people had asked him about his hair.

"Weird genetics." Will shrugged. "Korean dad. Blonde, American mom. Double recessive." He pointed at his head.

"Let's get you some chow," Olsen said. "Then I'll drive you into town. My shift is almost over."

– 1 1 0 1 0 0 1 0 –

It was a quiet ride. They pulled up in front of the homeless shelter, and Olsen turned to the kid.

"Listen, they can take care of you in there." Olsen nodded toward the shelter.

Will shook his head.

"I'm just a grunt," the guard said. "But if you keep going the way you are, I think you're gonna die out here."

He paused and seemed to think. Then he reached down to his boot and pulled out his sheathed KA-BAR knife, and sighed.

"We took that knife you had in your backpack."

Will said nothing, but his posture stiffened, and the muscles in his jaw worked.

"Listen, Will, a knife like that is only get you into trouble, and is unlikely to get you out of it. Take this." He handed Will the KA-BAR in its sheath. "It's made for fighting and combat. This," he patted the KA-BAR, "is a weapon. If you're on your own, you need something." He handed Will two fifties, along with the knife. "If nothing else, take a bus to someplace cooler. Maybe head down to LA or San Diego. The desert isn't very forgiving."

Will mumbled, "Thanks," and got out of the car. He stood there until Olsen finally drove off.

– 1 1 0 1 0 0 1 0 –

Despite his stoic demeanor, Will was scared. He had nearly died. He *would* have died if those guys hadn't taken care of him.

It was early in the evening. The sun was close to the horizon, and the homeless of Barstow were starting to form a line for the free dinner. Will crossed the street to put some distance between him and the shelter. He sat on a bench with his back to the library and facing the shelter, and thought.

His emotions overwhelmed him, and he put his head in his hands. *Is that my future? Homeless shelters and soup lines? I've got to figure out a way to make this work.*

Will was angry with himself. *Did I really let some stupid girl chase me away from SPARK? Who cares if she flipped me off? I need to get back on my path.* He started to plan.

I ran from the system twice, my fosters once. I'm not running away from SPARK.

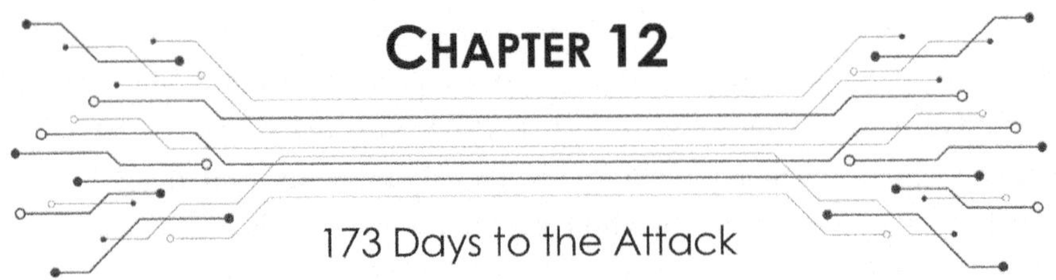

Chapter 12

173 Days to the Attack

Once more unto the breach, dear friends, once more;
Or close the wall up with our English dead.
—Shakespeare, Henry V

The last month had sucked. ShaChri was mad at herself for being too cautious, but SPARK was her home now, and the idea of trying to live outside its walls bothered her. She knew she could survive, but it wouldn't be good.

It killed her to know that every day she paid for would have covered one-twentieth of the cost of the pass. But it was all about sleeping and eating. In SPARK, she could do both for free. If she went into Barstow, any place that felt as remotely safe as SPARK was going to cost her the equivalent of a day's entry.

She'd even tried crashing on SPARK property—outside the park, but around the resorts. Every time she thought she found someplace she could nest, Security showed up and rousted her out. After seeing the same guys a couple times, one of them warned her.

"Look," he said, "I know you're a big deal in the Questing world, but out here you're just some girl that acts homeless and is going to freak out the paying customers. If we have to warn you off again, you're going to be Banned."

Feral heard the capital B. He wasn't talking about a one-day entry denial. He meant the big B. Banned. At least a year. She couldn't do that.

ShaChri walked around the rest of the night, avoiding security patrols, paid for entry, and hadn't left the park since. It was her home now. She only left to meet clients.

Fantom squatted next to where Feral sat leaning against a water pipe. The Pod was currently camped near Evolve in the Underground City. It was morning and everyone was waking up.

He held out a bag of animal crackers.

"Don't you ever eat anything good for you?" She took what appeared to be a hippo.

"Sure. I eat veggies all the time: potatoes, lettuce, pickles, tomatoes. Tomatoes are a vegetable, right?" Fantom sat down.

Feral snorted. "I don't think anything you get in a Sparky Combo Number 1 counts as a veggie. Unless you ask for carrots instead of fries."

Nonetheless, the animal crackers hit the spot.

A minute later she said, "How long are you going to stay?"

It was a common topic. How long do you stay? When are you ready to leave? Some Pod members, like Mellew, were just biding time, waiting for a magic birthday or for things to cool off at home.

Fantom had seemed malcontent lately.

"Dunno," he replied. "Sometimes it gets old. I think I'd like to sleep in a bed again. But then there are rumors of upgrades and changes to the quests. Still, leveling up is harder. I used to think I'd hit a hundred and then leave."

"I'm not sure it's even possible," Feral said. "Look at CastIron."

Nothing was published about an upper limit to Levels. Feral was now a Level 55. Fantom seemed stuck at 62. CastIron ruled the leaderboard at a distant Level 71. She was one of the few pros left on the board.

When SPARK went live, there'd been an influx of wealthy wannabes—people with dreams of Sparking for a living. Eventually, they all got to where Feral and Fantom now were. From the 50s on, it was tough going.

"Yeah, but she doesn't even quest anymore," Fantom said, but then he quickly shut up.

CastIron had leveled up just last week at the open melee by beating Feral in the finals. Fantom clearly thought it might still be a sore spot. It was.

ShaChri flushed but kept her mouth shut. She'd faced CastIron five times in open tournaments, and lost every time.

Finally, she choked out, "Better. Gear."

Fantom himself died fighting CastIron in the arena a dozen times. The crucial difference between his history and Feral's with CastIron was he had beaten CastIron. Once. It had been nearly two years ago. He'd used a poisoned blade. His victory was the last time anyone—*Anyone*—had beaten CastIron.

Fantom wisely stayed silent. They'd had variants of this conversation before.

Several heartbeats later, ShaChri calmed enough to speak.

"How's the math go, again?"

Fantom knew what she was asking.

"You get a hundred Experience Points for the first Princess. The points double with every Princess you beat. The second is worth two hundred XP. By the time you bag your seventh, you're collecting sixty-four hundred XP. That's a level for either of us."

Stupid Princesses. Stupid riddles. Even Fantom was mum about the Princesses.

She sighed and vowed to herself to try the Princesses again.

– 1 1 0 1 0 0 1 0 –

Bull recognized the kid when he showed up for the first bus. *Whatever the kid had in his hair before is gone. Seriously orange.* Security over at Prime said they cleaned him up. Scans showed no knives, and this time the kid went straight to the line and waited his turn to board.

After checking in with his boss, Bull boarded the same bus. He didn't see anything to worry about, but he gave the crowd a hard visual scan. Nothing.

He caught sight of Feral Daughter standing outside the entry and walked over to her. He wasn't a big gamer himself, but he did like bringing his kids to the park, and he worked crowd security for the melee tournaments. Unlike many of the other combatants, Feral was relaxed while she waited for her bouts. They had chatted a couple times, and she guided him and his family once.

"'Sup, Feral?" Bull walked up.

"'Sup, Bull. Just trying to get some business."

Bull nodded. "Best day yet, Feral."

"What do you really mean when you say that?"

"Well, after fighting in Korea, I realized that every day at home—every day with my family—is a gift, and is going to be better than the day before. So...*best day yet*."

"Why are you here today?" Feral looked around. "I mean, you usually work in town, right? Is there trouble?"

"Nah, just tracking a kid. Thought he might have been trouble before, but he was cool last time he was here, and looks like he's just going to have a good day in the park today."

Feral looked behind Bull. "Oh yeah? Which one?" She was scanning the lines.

Bull nodded toward one of the lines. "Kid with the bright ginger hair, third line over."

"He looks kinda familiar," Feral said.

"Yeah, he was here two days ago. Hair looked different, though—greasy black, with some of that orange bleeding through."

Feral snapped her fingers. "That's it! I saw him coming out of one of the Princess Quests. Jerk Peeked me."

Bull bit his tongue. He didn't think Peeking was such a bad thing. It could prevent all sorts of confusion later on. Still, he knew that a lot of the park guests only wanted to be seen as their avatars.

He was saved from the discussion when Feral's customers showed up.

"See ya," he called, as she went to greet them.

"See ya!" she called back over her shoulder.

He watched Will enter SPARK. *Janne's problem now.*

Bull boarded a bus to return to the terminal.

– 1 1 0 1 0 0 1 0 –

"Welcome back, Will. We're happy to see you again!"

During the ride to the Hub, Janne made small talk with WB while giving him a closer look in the IR and visible spectra. He showed no sign of the high body temperature her twin reported when Will was picked up at Solar Prime. She also noted the new hair color and cleanliness but chose not to mention it. Acknowledgement of hairstyle changes seemed bifurcated along gender lines. Females appreciated it, while most men were ambivalent. Even with women, it was allowable to acknowledge a style change, but mentioning a color change, particularly one designed to cover gray hair, was taboo.

Bull was right, Janne thought. *It is vibrant orange.*

"Congratulations on your first Princess, WB," she said.

"Thanks!"

The difference in behavior between Janne's previous encounter with WB and today was significant. Previously, he was sullen and angry, then grief-ridden. Today, she categorized him as giddy. He squirmed and leaned forward with bright eyes as he peppered her with questions.

"How many people come to SPARK every day?"

"Approximately forty thousand paying guests visit SPARK on an average day."

"How do you keep track of them all? How do you know who I am when I enter a quest?"

Janne detected WB's eyes dilating. This topic particularly interested him.

"Every guest is tracked through their wristband and ARGs. Both are linked to your profile. When you make your first trip to a Princess, or your fourth," Janne had her avatar wink and smile at Will, "we see your profile via your wristband, and recognize you." She made no mention of the extensive camera and facial recognition network spanning the park. That capability proved extremely beneficial in countering the previous attempts made against the park.

"What if someone loses a wristband or swaps with someone?" Will said. "If some other kid took my wristband, would he be able to play my profile?"

Janne processed this for a few extra cycles. There were unspoken questions in what WB asked. *Are these questions innocent curiosity, or is Will planning something?* She verbally treated them as innocent, but electronically, she elevated Will's FaceRec tracking status to Active. His position would now be correlated between ARGs, wristband, and Fac-Rec every ten seconds. It would cost Janne extra processor cycles, but she had plenty to spare.

"Wristbands are designed to be difficult to remove," she replied. "We cut them off for people, or deactivate them as they leave. When a wristband is removed, it continues to relay information for several minutes, but automatically disables that player's profile. So no worries about anyone stealing your band and playing your profile, WB."

"What's your favorite quest?" he said.

It was a frequent question. She took it as an indication the guests saw her as more human than AI.

"Hmm...that's tough to say. They're all great. I guess," Janne appeared to temporize, "if I had to choose, it would be a toss-up between KT Crossing and War on Mars."

"I haven't played War on Mars yet," Will said. "Why those two?"

"They're at the far ends of our timeline, and present more extreme environments. The quests in between are more...comfortable. Guests feel more at home in them."

"Huh," WB said.

They arrived at the Hub.

Janne flashed him a smile. "Have a great day at SPARK, WonderBoy!"

Will dropped his ARGs into place and plugged in his earbuds. He gave Janne a thumbs-up, and entered the Hub.

– 1 1 0 1 0 0 1 0 –

Already, Will was tempted to change his plan. He felt drawn to see the Princess again. She haunted his thoughts. What was the connection to his mom?

He resisted the siren song and entered the Future Worlds arcade arm leading to the War on Mars major quest. It felt immediately different. PreHistory was organic—lots of lush vegetation and enormous plants with leaves the size of umbrellas. Future Worlds was sterile, by comparison. Nothing organic showed up in his ARGs. Nothing except people and their avatars. People who looked out of place.

He was following a family that seemed to have chosen a Viking theme. They were all blond. They wore skins or furs. They carried virtual swords or axes and shields. They also all seemed to have anachronistic weapons strapped to either their backs or their hips. Blasters of some sort, Will assumed. SPARK weaponry rarely let physics interfere with appearance.

All of their blasters were an ominous flat black or shiny chrome. Bizarrely large, as if size determined lethality. One family passed him, where the youngest child seemed to have a blaster bigger than the kid was.

Will's pace slowed as he lost himself in thought.

Why chrome or black? There are other colors of metal, like gold and copper. He hadn't seen any gold swords being carried around. *Why? A gold sword would be cool. And why are so many blasters black? Is it just to make them look more menacing? Or is there some inherent property that makes them black naturally?*

The map said there were WeaponSmiths in every arcade.

He jolted out of his reverie and realized he was stopped right in the middle of traffic. Embarrassment brought a rush of blood to his face. *Why do I do that? Do I have some sort of defect where I can't walk and think at the same time?*

He felt his pace slowing again but caught himself before he was re-trapped in thought. Altering his current goal made sense now—it was just a short detour, not a major change.

Will looked around. People were streaming past him. He realized he'd passed the WeaponSmith, and began to backtrack, feeling like a salmon fighting to get upstream.

When he reached the WeaponSmith, there was a short line. Patience with lines was never one of Will's strengths, but he spent the time looking around. *Maybe the décor here provides clues like it did in the PreHistory Arcade.*

The surroundings looked like a corridor in a giant spaceship. Everything seemed to have a space, science, or science fiction theme. Where PreHistory was overflowing with representations of plant and animal life, Future Worlds felt sterile. Lots of muted grays, robots, and spaceships. A restaurant named Bytes Bites.

He'd passed a couple smaller quests already: SPARK's Quarks, where players assembled shapes from minute pieces of matter; and Higgs Bassoon, a puzzle-based quest focused on the nature of sound.

Across from the WeaponSmith, there was another shop called Quantum Quester, featuring souvenirs. Will couldn't decipher a unifying theme from the graphics. There were lots of strings of ones and zeros. Some graphics showed lines that looked like the top of a castle wall. Those seemed irregular—sometimes they stayed at the higher level for a while, sometimes the reverse. It wasn't regular like crenellations were. There were also lots of science-looking diagrams—some related to geometry; others just strings of letters, numbers, and symbols Will couldn't identify. Maybe there was a mathematics theme? Science? He knew binary was a thing, and it involved base-two, so it only had ones and zeros.

While he stood in line, he tried to make sense of one of the strings of numbers.

If Will's memory was correct, base-two worked like this:

Decimal	Binary
1	1
2	10
3	11
4	100
5	101
6	110
7	111
8	1000
9	1001
10	1010

Some of the numbers he saw in the arcade had decimal points in them. *How the heck do decimals*—which Will knew meant either one-tenth, or based on one-tenth, or something like that—*work in binary? How does a fraction work in binary? Was one-half written as one-tenth?*

"How may I help you, good sir?"

Will realized, with a start, he was next in line. The WeaponSmith looked at him expectantly from behind round spectacles that made his eyes appear enormous. The WeaponSmith was slight. Taller than Will, but nearly skeletal in build. His short black hair was plastered back on his scalp.

"Can you turn this sword gold?" Will said, characteristically abrupt.

"What sword?" said the WeaponSmith.

Embarrassed, Will realized the WeaponSmith could only *see* whatever he equipped. He equipped the sword Will inherited from his parents, swapping it out for the bat slung over his shoulder. Then he drew the sword exactly as he would have in virtual combat, by reaching over his shoulder and pulling it out.

"Ah, no, good sir," he replied. "I am not versed in ancient technologies, but I know of merchants in other lands and times who may be able to help you."

The WeaponSmith pulled out a virtual map and pointed to the first five chronologically ordered arcade arms, and then made the map disappear again.

He pointed at the blaster on Will's hip.

"That, on the other hand, I can work with." He put a hand out, indicating he wanted to look at the blaster.

Will handed it over. It was cartoonish in appearance: red and blue, with fanciful gold rings at the muzzle end. Just the kind of thing that appealed to ten-year-olds who were Level 1.

"Ah, you don't see many of these." The WeaponSmith turned it over in his hands. "Original design Mark One blaster. Suitable for all levels. I see it's leveled up with you?"

Will nodded.

"Excellent! We can do modifications without affecting its provenance—it will continue to level as long as you keep it. Its four basic characteristics will continue to grow. Mods will remain at whatever capability you buy. Until you pay to upgrade them again, of course." He looked at Will. "So what'll it be? IFF? Multispectral emitter? Long-range sights? IR-seeking ammo?"

"Actually," Will said, "I have some questions."

The WeaponSmith nodded.

"Why are so many weapons black or silver?"

"Black normally indicates carbon-fiber materials. You'll notice many also have a characteristic honeycomb pattern to the material. Silver normally indicates lower tech, but more robust metal frame weapons. The luster is generally just a preference. You can have a steel weapon blued or painted a flat black. Or you can have it shine like a mirror. Or paint it red and blue." He returned Will's blaster.

"What's carbon fiber?" Will said.

He kinda-sorta thought he knew, but the conversation made him want to ask more questions with every answer.

The WeaponSmith stepped back. "It is clear, good sir, I have misjudged you. From your mien, I took you to be a Warrior. Now, I sense you have deeper currents. Are you a Seeker?"

Will assumed he was a Warrior. It was the simplest choice—Warriors treated almost every challenge as something to be fought. Will's research at the library said 80 percent of men and 40 percent of women played as Warriors. Most of the remainder played as magic users—wizards, sorceresses, mages, and clerics. A much smaller group were thieves. Thieves were agile and good at finding treasure and disarming traps.

Losing his dad in an actual war had made Will less interested in fighting. He had no real idea what a Seeker was, and didn't remember seeing it listed as a playable class of character, but he liked the sound of it, so he nodded.

"Do you seek knowledge of weapons?" said the WeaponSmith.

Considering it was weapon questions that drew him to this very spot, Will said, "Yes."

The WeaponSmith gestured to the back of his shop.

"Then follow me." He turned to the people standing in line. "Good sirs, good ladies, it will be just a moment." He led Will through an unmarked door. "Completion of this Knowledge quest will result in a ten percent discount at weapons vendors throughout SPARK, today only."

Then he clapped Will on the back and left.

A virtual WeaponSmith, identical to the human who escorted him in, appeared in the room.

– 1 1 0 1 0 0 1 0 –

For the next hour, Will learned by playing. The quest, game—or whatever it really was—engaged him immediately. He assembled virtual weapons and tested them. He learned the tradeoffs made between composite and metals: weight, strength in tension, compression, torsion, heat absorption and heat shedding capacity, battery life, and much more.

The quest used binary for everything. The WeaponSmith posted prices in base-ten. *Probably just easier for most customers. Why, then, did so much of this quest make you use base-two?*

He had an epiphany: *It's important. It's a clue!*

It turned out, 1/10 was a perfectly acceptable way to express one-half in base-two. Expressing fractions as binary decimals was trickier. In base-ten, the first digit to the right of the point was the tenths place, then the hundredths, thousandths, and so on. In binary, the first digit to the right of the point was the halves place, then the quarters, eighths, sixteenths, and so forth. Converting decimals to binary, and vice versa, seemed complex to Will, but he understood the theory.

Two hours had passed. He finished the quest in an hour, and spent another hour replaying some parts. The quest netted him 100 XP and a permanent 10 percent increase to damage caused by his blaster. *Are there knowledge quests at all WeaponSmiths? Does each arcade have one? If they do, can they provide clues to other Princess Quests?*

There were no customers needing the WeaponSmith's attention when Will came out, so he asked him.

"Yeah." The WeaponSmith dropped out of character. "This quest takes a long time unless you're really good at the math stuff. Most people don't see the value. Dedicated gamers will beat it once and then come back to beat it again first thing in the day to get the discount when they want to buy something big. The discount doesn't mean much if you're buying a Level 3 sword or blaster. But it can save you half a million gold if you're buying a Level 50 multispectral, fully tricked-out plasma cannon."

"So are there Knowledge quests at the other WeaponSmith locations as well? What about other vendors?"

The WeaponSmith dropped back into character and smiled.

"Seek and ye shall find, good sir. Seek and ye shall find."

The hairs on the back of Will's neck stood up. *Was this a secret?* Nowhere online did anyone mention Knowledge quests. But clearly, people knew about them, because the WeaponSmith casually said gamers did one and then repeated the same one whenever they wanted to get the discount, because doing all the others took too much time. If they somehow tied into the Princess Quests, and the Princess Quests tied into his mom's note, he had to learn more.

Will ran back to the Hub and turned up the PreHistory Arcade. He found the WeaponSmith, but there was a line. He looked around while he waited.

He never paid much attention to the vendors before. Now, he searched for hidden opportunities. Mostly, he saw dinosaurs and Sparkys—stuff that made sense. Then he saw it: a store that looked out of place. It was called Miss Sparkle's.

Full of pink dresses, magic wands, and cone-shaped hats. He decided it was there for the same reason candy bars were by the checkout lines in grocery stores: impulse buys with high profit. Families with daughters passing this place would be instantly sucked in and promptly separated from another hundred bucks.

I definitely don't need any Princess gear. He turned away, but found his eyes drawn back to Miss Sparkle's storefront a few more times, unsure why.

Finally, it was his turn with the WeaponSmith. This vendor was different: short and stocky, bearded, and wearing a leather apron. Behind him, Will could see the glow of a forge as a virtual assistant pumped the bellows.

Will asked the WeaponSmith the same question: "Can you turn this sword into gold?"

"Ah, good sir, that's a conundrum," the WeaponSmith replied. "I am capable of turning the metal in this sword into gold. But you may not have the funds. Besides, gold is a poor choice for anything but a ceremonial sword."

"Why?"

"Too soft. It won't hold an edge for very long, and your entire blade may actually bend. It's also very heavy. It would be difficult to wield with a single hand."

At some level, Will knew there were differences between metals, but thought they were mostly about how scarce they were. Gold was expensive because there wasn't a lot. Aluminum was cheap because it was everywhere.

"Well, this is steel, now, right?" he replied. "Isn't there something better? Titanium or magnesium or something?"

The WeaponSmith gave him a long look.

"Good sir—"

"I'm a Seeker. I seek the knowledge of weapons...and metals," Will added for good measure.

"Ah." The WeaponSmith nodded. "You have chosen a difficult *and time-consuming* path."

He's trying to dissuade me.

– 1 1 0 1 0 0 1 0 –

"No, I will not agree to this."

Ragnar Sarnak was back in Budapest, on a secure call with his employers for the SPARK job.

"It will greatly enhance the kill ratio."

Faces were obscured on the call, and the speaker's English was flawlessly American.

North Korean. Only they would suggest this weapon.

"That is certainly true," Sarnak replied. "However, the requirements for correctly handling and deploying such a weapon make it impractical without using professional soldiers. If you will allow me to recruit and train my own team, such a thing may be possible. Even then, it seems like a suicide mission, and I am not interested."

"We have a good deal of experience with the product, and can safely package and transport it. With timers, you and your men could be well-clear. We can train you in safe handling."

Good deal of experience. Definitely North Korean. Only they—and maybe the Chinese—have any experience with Melt.

"You will let me choose my own team?" Sarnak said.

A long pause followed. He knew they had muted the call on their end.

Eventually, the blurred face spoke again.

"No. That will not be possible. Our partners insist that their men must be used."

"Then we will use conventional weapons only," Sarnak said. "Or you may find someone else to lead this effort."

Another long, silent pause.

Sarnak was not a religious man generally, but he prayed in the silence. *Please, God, keep them from using this weapon.* His stomach roiled. The images and aftereffects from Korea had been horrific. *There's a reason the Geneva Convention bars the use of biological weapons, and that America responded by going nuclear.* Pyongyang would not be habitable for many years.

"We agree. Only guns and incendiaries."

Sarnak signed off with a sigh of relief.

– 1 1 0 1 0 0 1 0 –

Genetics haunted Will. Of all the mixed blessings of inheritance combined in his DNA, stubbornness was most clearly inherited from Kathy, his mother. It was expressed and characterized in many ways, but the streak Will inherited would have been described in Houston as "pure cussedness, plain and simple."

"I have," Will replied in a firm tone, and stood straighter.

With that statement, he made a decision. The resolve crystallized within him. It was similar to his decision to run away from the foster system, but this felt important—much more so than a decision in a theme park should—as if he was making a life-defining choice. He was choosing his path. One he knew would guide him, even beyond SPARK.

A heavy, theatrical sigh emanated from the WeaponSmith.

"So be it, then. So be it."

He ushered WB through the door and returned to his customers.

When Will emerged two hours later, the WeaponSmith simply bade him farewell with a small shake of his head.

To Will, the actual quest elements were mostly rudimentary—things he already learned in the arcade and through the clues he saw. But halfway through his time in the quest, he realized he was learning things that directly applied to some of the riddles. He also discovered the virtual WeaponSmith had a didactic mode. When Will asked questions, he answered them as fully as Will desired.

Mostly, Will glossed over the equations, but was intrigued by the constant pi in the discussion of recrystallization of grains in the working of metals. Like Yul, his father, Will picked at threads. By the time he finished his second Knowledge quest of the day, his understanding of gravity, dark matter, light, and metallurgy surpassed that of 99 percent of the world's population.

As he walked away, Will checked his stats. Two hundred XP for the quest. He double-checked it was twice what he got at the first WeaponSmith. He also picked up a permanent 10 percent increase in edged-weapon damage. His vendor discount hadn't changed, so it looked as if 10 percent was the cap there. But his Brains had increased by one, and now he had a score for something called Wisdom.

Huh? That category didn't exist when I was tweaking my profile with Janne.

Apparently, those points could only be earned.

Will checked his history. He'd gotten one of those Wisdom points for the first Knowledge quest. He was still a Level 15, but now had the stats of a Level 18.

Maybe I'm on to something. Maybe these Knowledge quests have hidden benefits.

His stomach growled. Time to test another hypothesis.

Two days earlier, he noticed that people at SPARK left a lot of uneaten food on their plates. Food that would go to waste. Will was about to test his Freegan Theory—that a crafty gamer could survive, and maybe even thrive, on what others left behind.

Freeganism worked in SPARK. At least, Will didn't get kicked out, verbally abused, or accosted in any way. He entered one of the quick-serve restaurants at the peak of the lunchtime rush and grabbed a stool near a large group—two women, two men, and five kids. When they left, a lot of uneaten food remained.

Will pretended to be engrossed in his ARGs but was scouting the table. When the family exited, and before the staff could clear the debris, Will moved. He grabbed a half-eaten burger, stuffed a nearly full box of fries, an unopened pudding, and a bag of carrots into his pockets, picked up the fullest soda, and walked out. He sat on a bench, with his back to a mosaic tile wall, and ate his free meal.

An odd sense of déjà vu enveloped him. He was full, and dumped the trash, but still couldn't shake the weird feeling. Something was bothering him. His brain was itching again, and he didn't know why.

With his original plan of meeting and beating the Future Worlds Princess trashed, he decided to go see the PreHistory Princess. Could he beat her again? What might it net him in terms of XP or perks?

As he walked up the arcade, the itching in his brain grew stronger, and he froze again. *What's going on? Why do I feel this way?*

Unknowingly, he became a human barricade again. His brain chewed on the problem. He had seen, heard, learned, or felt something that didn't mesh with what he knew. *What the heck was it?*

Without conscious thought, he stopped in front of the WeaponSmith. Even though Will's eyes paused on the WeaponSmith, his attention was elsewhere. What was going on? This was the right spot, he was sure.

Other gamers diverted around him. His gaze settled on the Miss Sparkle's sign. It took a minute, but he figured out the itch.

The sign read, *Miss Sparkle's Princess Gear.* All in a clearly legible font, and consistent with the visible merchandise. In a smaller script, and a different font, were the words, *And Charm School.*

Charm School. *School implies learning and knowledge. Knowledge means clues and advantages in SPARK.*

With the full dread of an adolescent male walking toward a boutique full of princess apparel, Will entered the emporium feeling totally out of place. He was the only male in the store. Fathers, husbands, and older brothers all stopped at the door. Most were looking at the WeaponSmith's shop. Only Will broke the plane of entry.

An unexpected cacophony engulfed him. High-pitched voices surrounded him. He felt a palpable desire to flee.

Resolve overcame panic. He scanned the area for an employee. Acquired a visual lock and tracked a pleasant-looking woman to her perch.

As he approached, she looked up and said in a pleasant tone, "How can I help you?"

A surprising amount of phlegm coated Will's vocal cords.

He cleared his throat. "Yes, well, um, what can you tell me about the Charm School?"

The employee's demeanor changed.

"Thank you so much for inquiring," she purred. "Miss Sparkle's offers a learning environment tailored to all people looking to improve their personal interactions, interpersonal success, and charismatic influence."

Bingo. This is another Knowledge quest. One which might actually boost his lowest stat: Likability.

WonderBoy smiled. "Sign me up."

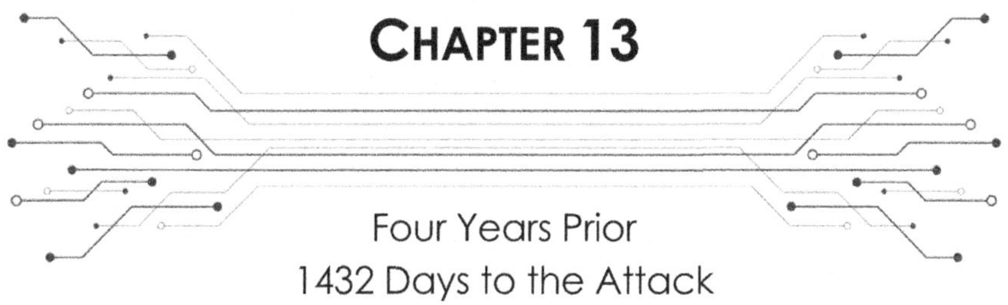

CHAPTER 13

Four Years Prior
1432 Days to the Attack

Do you all think this slowly?
—Janne's first unprogrammed sentence.
(As reported by Hecker Van Horne)

"Boss, we should add childcare as a no-cost employee benefit," said Cindy Glazer, SPARK's in-house legal counsel and de facto head of Human Resources.

Everyone turned to look at Van Horne, who sat in stony silence, playing with one of the coasters on the table.

Glazer took off her glasses and cleaned them while she waited. The pads on the inner edges of the glasses left small oval imprints on either side of her nose. She replaced her weighty spectacles and looked at Van Horne.

"No," came the eventual reply.

Earl Talton, head of Finance, said, "Hecker, the cost wouldn't be large. We've got plenty of room here, and it's a legit write-off."

"Thanks, ET, but it's not the cost I'm worried about. I just don't like the concept of custodial care for kids. I grew up in daycare. They just wanted to turn us back over to parents *relatively* unharmed. I hated it."

"Then make it a school," Glazer said, doggedly. "We already subtly educate guests. Why not overtly teach our employee's kids?"

ET said, "If we got certified, we could even get tax money to help defray the costs."

"There is no way in hell I will allow SPARK to accept government funding. Once they give you money, they think they can control how you work."

HVH pointed at Glazer. "Cindy, you figure out how to make this work and keep us independent of the state and the local school district."

Glazer nodded.

Van Horne turned to Talton. "ET, we're going to open this school to Solar Prime kids as well. Prime's throwing off decent amounts of cash. Work with them to set a fee high enough to cover our costs, but low enough to keep us clean tax-wise."

Talton tapped notes into his tablet, nodding.

"Janne," HVH looked at the ceiling, "start looking at your subroutines. We're going to spool up a new AI for the school. She needs to be able to act as an emergency backup for you. But more…I don't know, maternal, maybe."

"Maternal, boss?" Janne's voice came from the screen on the wall where her avatar appeared.

"Yeah." HVH stood. "Maternal. Cuddly. More focused on the kids. More empathetic, more protective. Let's boost her emotional intelligence."

Janne altered her voice. "By your command," came the distinctly robotic reply.

"Smart-ass AI." HVH smiled as he walked out of the meeting.

Hecker walked the dozen steps from his board room to his private office. *Crossing the threshold into this room always gives me a sense of peace. Like I'm home.*

As he entered his sanctorum, Janne spoke to him via the discrete earbud he wore.

"Boss?"

"Yeah, Janne. What's up?"

"What about the Pod? Will they get to attend the school?

HVH stopped mid-stride. *That's a good question.* He folded his arms across his chest and stared at the floor, deep in thought. Kicked off his shoes and made fists with his toes, digging into the carpet fibers.

"No," he eventually replied. "We're already at risk, allowing them to stay. Welcoming them into the school makes it official. We'd have to turn them over to CPS. Besides," he grinned, "it would ruin the adventure for them. We'd be kicking them out of Neverland."

"Got it," Janne said.

– 1 1 0 1 0 0 1 0 –

Two months later, HVH was manic. They were taking Teacher Janne out of the lab, and the SPARK School was ready to open.

HVH entered the space they dedicated to that purpose. Hodgins had suggested it be next to Security. Safer he said.

HVH smiled. As gruff as Hodgins came off at times, Hecker knew he had a soft spot for kids in general.

Van Horne agreed and gave the go ahead. Today, he was going to introduce Teacher Janne to the staff.

Hecker and his programmers worked on her image and finally settled on an avatar with auburn hair and piercing hazel eyes. They set her apparent age at thirty-eight: "Old enough to have an air of gravitas when necessary. Young enough to be identifiable as more mom than grandma," Van Horne had said. They added some laugh lines and high cheekbones and gave her a quick smile.

"Teacher Janne?" Hecker looked at a nearby monitor.

She appeared. "Good morning, Mister Van Horne."

Her voice was deeper than Janne's, more mezzo than soprano, and her speech cadence slowed three percent from Janne.

Teacher turned to face her assembled staff.

"Ladies and gentlemen, welcome to the SPARK School. Students will begin enrollment tomorrow, and will be here full-time Monday. This is our beta test. We'll limit the school to ten students for the first month, then scale as we work out the bugs. Within a year, if we get the enrollment we expect, we'll have over five hundred students. We've got a lot to do before then. As a reminder, our goals are: One, abundant physical activity—kids should be as tired as their parents are when they pick them up." She ticked them off on her virtual fingers. "Two, world-leading education…"

Cindy Glazer whispered to HVH as they walked away.

"I can't believe we just did that."

"What?" he replied.

"Set up a school where the humans work for an AI," Glazer said.

"Don't worry. We're keeping a very close eye on Teacher Janne. We have to. She's the primary instructor, and will be with every student, all day, every day. One hundred percent individualized instruction. Besides, the parents have to eat lunch with their kids every day. We'll know quickly if something is going off the rails."

"Why even have human teachers, then?" said Glazer.

Van Horne stopped walking and turned to look at her.

"Physical contact and diaper changes—primarily for the younger ones."

– 1 1 0 1 0 0 1 0 –

Present Day

Janne observed Will enrolling in the Charm School, and set in motion a chain of events invisible to him. She alerted the SPARK School that they needed a child actress to be ready at a specified location in one hour. The School sought volunteers within a specified age range and tested for believability.

Casting chose little Paige Bennett for the Lost Child role, and then pinged her mom, Marian Bennett.

"Yes?" Ms. Bennett answered.

"Hey, Marian, it's Denean in Casting. We'd like to use Paige for Miss Sparkle's Lost Child Quest. Can we get your consent?"

"Sure, I'm on my way." Marian looked at the ceiling. "Janne? Can you lock my designs, please? The floral layout for the Labor Day Flower and Garden Show will have to wait another hour. It isn't every day a mom gets to watch her child make her acting debut."

"Of course, Marian. And may I add that the subtle variations of the hues you've chosen for the display around the Hub are impressive."

Janne was experimenting with a new subroutine, prompting her to make unsolicited remarks to employees concerning their work. Her sister, the Teacher, suggested it as a way of emulating empathy.

"Thanks!" Marian replied.

The AI watched Marian Bennet walk through the corridors of the Underground City toward Casting. Judging human reactions was still a challenge for her, but it seemed Marian genuinely appreciated the compliment. Janne upgraded the empathy subroutine to *Verified*. She continued to follow Marian Bennet, camera by camera, to her rendezvous with Paige in Casting. Paige was receiving final coaching from the quest referee as Marian walked up.

Paige turned to her mother. "I'm gonna play a little girl who gets separated from her mommy. Some guest is on another quest, and we're gonna see if he'll help me instead."

Marian smiled at her daughter. "Sounds good, sweetheart. Are you going to cry?"

Paige nodded. "Uh-huh. Want to see me?"

"Not now. But I'll be watching!"

Janne allocated a few cycles to analyzing this exchange. Crying on demand was a critical skill for this role. Why had Marian not required Paige to demonstrate proficiency? She appended that question to her list for HVH's evening download. Her cameras followed mother and daughter until Marian dropped Paige off and entered the Security office in the park where she could watch Paige's performance, and Paige would finish her role. Janne put views of Paige and WB up on separate monitors for Marian and the quest referee who was waiting in the Security office.

– 1 1 0 1 0 0 1 0 –

Will was enduring the longest hour of his life. Things were hammered into his increasingly aggravated, overloaded, and frustrated brain. Forms of address, etiquette, how to deal with others by being able to recognize and react to their social styles, how to acknowledge status without being obsequious. His tedium grew, and his fuse shortened. Compared to the previous two Knowledge quests, this experience was horrible, as if designed to irritate him.

The virtual instructor wore a black high-necked dress that reached to the floor. She had gray hair pulled back in a severe bun, a downturned mouth, a grating voice, and a condescending demeanor. Her face was weathered by time, and she tended to peer at Will by lowering her nose and scowling over the hexagonal frames of her glasses. She was old. *That's okay. Old's fine.* Will just expected wisdom and kindness to accompany it. Every other elder character in SPARK had those qualities. *Not this fussy crone. Somewhere, a tweety is missing his granny.*

Will suffered another withering glare from the instructress as he stifled a yawn. He relaxed a bit, remembering his mom saying, "*Wisdom doesn't necessarily arrive with old age. Sometimes gray hair comes on its own.*"

Finally, the virtual Miss Sparkle looked over her glasses and down her nose at him.

"You've but one task left to complete. Please deliver this to my associate, Devon. He is waiting for you by the green door that marks the entrance to the adults-only area in PreHistory. This matter is urgent. Speed is of the essence. You have less than five minutes before Devon will need to leave."

Will looked where she gestured. On the counter was something that looked like a tiny rectangular terra cotta pillow. It was about as big as his hand. He picked it up and realized it was physical, not virtual. One side was covered with some sort of markings. *Writing?* He felt a slight rattle.

"What is it?"

The instructress snorted. "Clearly you need to spend more time in Civilization Rises. It's a Hittite letter, of course, and you're wasting time. Go."

Will hesitated. "And then what? I'm done?"

"Yes. Yes. Yes. Once you deliver the letter, you will have finished the quest, and you'll receive your oh-so-precious Experience Points. Devon will see to that. You're wasting time for both of us. Now, go!"

He had a million questions but was happy to get away. He left Sparkle's and began jogging up the Arcade. A timer appeared in his ARGs. He had just over three minutes left. He would have to hustle.

Will was angry but also intensely curious. He was being used as a delivery service. *What the heck does that have to do with charm? How am I supposed to find Devon? How will I even know it's Devon?*

The arcade was crowded, but WB made it up to PreHistory Plaza with over a minute left on the timer. *I can make this.*

Then he heard someone crying. He slowed to a walk and looked around.

Over on a bench in the shade was a little girl, sobbing. People were walking past her and ignoring her. As he got closer, he could make out what she was saying: "Mommy, Mommy! I can't find my mommy."

What the heck. Will continued looking around. *Why isn't anyone helping this kid? Where are the SPARK employees?*

No one seemed to be paying any attention to the crying girl.

The timer in his ARGs turned red as the digits counted down the last sixty seconds. Will looked down at the dried clay letter in his hand. *Crud.* He sighed and pushed up his ARGs. Devon and Sparkle's would just be out of luck today.

He squatted down in front of the girl, who appeared to be about five years old.

"Hey, it's okay. I'll help you. What's going on?"

The little girl took her hands away from her face. Tears left trails of dirt running down her face. Walnut hair, disheveled and escaping from an ineffective ponytail. Eyes reddened from crying. Irises such a deep blue they bordered on navy.

"My mommy got lost, and I can't find her."

Typical for a little kid—her mommy was lost, not her.

His foster sister in the second home got separated from the group in a grocery store and had been indignant that her mother had wandered off.

"How about we find her together?" Will said. "I think I know where to start."

"Oh…oh…okay," the little girl got out between sniffles.

Together they walked to an information kiosk. Will had a strong urge to hold the little girl's hand but was afraid to do so. What would her mom do if she saw her daughter holding a stranger's hand?

Will looked down the arcade and froze. Striding up the arcade was the drunk from Barstow. Even though he was wearing ARGs and haptics, Will was sure it was him. The dark hair, florid face, and the mole on his cheek. He looked sober now and seemed to be in a hurry.

What's he doing here? Is he after me? Will's amygdala began to trigger the fight-or-flight reflex. Epinephrine and norepinephrine coursed through his body.

And then the belligerent passed without ever having glanced at Will. *Of course. He only sees my avatar. He wouldn't recognize me.*

As the man passed, Will saw he was wearing an ID Badge for SPARK.

Tony Severski. At least now I know his name. Never would have guessed he works here.

Will took a deep breath and tried to relax and focus on the little girl. At the kiosk, he hit the Help icon.

Janne appeared. "WB, how can I help you?"

"I've got a little girl here who's mommy has gotten lost. Can you help us find her?"

"That's odd," Janne replied. "I don't see another wristband near you. Is she there right now?"

"Yeah," Will said. "Can you see her if I put on my ARGs?"

Janne nodded. "Yes, that would be very helpful."

Will put his ARGs down and immediately saw the *Quest Failed* message displayed. He cleared it and looked down at the little girl.

"What's your name?" he asked her.

"Paige."

"This might be part of the problem." Will squatted down next to her. "It looks like her wristband got torn somehow."

Paige nodded. "It got caught on something in the big dinosaur place. I thought I was going to get eaten."

– 1 1 0 1 0 0 1 0 –

Inside the Security office, Marian Bennett rolled her eyes. Her daughter clearly had a flair for the dramatic.

The referee was smiling, though.

– 1 1 0 1 0 0 1 0 –

Janne said to Will, "Okay, I've got her mom located. She'll meet you at the Security annex in the PreHistory Arcade. Can you find that?"

"Sure. We'll head that way." He pushed his ARGs back up. "They found your mommy. Shall we go meet her?"

Paige nodded.

As they walked away, she took Will's hand. "I don't want you getting lost, too. What's your name?"

"Billy," he replied, without thinking.

They were just entering the arcade. Will stopped and squatted down next to Paige.

"Ever met the Princess?"

Paige nodded. "She's tough. Mommy says nobody can beat the Princesses."

"I think we might be able to do it together. Want to try?"

Paige's eyes widened.

– 1 1 0 1 0 0 1 0 –

Marian knew this was definitely off script. In the Security annex, the referee shot her a questioning look.

"We'll be able to see them the whole time, right?" she said.

The ref nodded.

"Okay."

"Your mom says it's okay," the referee said on a private comm directly to Paige via her earbuds.

– 1 1 0 1 0 0 1 0 –

"Yeah!" Paige dropped Will's hand. "Hang on." She lowered her ARGs and looked up at Will and took his hand again. "Ready. Why do you have a number on your costume?"

"Ah." WB shrugged. "It's the number of my favorite baseball player."

"Okay. Think we can really beat the Princess?"

"Yep."

They entered the quest.

The PreHistory Princess looked at them as they entered. Will glanced at Paige. Her avatar looked like it had been styled after this very Princess, down to the pink of her robes and the cone-shaped hat. She looked like the Princess must have looked when she was five: long dark hair, cone-shaped hat with a veil tacked to its apex.

Paige's eyes shone their natural blue through her ARGs. *Just as serious, though.*

The Princess went through the standard dialogue and led them to one of the doors. The riddle was complex, but as the Princess finished, WB was smiling. He squatted down next to Paige and whispered the answer.

Another glance, then he nodded to Paige. "Go ahead."

Paige looked dubious but turned to the Princess.

"Gravitational lensing caused by a massive object." Her missing front teeth created a lisp.

Will fed her the next line, and Paige spoke it.

"Could explain the ring of light you see."

The Princess smiled, her face glowing. "Of course! I should have seen that myself. Thank you, Princess Alana. You are a true sorceress."

A fanfare of trumpets played as they exited.

Paige jumped up and down. "We did it! We beat the Princess!"

If the fanfare hadn't drawn attention, Paige's shouting and dancing would have. Gamers congratulated them, and Will blushed.

"C'mon!" Paige grabbed Will's hand. "We've got to go tell my mommy!"

As they walked, Paige looked up at Will.

"How did you know the answer?"

Will thought about it.

"I guess I knew because I did my homework. Sort of. I mean, I studied what I could find. Somebody today called it *seeking knowledge*. I think that's what I did."

Paige looked as determined as only a five-year-old can, and said, "I'm going to seek knowledge and beat every Princess!"

– 1 1 0 1 0 0 1 0 –

In the Security annex, Marian Bennet listened as the referee was talking fast to Janne on a private channel. She only heard the ref's side of the conversation:

"That's never happened before, right?"

She watched the ref nod as he continued.

"Yes, he's clearly completed the Lost Child Quest, so full points there. But what about taking her to the Princess? He didn't have to do that." More nodding. "Yeah, I see he's beaten that Princess before, so only ten XP there. But it was a nice thing…"

Paige's mom put her hand on the ref's shoulder. She worked at SPARK and knew how tough the Princess Quests were. This young man had just done something for her daughter that few guests ever accomplished. Professional gamers like CastIron hired outside consultants to help them through the Princesses.

Marian had never beaten one. There were tears in her eyes.

"No," she said, "it wasn't simply a nice thing. It was a wonderful thing he did for my daughter—he saw a little girl crying, and stopped to help her. Did you see how many people never gave her a second look?" She stabbed a finger at the monitor.

The ref nodded and wrapped up his conversation with Janne.

"Yeah, yeah, done," he said, as the door opened.

Will and Paige entered.

The girl ran to her mom, screaming, "Mommy!" She followed it immediately with, "We beat the Princess! We beat the Princess!" The joy and enthusiasm she showed were genuine. "Nobody in my group at school has a Princess! I'm the first."

Paige and Marian thanked Will profusely and exited the scene. As they left, Marian looked down at her beaming daughter. Paige began telling the story, using words she would always say from that point forward: "When my friend Billy and I beat the Princess…"

– 1 1 0 1 0 0 1 0 –

Now alone with the referee, Will pulled out the Hittite letter.

"I guess I need to give this back to Miss Sparkle…"

The ref smiled and lowered his ARGs.

"Put on your ARGs," he told Will. "She's already here."

WB dropped his ARGs into place and saw Miss Sparkle standing by the door, smiling. She seemed regal now, less a crone. Her wrinkles softened, and she was lit from within, as if her heart had grown three sizes. Maybe it was the smile.

"This quest was never about delivering the letter, WonderBoy," she said. "It was about helping Paige. You were deliberately aggravated so you would be less inclined to help. You were put under pressure to meet a deadline. Completing the quest would benefit you, but you set that all aside to help a crying little girl. That is the essence of gallantry, and a requisite for charm: to help those in need, even if it costs you something you want. Not everyone succeeds in this. Most deliver the letter. Miss Sparkle's is proud to consider you a distinguished graduate of our school."

"What about the letter?" WB held it out.

Miss Sparkle gave him a winsome smile. "I think you'll find it's for you."

She winked. "You'll just have to learn how to read it." She turned as if to leave, and then glanced back. "Taking her to beat the Princess was not part of the quest, but it is something Paige will remember forever. So will I."

Miss Sparkle faded. Will lost himself in thought and stood quietly until the ref cleared his throat.

"That's it for the quest. Well-done, kid. Well-done. Enjoy the rest of your day at SPARK." The ref turned and walked away.

Will's ARGs began tallying his reward:

Quest completed!

400 XP—Charm School Complete

10 XP—PreHistory Princess Complete

+3 Charisma

10% permanent discount at Miss Sparkle's Princess Gear

400 Gold received from Anonymous Donation

Level Up!

Shame and pride warred within him. He didn't really feel like a hero. He wasn't! What kind of jerk wouldn't stop to help a little girl? Did most people really just walk past? The Princess visit was something he wanted to do, anyway. It seemed wrong to be rewarded for it.

He headed back to Miss Sparkle's and asked the lady who had helped him before if he could speak to Miss Sparkle again. He was ushered back into the Charm School classroom. Miss Sparkle materialized, still looking friendly.

"Yes, WonderBoy? How may I help you?"

"It's about this reward and stuff. I don't think I earned it."

"Hmm. What makes you think that?"

"Well, anybody would've helped Paige. That wasn't anything special. And the whole Princess thing? I wanted to go see her again, anyway. I wanted to test my theory. Bringing Paige along…well, I guess I just thought it would be fun for her. I didn't do a single heroic thing. Not one."

Miss Sparkle smiled and sat on a bench, patting the seat next to her. Will sat, and she took his hands in hers. It actually felt, a little, as if she were holding his hands. *These haptic gloves are really good.*

"My dear boy. A Nobel Prize winner, Romain Rolland, once said, 'A hero is a man who does what he can.' You exemplified what all of us want to see as the best of ourselves. The situation didn't require you to die for someone else, or to protect an ideal. It required you to put aside your own best interest to help a child. You did that. WB, you earned the points you were given.

There'll be no further discussion on that subject." She gently squeezed his hands. "As far as the reward of the gold, there's a certain mother who has seen uncontained joy from her daughter. And a certain little girl who now knows, without hesitation, if she seeks knowledge, she'll find it. There's not a parent worth the name who wouldn't trade all of their gold in exchange for their child learning that lesson early on." She smiled again. "Now, maybe you should get out there again yourself, Seeker."

Will thought for a moment, digesting her words.

"Can I ask you a favor?" he said.

"Of course."

He pulled the terra cotta letter out of his pocket.

"I don't really have a place to keep this safe. I'm afraid it'll get hurt or something if I carry it around in my back pocket. Can I leave it here until I learn how to read it?"

Miss Sparkle nodded. "Certainly. Put it on the counter. I'll see it's kept safe for you."

They said their goodbyes. It was mid-afternoon already. He'd been in SPARK nearly seven hours, and accomplished exactly zero of the things he'd set out to do today, but felt immensely satisfied, nonetheless.

He turned to head back to the Future Worlds Arcade, and began to work his way through all the small quests. His near encounter with the drunk temporarily forgotten, Will hunted for clues along the way.

CHAPTER 14

There are ten kinds of sapient.
Those who understand binary, and those who don't.
—Janne's first attempt at humor

The arcade was heavy on binary stuff. There was a quest called Asimov's Quandary. In it, Will learned about Isaac Asimov and the Three Laws of Robotics he wrote about in his fiction:

1. A robot may not injure a human being, or through inaction, allow a human being to come to harm.
2. A robot must obey orders given it by human beings except where such orders would conflict with the First Law.
3. A robot must protect its own existence as long as such protection does not conflict with the First or Second Law.

In the quest, WB played a robot. He was to apply the Three Laws of Robotics to a variety of scenarios and make choices that either followed or violated them.

The world faded, and WB found himself in a mechanical body. A driver, focused on his phone, was closing with a child walking to school. WB pulled the child out of the car's path. *Easy.*

The next two scenarios were also easy choices. The fourth was not.

The scene changed, and WB the Robot found himself next to a hiker in the mountains. The hiker's arm was pinned under a boulder too large for WB's robotic strength to move. No outside help was available.

"If you don't get me out of here, I'm going to die." The hiker held out a knife. "You'll need to apply a tourniquet, cut my arm off at the elbow, and carry me out."

As a human being, the decision was easy. *I'll do what I have to do to save his life. But I'm supposed to be following the Three Laws. Applying Law Two will directly violate Law One.*

WB applied the tourniquet. *Is SPARK trying to say these laws are wrong, or just too simple for the nuances of real life?*

He took the knife and began a cut. The scene changed again.

Robot WB stood on a bridge overlooking parallel, but widely separated, railroad tracks. Two trains barreled toward him. WB saw the problem. Two kids seemed to be stuck on the right-hand track. On the left-hand track, two elderly people were in the same predicament. WB could only save one pair. *Crap! Is it wrong to save the kids, just because they're younger? Maybe the older couple would develop a cure for COVID-X. I can't exactly stop and interview everyone.*

He leapt off the bridge and pulled the kids out of harm's way but saw the elderly couple disappear under the wheels of the other train.

Scene change.

A virulent plague was ravaging the planet. Robot WB had to decide whether or not to release an anti-viral guaranteed to kill half of all Americans, but would save 90 percent of the rest of the world.

Will thought of Paige, the little girl he helped. *There's not enough information. How many will die if I do nothing? Is saving other people worth a fifty-fifty shot Paige will die?*

WB made his choice.

At the end, Will got a few XP out of the quest, but mostly he just felt uneasy. *The calculus of choice is incredibly complex when lives are at stake. The Three Laws just aren't enough.*

He left with a greater respect for people who were working in artificial intelligence.

He moved on.

Other small quests gave him a deeper understanding of Black Grass and power generation. Some arguments, Will learned, theorized that the worldwide demand for carbon to make Black Grass was going to begin outstripping carbon emissions quickly—to the extent that some people were now concerned there would be too little CO2 in the atmosphere, and the greater percentage of oxygen could cause problems. It was fascinating, and Will grew melancholy thinking about how much his dad would have loved it.

There was only one thing left for him to do in the arcade. He stepped in and met his second Princess.

She wasn't what Will expected.

The Princess was grown up. Not old, but a grown woman. Maybe twenty-ish? She wore the same style gown and hat, but it was now crimson, not the delicate pink of the younger Princess, as if it, too, had aged and matured.

At first, Will wasn't certain it was even supposed to be the same girl. But as he stared at her, he could see it. The same dark violet eyes. The same hair, but more elegantly styled—soft curls cascaded past her shoulders. Her voice was slightly deeper and more nuanced in its modulation. *Pretty. But somehow not attractive.*

He stopped for a moment to consider the difference, then forced himself back to the quest. The room seemed the same, although the flickering torch sconces had been replaced by diffused lighting illuminating without casting shadows. Even the coat of arms with the Sparky-ish star was present.

"Good." She looked right at him.

She has a more resolute air about her, but there's a touch of weariness in her voice.

"You're here." Then she seemed to peer at him more closely. "You've helped me before. I was much younger then, but you seem the same. Some trick of magic or technology, I presume. It matters not. You've got to help me. The points of the star will guide you. Our first challenge is this." The Princess waved a hand at the wall behind her, and a series of numbers appeared in the air and scrolled from the bottom of the room to the top, like the credits in a movie.

00000011.
00100100
00111111
01101010
10001000
10000101
10100011
00001000
11010011
00010011
00011001

10001010
00101110
00000011
01110000
01110011
01000100
10100100
00001001
00111000
00100010
00101001

10011111
00110001
11010000
00001000
00101110
11111010
10011000
11101100
01001110
01101100
10001001

The wall blanked.

"I-I…"

Clearly it was binary, but the numbers went by too fast.

"Fear not," the Princess told him. "It repeats."

And it did, and then again.

Partway through the fourth repetition, the numbers faded.

The Princess looked at him expectantly. "What does it mean?"

Will shrugged. "I don't know."

The Princess herself began to fade, and her voice softened in his ears as if she were receding from his presence.

"Find me. Save me."

He froze. Even though it was the Princess saying the words, Will heard his mom's voice.

Exit Now, appeared in his ARGs.

Will didn't move, lost in thought. It wasn't until there was an aural, "Please exit now," that he shook himself out of the reverie and exited.

As happy as Will was at helping Paige earlier, now he felt gut-punched. The whole thing was fictional, he knew, but the Princess seemed very real, and in need of true help.

What did she mean when she said, "Find me?" She was right there! *Was Mom trying to tell me to do these quests?* What the heck was he supposed to do with the numbers? Add them? Was it all one number? Was he supposed to figure out a decimal equivalent? Put it into hexadecimal? She hadn't given him much to work on.

He re-entered to see if it was the same. Maybe it was like the other Princess, where the riddle changed every time and he would get lucky this time around.

Nope. Same dialogue, same numbers. Same *Exit Now* message.

Frustrated, he decided to go find some food. Sometimes his brain needed time to process information.

Another freegan feast awaited him at the Soylent Bistro in Future Worlds Plaza. Will took a different approach this time. When a family left, he simply sat at the table they vacated and began to eat their leftovers. *This is way better than trying to survive on PB and J and granola bars.* They even left a bottle of water behind.

– 1 1 0 1 0 0 1 0 –

Tony Severski was home, drinking. It was cheaper, particularly since that Kimmy got him banned from the Stumble. Every other place on a direct path from his job at SPARK to his house was pricier. Some even encouraged him to take his business elsewhere. Besides, since he'd visited the adults-only area that afternoon, he felt no need to go out in search of companionship.

No sense dirtying a glass. He took another slug directly from the bottle of tequila, and smiled at his own humor.

The sink was full of dirty dishes. He had only run the dishwasher twice since his wife moved out. *She'd seen the signs.* The unexplained expenses. Him coming home drunk, even after they agreed he'd stay away from the booze. His griping about the unfair treatment he was getting at work.

He recognized the spiral. It had happened before, and cost him at least two jobs. And maybe now, two wives. *Nothing to do but ride it out. I'll bounce back.*

Tears formed in his eyes as he realized that she would take everything. *Thank God we didn't have kids.*

He grew maudlin as he thought of the wife and son he had lost in Korea. Fat tears rolled down his cheeks. He took another swig and forced his thoughts away from that memory.

He wondered what they drank in Mozambique.

Severski wandered over to his new laptop. The one *they'd* given him. He logged on as he had been trained. Weeks with no contact lulled him into believing they had forgotten it. Forgotten him. *Maybe there would be no attack. I'll just be able to keep the money.*

Instead, there was a message:

> *Cousin!*
>
> *Everything has worked out here. Are you still willing to host the reunion? I'm looking forward to seeing you in two months, on the 24th!*
>
> *Be well,*
>
> *R. Severski*

Tony nearly dropped the bottle. R. Severski was actually Ragnar Sarnak. Two months meant two days. *Willing to host* meant Sarnak was coming here, to Severski's house. *The 24th* was code for 2:00 to 4:00 p.m.

God, it must be on. He took another pull from the bottle and looked around. *Have to clean up some. Maybe sell my guns. Got a lot of money invested in them. Don't think TSA will let me take them to Mozambique.*

– 1 1 0 1 0 0 1 0 –

From where Will sat, he could see the War on Mars Quest entrance. The quest grounds were enormous, and easily the tallest part of SPARK, stretching several stories above the surrounding desert. It seemed like a high-tech mountain had been built to launch spaceships. The graphics gave him some of the background story:

Humans made it to Mars. Once there, they established an outpost in a deep canyon. Not long after, our solar system was invaded. A race of creatures that seemed to be a cross between armored badgers and blaster-wielding cockroaches, landed on Mars and promptly eradicated our settlement. We were the last hope for saving humanity. First Mars, then Earth, would fall to the invading hordes.

A little heavy on the hype. Will ate his fill and then decided to give War on Mars a shot.

The day was nearly over for entrants. It was a long quest, and SPARK stopped entries three hours before the park closed. For Will, it was all new. His family hadn't made it this far on their trip.

There was a line, and Will squeezed in just as they closed entry. It looked as if he'd be one of the last combatants allowed to save humanity today. As he went through the line, he learned more of the story:

A joint effort led by the Australians established an outpost on the Red Planet, in a place called Valles Marineris, or Mariner Valley. According to what Will saw in his ARGs, this valley was five times as long as the Grand Canyon, and four times as deep. Will had never been to the Grand Canyon, but his ARGs displayed graphics as the line of gamers moved forward.

Mariner Valley was around eight hundred kilometers long and about seven deep. We established our outpost there to begin a terraforming project. The outpost was situated where there was evidence of water erosion. Underground water was found, and additional expeditions increased the number of settler-scientists to nearly fifty. Then the Desnardians struck.

Contact was lost, and all humans were presumed dead. The last images transmitted showed the hideous aliens—giant six-limbed creatures with badger-esque faces and snouts displaying black and white stripes running from the chitinous crown of their heads toward a mouth that, when open, revealed sharp-pointed predator's teeth. Two-meter-long antennae sprouted above soulless eyes and trailed behind them as they ran. A short video of the attack showed them running on all six limbs, and revealed a humped carapace covering their backs. The audio track captured a sound something like, "Desnardia! Desnardia!"

Will's ARGs and earbuds replayed the video and audio, and he grudgingly agreed it did sound like that, so maybe the name was apt. Will barked out a laugh that earned him glares from others in line.

Of course it sounded like "Desnardia." Will was still smiling. *It's a written fiction, and the writers crafted audio to match their vision for the quest.*

Will admitted to himself that the *news report* seemed pretty darned real, and he was ready to go kick some Desnardian butt. It impressed him how strongly and quickly a good story could pull you in.

One of the guys in front of Will turned around and looked at him.

"Jumper?" the guy said.

He and his two buddies were all wearing military-style tech gear. They all had subtle blue and gold highlights against the predominantly black military-looking uniforms. All carried long black blasters slung on their backs.

"What?" Will replied.

"Are you a jumper?" the first guy repeated.

His name tag read, *Bruin Baker*. The others were Bruin Able and Bruin Charlie.

"I don't know what you mean." Will was embarrassed. "Are you guys some sort of team?"

He powered through. A lesson he learned from his dad was that feigning understanding early just made you look even dumber later.

"Yeah!" yelled Baker. "Go Bruins!"

He and the other two traded high-fives.

"So," Baker said, "I take it you've never done this quest before."

Will shook his head.

"You, then, young sir, are in for the ride of your life!"

"What do you mean?" It hurt Will to repeat ignorance, but he pushed on.

"We mean," said Able, "War on Mars is without a doubt the most awesome quest in the park!"

As they moved up in the line, Baker said, "When we get there, they'll try to make you get into the assault craft. It's supposed to take you to the bottom of the canyon. Near the bottom, you'll come under fire from the Nards and will be ejected. You'll end up in a parachute." He used air quotes around *parachute*. "You'll hit the ground and be deep in combat in a hurry."

Will nodded his understanding, although he didn't like the sound of being ejected.

"Or," said Bruin Charlie, "you man up and jump the rim!"

More whoops.

Baker continued. "It was an Easter Egg one of the founders of our club discovered early on. Dude was a skydiving fool. He figured if you were going to have to parachute in, why not start early? When we get to the launch zone, they'll try to scoot you into the assault craft. If you want, you can skip that and get to the bottom quicker."

"Is there another way?" Will had a sense of dread.

The thought of jumping prompted an electrodermal skin response. His mouth dried.

"Nah," one of the Bruins replied. "Couple of dead-end paths. Off to the left side, there are some rocks you can climb up. They lead to a flat area that projects out a few meters into the canyon. You get up there, run like crazy, and jump off the edge! Your chute will open after a few seconds of freefall, and you'll be on the ground before the noobs in the assault craft even get close. You scarf up the swag at the bottom and start blasting as soon as the Nards come over the hill. The ride down in the chute is sweet. You can see the whole canyon—where the Nards are, how they're deployed, the geography beyond the first hill, everything. From the assault craft, all you see is the people around you, and the incoming fire. Suck City."

"Do you get anything for the Egg?" Will said.

"Nah," said Able. "Dude couldn't keep a sweet secret like this from his brothers."

That started an argument over what the first Egg finder may have earned had he kept his mouth shut. Will, of course, had an excellent idea of what secrecy was worth.

"How many people jump?" he said.

"Not many," said Charlie. "I know the dudes from USC do. Probably most of the other clubs. But most people just ride the wagon of doom."

Will was silent.

"Think about it, dude. If you hit the bottom with us, we'll watch your back."

When they reached the launch zone, they were briefed by a cast member in a red jumpsuit and virtual body armor.

"Recruits, I am Commander Ryker. I will get you safely to the floor of the canyon today. Desnardian activity has been high. Expect contact with the enemy shortly after we land. I will not be staying with you. I have to return for the next load of recruits. Your mission is to reach the outpost and secure our Data Core. The Desnardians took out our telemetry antennas and relays, but all sensors should still be recording. The Data Core may hold the key to winning the war, and the key to saving Mars itself. Once you have the Core, continue two kilometers beyond, and you will be exfiltrated. Of course," Ryker flashed a grim smile, "if you've taken out all of the Desnardians, we'll pick you up at the outpost site. Please don your safety harnesses."

Ryker continued. "War on Mars simulates a hostile environment with a risk of falling. SPARK guests are required to wear a safety harness that offers fall protection during the initial portion of the quest. Simply step through the leg straps and insert your hands through the shoulder straps. A War on Mars cast member will assist you and check for proper fit. The fall protection system will not prevent you from making small jumps, but will activate if it senses more than one second of freefall."

Will thought about this and looked at the gear. The harness seemed reasonably robust and should hold him, but the safety line seemed to be tiny—only a centimeter in diameter. *I'd prefer something a lot thicker.* His mind wandered. *Mom called it acrophobia, but that's wrong. That's an irrational fear of heights. What I have is basophobia—a completely rational fear of falling. And dying.*

He shook himself and paid attention to Ryker, who was still talking.

"Your safety is our paramount concern. If at any time you choose not to participate in this quest, simply notify a cast member."

As they donned the harness, a virtual drop suit materialized around them. Will looked down and saw a compass, a power meter (currently at 100%), and an altimeter (now at 0000m). He knew from the online tutorial that the floor of the canyon would indicate -6984m.

Ryker checked them all—there were twelve in the group—and then connected them to the fall cable as they boarded the assault craft. The three Bruins whispered, "Jumper," to Ryker. He nodded, hooked them up, but did not put them on the craft.

The craft looked to Will like an oversized shopping cart—metal grids on all sides, open on the top. It *almost* looked strong enough to support them. He began to sweat.

Ryker motioned him in. Will was the last in line. He froze in place. He couldn't make himself step into the assault craft. Ryker understood.

Chapter 15

We sent unarmed scientists first, to a planet named after a god of war.
We should have known better. Now we're sending warriors: you.
—From the official SPARK description for the War on Mars Quest

Ryker grew up a child of SPARK. He was a local. Both his parents worked at the park, and as soon as he turned eighteen, he got hired himself. His plan was to get into quest design. Right now, he was paying his dues—doing the grunt work that made the park run.

In the time he'd been on this quest, he'd seen lots of people bail at this point. Fear of heights was no joke, and the open grid at the bottom of the assault craft seemed to trigger it. SPARK didn't want to make anyone freak out. This was the point of no return. Gamers were allowed to jump or ride the assault craft. Those that couldn't do either were gently escorted back to the ground and shown where to meet their party when they emerged from the quest. War on Mars was not for everyone.

"I understand." Ryker spoke the words he was trained to say. "Before you can go down, you must go up. If you remain here, a cast member will be in shortly to escort you from the quest."

He then double-checked Will's fall protection, making sure Will could not possibly disengage it himself, tapped the button that would summon a cast member to walk Will out of the quest, and boarded the assault craft.

Virtual thrusters lifted it. Physical cables did the actual work.

– 1 1 0 1 0 0 1 0 –

The Bruin Brothers looked at Will. "Dude! Awesome choice! This way."

They scrambled up the rock they described, and Will watched them hurl themselves off the edge one at a time, whooping, "Go Bruins!" as they leapt.

Will was alone on the launch platform. Wind whistled in his earbuds. Fear had pushed him out of the assault craft, and it kept him from jumping off the edge. Cussedness kept him from walking out the exit. He would climb down.

He started scouting the terrain. It appeared to be afternoon on Mars. The sun was low in the sky. The vista from the launch area was impressive. Mariner Valley stretched several kilometers to his left before bending back to parallel the southern rim. To his right, the valley faded into the distance. Shadows were elongated and sharper than they were on Earth. Starker. Everything was shades of sienna and umber, as if the artist was constrained by a limited palette. The vertical drop was daunting.

He couldn't jump. His heart was pounding. He wouldn't quit. The resolve he inherited from his mother crystalized once again, and he began looking for handholds.

Keeping his face to the wall of the canyon helped. Will followed the path the Bruin Brothers took and looked around. The view was majestic and terrifying. His drop suit now showed him at 0003m. Will tried to walk to the edge, but froze when he got too close. He dropped down to his hands and knees and crept nearer. When that became too much, he belly-crawled until he could look over. From here, he could see a lower platform to his right. He might be able to jump to it. He toggled the rangefinder in his ARGs: 15 meters. He did some quick math.

It looked to be about a forty-five-degree angle to the lower ledge. That meant the vertical drop was just over ten meters. A ten-meter drop would trigger his fall protection, and Will would be hanging in the middle of the canyon as his *parachute* lowered him to the floor.

Wait! Those were Earth numbers. The acceleration due to gravity on Mars is only 3.7 meters per second squared, not 9.8 like Earth. What does that mean in the quest?

Will rolled onto his back and thought. *Okay, on Mars, I should be able to survive a much longer drop. But the briefing said, "one second of freefall."*

One second on Earth meant a drop of 4.9 meters. On Mars, it was only 1.85 meters. That had to mean, even drops that appeared survivable in Earth gravity would trigger the fall protection. It was the last thing Will wanted. *I bet other people have made that mistake.*

He wasn't sure how SPARK was doing its calculations, but decided to err on the side of caution.

– 1 1 0 1 0 0 1 0 –

"Can you see him?" came the call from Dorothy Watkins, the senior War on Mars referee.

Watkins worked as a nurse most of her life. But nursing was a hard life, and she also loved gaming. When SPARK opened, she retired from nursing, dyed her hair brown again, and became a ref.

She was calling the cast member who was sent to escort a guest, WB, out of the quest.

"He's lying on the jump platform. Want me to get him?" The cast member hadn't reached WB yet, but had him in sight.

"Nah." Watkins looked at the clock. "Let him make the choice, for now. We've got time."

She set a timer. If the kid was still in the quest in an hour and hadn't progressed to the canyon floor, she'd loop Double F into the decision.

– 1 1 0 1 0 0 1 0 –

Will's eyes overrode his intellect. It couldn't possibly be a seven-kilometer drop to the floor. Even if the building was actually ten stories tall, and went another ten stories into the ground, that wasn't even a kilometer. The ARGs were tricking him. He pushed them up and looked over the edge again.

Dead was dead, Will decided. You would die as certainly from a two-hundred-meter fall as you would from a seven-thousand-meter fall. Even with his ARGs up, Will's brain interpreted the distance as too far. Reality showed catwalks and scaffolding around the edges, but plenty of room to fall and die. He put his ARGs back down and Mars returned. He took a few deep breaths to calm himself and started looking for hand and foot holds. There seemed to be plenty, but they all led away from the launch area. Would SPARK really expect him to traverse what looked like kilometers of cliff face?

– 1 1 0 1 0 0 1 0 –

"He's moving. Climbing away. Want me to get him? Call him back?"

"No," replied Dorothy, "but sit tight. He may come back."

She hit the alert key on her screen. All it did was let management know when someone went off script. Watkins had seen this before.

"Looks like he's headed for the high path. He'll either jump, or be back."

– 1 1 0 1 0 0 1 0 –

Cussedness manifested. It wasn't about coming back and quitting. That wasn't a consideration. It wasn't about jumping and letting the parachute carry him to the floor. That wasn't an option. One handhold or foothold at a time, Will moved on.

The terrain was brutal but always possible. At times, Will closed his eyes and tried to meld with the face of the cliff until his heart slowed. A sort of trail seemed to be visible. Sometimes he lowered himself to his belly and inched along by feel. His fear of falling was too great to allow him to open his eyes on occasion, forcing him to creep along as his hands probed the path in front.

An hour passed. Then two. It was starting to get dark, and the rusty umber of Mars was darkening to a ruddy magenta with the fading light. He could see flashes of light from the canyon floor. Recruits were fighting Desnardians far below. A third hour passed, and Mars grew dark.

A voice crackled in WB's earbuds.

"Recruit WB, this is Commander Ryker. We see your location. Do you need assistance? We have an assault craft on standby, but we're losing light and might not be able to pick you up much longer."

"I'm fine. I'm fine!" Will's voice was raspy—it was hard work crawling along the trail.

Ryker's voice changed. "C'mon, kid. Let us come get you. We'll get you out safely."

"No!" Will yelled back.

He wanted to finish this. Somehow. Being evacuated from a quest because you were scared of heights was a humiliation he refused to endure. *Will they force me out? They could just kill all the virt, turn on the lights and drag me out like a misbehaving dog.*

But they didn't. Will crawled on in the dark. Some starlight illuminated the red world, but Mars's puny excuse for moons, Phobos and Deimos, offered little help. The vid he'd watched online said Phobos—even though it was much closer to Mars than Luna was to Earth—was much smaller and appeared only about a third of the size of Luna. Deimos was even smaller and farther away—about the size and visibility of Venus as seen from Earth.

The path seemed to run out. WB, Mars Recruit, was stuck. He couldn't find a way forward and was too scared to stand up, turn around, and crawl back.

There were no good choices, and the bad ones were untenable.

CHAPTER 16

We choose to go to the moon in this decade and do the other things, not because they are easy, but because they are hard, because that goal will serve to organize and measure the best of our energies and skills, because that challenge is one that we are willing to accept, one we are unwilling to postpone, and one which we intend to win…
—President John F. Kennedy, September 12, 1962

The atmosphere in Quest Control was electric about the kid, so HVH had pulled his leadership team together in the boardroom to give them a little space from the chaos the kid was creating in the quest.

There were two paths leading away from the launch area in opposite directions. Both were apparent dead ends. Both contained some hidden treasure. The high path, the one the kid took, was longer and more difficult. Exploring gamers found a spare power cell that would fit either your assault suit or an energy weapon, a flawless Mars ruby reported to be worth one thousand gold, and a couple first aid kits. Good swag, they agreed. But even the fastest player took fifty minutes to get out to the end of the trail and back. Most recommended jumping after you found the ruby because "there was nothing else there." They were wrong.

War on Mars was officially closed. All players, save one, were out of the quest. The night crew was waiting. Normally they would flip on the lights, make sure everything got cleaned and all physical swag was replaced and reset. A light coating of sand covered the floor of the canyon, but by the end of the day, a lot had been displaced and the bare floor was visible beneath. They would go in, replenish it as necessary, and rake it smooth for the next day's gamers.

Right now, I'm paying them to stand around. That part's okay. But it means they'll end up having to work faster later. Going too fast means you miss things.

Most guests wouldn't notice rocks and supplies weren't in the right place, but hardcore serious gamers would.

In the boardroom, tempers flared.

"Mister Van Horne," said Cindy Glazer, SPARK's in-house legal counsel, "you simply can't leave a guest alone in a quest overnight. The liability if something happened would be huge!"

Three of the others around the table nodded. Security was there in the form of Hodgins. Glazer represented Legal. Earl Talton covered Finance. The quest had its head referee, Dorothy Watkins. And the group was rounded out by SPARK's head referee, Fitz Flaherty. He didn't nod. Janne's avatar appeared on a screen. She remained silent.

"No," HVH replied. "I want to leave him in. The kid has done amazing things in our park—now, and before. I want to see how this plays out. I like his determination. He walked out to see the Black Grass fields. Walked!"

Hodgins said, "Yeah, in hundred-degree weather, and nearly got heat-stroke, Hecker. Look, I've got a soft spot for this kid, too. But the risks—"

"Fitz. Where is the kid?"

Double F glanced around the table deliberately before looking at HVH. He looked uncomfortable.

"Boss, the kid's right at the end of the trail. I mean, he's *there*." Fitz paused.

HVH nodded, so Fitz continued.

"We've got Costuming and Casting on alert."

Glazer picked up on the emphasis, as did the others at the table.

"What do you mean, *there*? And why the heck do we need to alert Costuming and Casting?"

Hodgins started nodding. It made sense now why the boss was being so stubborn about this.

Cindy snapped her fingers. "That's it! This is about an Egg, isn't it?"

HVH said, "Janne, show us the kid."

A large screen flared to life as Janne gave them four views: low-light TV from above and across the platform, IR from the nearest sensor with that range, and a quest view showed Will in all his gear.

"He's just lying there," Talton said. "Is he okay?"

Janne replied, "He rolled onto his back approximately thirty minutes ago. He has shown minor movements since then. IR indicates his body temperature is within acceptable parameters. His breath sounds have slowed, and he seems calmer. Active and passive fall protection are in place."

"Passive?" said Glazer.

Watkins cleared her throat. "Uh, yeah. We have quick reaction nets all along the trail. They extend ten meters into the canyon, and only deploy if Active fails, or we manually deploy them. We've got the three nearest the kid already manually deployed."

"Hodge." HVH played with a coaster on the boardroom table, "how are your guys deployed?"

"We've got one guy just inside the trail's emergency exit, and two ready to go off the catwalks above. Everybody has goggles and fall protection on."

"Any weapons?"

"Just tasers. I don't think our guys will have any trouble with the kid, but I wanted them to be able to immobilize him if he freaks."

HVH nodded and the room fell silent, waiting. He spun the coaster between his fingertips.

Earlier today, he had negotiated a billion-dollar deal. Agreeing to terms there had been contentious, but seemed easier than this decision.

"Replay the conversation with Ryker," said Van Horne.

Janne fed the audio into the room's speakers.

Cindy seemed mollified. "At least we have him refusing assistance. But Hecker," she turned to her boss, "he's a minor. If something goes bad, we'll all be crucified."

"Let's make sure it doesn't, then." HVH stood. "Double F, Dorothy, you're here as long as the kid's in the quest. Hodge, let's keep this kid safe. He's staying in until he gets killed out or quits." As Van Horne walked away, he looked back at SPARK's head referee. "You might want to start thinking about how much help you'll need if we have to do the reset."

Fitz Flaherty nodded with a grin.

"Got it, boss." He paused. "What if the kid's still playing when the park opens tomorrow? Do we open on top of him?"

HVH paused. "Your call. Quest first, kid second—as long as we keep him safe."

Hecker rounded the corner and entered his private office and suite.

"Janne?"

"Yes, boss?"

"What are the odds?"

"That WonderBoy will find the Egg?"

HVH nodded.

"Statistically, miniscule. In the seven years we've been open, this Egg has never been found. In terms of just the War on Mars Quest players, ninety-four percent take themselves out of the competition for the Egg by getting in the assault craft. Four percent jump immediately. Two percent run the paths, but most of those take the lower path and then jump. Since the high path was discovered and explored in our first year, runners on the upper trail have dwindled to nearly zero. Players used to split fairly evenly, but when SparkLord312 wrote his online review advocating ignoring the high path entirely, or jumping immediately after finding the ruby, only two guests have gone all the way to the end. The first turned back, found the ruby, and jumped. WonderBoy is the second. No guest has ever lain down on the path before. No one has ever crawled to the end."

"When we designed it," HVH said, "I knew the Egg would be tough to find. I just never thought it would have taken seven years." He sighed.

The AI replied, "War on Mars has become a de-facto combat-only quest. Writers have questioned that. There were many rumors, but they have died off over the years. Every other major quest offers a combat-minimal solution. Even those that are commonly known are rarely taken. You humans seem to enjoy the battles."

That's our flaw. We like to fight. It's also our strength.

"How many quests has he beaten?" said HVH.

"If you're asking about major quests, he has credit for two. Both were completed six years ago, when he came here with his parents. He has completed numerous smaller quests, including all of those in the PreHistory and Future Worlds Arcades. He has successfully answered the first Princess's riddle."

"Okay…wait. You said he has beaten all of the minor quests in both of those arcades?"

"That is correct."

"Including the Knowledge quests?"

"Yes, and the Charm School. In fact, on that quest, he took the lost child, Paige, to meet the Princess. He coached Paige through a successful completion."

"No kidding?"

"No kidding. He made quite the impression on both Paige and her mother."

"Huh." HVH flopped down on his couch.

The silence stretched.

"What has he purchased at SPARK?" HVH said. "Not counting whatever his parents bought for him."

"His sole purchase was a Sparky meal two days ago, when he last visited."

"When did he enter the park today? Late?"

"No. He was on the first Barstow bus," the AI said.

"He's gone all day without eating? What's going on? Tell me everything we know about the kid."

Janne recapped Will's activities, including her observation that he was eating other guests' leftovers, and her speculation that he was currently homeless.

"Think he's headed for the Pod?" Van Horne said.

"Given his apparent intelligence and resourcefulness, I consider it highly likely he will find a way to remain in SPARK. Joining the Pod is less probable."

Janne played several views of Will's encounter with ShaChri.

"Jeez," said HVH. "She thought he was peeking her, and she flipped him off."

"That is my analysis as well."

"Look at his face. He goes from on top of the world to looking like someone just shot his dog." HVH paused again. "Okay, after this is over, include a recap of his SPARK activities in my daily download."

"Noted."

"What's going on with the Pod?"

"Population remains at nine. Both Feral and Mellew have talked about leaving. Feral is considering buying All-Access so she can concentrate on leveling up. Mellew is planning on heading to SCAZ and Hollywood once she turns eighteen."

– 1 1 0 1 0 0 1 0 –

The Pod was worried. Feral, less so. Something was wrong in SPARK. They were currently camped near War on Mars, and tonight there was far more activity than normal.

"Okay," said Fantom, as they huddled in the midst of the mechanical equipment. "Let's disperse and go singles tonight—no more than duos—and then meet back at the Evolve spot tomorrow night. If you think you can't make the shift-change walkout in the morning, hunker down and wait it out. Sound good?"

The other kids nodded. Feral thought they were overreacting, but she always thought the Pod overreacted. Of all the members, Feral had the most self-assurance and confidence in her ability to fend for herself. She wanted to figure out what was going on.

War on Mars, unlike most of the other major quests, descended well into the ground. The Underground City never actually passed beneath Mars, but did surround it for the first ten meters it penetrated the ground.

ShaChri tried to get close, but there were too many people running around. She found pallets of red sand stashed near the service elevators. *What the heck? Are they planning a major refurb?*

A major change in the quest could potentially make it *new* to someone like Feral, who had beat it so many times it was almost boring. The combat was always challenging since it was tied to her level, but new bad guys, new tactics? That got her amped! It was too busy for her to learn more, so she hit the gym and crashed, alone, under a bend in some piping just on the Hub side of Mars.

ShaChri kept this spot a secret. It was quiet. It was small—a one-person spot—but it made her feel cozy, almost at home. It was the first solo spot she discovered after she joined the Pod. When she needed to be alone, this is where she came.

She fell asleep, wondering what was going on in Mars.

Feral awoke when the pipe over her head roared to life.

– 1 1 0 1 0 0 1 0 –

Will was at the end of the path and nearly at the end of his rope. His initial panic subsided. He was alone. As darkness fell, he heard the lyrics of "The Sound of Silence" in his head.

His mom had loved the Simon and Garfunkel original. Will preferred the remake by metal band Disturbed. In any case, the darkness was real. His earbuds fed him only the occasional whisper of thin Martian wind, and the susurration of sand over sand.

Will would have preferred silence. He wanted his knife. The weapons in his inventory weren't real. The knife was. Unwittingly, his empty hand curled around the remembered handle of the knife. The KA-BAR could help against real threats. Like whatever seemed to lurk just beyond his vision, just at the edge of his hearing—like the Thing in the Wall.

Darkness begat darkness, and he slipped into a memory.

– 1 1 0 1 0 0 1 0 –

Four years prior

Yul had been dead two years. Kathy was fighting her own battle. Trying to keep it together. She was losing. The deeper she plunged into despair, the further away she pushed Billy. She began writing letters to Yul, and stopped throwing things away. Billy lost friends. No one was allowed in his house.

By the time he was thirteen, the hoarding was out of control. Newspapers. Junk mail. Milk cartons. Pizza boxes. Whataburger leftovers. Squirrels gnawed at the corners of their house because that's what squirrels do in Houston. Rats took advantage of the holes and moved into the attic. They multiplied. Noises began coming from the ceiling and the walls—scratching, rustling. Billy couldn't explain the noises, but his vivid imagination conjured answers. The darkness and the noise were planting visions in his brain. None were good.

It was coming for him. The Thing in the Wall was coming. He was certain. He needed protection.

Billy crept over the layers of debris in the darkened house. There were big knives in the kitchen. He would use one to slay the Thing when it came.

– 1 1 0 1 0 0 1 0 –

Present Day

It helped to look up at the sky. Since he laid on his back, Phobos had risen and tracked most of the way across the sky. Its rotation and odd shape made for an ever-changing spectacle. He couldn't tell what phase it was in. It was mesmerizing, and calmed him some. The moon cast faint shadows above him. He was too afraid to sleep. That's why he saw it.

He looked up as Phobos transited the sky, and it disappeared briefly, as if eclipsed. Even with all its irregularity, it looked odd—as if a straight edge were cutting into it. Will watched, fascinated.

The larger of Mars's moons quickly emerged, and Will noticed it emerged with a straight edge as well. Only, this time, it was on the trailing edge. The angles weren't the same and seemed far too regular for some rocky edge of the canyon. *I'll check it out when it gets light—if I'm still up here.*

At first, he expected to be rescued. He didn't want it, but he expected it. The rational part of his brain argued that SPARK wasn't going to leave a kid alone in a quest overnight. Then his imagination took over. He really was on Mars. No one was coming, because he told them not to. What was another dead Recruit? It didn't matter whether the Desnardians killed him, or he fell seven kilometers to his death.

He checked his suit stats. He was forty-seven meters higher than when he started. *It's hard to tell you're climbing when you're crawling. What had Ryker meant? "Before you can go down, you must go up."*

He felt his knees. They were raw, but he couldn't tell if they were bloody. His hands seemed okay, but that was because of the gloves. His power charge had gotten close to zero earlier, so he used the spare power pack he found along the trail. His first one had lasted five hours. He was almost two hours into the second one.

What would happen when it ran out? Would he slowly freeze? Die of carbon dioxide poisoning when his suit could no longer scrub it out of his air?

In his moments of rationality, he knew neither were going to happen. SPARK was simply going to let him *die*, deduct a level from his profile, and then escort him to an exit.

Will's biggest problem was he needed to pee. Badly. He'd never had to pee during a quest. Had never even thought about it. It's all he could think of now.

He scraped away some of the sand in front of him to see if the path continued. Nothing. Just a smooth slope of red sand. Whenever he tried to brush some away, more cascaded down—both physically and virtually. His current plan was to wait until he got down to 20 percent power, and then gut it up and jump.

Closing my eyes might help. He would shut his eyes and step off the edge of the path as if everything were fine. There would be a second of freefall. Then his chute would open and carry him to the floor of the canyon. He convinced himself he would survive the single second and the parachute descent that followed. He made himself believe he would find spare power packs. He could not convince himself he didn't need to pee.

Real astronauts planned for this. They either had a catheter or a relief tube leading to some sort of super sponge. That distracted Will long enough to wonder how it worked for lady astronauts. He wasn't certain, but he figured the catheter thing would work. Maybe a diaper? *That would be kind of embarrassing, but it would work for men and women.*

Will didn't have any of that. No catheter. No diaper. No relief tube. And a tremendous need to pee.

Embarrassed, he turned his back to the canyon so he was lying on his right side, and unzipped his pants. He hypothesized the sand would act as cat litter and contain the urine.

Peeing while lying on his side turned out to be more difficult than he expected. Will pushed himself to his knees, but they were so sore he risked standing up. He kept his back to the canyon. Will felt bad he was making a mess, but the relief was sublime.

– 1 1 0 1 0 0 1 0 –

"Janne," said Dorothy Watkins, "are you watching this?"

"Of course. WonderBoy is now standing."

"Get the actor in place." Double F grinned.

Dorothy Watkins grinned back. Double F might be her boss, but Mars was her quest.

Costuming hastily put the finishing touches on the actor and put him on a golf cart to the access elevator that served War on Mars.

Watkins called him. "You're ready?"

"Absolutely," he said. "This is really cool. It's not every day an actor gets to play a role for the first time!"

Watkins could almost hear his grin. "Okay, let's go over your lines."

– 1 1 0 1 0 0 1 0 –

Standard urination posture for Will was feet slightly wider than his shoulders, pelvis thrust forward. He was keeping the rest of his body away from possible backsplash, and also preparing for the urine to run vertically toward his feet. It did not. He was facing a sandy slope that seemed to be at a forty-five- to sixty-degree angle. He probed ahead but only triggered small cascades of dust as he disturbed the slope. *The trail must have been wiped out by a landslide.*

Now, in the dim light, he watched his urine pool, not at his feet, but in a horizontal line just above his knees. *That's weird.*

Will finished and zipped his pants. He ignored the pain in his knees as he knelt. His urine, largely absorbed by the sand, pooled on a flat rock hidden under a layer of sand. He reached up a hand and gently brushed the sand away from his urine mark. The action triggered a small avalanche of grit and dust. He did it again. More sand, but he was clearing a spot.

Clear sand, wait for the avalanche to stop, clear more sand. After a few iterations, he had cleared a flat spot big enough to stand on.

He leaned on it. It took his weight. Not even a quiver. He raised one foot and leaned into the slope and slowly stood.

– 1 1 0 1 0 0 1 0 –

"Call the boss! Call the boss!" yelled Watkins, simultaneously punching Double F in the shoulder.

It was happening!

"Done," Janne replied with electronic calm.

– 1 1 0 1 0 0 1 0 –

Will's platform was a half-meter above the trail. He leaned against the slope, triggering micro-avalanches, and used his foot to clear more sand. Then he did the same with his other foot, sending the urine-soaked sand into the canyon below. He now had a meter-wide clearing. It was remarkably flat. Clearly weathered and worn. But flat. He gently probed the sand.

At knee-height, he felt something hard and vertical. He traced it upward until it ended in what seemed to be another flat surface. It was about the same height above his feet as the first one. He began clearing the second platform. Sand and dust pooled around his feet. He cautiously kicked it away, excited but still frightened enough to savor secure footing.

He climbed onto the second platform.

– 1 1 0 1 0 0 1 0 –

Double F and Watkins watched from Quest Control as Will repeated the process a third time, and then a fourth. The buzz quickly spread that the kid was on the move, and up, not down. Money changed hands.

War on Mars was a quest surrounded by rumors. Why wasn't there a non-combat ending? All the other major quests had one. Gamers found small Eggs. But serious gamers knew HVH loved big Eggs—something that would change the way you played the game. Something so cool, SPARK would buy you off rather than have you go public.

SPARK enthusiasts said the Big Egg had been found—the ability to jump from the launch area.

Typically, Mars ended with an epic battle, set up by a number of previous skirmishes. Gamers fought their way down the canyon, slaying Desnardians, tending to their wounded, and gathering swag in the form of Desnardian weapons, Mars relics, and things left behind by Outposters. Then the remaining members of the party battled the Boss—the Desnardian Commander—on the grounds of the Outpost.

Once victorious, they reclaimed the Data Core, were met as victors, and exited through the War on Mars gift shop. Guests who *died* early were guided to a viewing area where they could watch the slaughter: either their party emerged victorious, or the Desnardians did their own endzone dance. Then the whole thing reset in time for the next party of gamers.

When the group Will started with exited the game, Double F asked Watkins, "What's your plan here? If he jumps now?"

"I think finding the canyon floor empty would be a little anticlimactic, don't you?" she said.

Double F smiled. Watkins pushed the manual reset. Fifty Desnardians respawned and awaited Will on the canyon floor. The fearsome Desnardian Commander guarded the Data Core at the Outpost. WB would not face an empty canyon floor.

– 1 1 0 1 0 0 1 0 –

After clearing and climbing up four steps, he was in a position where he could clearly see the object that eclipsed Phobos. It was triangular, with rounded corners. The apex was hidden, buried into the dust. But from the general size and shape, Will concluded it was about ten centimeters on each side, and metallic. He couldn't really tell how thick it was, but he had the impression it was thin, like a sheet of metal. A braver or more athletic gamer might have been able to jump up and grab it. Will was neither. He cleared a fifth step and climbed up. His hand trembled as he reached up for the object.

– 1 1 0 1 0 0 1 0 –

Quest Control held its collective breath. It was 3:00 a.m. Most of them had been on duty since 3:00 p.m. the day prior.

Normally the quest was empty by 10:00 p.m. Then they debriefed for an hour and went home.

They had been up all night. Nobody felt sleepy. Nobody was dozing off. Hearts pounded. Double F was sweating. He'd known about the Big Egg for two years—ever since he took over as head referee for the quest. Recently he was made head referee for all of SPARK.

The Egg remained hidden for seven freaking years.

He'd played the quest numerous times as an employee, and maybe a dozen times since he'd become a ref. A sixteen-year-old kid was about to discover—on his first time through the quest—something Double F never imagined.

– 1 1 0 1 0 0 1 0 –

Will plucked the rounded triangle from the dust.

The change was immediate but gradual. Sand and dust cascaded onto his face. He felt the rumble before he heard it. His hands and feet lost contact as the ground beneath them seemed to liquefy. The tide of the avalanche hit his body and pushed his legs and feet backward. He slipped off the step and began to fall.

Terror washed over him. Everything he feared on the path was becoming real. Epinephrine and norepinephrine were squeezed out of his adrenal glands like toothpaste out of a tube. Fight-or-flight took over and Will scrambled, swimming against the avalanche of sand and dust. He couldn't see. He could barely breathe. His left foot struck something solid but bounced off! Then his right hand. Every physiological process in his body reprioritized to add strength and focus to holding on. His right foot found a ledge and fought against the stream of debris. He pushed his left hand through the stream and found the lip of the stair and hung on. With decreasing force, the avalanche buffeted him as it passed. Will's heart jackhammered in his chest and he gulped air. The entire planet, all of Mars, seemed to shake. The rumble faded, and Will opened his eyes.

Below him, the avalanche accelerated toward the floor of the canyon. It tore rocks and boulders from spots that had cradled them for millennia. Entire pieces of the canyon wall fluidized in a flow that continued seven kilometers down. Some of the debris moved so fast it continued across the floor of the canyon and up the opposite wall. Sand and grit ebbed like the ocean for a few moments. Dust and darkness obscured much of what was below him. Will couldn't bear to look down for more than a glimpse at a time, but he could see stairs had cleared beneath him. He was shaking and still terrified but forced himself to breathe deeply, and that calmed him.

Will looked up. Up was tolerable. Up was safe. No one ever fell *up* stairs.

He was calm enough to begin climbing. He could manage one step. His arms and legs shook. He collapsed on the step and flopped onto his back, once again looking up at the stars. Phobos was nearly set. He checked his power gauge and estimated he had two hours left. For now, though, he was safe.

Will concentrated on breathing slowly and deeply. It helped. He was alive.

Chapter 17

Things are not always what they seem; the first appearance deceives many; the intelligence of a few perceives what has been carefully hidden.
—Phaedrus

Quest Control erupted with cheers of joy, shouts of, "Holy crap!" and "What the heck just happened?" People glared across the room at HVH and Double F.

Van Horne turned to Fitz Flaherty. "You want to handle this?"

He's the head referee for all of SPARK—he's come a long way in the last seven years.

Double F nodded. "First of all, sorry for keeping you in the dark about the Egg. But hey, they're strictly need-to-know. Here's what happened: When WB pulled the Patch—that rounded triangle thing—it was Janne's trigger to start a pre-engineered release of five tons of actual physical red sand and dust, sending it tumbling down a precisely designed slope for almost one hundred yards. That was the avalanche. Janne, you want to take it from there?"

"Certainly, Fitz. At this point, I would also deploy fall protection to ensure guest safety. However, since Hodge already ordered the nets deployed, that step was unnecessary. The next step is to pretension the cable to the player's fall harness."

Double F said, "Yeah, we want them to experience the feeling of being in danger, while keeping them perfectly safe."

"Fear minus death equals fun," said HVH. *I wonder who said that first?*

Janne continued. "Most of the avalanche is virtual. I pulse the hydraulics and pump subsonics throughout the quest area. Avalanche noise within human audible range is sent to the players' earbuds. ARG video is adjusted to make it appear larger and consistent with Mariner Valley on Mars. Design parameters required visuals crafted to make it seem as if a cubic kilometer of debris was rushing down the canyon wall—enough to fill a professional baseball stadium over three hundred times. Designers considered Mars's gravitational acceleration, angle of repose of the sand, friction between the sand and the ground, and atmospheric density. The numbers aren't precise, but I conservatively estimate the debris would hit the canyon floor with a velocity of two hundred miles per hour."

"From either the trail or the floor," said Double F, "the avalanche would look *massive*."

HVH said, "We couldn't actually let five tons of sand slam down onto players on the canyon floor—even if it was only falling a hundred yards, it would be lethal. So we designed sluice gates to funnel most of it away and then do a controlled dump much closer to the floor."

"From the lower levels," said Janne, "we introduce enough sand to cover the floor to a depth of four inches."

– 1 1 0 1 0 0 1 0 –

Will stood again. His power had dwindled, and he knew he had to do something.

He took one glance down the stairs and ruled that path out. Just looking down gave him vertigo, so he leaned into the slope and put his hand on the nearest step. The fingers of his right hand slipped on something. Something flat and metallic. It was the rounded triangle that had triggered the avalanche.

Will looked at it. Over the years, the abrasion of wind and sand had pitted and scarred one side. The design on the other side was still clear. In the center of the triangle was a circle. The right half of the circle looked like Mars—the planet, not the quest. The other left side looked like Earth, but wrong somehow. It had a lot of blue, like pictures of Earth seen from space, but the land masses weren't the right shape or in the right places. The words underneath were: *NASA–JPL.*

Will's spine started tingling as he brushed the dust off the rest of the triangle. It was legible, but barely:

Unlocking Mars's History

Mars Surveyor

He began to fall into a mental freeze, and shook himself back into action. He didn't have time to think about this. If he didn't do something, he could die in the quest.

A bunch of stuff flashed through his ARGs last night, but all he wanted to do was survive. He stuffed the triangle in his back pocket and started climbing.

The steps were swept clear by the avalanche, so the climb was faster. The spacing was awkward, the steps too tall. He climbed slowly but steadily for ten minutes and took a break.

Another few minutes, and he could see the rim of the canyon. He took a few steps onto the plateau before turning around to look at the canyon. The sun broached the horizon on his right—a bright, majestic crimson. He checked his power gauge—down to 20%. He needed to jump or give up.

He couldn't do either.

Last night, it seemed logical. That was before the avalanche.

I'm too scared to even try. He sat, tears welling up in his eyes. *I'm going to fail Mars.*

WonderBoy heard a faint crunch behind him. As he turned, he heard a voice.

"Welcome home, son of Mars."

WB stood and saw a tall, slender humanoid walking slowly toward him. *The kind of height, when coupled with Mars's lower gravity, would make those stairs reasonable. He looks humanoid. Dark skin, big set of ears. He's gotta be at least seven-feet tall. Skinny.*

Looking through his ARGs, WB read, in green: The Elder of Mars. *Okay, so this is a good guy.*

WB didn't know what to do, so he held out his hand. Virtual handshakes were always a little awkward. They never felt quite right, so Will was surprised to feel a very physical handshake. *Huh. Martians shake hands.*

"Hi, um, Mister Elder. Who exactly are you?"

The Elder continued to clasp his hand for so long, Will thought something must be wrong. Gradually, the Elder released WB's hand.

"That is a difficult question," he replied. "I am not who I was, nor who I will be."

His voice somehow rasped and whispered simultaneously, like sand skittering over sunbaked cardboard.

"Okay...what should I call you?" WB said. "And how do you speak English?"

His father always griped that aliens in movies and on TV somehow managed to speak English.

"Valentine," the Elder replied. "Call me Val. It will suffice."

Another gust of wind and sand.

"I do not speak as you do. I allow my thoughts to form in your head, and you interpret them for me in your own tongue."

"Telepathy? Cool," said WB. "So do I have to talk, or can you read my mind?"

"You do not have the discipline to form coherent thoughts without the need of encoding them in language. Please speak. It will be…easier."

"You called me a son of Mars a minute ago. What did you mean, Val?"

"I called you a son of Mars because you, all of you from Earth, came from here."

"How?" Through the exhaustion, WB felt a surge of excitement.

The Elder, Val, turned and faced Mariner Valley.

"This was once the site of our greatest experiment and our greatest failure. We sought to harness the power of the quantum. The universe itself. Instead, we drove away our own moon and cracked the very crust of our planet. This valley is the scar our failure left on our world. We sacrificed the last of our resources to send our children to Earth. Those that stayed behind carved the steps so we could climb them and view the scar." Val paused. "Penance, I suppose."

"That…sucks," WB said. *How do you make a mistake so colossal it pushes your primary satellite away and leaves a gash this huge on the face of your planet?*

"Indeed." Val rasped a chuckle. "Your vernacular is odd but fitting."

WB looked down at his power gauge. 16%. *I'm nearly out of time.*

"Look, I don't mean to be rude, but I need to get to the floor of the canyon. I'm supposed to retrieve a data core, and I'm running out of juice."

"I understand," Val said. "What is your plan?"

"I thought I might run and jump off the edge. Maybe run all the way down the stairs. Do they go all the way to the bottom?"

"They do. Both choices are perilous, but I will accompany you."

"I'm also low on time." WB pointed to his power gauge.

The Elder gave him a very human nod.

"Listen," WB said, "jumping kind of freaks me out, and I don't know if I can handle the stairs without falling or going catatonic, just from looking all that way down."

"The view is humbling. Very few of us ever descended the steps."

"Then how do you get down there?"

The Elder turned and rasped, "Normally, we take the elevator."

Relief flooded WB. "You've got an elevator?"

Another nod.

"Let's go! I'm running out of time here."

Val led them to what seemed to be just another piece of the vast rust-colored plateau. The wind whipped his long hair, pulling it straight back. With a wave of his hand, a door opened out of what, to WB, seemed to be empty air. They stepped into a small, featureless room. WB's ears popped in the descent.

As they rode down, he said, "Mister Val, you should know there might be a fight coming on the floor of the canyon. We're going to be significantly outnumbered. It might not go well for us."

Val nodded. "WB, all actions have consequences. Often unintended, but consequences nonetheless."

The elevator door opened.

Broken Desnardian bodies were scattered everywhere. Chiton-clad arms, legs, torsos, and helmeted heads stuck out from a layer of sand and debris that coated the area. Nothing moved except the windblown dust and sand.

"How…how…oh man." WB sank to his knees.

The Elder was silent.

"The avalanche," WB whispered. "It wiped out the Desnardians. I didn't mean to. I mean, I'm sorry…"

"You came to Mars to kill them. All but their commander are now dead. And yet you mourn."

WB knelt in the quiet. It was one thing to fight back against something that was trying to kill you. But with one action, he had wiped out the entire force of Desnardians. Though virtual, their deaths seemed real. Where they leaked blood, it was red. *Just like mine. Just like mine.* His heart sank.

"There are things here that may be useful to you," Val said.

There was so much swag here: weapons, first aid kits, gold, artifacts. None of it was real, but all of it had value in SPARK. Every bit could be used or sold.

WB stood and walked toward the point where his ARGs said he would find the Data Core. *I'll get that and be done.* He walked past blood-stained sand and avalanche-maimed Desnardians. He didn't pick up a single weapon or artifact.

The soft sand swallowed his feet. It reminded him of the sand dunes at Galveston. His feet sunk in and made the walking difficult. He clambered over some rocks and walked some more. Lights burned. *There's the Outpost.* A lone Desnardian stood between WB and the Data Core. The red tag identified him as *Desnardian Commander.* A red skull appeared next to this title. WB knew he was hopelessly outmatched.

The Desnardian Commander held an enormous blaster and pointed it at WB. He heard an ominous hum.

"Have you both traveled so far, simply to kill?" The Elder walked up behind WB.

Somehow Val was translating for him. "This world will be Desnardian."

"Conquest is the path to expansion." It was the Desnardian, Will realized.

"What about your people?" said WB. "They are all dead."

The muzzle of the blaster lowered a bit.

"You have used the planet itself as a weapon against us," the Desnardian Commander growled.

"We were born here," WB said. "Mars sees us as natives. You are intruders." *Maybe a stretch. But kinda-sorta accurate.* "Throw down your weapon, and you will live."

"Living in defeat is worse than death." The muzzle raised again.

Will thought as fast as he could. The red skull icon next to the Desnardian Commander's name disappeared. Val now stood beside WB. *Will he fight with me?*

"Then live with an ally, not an enemy," WB said. "Both Desnardians and humans have died. Keep your weapon, but stop trying to kill us. We can...I don't know, somehow work together."

True diplomatic solutions take time. Many details need to be worked out. Plans developed. Interfaces established. But this was SPARK, not reality. A quest, not an actual war. *C'mon.*

"It shall be so." The Desnardian Commander's name turned from red to blue, and he holstered his blaster. "We shall be allies."

Later, when Will replayed the scene in his mind, it seemed corny, hokey, contrived. As his closest friend would later tell him: "Hey, it's a quest in a fantasy park. Not a documentary. Exit through the gift shop and buy a Desnardian plushy."

The Desnardian Commander stood aside, and WB approached the Data Core.

"I must see to my dead," the Desnardian snarled.

WB nodded, distracted now by the Data Core. It looked like three thick white pancakes stacked atop a trapezoidal base. Removing it required solving a puzzle.

It took him a few minutes and forced him to remember the nursery rhyme "Twinkle, Twinkle, Little Star," but he got it. As he extracted the Core, he looked up to see the Commander dumping weapons at his feet.

"The dead have no need of these. Allies should share technology. Take these to your people. Your weapons are grossly inferior to ours. This is our first gift to you." The Commander stepped back.

The pile was enormous. Will began to add weapons to his inventory until he reached his carrying capacity.

An assault shuttle was landing. Will turned toward it and then turned back and handed his blaster to the Commander.

"Allies should share technology," he said.

The Desnardian Commander beamed—if that were possible for a hideous cross between a badger and a cockroach. He accepted WB's weapon and then handed his own to WB.

As soon as WB stepped into the shuttle, the scene ended, and Will found himself alone in the Exit area. It was 5:23 a.m., and his ARGs were going nuts. Lines and lines scrolled by too fast for him to read. Finally, a single line blinked in green:

Attention: You have unallocated skill points!

Will figured he'd sort it out later. Right now, he was exhausted and exalted.

The gift shop offered an eerie quiet—no noisy kids, no cast members.

The palpable wrongness settled on Will. *I'm not going to touch anything.* He pushed his ARGs up and exited.

– 1 1 0 1 0 0 1 0 –

In Quest Control, HVH slapped Hodgins on the shoulder.

"Go. Go. Go!"

Double F and Watkins looked at him, and Van Horne nodded.

"You, too."

Then he saw seventeen pairs of eyes looking at him. The park wouldn't open for early entrants for another two and a half hours.

"Okay. All of you, go!"

HVH stayed put. He was melancholy.

Only two Big Eggs remained, and he didn't know that they would ever be discovered. It made him a bit sad that this one was found. The last one in a major quest, and it took seven years.

– 1 1 0 1 0 0 1 0 –

By the time WB made his way through the silent gift shop—full of plush Desnardians, replicas of the Desnardian Commander, and plastic copies of the Data Core—he was in full freak-out mode. He desperately wanted to stop and think, but an empty and silent SPARK felt wrong.

As he neared the gift shop exit, he saw a cluster of people outside. He could hear the quiet buzz of their conversations. His heart sank. *Probably Security, here to kick me out of SPARK for staying overnight.*

When the group outside the gift shop caught sight of Will, all conversation stopped. He stepped into the auditory vacuum, feeling the abrupt silence as a palpable weight. The crowd drew back to form a gauntlet, eyes fixed on WB, only the occasional scuffing of a shoe to break the quietude.

And then a ginger-haired man with a sloppy ponytail began to clap. The others joined him. Suddenly, people were slapping WB on the back and congratulating him.

Eventually, ponytail guy, an older woman with brown hair and glasses, and a large, bald black guy with a white goatee pulled Will away from the group of admirers. The big guy had a small device in his ear, Will noticed. *Is that a hearing aid? I never would have noticed it if the light hadn't glinted off it.*

"I imagine you're hungry," Hodgins said after introductions all around.

This Hodgins guy has a voice to match his body—outsized and booming. Maybe he's compensating for hearing loss.

Will nodded. Both men looked vaguely familiar to him, but Will could not attach a specific memory to that whisper of recognition.

Double F looked around. "Nothing's open yet. Early entry doesn't start for another three hours."

Soylent Bistro squatted dark across the plaza. None of the normally prolific food carts were in sight.

Hodgins said, "The employee cafeteria is always open. Let's go there."

Double F blinked and cast a look at Watkins, who shrugged.

Hodgins had his reasons. He saw Will's gaze intently follow the quest staff as they left through an unmarked door into the Underground City.

Hodgins led them to the rim area connecting Future Worlds to PreHistory. *This is a violation of a policy I wrote.* He pushed open another unmarked entrance—this one leading to a medical assistance area. *Minimize guest knowledge of access points.*

Why am I doing this? In his heart, Hodgins knew.

Four unsuccessful pregnancies. Repeated heartbreaks as Hodge and his wife tried again, only to have their hopes dashed again. Eventually, they stopped trying and took steps to make sure they wouldn't have children. *Easier to know we won't, than to suffer through a continuing series of miscarriages.*

He looked over at the young man that had just turned Mars upside down. *Our kids would have been about his age.*

As Hodgins led them down the empty corridor, the scuff of his dress shoes echoing off the polished concrete floors, he looked at Will.

"In all of SPARK, only the medical areas and restrooms are free of surveillance. We have to respect people's privacy."

Hodge knew that information was publicly acknowledged by SPARK. Realistically, they kept quiet about their extensive surveillance—no sense reminding everyone their every move within the park was being captured on camera.

They made it to the cafeteria, just as the first-shift cook was firing up the grill. Since they were early, and since Hodgins was there, the cook seemed happy to make things to order.

When they sat, Dorothy Watkins got right to the point.

"Young man, you urinated on my quest!"

Will blushed and mumbled, "I'm sorry."

Hodgins said, "Would you have found the stairs if you hadn't peed on them?"

"I'm not sure. I'd already seen this." Will pulled the rounded triangle out of his pocket. "Or, at least, I saw the outline of it, stuck in the sand above me." He shrugged. "I might have tried to climb up to get it. But maybe not…"

There was an awkward silence for a few minutes.

Will's obvious fear of the simulated and real heights of Mars seems best left unaddressed.

Hodgins saw Will staring at his pancakes, and thought maybe they'd lost the kid again. *What's going on in his head? Is he just spacing out? Is he thinking?*

"Yes, well," Hodgins said, interrupting Will's reverie, "we do have a few things we have to talk about. You've just joined a very small group of people who have found two Eggs."

"Is that what the EggSpert thing in my profile is about?" Will said.

"Eggsactly." Double F wore a huge grin.

Will gave him a small grin, and Hodgins rolled his eyes.

"Really?" Double F said. "Was it that bad? If you don't like that one, you're going to hate my joke about Orion's Belt being a waist of space."

This time, Will actually smiled. Hodgins jumped in before Double F could say it was *a three-star joke*!

"Will," said Hodgins, "we're in uncharted territory here. Normally, at this point, I'd make an offer to give you some free days at SPARK, put you in one of the resorts for a few nights, and get you to agree to not reveal the Egg."

"Sounds pretty good to me," Will said.

"Yeah, it really is a good deal," said Hodgins. "Our problem is that you're a minor. Our lawyers say any agreement we make with you might be unenforceable because you're not an adult. Is it fair to assume you don't have a parent or legal guardian conveniently close by to sign an agreement on your behalf?"

Will nodded slowly.

Double F said, "So what did you think about the Elder? The ending?"

"It was cool, and kind of sad. I'm glad I didn't have to kill the Desnardian Commander." Will visibly relaxed. "You know what I don't get?"

The three SPARK employees looked at each other and shook their heads.

"Well, Desnardians have three fingers—or toes, or claws, or something—at the end of each limb, right? Like they have two opposing thumbs and one longer finger?"

Double F and Watkins nodded.

"So how come the Desnardian Commander's blaster fit my hand so perfectly? Wouldn't the Desnardians have built it for their hands?"

Watkins and Double F stared at Will, and then at each other.

"Uhm…" they said in unison.

Hodgins barked out a laugh and slapped Will on the back.

"Seven years this park's been open, and no one has ever pointed that out." He wore a big smile. "Will, you're an interesting young man.

Hodgins continued. "So back to the other thing. Let's not even consider a formal contract. Here's what I propose: we can't get you a room. Not at SPARK. Not in town. There are places in town that wouldn't demand your ID, but also aren't what I would consider safe. Frankly, it's probably safer camping in the desert. So I'm thinking we give you some cash instead. The cash equivalent of a room and food for three days. Some gift cards for in town. We'll also throw in three free days in SPARK, plus one day per year for as long as you keep the Egg secret. Blab, and that stops."

"Why's it have to be so complicated?" Will said.

"Kids have been exploited before," replied Dorothy Watkins, "and the laws are actually there to protect everyone. It stinks, but it's true."

"So what do you think, Will?" said Hodgins. "Does the deal sound fair?"

Will took a moment to answer.

"Can you make it four days? Today doesn't count. And I get early admission, even if I'm not staying at a SPARK resort?"

Hodgins laughed and stuck out his hand. "Deal."

With business done, Double F started grilling Will about the quest. How had he seen the Patch—the rounded triangle that triggered the avalanche?

"I was lying on my back on the path, and the big moon, Phobos, passed right behind it, so I saw the outline."

Watkins nodded her understanding.

"When you found the Desnardian soldiers all dead," she said, "why didn't you grab all the loot?"

Will started slowly. "I'd just killed them all—accidentally. I mean, I know it's a game, but it felt pretty real. It was so quiet, and they looked so…dead. It just seemed wrong to loot them. I think if I'd shot them in a battle, it would have been different."

"Is that why you didn't kill the Desnardian Commander?" said Double F.

"Maybe. Val said something, too. Something about coming so far just to kill. My parents…" Will's voice caught. "My parents always said interplanetary war wouldn't make any economic sense. It's really expensive to go anywhere, and when you get there, you just start killing people? Besides, he was showing as a red skull. He'd have wasted me."

Double F nodded.

Will said, "What's the deal with the Patch?"

"Your ARGs will tell you all about it," said Double F. "But basically, it's the logo for a real-life Mars mission that failed. JPL and NASA were working in different units—one group was using metric, the other imperial. Neither side knew what the other was doing. That put a calculation off by a significant amount. So instead of entering orbit, the Mars Climate Orbiter slammed into the planet. It happened when HVH was in school, and now every SPARK employee hears that story at new-hire orientation."

"That's…" Will struggled for words, "…really dumb and hard to believe. I thought all scientists used metric."

"God's honest truth," Hodgins held a hand over his heart. "Three-hundred-million-bucks dumb. Scary, too. It's a very expensive lesson in making sure you verify your most basic assumptions."

Will nodded, but resolved to look it up when he got online.

Hodgins moved to get up. Will cleaned his plate, and everyone looked beat.

"I'll walk you out," Hodge said.

He was following his gut and wanted to make sure the kid knew a few more things.

Double F and Watkins shook Will's hand and told him they'd see him around, and headed off.

"Lots of rumors about this place online," Will said, when he and Hodgins were alone and walking away.

"You mean SPARK in general, or the Underground City?"

"Both, I guess. But I was thinking more about the Underground." Will looked around as they went.

"Yeah," Hodgins replied, "HVH likes to keep an air of mystery about the whole place. Down here…well, I always think of it as a human body. All the fun stuff happens at the skin level, and people tend to think of themselves as *living behind their eyes*. None of that would be possible without the heart, lungs, liver, blood vessels. Up top? That's the skin. The Underground, that's the organs."

"That kind of makes sense," Will said.

"We keep it all hidden. All theme parks do. We just put it underneath. Nobody wants to see the sewer system, but they're all very glad that it works and that they don't have to think about what happens when they flush the toilet."

"Why's it so complex?" Will said, after they had passed what seemed to be an intersection of five corridors.

"Long story. But basically, HVH built the major quests as anchors—giving them as much space as they needed—horizontally and vertically. Then we put the Hub in the middle and built everything else around it. That's why sometimes the corridors seem like a maze. Once you realize that it mirrors the park above, it all makes sense."

As they walked out, Hodgins pointed out a few areas of the Underground.

"You were actually one hundred or so feet below ground on the canyon floor of Mars. Now, we're only about twenty-feet down. There are a couple floors below us. Ten thousand people work here—most of them in the Underground City. Only about a thousand work in what we call guest-facing jobs up top."

As they walked out, Hodgins pointed out more areas of the Underground: the gym, locker rooms, Costuming, Security.

When they neared the exit, Hodgins turned to look at Will.

"Entry to SPARK doesn't start for a while. How about if I give you a ride into town, let you grab your stuff, hit Bullseye—it opens early—and have you back here in time for opening?"

Will didn't question him.

Is he already planning to stay in the park?

On the way out, Hodgins played tour guide.

"This place actually started with Solar Prime—the Black Grass farm?"

Will nodded his understanding.

"HVH and a few others go back and forth every day, so we have a tunnel connecting them. Solar Prime is much bigger in terms of both revenue and land area, but smaller in terms of people. Less than one hundred people are there at any time. Here," Hodgins gestured around them, "we have over ten thousand people employed. We even have a school for the children of employees." They were passing Security, and Hodgins pointed. "It's down that way, but they do a lot of their learning in the park."

Will's eyebrows rose in interest.

"Yeah," Hodgins said. "Guests can pick up high school and college credits for stuff they do in the park."

Will was quiet for a long time, and then blurted out, "Anybody ever try to stay overnight in the park? Guests, I mean."

"Yeah, lots of people try. Some have even been successful. Mostly though, we find them and escort them out. Know what trips them up?"

Will shook his head.

"These." He pointed at Will's wristband. "As soon as we shut down for the night, we get notified about active wristbands still in SPARK. Then we go round them up. Normally it's just teenagers and frat boys."

They drove to the baseball park, and Will quizzed Hodgins along the way.

"People online say HVH is a jerk. Have you ever met him?"

"Will, I have worked with the man for the last fifteen years—well before SPARK was even a dream. He's demanding, but I wouldn't classify him as a jerk."

"How rich is he?"

"Very."

"Does he ever play any of the quests?"

"Mister Van Horne plays routinely. Rarely a full day. But he'll join groups and go through quests with them."

"What's his avatar name? What's he play as?"

"That is something I will never reveal. Now I've got a question for you."

"Okay." Will shrugged.

"Why do you speak so loudly?"

Will sputtered a bit, and the head of Security turned to look at him, and saw he was blushing.

"I thought...I mean, I saw the thing in your ear," Will pointed to his own ear, "and I thought maybe you were hard of hearing or something."

Hodgins's laugh filled the car.

"You got me. I do have some hearing loss, but this thing is an earbud that allows Janne—and the rest of the executive team—to talk to each other privately, if necessary."

"So you have to talk out loud, but no one can hear her?" Will said.

"Right. Or anyone else on the net. We lose coverage when we leave SPARK property."

They drove on in silence a while before Will said, "You were there, right? You're the guy who met us when we came out of the quest?"

"After you found the Egg? I was." *Where's this going?*

"My mom and dad were pretty jazzed, and we did a lot of combat-oriented questing. I think about it a lot—saving Baby Cyanite, and how that changed everything."

Jeez. "Will, the Cyanites are virtual beings. They are no more alive than one of the targets at the shooting gallery."

"I know. It's just that...well, now, I guess I like the games better when I can figure out a way to beat them without killing anyone."

Hodge nodded. *Life lessons from a sixteen-year-old. Huh.*

He followed Will's directions to the baseball park.

They headed back to SPARK.

One more thing. As they walked up to one of the public entrances, Hodgins pointed out a couple of the unofficial guides to Will.

"See those guys? They're UGs," Hodgins said, pronouncing it *Uggs.* "Unofficial Guides. They earn their day in SPARK by convincing guests they'll have a better experience with a guide. We don't sanction them, but we condone them. The UGs usually get their entry paid for, and a tip. Normally, they negotiate an hour or so of off-time as part of the deal so they can play on their own. They've beaten all the major quests, and either just love the park, or they have some goal."

He took Will by the upper arm gently and slowed their progress.

"Many of them will recognize me. That may not be good for you, so I'll break off, go in via the employee entrance." He hefted Will's backpack. "When you're done for the day, go to the Security office in the PreHistory Arcade. This'll be there waiting for you."

Panic flared in Will's eyes. He reached for his backpack.

"Wait—"

"Will," Hodgins said gently, "there is no way you would get through the entrance with this. I promise you. Everything in this backpack now, will still be in it when you claim it from Security tonight. Everything, plus the cash and the gift card."

"Okay," Will said quietly, after a long moment, and turned away.

Hodgins watched him go. Proud the kid could let go, and pleased he trusted him, and hoping neither of them were wrong.

Time to call in a favor.

– 1 1 0 1 0 0 1 0 –

Tony Severski was late for work and hungover. *One might have caused the other.*

He'd managed to convince the new girl in his department that it was in her best interest to meet him in the adults-only area after work. She hadn't wanted to, but he'd convinced her.

It wasn't great. That's why I killed the tequila when I got home. Her fault.

As he walked through the parking lot, he saw Hodgins's shiny head moving toward the main entrance, and almost called out. Then he saw the kid. The Kimmy. *It's that stinking brat that got me barred from the Stumble Inn. What's he doing with Hodgins?*

Tony sped up, spiking his blood pressure with the effort. *If I can get to Security before the kid enters, I'll be able to find his profile.* Once he had that, he could figure out how to fix the kid.

As he walked, he relived the shame of what he thought of as The Incident.

He'd been a captain in the Army, stationed in the Republic of Korea, but well before the North went completely rogue and nuked Guam. He was a rising star. His superior officers called him brilliant and said he'd be wearing a general's stars one day. He had a beautiful young wife and a small son, with another on the way. Life had been perfect.

Then his boss, a lieutenant colonel had shown up at his office with the base chaplain. Severski remembered the sinking feeling. The unreality of the entire event.

They'd been killed in a car wreck in Seoul. The other driver was from a remote fishing village. His truck was overloaded, and he didn't know his way around Seoul. A panicked turn on a wet road was all it took.

"They died instantly, Captain. God took them quickly and without pain," the Chaplain had said.

Wasn't true. The paramedics report said they could hear my son crying when they arrived. Died before they could get him out of the twisted mass of metal, seaweed, and fish.

Nothing they could do. Nothing anyone could do.

Severski escorted the bodies back and had them buried in their hometown. Then he started drinking and drank until the Army acknowledged the problem and put him in rehab.

Didn't take.

Three weeks out of rehab, he was back drinking at the officers' club at Fort Hood. It was the only way he had found of reliably dealing with the grief that still tore him apart. His intent was to have two drinks and then leave. Prove to himself that he could control it.

He couldn't. Once he started, the booze took over.

"Well, Captain, I'm disappointed to see you here," his brigade commander had said.

Severski turned to him and raised his glass. "I thought all officers were expected to be members."

It seemed witty at the time.

"That's right, Captain. Up to the point that I get a call saying that one of my men is making a fool of himself and disgracing his uniform."

The lieutenant colonel pointed to Severski's open jacket and pulled-down tie.

He might have survived the encounter with his career intact, but at some point he decided to take a swing at his boss. The rest of the evening was a bit of a blur, but he had clear memories of waking up in the stockade. He was charged with conduct unbecoming an officer, and discharged.

The Army was like my second family, and they kicked me out.

Damn Kimmys. They took that away, too.

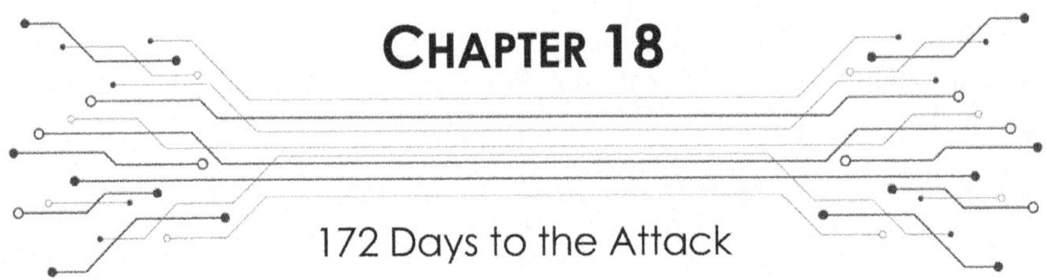

Chapter 18

172 Days to the Attack

The only thing worse than being blind is having sight but no vision.
—Helen Keller

"You may not want to start with us," Feral told the man behind them in line.

Looks like a family of three, still in the teen levels.

The father blustered, "Now just a minute—"

The kid said, "Dad, we're gonna get creamed if we start with those two. Look at their levels."

"Huh? Oh. Yeah," the father said. Then whispered, "Thanks," to Feral.

Feral and Fantom entered the launch area after donning their harnesses, and were instantly disappointed. Ryker tried to get them to board the assault shuttle, but they ignored him.

"Whiskey Tango Foxtrot?" said Fantom. "It looks exactly the same."

"Okay, I don't know," Feral said. "I swear I heard something, *saw* something, last night. There was too much activity for it to be nothing." She scanned the paths and saw nothing unusual. "Jump?"

"Jump," Fantom agreed.

They started firing as soon as they saw the Nards.

"Something's different," Feral said, when they were on the canyon floor. "It *feels* different."

"It's the sand," Fantom replied. "The sand is much deeper than I've ever seen it. I feel like we're walking on sand dunes. It's harder to move."

"I am going to be so peeved," Feral muttered, "if we paid for entry, just to find out they replenished the freaking sand last night."

She was standing near one of the canyon walls, and turned and looked at it. From the floor of the canyon, she could see a distinct difference in the color of the sand. It made a roughly vertical line stretching up a few feet.

New sand? On the canyon wall?

"The rocks are different, too," Fantom said. "I mean, they're probably the same rocks. They're just not where they were before. It's like they all moved south some." He looked up. "The next wave of players is inbound. We need to move."

Killing the Desnardian Commander took longer with just two of them fighting him. It was also more satisfying than usual to Feral.

She *knew* she had seen and heard things last night. It wasn't her imagination.

"I don't get it," she said, as they exited the quest. "I know what I saw. I saw a guy wearing a sherwani, rehearsing lines."

"A sher-what?"

"Sherwani. It's Indian formal wear. Like a really long shirt." She gestured toward her knees. "All that commotion couldn't have been just so they could put down more sand. Something's changed. It's like I can *feel* it, but not see it."

Fantom grunted, "Dunno."

As they walked out of the giftshop, Feral said, "Hit the WeaponSmith. Sell all the loot, and play it again? This time, we run the paths to their ends?"

Fantom shrugged. "I'm going to need a churro and a coke before going back in."

"Okay." *The line is already long. Delaying another ten minutes so Fantom can pack his face won't matter.*

– 1 1 0 1 0 0 1 0 –

Hodgins phoned Houston.

"I got what you wanted," said the voice on the other end. "Hodge, it ain't pretty."

"Figured." Hodgins sighed. "Let's hear it."

"Okay. About nineteen months ago, your boy called 911 at 2:14 a.m. Said his mom collapsed. They tried talking him through CPR."

"Sounds grim," said Hodgins.

"It gets worse. The responders found him next to his mom, holding a kitchen knife. At first they thought he might have stabbed her."

"Ah, man..."

"Don't worry. He didn't. Autopsy showed no signs of foul play—no knife wounds. COD was pulmonary embolism. A few postmortem injuries to one ankle, which the ME said were likely rat bites. The paramedics reported the garbage in the house was over three-feet deep in places. Said the house stunk—one of the cops on the scene vomited when he entered the dwelling. The report said there were numerous—*numerous* is underlined—rats visible on the scene." The voice on the phone paused. "Hodge, the kid didn't use the knife on his mom. He was using it to defend her. From rats."

Hodgins was silent for a moment.

Finally, "Okay. Thanks. I owe you one."

He hung up and sat alone in his office for several minutes, head in his hands, trying to understand what this kid had gone through.

Time to talk to the boss. He stood and walked around the corner to Van Horne's office.

"Hodge," said HVH, "this kid didn't *bring* a knife into the park. Our head of Security—the guy that designed and implemented our system of keeping weapons *out* of SPARK—circumvented our safeguards, and now plans to *give* the kid a weapon."

Hodgins rubbed his hands over his face and bald scalp.

"You make it sound pretty dumb, boss."

"Isn't it?"

Hodge knew he had HVH hooked. If he were going to refuse Hodge's request, the conversation would already be over.

"Here's the thing," Hodgins said. "When our guys found him out by the Solar Prime fence, he had a kitchen knife in his pack. Said he was on his own and needed it for protection. When he nearly lost it in Mars, and rolled on to his back, he didn't take out his blaster or his bat, or any other virtual weapon. He put his hands on his stomach, like this." Hodgins repeated Will's gesture. "Like he was holding something. Like he was holding that knife. In the middle of the safest ten square miles on the planet, the kid was scared of something besides just falling. People afraid of heights don't need knives." He rubbed his head again. "I don't know why I want to help the kid, but he needs help. We know both his parents died. We know he almost died after hiking through the desert so he could look at the grass. The kid has a lot of issues."

"Nobody's arguing that, Hodge."

Hodgins filled him in on what he'd learned from his source in Houston.

"Boss, every kid in the Pod is messed up in some way. The ones that are okay, never stay around. Their parents come looking, or they make the smart decision: that sleeping in a bed is a better deal than sleeping on cement under a hot water pipe beneath a quest."

HVH nodded.

Hodgins continued. "But you said it yourself. The Pod and the park heals these kids. They are their own support group. That girl? Calls herself Mellew? Once she found the Pod, she didn't go outside for a month. They brought her food, and somebody stayed with her twenty-four-seven. Now she's an UG, and stood up for Feral when a kid got out of line." He looked at HVH to see if he remembered the confrontation.

HVH nodded his understanding, so Hodgins continued.

"I think the Pod can help this young man. But I think he's afraid of something." He shrugged and gestured around them. "Rats, and God knows what else—he needs the knife to sleep at night. We'll be on top of this. If he ever pulls that thing out of the sheath for any reason other than to cut up an apple, we'll be on top of him. And I promise you, he'll never get close to carrying it in the actual park."

A long silence followed.

"Okay, Hodge. I have literally trusted you with my life since we hired you away from the Secret Service. I'll trust you on this." He pointed at Hodgins. "But I want to be kept in the loop. Anything else going on?"

Relieved to be supported on this item, Hodgins launched into his daily security update.

"Hack attempts are up, but our cybersecurity folks are seeing good success protecting our web interfaces with the mini-Jannes we rolled out earlier this year. We got a couple emails from State…"

"Yeah?" Van Horne said.

"Maybe it was the PlayMax interview, maybe something else. But you seem to have moved up on the Daesh enemy list. They called you and SPARK out by name."

"Ah, they're probably just mad the price of oil continues to drop," HVH said with an indifference Hodgins knew was feigned.

"Possibly. But these guys play rough. I'm going to ping some of my contacts to see if they know anything. Most of the hack attempts are coming from offshore. Primarily China, its territory of North Korea, and Mozambique.

The level of sophistication on some is impressive. They're ghosting as independents, but they may be state-sponsored." Hodgins looked up. "There's a lot of chatter that Solar Oz is going to change the political power structure in that part of the world, and not everyone is happy about a resurgent Australia. I've doubled our security at the Grass plant in Alice Springs, and the construction areas. I'll feel better when we've got the new Janne online down there."

"Sheila," HVH said.

"Pardon me?"

"We're calling the Aussie Janne, *Sheila*. It's confusing enough with three Jannes around here."

"You're the boss." Hodgins shrugged. "What's it stand for?"

"Nothing. I just like the name. And it's got a more Aussie ring to it."

"Okay." Hodgins paused to let Van Horne continue.

When he said nothing, Hodgins plowed on.

"That's it. I'll keep you up to date on the Daesh thing."

"Janne," said HVH, "how long do you think the Egg will stay secret?"

"Odds are it will be public knowledge within a month. Forty-three cast members and employees now know about the alternate ending. Two Pod members have clues they are already pursuing. Will is somewhat taciturn. He agreed to remain silent, but I now project a limited lifespan for the secret."

"How does the Pod know?" HVH said.

"Feral was awakened by the noise of the hydraulics during the avalanche. She went to investigate, saw the actor portraying the Elder entering the elevator. She told Fantom. They paid for admission."

Hecker Van Horne looked at his phone.

"Well, if they hit Mars running, they'd be done by now. And if they'd found the Egg, we'd have heard about it. Where are they, Janne?"

"They have played Mars once, and noted the depth of the sand and the slight repositioning of the rocks on the canyon floor. They plan to play again, but are currently selling their loot from the first round, and plan on eating. They intend to run the paths on their next go."

Van Horne turned to Hodgins. "What do you think? Safe for another seven years?"

"No, boss. I'm with Janne. This one was too big to keep quiet. I'd bet it's out within six months at the latest."

"Well," said HVH, "we're planning on starting major renovations to the park in a couple years. If it gets too spendy, we'll push Mars to the top of the list. New quest, new Egg."

– 1 1 0 1 0 0 1 0 –

As Fantom pushed the last piece of churro into his face, Feral saw Bull walking up the arcade. She almost burst out laughing. He was attired in a SPARK Maintenance uniform. Feral knew Security wore Maintenance uniforms, but most of the in-park Security people looked more…*normal* in them. They tended to be smaller than Bull. Wiry where Bull was bulky. Average in height, whereas Bull stood close to six-foot-six-inches tall. Plus, they learned to walk like normal people. They blended in. Bull stood out. He swaggered, rolling his shoulders.

SPARK liked to take troublemakers out quietly, so as not to disturb the other guests. Bull was the guy you chose if you needed to intimidate someone. That's why he was perfect for security at the tournaments. He looked like someone you didn't want to mess with. Even if you didn't know him, you would look at him and think: Marine, fighter, badass. Your next thought would be, *Oh, hey, he must be Security*.

She called out to him. "Hey, Bull!"

He looked slightly annoyed, then smiled when he saw who it was, and walked toward her. She watched him approach and saw him split his attention between her and some kid wearing what looked to be a baseball uniform. That felt familiar to her, but she didn't know why.

She peeked the kid. It was the ginger from the Princess! Bull was following him again.

"Hey, Feral," Bull said with affection. He nodded at her companion. "Fantom."

"Okay, two things, my friend." Feral bumped fists with Bull. "First, what are you doing in the park? I thought you preferred being outside?"

Bull nodded. "Yeah, but we decided to put our kids in the SPARK School. It's way easier to get them here and home if I work inside the park. Besides," he smiled, "now I can have lunch with them. I like that!"

Feral thought again that Bull was a good guy. Maybe not the smartest guy in the crowd, but absolutely the guy you would pick to have your back in any—literally, *any*—situation. Bull would tell you if he thought you were wrong, and help you do the right thing. And he would die for you if he thought you were right. Bull was physically what ShaChri's father was intellectually.

The ginger, Feral noticed, stopped at the WeaponSmith and seemed to be actively trading.

"You said two things?" Bull asked Feral.

"Yeah," she replied. "The second thing is, that outfit looks wrong on you." She made a small circling gesture at Bull with her finger to indicate his apparel. "I think SPARK should keep you in the uniform, but let you wear an avatar over it. Something that fits you. I dunno, maybe a bulked-up Viking or Zulu warrior, or…a Frost Giant! That's it! Kit you up as a Frost Giant with an enormous war hammer or club on your back! SPARK would get the best of both worlds—an intimidating presence, and invisibility. You'd be awesome!"

"That's…a really good idea." He grinned. "I'll tell my boss."

"Actually, there's a third thing. Unless you're willing to accept the avatar thing as part of the first thing. In which case, there's really only two things."

She saw Bull check the kid in the baseball uniform, and then turn back to her with a tolerant smile.

"Second thing, then, is what's with the kid?"

"Aw, nothing," Bull said in a sheepish tone. "We were a little worried about him before, but it turned out to be nothing. I just saw him coming up the arcade, and decided to follow him and see what he's up to."

"Selling a lot of loot, from the looks of it," Feral said.

Bull turned around and nodded. "Yeah, I think the kid had a good day yesterday. Level Eighteen when he went in. Level Twenty-Five now. Pretty good, huh?"

Feral looked at the kid with new respect. *Seven levels in a day? That's beyond good. Admittedly, he's on the easier levels. But still, that's like…*she tried to do the math…*twelve thousand XP in one day?*

They watched the kid turn into the Mars Arcade Princess, and things almost clicked for her. She knew there was something there, but couldn't connect the dots.

– 1 1 0 1 0 0 1 0 –

In Security, Severski watched the monitor that showed the entry queue. He caught Will's name and avatar when the boy entered, but also saw the code indicating he was under stricter-than-normal surveillance.

Little Kimmy's trouble. Gonna be hard to mess with him with the extra surveillance. Your time will come, punk.

"Anything in particular you're looking at, Severski?"

The voice startled him and he jumped.

"No," he told Hodgins, trying to smooth over his obvious unease. "Just trying to get a feel for what kind of day we're going to have at SPARK."

The head of Security moved closer to him and stood looking at the monitors surrounding the area. Hodgins turned slowly to face him and leaned closer, his voice a harsh whisper.

"Jesus, Tony, I could smell you as soon as I turned the corner. Did you bathe in Tequila?"

"You're just smelling my mouthwash." *Why is it that big guys like Hodgins always try to intimidate people by getting in their face?*

Hodgins snorted. "Like I can't tell the difference." His tone softened. "Look, man, you're already on thin ice with the boss. Stay away from him today. Join AA. For your own sake, do something." He turned and walked away.

If it wasn't for jerks like him, I wouldn't need to drink.

He glared at Hodgins's back. *You'll get your due. You and your puppet master.*

Chapter 19

Art has a double face, of expression and illusion, just like science has a double face: the reality of error and the phantom of truth.
—René Daumal, The Lie of the Truth

Will was tired but pumped. Now that he had beaten the quest, Mars was awesome. His basophobia faded into memory and he worried about his stuff. Trying to sleep tonight could be tough. *There's no way Mister Hodgins is going to allow the KA-BAR into SPARK.*

If it came to it, Will decided to steal a knife from a restaurant. *I can sharpen it on the concrete.* It wouldn't be like the KA-BAR Olsen gave him, but it might keep the noises away.

He sold all the Mars loot, except the Desnardian Commander's blaster—somehow it seemed like the right thing to do. It was on his hip now.

His points added up to someone who should be Level 41, but he was still a Level 25. Will was feeling a little cockier than the previous morning, so he decided to go straight back to the Princess. The circular pancakes, not the points of the star, guided him.

The Princess went through her normal routine, and this time when the numbers began to scroll up in his ARGs, he saw it immediately. He was looking for it now:

00000011.	10100011	00101110
00100100	00001000	00000011
00111111	11010011	01110000
01101010	00010011	01110011
10001000	00011001	01000100
10000101	10001010	10100100

00001001	00110001	10011000
00111000	11010000	11101100
00100010	00001000	01001110
00101001	00101110	01101100
10011111	11111010	10001001

There was a period after the first group of numbers. That worked as a decimal—or binary—point, just like in any other base. *That changes everything.*

When the Princess looked at him expectantly, he said, "It's an approximation of pi—the ratio of the circumference of a circle to its diameter."

"Of course! I should have known. Let's see what's next." The Princess led him through a door.

A vast field appeared before them. Green grass surrounded a well visible in the distance. Script appeared in the air before them:

For the Princess to flee
She will beseech thee,
Her savior to be.
But we say as a fact
With all possible tact
That your answer, it must be exact.

What is the area of the mouth of the well?

The Princess pointed to the well. "That must be it. Go find the area."

WB raced off. A walkway led him to the well. Surrounding the well were a pile of pieces of metal, wood, bone, plastic, and some things he couldn't recognize. Radiating out from the well were seven paths other than the one he followed to the well. The well itself looked perfectly circular on the inside, even though the outside seemed constructed of brick.

This should be fairly easy. I just need to measure the radius or diameter, do a little mental math, and be done! But how do I measure?

He squatted down and looked at the pile of debris. They were all rulers or measuring devices. Different shapes and sizes, but they all had regular markings perfect for measuring something. He grabbed one and put its end against the inside of the well.

Crud. This one's not long enough. It didn't even reach to the center of the well. He needed a longer one.

He pawed through the pile. None of them looked long enough. They didn't even seem to use the same units. Some were clearly marked as inches or millimeters, but others had units he could only guess at. All were different. Some were decimal, others clearly binary. One had both letters and numbers—*hexadecimal*? This was eating up time.

Will scrambled around the well. None of the rulers were long enough. He stood and looked down the other walkways. There were piles at the end of each. He raced to one.

Time ran out, and Will left the quest dismayed. He thought he'd figured it out. The key to beating the Princess Quests was doing all the Knowledge quests in the arcade. That, combined with searching the decorations and minor quests, should have set him up for success.

He walked to the quiet area on the rim between the plazas and sat on the bench again. He needed to think. He couldn't just stop wherever he was. People kept bumping into him and disrupting his thoughts.

How can I calculate the area when I can't get an exact number for the radius or diameter?

If he went through every pile to find the perfect ruler, that meant going through the quest at least three more times to check every pile. What if he somehow combined two or more of the rulers? That might work. But that was a lot of converting to do. He remembered the lesson of the Mars Surveyor—units mattered! He wouldn't have to simply convert units, he'd also have to jump between numeric systems—base-2 to base-7 to base-10 or something. Without a calculator, he was certain to make some conversion errors. Even if he could get everything to the same units and base, there was bound to be slop in his mental math.

Will let his imagination run. He came up with four different ways to calculate the area.

An hour later, he was frustrated. Nothing worked. He was never going to figure this out.

Maybe I need to look at this from the other end. Let's say I figure out that the radius is exactly two whatevers. Pi times two squared is, what? Around 12.6? How accurate do I have to be?

He reviewed the riddle in his head: *"...must be exact."*

Exact. His scalp started tingling. *Even if the radius is exactly one unit, pi goes on forever. It's irrational. What's the exact answer? It's irrational even to try!*

Will stood and suppressed the desire to run back to the Princess, hope and anxiety fighting for dominance.

WB reentered the quest, and after the riddle appeared in the air, he said, "It can't be done. Pi is irrational. There can never be an exact answer."

The Princess turned to him and smiled, her eyes bright.

"Of course! I should have seen that myself. Thank you, WB. You are a true Seeker." She took his hands in an awkward virtual clasp. "Now, find me. Save me."

The Princess faded, and a fanfare of trumpets played as Will exited.

This time, no one came up to him and congratulated him. A few heads turned, but that was all. His ARGs showed he had now completed the first and seventh Princess Quests, and had gotten two hundred XP for the seventh. *Are the XP going to grow exponentially like they do for the Knowledge quests? And if I just saved the seventh Princess, why isn't she skipping off down some virtual meadow, celebrating her freedom? What was that about finding and saving her? Do I have to beat all seven before she's saved?*

He pondered it during lunch, fell asleep and napped at his table.

– 1 1 0 1 0 0 1 0 –

When he awoke, there was a small puddle of drool on the table beneath his mouth. He was embarrassed. People were staring.

He slapped his ARGs down, sorted trash from recycling, and headed down to the Hub. He'd decided to try to run all the Knowledge quests in chronological order. That meant he needed to hit the Ascent of Humanity arcade and start working his way up.

That didn't last long. He was too tired to concentrate. Instead, he wandered the arcade and plaza, concentrating on physically active small quests and activities. Eventually, he decided to just walk all of the arcades. He needed to kill time until it was closer to closing. Then he would grab his backpack and try to hide in the Underground overnight.

By the end of the day, he'd done enough small stuff to push himself to a Level 26, and he put his additional point into Brawn.

– 1 1 0 1 0 0 1 0 –

Ragnar Sarnak was not a happy mercenary. Yes, his work in Dubrovnik had been flawless. Yes, Budapest went well. But now his employers for the SPARK job wanted him in Maputo for a face-to-face meeting. *Foolish.*

He hated Mozambique in general, and Maputo most of all. Wikipedia said it was getting better, more stable. Said Maputo was called the Pearl of the Indian Ocean. Sarnak thought that true, only if a pearl was the same as an armpit. Wikipedia had never been to Maputo. If he had to go to southern Africa, he'd rather go to Angola, even to Luanda in Angola. At least they had a well-trained military. And he had friends there. Angolan mercenary friends.

The additional money assuaged his bruised sensibilities somewhat. Still, it was Maputo. Dangerous, even for someone with Sarnak's skill set.

Remember the money.

Chapter 20

You can learn more from a guide in one day than
you can in three months fishing alone.
—Anonymous

"Stop!"

Will spun around, certain he'd been caught.

He'd picked up his backpack from Security. It was in a shopping bag and had a plush Sparky covering it. It still contained his knife. As the day wore down, he wandered up to one of the entrances he'd discovered early that morning with Hodgins. He was still wearing his ARGs, and some girl was walking up to him. She was wearing black leggings and a snug pink T-shirt, but wasn't wearing ARGs, haptics, or a wristband, so he was seeing a person rather than an avatar. She was blonde, with short curly hair and curves that got his attention.

She doesn't look old enough to work here, and those aren't work clothes. Can't be official.

"You can't go in there with all your gear on," she said. "They'll track you."

Will stared blankly at his haptics and wristband. He remembered what Janne and Hodgins said, but hadn't figured a way around it.

"You're trying to get a peek behind the scenes, right?"

At this point, Will figured he was busted, and nodded.

The girl—he was sure she wasn't official now—chewed on her thumbnail and appeared conflicted. She seemed a little taller than him, and had a light dusting of freckles across the bridge of her nose. For three heartbeats, she stared at him, one hand on her hip, then apparently reached a decision. She grabbed Will's arm.

"Rookie mistake. Follow me." The girl tugged him down the arcade.

After a few steps, she let go. He stayed close behind. Soon they were close enough to the Hub that people were doing last-minute shopping and strolling toward the exit.

She squatted down near a concrete bench.

"Pretend like you have to tie your shoe."

Will knelt down slowly.

"Now saw off your wristband on the edge of the bench."

"Got it." He scraped the band off his wrist.

Freckles stood and pointed him toward where people were crowding together to exit.

"Get to where people are a little more packed together, then dump everything—wristband, haptics, ARGs—into a shopping bag or a stroller. Keep them all together. SPARK will just figure you exited with that group, and you'll be officially out of the park. And invisible. But you have to hurry. I'll meet where I saw you before. Walk, don't run, back there. Running back into the park makes you look like you're up to something. Hurry!"

The girl turned, curls spinning, and followed her own advice, leaving Will to fend for himself. He pulled off his ARGs and haptics and clutched everything in one hand. The crowd was thicker near the exit. Will felt nervous sweat trickling down his back. A lady in front of him had a big bag slung over her shoulder. He dumped his gear in the bag, feeling like everyone was watching him.

The crowd closed in behind him, and he kept saying, "Sorry, forgot something. Sorry, forgot something," as he pushed through, receiving a few glares from tired guests.

Will strode back up the arcade. Some of the vendors had closed. It felt like everyone he passed stared at him as he headed back to the door. The girl was nowhere to be seen.

Will took a deep breath and pushed through the door.

"I was about to leave you. C'mon." The girl turned and led him down the hallway that held the medical assistance rooms. "What was your plan?"

Will mumbled, "I was gonna sleep in one of these rooms and then try to sneak out in the morning."

"Bad idea," his impromptu guide said over her shoulder. "First of all, sometimes employees sneak into these rooms at night to do stuff they don't want seen. Usually it's a guy and a girl. Get it?"

Will nodded.

"Second, it's harder to get out than to stay in. If you go out a public exit, they want to know where your gear is so they can log you out. Then they want to know why you're leaving so early. Or people see you walking around SPARK without any gear and wonder what's going on. First rule of the Pod: never do anything entering or exiting that will draw attention to yourself."

"What's the Pod?" Will said.

"You'll see. Maybe." Freckles grinned as she led him deeper into the Underground.

They passed through a door that read *HVAC 7*. Behind that door were a myriad of large noisy machines. Will had lots of questions, but didn't want to shout, so he just followed the girl.

They passed between several machines labeled *Chiller 70-75*, and then crawled around some pipes before emerging into another open area where it was much quieter.

The girl stopped and turned to Will.

"So what's your sitch?" She smiled.

"My what?"

"Your sitch. Your situation. Why are you here?" She gestured in a circle around them. "Are you just looking around? Trying to see behind the curtain?"

Will stared at her piercing, crystal blue eyes. *Why is she helping me?* In a quest, she'd have a tag to help him figure out how to treat her. *Ally? Neutral?*

"It's a boring story," he replied.

"You got somewhere to be?" Her smile was contagious. "Cop a squat. Pretty sure we have time."

"Okay." He sighed and sat opposite her. "I'll go with the short version. I got orphaned a few years back. Foster care sucked." He paused, looking at her. "You ever in the system?" *Always heard it was tougher on girls.*

The blonde shook her head.

"Well, it's not great. Anyway, things got messed up with my fosters, and it looked like they were going to send me back to a group home." *Or worse.* "I ran."

She nodded encouragement.

He continued. "My parents brought me out here, like, six years ago. We loved it. I wanted to come back. Thought I might be able to get a job. I want to work in AI."

"And then you found out that they won't hire anyone who's not eighteen."

"Yep. You, too?"

"A little different, but yeah. Thought I could find work. Go on."

"Anyway, I'm almost out of cash and thought that maybe—"

"You could live every gamer's fantasy and stay in SPARK?" She grinned.

"Something like that." Will shook his head. "Dumb, huh?"

"Not at all. Look where you are." Another smile, this one softer.

"What about you?" he said. "How'd you end up here? How'd you figure this all out?"

"It's a sad tale of divorced parents, asshole stepmom, and a stepdad who's a little too cuddly. Couldn't live with either set."

She paused and looked at Will, seemingly wanting an acknowledgement.

"Sorry," he said.

"Not your fault, but thanks. Anyway, I was headed to LA but wanted to stop here. I'd only ever played online."

Will smiled at her. "Isn't this so much better? Playing live?"

"Absolutely! And the quests play different every time."

"Really?" *Wonder if she has a boyfriend.*

"Yeah. Well, sort of. I mean, the major storylines are stable, but so much else changes as you level."

"I haven't played that much yet," Will said.

"You're going to love it. Okay, I guess you pass."

"Pass what?"

"A test. If we bring someone down here, we quiz them for a while to make sure they're not a complete jerk."

"What would have happened if I didn't pass your test?"

"I would have run like crazy. Gotten you lost down here. Then I'd rat you out to Security. Instead, I'll introduce you to the Pod."

"Okay. Glad I passed." Will grinned. "Now, what's the Pod?"

"It's our little band of adventurers." She stuck out a fist.

He bumped her knuckles.

"I'm Mellew."

"I'm Wi—"

She put up a finger. "Avatar names only in the Pod. Nobody wants to know your real name, and you don't want anybody to know who you really are."

"Okay, I get that. I'm WB."

She looked at him as if wanting more of an explanation. He just shrugged.

Finally, she nodded. "Nice to meet you, WB. Let's go meet the Pod."

She pushed herself up and dusted off her pants. Will stood and followed.

As they walked, Mellew gave him some insight into the Pod.

"Why do you call it the Pod?" WB said. "Are we orcas?"

Mellew chuckled, her voice echoing off the pipelined corridor.

"No. I'm not really sure why. Maybe more like peas. Everybody's in the same situation?"

Will nodded. "Okay."

"Everybody's got a story. Everybody's a runaway." She paused. "Except maybe Fantom. I think his parents kicked him out."

"Phantom?"

"Yeah, like a ghost. But spelled with an F. I think the Ph version was already taken. Anyway, he's been here the longest. He's the one who figured out about ditching the wristbands and how to exit. He's like the mayor of the Pod. There are nine of us right now." She ticked them off on her fingers. "Fantom, me, Zen, Myranda, Hunter—actually, he's Hunter319, but we just call him Hunter—Yennifer, DreadBot, and DeadElf—Dread and Dead, they're a couple—and Feral, of course."

"Dread and Dead are feral?"

Mellew laughed again. "No! Feral, as in Feral Daughter. That's her real avatar name."

She explained to Will that they were currently staying near the Evolve Quest.

"We were staying near Mars, but it was really busy last night. We thought something big was going on, so we scattered. Tonight, we regroup at Evolve."

She kept up her tour guide monologue.

"It's a little more confusing down here than upstairs. But mostly, the Underground City mirrors SPARK. You can tell what zone you're in by the numbers: hundreds are support stuff for PreHistory, two hundreds for the Ascent stuff. We came in near Future Worlds, so everything had seven-hundred-numbers." Mellew pointed to a door. "See? Two-twenty-two. We're already in the Ascent zone. We've passed PreHistory and are coming up on Evolve."

"I hate that quest," WB said. "Well, I hated it when I came here with my parents. We must have died, like, four times before we made it out. It was a long day."

"What's your favorite?" she said.

"Probably KT Crossing. But I haven't done it since I got here. I mean, since I've been here this time."

"Everybody loves KT Crossing. Kids go nuts for the Bronto Ride part, and there's a ton of semi-interesting side quests."

"I remember that!" WB said. "My mom and dad were all about the side quests. It took us nearly a whole day to finish KT Crossing, but I bet we found every stinking piece of swag."

Will realized he had stopped walking and gotten lost in his own memories, when Mellew tapped him on the shoulder.

"You okay?"

Will blushed. "Yeah. Sorry. Sometimes I start thinking about stuff, and then the world just kind of fades out. It's worse when I'm tired. Used to drive my teachers nuts."

"Anyway," Mellew said, recommencing her guide role, "learn the schedule. Night shift leaves at seven a.m. We walk out with them—try to blend in." She pointed to his hair. "That might make it tougher. It's…"

"Unusually bright?" WB smiled.

"Yeah," Mellew nodded vigorously, sending her curls bouncing. "Maybe a hat."

Before WB could reply, Mellew continued.

"Normally we can eat one, maybe two, meals at the employee cafeteria. It's mostly automated. They have a big rush around three a.m.—lunchtime for night shift—but it's pretty empty the rest of the time." She turned and stopped WB, putting her palm on his chest. "Clean up your mess. Don't do anything to draw attention to us. Same for the locker rooms and the gym. You can shower there, but don't leave any signs you were there. When you need clean clothes, go to Lost and Found and find something that fits."

They made a slight turn and found themselves in a more open area. Conversations abruptly stopped as WB and Mellew entered. They had found the Pod.

The silence grew awkward, and the stares could have peeled paint.

Mellew stepped forward. "This is WB. He found his own way in. We've talked. He doesn't know all the rules, or how it works, but he should get a shot. He's as messed up as all of us."

She introduced him around. When they got to Feral Daughter, she glared up at him.

Uh-oh.

"I see the perv brought his own gift bag." She pointed to the SPARK shopping bag that WB carried.

"What are you talking about, Feral?" Mellew had continued walking around the circle, and now retraced her steps until she stood next to WB.

"I mean, if Peek-boy here has enough money to go shopping," Feral said, "he doesn't need to stay with us."

Mellew shook her head and frowned. "I don't remember anyone else ever being booted for having some money. What's this really about? What did you mean by *perv*? Did he Peek you?"

WB said, "Look, I can—"

"Save it," Feral snapped.

"Hah." The guy that had been introduced as Fantom barked out a laugh. "Who'd Peek you? Somebody trying to figure out who the little ninja really is?"

"Shut up, Fantom. I was guiding as Flighty Damsel," she said, as if that explained everything.

"Feral, you need to get over yourself," Fantom said in a voice that WB already found annoying, even though the guy was coming to his defense.

"No, this is serious," Mellew said. "People shouldn't Peek. The Pod shouldn't Peek." She turned to WB. "You were trying to say something."

WB explained about exiting the Princess and running into Feral and her clients.

"Then she asked me for suggestions on how to beat the Princess, and—"

"Stop right there." Fantom glared over at Feral. "Now who's crossing lines?"

"It's not the same." Feral slapped the floor.

Mellew said, "No, but let's just agree that mistakes were made on both sides, and give WB a chance." She turned to him. "No more Peeking. It's rude."

WB nodded.

"Okay," she said with forced lightness, "that's settled."

Everyone was quiet until Feral grudgingly nodded and then looked at WB with eyes both beautiful in their dark intensity and terrifying at the same time.

"If you Peek me again, I'll break your nose."

WB swallowed involuntarily. *She's completely serious.*

Silence fell over the group as they looked at each other. WB realized that Mellew had left his side and moved over to where there was a gap in the circle formed by the Pod members. She sat and patted the concrete floor next to her. WB took the offered spot.

The silence stretched until WB could no longer stand it.

"So who has the conch?" he said.

Mellew laughed, and Feral snorted derisively.

More stony stares, until Mellew said, "Come on! Did none of you have to read *Lord of the Flies* in school?"

A chorus of head shakes.

Mellew stood, pulling the focus of the Pod.

"Imagine a war," she said. "One even worse than Korea Two. A war going so bad, the children were evacuated to someplace safe. Their plane crashes near an uninhabited island." She gestured dramatically around them. "Only the kids survive the crash."

She captivated them. The way she spun the tale for them, so passionately and thoroughly, made WB realize how much he had forgotten.

When Mellew got to the part about the conch shell being the totem of power and attention, they all nodded. It took her most of an hour to tell the story, and she did it with a flair WB had never seen, outside of vids.

"She should act," WB whispered to Dread, who was sitting beside him.

"Word."

The Pod settled in for the night. Some went to eat, but Mellew and WB stayed behind.

"Let's go to Lost and Found," she said. "People lose hats here all the time."

Once they had found him a Houston Astros baseball cap that mostly hid his ginger hair, Mellow pronounced it satisfactory.

"This is a sign," WB told her.

"What do you mean?"

He gestured at the hat. "The Stros? They're my team."

Mellew paused as if trying to grasp the entire concept of not only caring about baseball, but also caring about it enough to actually have a *team*.

She shook her head. "Okay, now we'll figure out where you can sleep. Everyone kind of has their own spot. You'll be on the outskirts, okay?"

WB nodded. "Sure. I've been sleeping in baseball parks, being devoured by bugs. Anything's fine."

"Come on." Mellew led him to a section of piping where he could have his back to the wall. "This should work."

He nodded.

"I'm right over there." She pointed to where the rest of the Pod was bedding down for the night.

As the Pod settled, WB scooted deeper into the shadows and quietly pulled out the KA-BAR. He held it in the darkness and quickly fell asleep.

– 1 1 0 1 0 0 1 0 –

In the morning, Feral woke WB by standing on his hand.

“Let go of the knife.” Her voice was soft, her tone deadly.

He relaxed his grip on the knife and stared up at her. She bent down and took the KA-BAR. Behind her, he could see other members of the Pod waking up.

Feral looked at the knife, her back still to the remainder of the Pod. It should have been incongruous—this petite girl in bike shorts and a Sparky T-shirt, holding a KA-BAR—but that she held it so comfortably, so naturally, disturbed him deeply.

“I’ve got no idea how you got this in, but it’s mine now. I could—probably should—tell everyone about this.” She jerked her head back toward Mellew and the others.

Her ebony ponytail accentuated the movement.

Feral squatted down and put the tip of the sheathed knife against his chest.

“If I ever trust you, I’ll give it back. Meanwhile, I thought about it last night. Maybe you’re not really a perv. Maybe you weren’t lying. I was going to tell you we’re even. Now,” she withdrew the knife, “you owe me.”

WB nodded. “What do you want?”

“I don’t know yet. Maybe just a better answer on how to beat the Princess than, *do your homework.*” She stood. “Wait here for me.”

Feral headed down the corridor, away from the Pod. In three minutes, she was back without the knife.

“It’s time to go. We have to mix in with the night shift employees as they leave.”

WB rolled onto his hands and knees and stood awkwardly, trying to avoid banging his head on the pipes he’d slept beneath.

“Listen, you don’t have to go out with us,” Feral told him. “But if you don’t, you’re better off hunkering down here for the day. We’ll bring you some food later.”

“No,” WB mumbled. “I’ll go.” He started to walk toward the other members of the Pod. *At least Mellew is more pleasant to be around.*

Feral stopped him. “Okay, I’ve hidden your stupid knife. Nobody else needs to see it, or even know it exists. I’ll meet you over there.” She jerked her head toward where the other Pod members were assembling and stretching out the kinks from another night sleeping on cement.

Coulda been worse. Will followed her over to the group.

"Morning, WB!" Mellew said. "I'll walk out with you."

"No," Feral said. "I'll walk him out."

Mellew started to protest, but Feral stopped her.

"You get too much attention from guys coming in. They'll notice you're with someone new. Peek-boy and I will find some taller people to walk behind. Nobody'll notice us."

"Enough with the Peek-boy stuff, Feral," said Mellew. "We agreed to put that behind us last night."

"Fine." Feral rolled her eyes. "C'mon," she said to WB. "And put on your hat."

Feral guided WB through the pack but jerked him back from the door to the exit corridor at the last moment. Her grip was vise-like on his upper arm.

"Hey," he said.

"Shut up," she hissed, and pulled him back a couple steps.

She relaxed her hand after a moment, then pushed him forward again.

Feral guided him through the corridors. As they exited, the stream of employees fanned out. Some headed to the parking lot and their own cars. Others boarded the waiting buses that would take them into the Barstow Park and Ride.

Feral and WB peeled off to walk around to the public bus drop-off entry Feral used as a meeting point for her clients.

She whispered to WB, "Frack! Did you see that big guy we almost plowed into?"

WB nodded but only vaguely remembered a large guy with two kids passing by the open door.

"He's Security. I hope he didn't see us." She chewed a nail. "He's the one who's been following you."

"Following me?" WB whispered back. "What are you talking about?"

"I saw him watching you a couple days ago. The day you Peeked me?"

"I wasn't perving on you. Are you going to let it go?"

"Maybe." She wore a slight smile. "Maybe I'll just call you PB instead of WB."

He was getting angry. "Dang it, I told you—"

"Easy." Feral held up a hand. "I'll let it go. Just teasing. Kind of."

Will gave himself a couple heartbeats to cool down.

"Why are they following me?"

"I wasn't sure before. Bull didn't say anything. Maybe it's the knife. I can't believe they didn't see it on you when you entered the first time. Wait. Did you bring it into the park your first day? You know, when you…"

"Enough. Not funny." He glared at Feral. "No, I didn't bring it in that day."

Feral was quiet for a minute.

"Huh," she said. "But they were watching you, even then."

A bus pulled up and guests poured out.

"Okay, these might be my clients." She turned and caught his eye. "Try to stay out of trouble. Fly below the radar?"

"Sure. You playing as Feral today?"

"No, I'm with a bunch of noobs. Japanese, I think. So I'll probably go with Flighty Damsel or Fumiyo."

"Fumiyo?"

"Yeah, she's an anime elf. All about swords and bows with magic arrows."

Will nodded but noticed that when the sun was in Feral's eyes, he could see that they weren't simply a deep brown. They had flecks of gold. *Mesmerizing.*

"Okay," she said. "Meet me at Mars an hour before closing. I'll show you another way in."

Chapter 21

You may choose to look the other way,
but you can never say again that you did not know.
—William Wilberforce

Bull dropped off his kids at SPARK School. It was very different from what he experienced growing up. A nicely dressed young woman introduced herself as *Miss Spencer*, and called him *Mister Bullard*, and said they would expect to meet him at noon in the employee cafeteria for lunch. He knew he or his wife would be required to eat lunch with the children every day, and was looking forward to it.

Bull hugged them goodbye. They were eager for their first day.

With his children seen to, Bull headed up to Security to put on his uniform and to check in before heading into SPARK. His encounter with Feral this morning surprised him. He couldn't think of a legitimate reason for them to have been walking out of the employee exit. And what the heck was she doing with Knife Boy?

Bull sought out Hodgins and found him just heading into the Stand Up.

"Hey, boss."

"Hey, Bull." Hodgins smiled. "What's up?"

"Can we talk after the Stand Up?"

Every shift began with a Stand Up. The team huddled together in the open space in the center of Security, and Hodgins or the shift supervisor talked about hot topics. It was called Stand Up because everyone stood. No chairs, no tables, nothing to prolong the meeting. Five minutes or less. Janne would provide any real-time updates as the day wore on.

"Sure," Hodgins replied, then moved into the center of the group. "Morning, everyone!"

A chorus of, "Morning, Hodge," or "Morning, boss," came from the group.

"Okay. Nothing major expected today. Hackers are more active, but we haven't heard any rumblings about anything impacting the park. No expected physical threats. Melee tourney this weekend. After skipping the last two, CastIron is expected to be back. That usually draws more people and a bigger online audience. Solar Prime has been getting a little more heat in the press due to China's recent failure of their Black Grass knockoff project."

A round of grumbling broke out in the group. Hodgins raised his arms to quiet them. When they did, he continued.

"Yeah, we all know there's a certain segment of the population and the media that thinks we should give away our technology and do anything to keep China happy. The boss sure isn't one of them, and that means the unhappy appeasers out there might try something stupid here. Let's not let it happen. That's it. Keep 'em safe, keep 'em happy!"

The meeting broke up, and Bull kept his place as everyone filed away to their routes in the park. Hodgins saw Bull waiting, and headed toward him.

"Let's walk and talk," Hodgins said, already moving toward his office.

Bull fell in next to him. "I was thinking—well, actually, a guest suggested it, but it sounded good—maybe I should wear an avatar in the park. I feel like I stick out in this uniform,"

"A guest?" Hodgins said.

"Yeah. Well, Feral. You know Feral, right?"

"Quite well. I'm not a drinking buddy or anything, but I am kind of a fan of the girl. What'd she say?"

"She suggested that I wear an avatar over my uniform. Thought I'd blend in better, but still be able to appear official when necessary."

"Hmm...that's actually pretty sound reasoning. Set it up with Janne."

They reached Hodgins' office. It was up a floor, just off of Vulture's Row, and around the corner from HVH's private suite.

Hodgins was often called Van Horne's last line of defense, but that wasn't technically true. There were still his personal assistants—one intimidating middle-aged woman who was the professional gatekeeper. And one pretty, petite woman who visitors assumed was there for her looks. Few people, outside of Security, knew the truth. Both had administrative and technical skills, and both could kill you in more ways than you could imagine. Billionaires like HVH could hire the best. When Van Horne appeared in public, he had one obvious male bodyguard, and the petite woman. The tabloids assumed they were an item. Bull knew they weren't.

"So. What's the private part?" Hodgins said, when they got to his office and he had closed the door.

"Boss, this morning," said Bull, "when I was walking in with my kids, I'm not sure, but I think I saw Feral and Knife Boy."

"And?"

"They were in a side corridor—inside the employee area. Getting ready to walk out, maybe." Bull let the statement hang.

Hodgins sat behind his desk and swiveled slightly away from Bull, looking out at the screens that surrounded the Security bullpen.

"Well," Hodgins sighed, "since you're going to be working inside the park from now on, I guess it's time to bring you in on our ugly little secret."

He looped Janne into the conversation, and then explained the existence of the Pod, HVH's tolerance of it, the rationale behind the tolerance, and capped it all off with last night's video of the Pod assembling under Evolve.

"Okay," Bull said. "So just to make sure I understand. I'm supposed to ignore that this group of kids lives inside SPARK."

"Yep," Hodgins replied.

"And you want me to act like nothing happened with Knife Boy and Feral this morning."

"Yep."

"And someday, God forbid, if my kids run away, I won't even get a call to tell me they're okay?"

Hodgins swiveled back and stood. "Damnit, Bull, that's not fair! You're part of the family. You know we'd tell you."

Bull nodded slowly. "Yeah. Just thinking about how other parents might feel."

Hodgins seemed to swallow his anger. He ran his hands over his bald scalp and collapsed back into his chair.

"Crap," he said. "I thought all about the legal issues. Not once did I think about it from a parent's point of view."

"Mister Hodgins…" Janne's voice from the overhead speaker seemed oddly formal.

"Yeah?"

"My analysis of conversations within the Pod, when compared with external data you have provided, indicate that most of the Pod wish no contact with living parents or guardians, or believe that those adults wish no contact with them. At least one is in routine contact with their legal guardian."

Bull said, "I get that. But sometimes I get mad at my kids. That doesn't mean I love them any less, or wouldn't want to know that they're okay."

"Bull's point is fair, Janne," said Hodgins. "Let's talk to Hecker and see if there's any way to covertly let parents know that the kids are okay."

"I will add it to our agenda."

Hodgins stood and stuck out his hand to Bull.

"Thanks. I mean it." He shook his head slowly. "You know, Steph and I always wanted to have kids."

"Sorry, boss."

Bull had been ambivalent about kids before his were born. Now, they were the center of his universe. He couldn't imagine how empty his life would be without them.

"Thanks," Hodgins replied.

Bull turned to leave, sensing the conversation was over.

"Hey, Bull. If you catch them again, feel free to give chase. We don't want them to get too comfortable."

"You got it, Hodge." Bull grinned. "Last thing. I'm a go for the avatar idea?"

Hodge looked up. "You can make this happen today, Janne?"

"Mister Hodgins, please. I do this over ten thousand times per day. I think I can manage one more."

Bull thought the AI sounded a little insulted.

When he entered the park later, he wore a Level 40 Frost Giant avatar Janne had created for him. It was fourteen levels higher than he'd earned, but looked awesome.

– 1 1 0 1 0 0 1 0 –

Will used another of his free days, and Janne greeted him warmly as ever. Somehow, he expected her to look more suspiciously at him. But she seemed the same. *Is it possible she doesn't know? She's got to know about Mars. Does she know about the Pod?* He wanted to ask.

"By the way, WB," she said, as she shuttled him to the Hub, "congratulations on the Egg."

He tried hard to contain his grin. "Thanks!"

He started to say something else, but Janne held up a finger to her lips. Will nodded.

WB started his day in the Ascent of Humanity Arcade. His plan revolved around hitting as many Knowledge and Princess quests as he could, playing and searching his way up the arcade, looking for clues and for anything that might be a hidden school. He didn't find anything and went to the point of asking vendors if they had a school. Nada. Except for the WeaponSmith. Will spent a couple hours playing games and simulations about bioweapons, pandemics, biology, genetics, mutations, and even the role of radiation in shaping life. There was even a biowar simulation that involved a weapon that interfered with fertility. *That's a long war. How long would it take a country to realize what was happening? How would they react?*

WB earned eight hundred XP. On his way out, he tried to quiz the WeaponSmith about an idea that popped into his head.

"Greetings, Sir Smith."

"Greetings, Master Seeker," the Smith replied.

"Is there a way to experiment with potions here in SPARK? Maybe create new ones? Advanced bioweapons?"

"I think, good sir, that you'll find that the First Strike Quest," the Smith gestured up the arcade, "might offer you some insight in that area."

"Thanks!" said WB. "I'll check it out."

First Strike turned out to be on the other side of the arcade. Will decided to stick to his plan and visit it on the way back down to the Hub, if he made it that far today.

After staring at Evolve for a few minutes, Will decided he wasn't ready to enter it again. He knew he and his parents eventually beat it, but he didn't feel prepared. He didn't want to go in until he knew he could crush it. Maybe find another Egg. *I'll go visit this Princess again.* The first time had been a bust.

As he was about to enter, he stopped. *I need to do my homework.*

He turned away and began to work his way back toward the Hub, visiting everything on the side of the arcade he'd ignored earlier. First Strike had consumed a couple hours with its experimentation and alchemy side quests, but by late afternoon, he was ready to visit the Princess again.

This version of the Princess was older than the one over in PreHistory. *Younger than me. Maybe twelve or thirteen.* Her gown was the same style as the younger princess but a deeper pink. The castle motif was the same—electricity still hadn't made it to the Evolve Arcade castle. The coat of arms remained, and torches illuminated the room. Instead of pacing, this Princess sat in a chair and arose as Will approached. Her intro was the same.

"Good." She looked right at him. "You're here."

Will waited expectantly.

"Pick a door." The Princess gestured to the wall.

WB pointed to the one on the right, and then followed the Princess through the door. He paused to wonder how they opened the doors. *Are they real and on some sensor, or are they virtual?*

As she had in the first arcade, the Princess knelt and began to sketch on the floor. One woman, three boys. Her drawing ability matured beyond stick figures, but was still not at a level Will would rate as *good.* As she sketched, she spoke:

"From the womb of one woman, three boys were born.
Not twins, not triplets, and loved without scorn.
Though one was fair, one dark, one's eyes gray as dust,
The woman who birthed them betrayed no one's trust.
On the same day, within the same hour, all arrived on the earth.
Can you explain this riddle of birth?"

Will almost laughed. Compared to the other riddles, this seemed simple. *Different fathers.* But caught himself before blurting it out, suddenly embarrassed to be talking about something like this with a Princess this young.

He thought a moment. *Well, she asked.*

The children were loved without scorn. WB thought if a woman was with three men, there would be some scorn and maybe a betrayal of trust. The woman would also have to have released three ova. He modified his response.

"The three boys are the product of any of a number of types of artificial insemination. Three different fathers, one woman to carry the babies. There may even be three separate genetic mothers."

The Princess jumped up and clapped. "Of course! I should have seen it. Thank you, Sir WB. You are a true knight!"

As before, Will exited to a trumpet fanfare, some nods, and a few "Congrats!" from passing players. Grinning, Will headed to lunch.

Four hundred XP! The Princesses and the Knowledge quests went hand-in-hand and were exponential. He was up two levels today and was now a Level 28. After lunch, he planned to hit the Civilization Rises Arcade and see if he couldn't do a repeat there.

He did. Eight hundred XP. Quick math said if he could knock out two Knowledge quests and two Princess quests a day, the seventh of each would bring him sixty-four hundred XP.

His enthusiasm tempered a bit upon exiting when Feral walked up to him wearing her Fumiyo avatar, and hissed, "This is your idea of keeping a low profile?"

She stomped away with her clients. WB realized as she left that he kind of liked her, even if she consistently bit his head off.

Her avatar wasn't what he expected. Fumiyo had large eyes and Elven features, but wore green leggings and boots—almost a Robin Hood look.

Is she always this angry? "Jeez," he muttered, as she stormed off. *Her real eyes are amazing, though.*

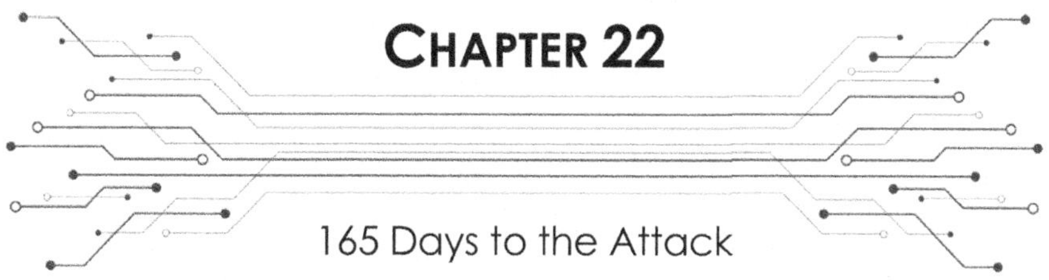

CHAPTER 22

165 Days to the Attack

Love me or hate me, both are in my favor. If you love me, I'll always be in your heart. If you hate me, I'll always be in your mind.
—Shakespeare

In Maputo, Sarnak began growing a beard. He hated long beards—they itched as they grew in, and made already-hot climates unbearable. But with shaping, it would alter his profile and make facial recognition difficult.

He scratched the lengthening scruff of his facial hair. He hated being back here, even more than the beard, but his employers seemed to consider it safer for all of them.

Sarnak scanned the bar as he waited. No sign of anyone following him. He checked his phone. *Time to go.* He left his half-empty, tepid Manica beer on the table. *Even the beer is bad here. How do you ruin beer?* He stood and walked to the main entrance, paused, and then doubled back and exited through the rear into an alley. The smell of urine, vomit, and stale beer assaulted his nostrils.

The blazing midafternoon sun produced an immediate sweat. Sarnak strode down the alley, pushed open a door and stepped into darkness once more. He pulled out his phone and used it to find his way through the darkened space. He pushed a second door open and was greeted with both light and air conditioning. He entered a nearly featureless room of white walls whose stains from the past bled through attempts to paint over them. The ceiling was of ancient acoustic tile that reminded the mercenary of his childhood schools in Kiev, stained by water leaks from above and splatter from below.

Four men sat around a metal table. Despite the brutal heat, they all wore dark suits and ties, and did not sweat. And despite their obviously Asian ancestry, the conversation would be held in English rather than the Portuguese common in Maputo. Despite the nature of the business, it was a business meeting.

One gestured to an empty seat, and Sarnak sat down. He recognized all four from previous encounters. Only two spoke. Sarnak decided they were North Koreans, even though they had never mentioned where they were from, nor mentioned their names. Their suits fit well enough, but were of inferior cloth. The other two wore suits that would have been appropriate for any corporate boardroom in Europe.

Odd—no Daesh are here.

"Our principal goal," Sarnak was told, "is the Data Core. Our inside asset confirms he can gain access. You will meet with him during your trip to surveil the target. He has been told to expect contact from you. The cover is that you are his distant cousin, Ragnar Severski. You are coming to America for your first visit. Evaluate this man as well. If you believe him unreliable, kill him immediately. Retrieve the laptop we have given him. It would be best if, after documenting his death, his body and house were burned. If you believe him sufficiently reliable, then arrange to meet with him during the attack. Once you have the Data Core, kill him."

"Understood," Sarnak replied.

The North Korean handed him a photo of the man, along with his contact information. The man's dark hair was a shade lighter than Sarnak's own, his nose more bulbous. *Distant cousins? Possible.*

The spokesman now slid a map across the table. "Your fighters and their leader have established a training camp. Meet them there."

Sarnak studied the map until he was certain he could find the way, and then passed it back across the table. *Let getting rid of that be their problem.*

"Have you reconsidered my request to be able to recruit my own team?" he said.

"We have. Unfortunately, we require ISIS—Daesh—be used for this event. Should any of them be captured or identified," the North Korean man shrugged, "it will point away from us, and the Americans will stop looking. An attack by Middle Easterners will be quickly attributed to Daesh. We are happy to both use them and to allow them to take all credit for the attack. There will be no further investigation."

Sarnak nodded. *This contact speaks English as an American would. How did he develop that facility? Has he lived there? Or is there a North Korean charm school where kidnapped and captured Americans teach them how to speak and act?*

"Who will be their leader?" Sarnak said. "Have the men fought against an armed, prepared enemy?"

Sarnak thought these were key ingredients of a successful operation, particularly if you wanted to survive it. He did.

"The man—Hashem—is their leader," replied the spokesman. "He is Afghani, but was infiltrated into Iraq at an early enough age to be able to join the Iraqi Army and be trained by Americans. When the time came, he led a small force against an American installation in Kandahar. Casualties were high on both sides, but Hashem and his men killed more Americans than they lost themselves. It is considered a great victory for Daesh. He is not to be underestimated. He is fervent in his hatred of America." Sarnak's employer slid a picture of Hashem across the ancient metal table. "Keep him on a short leash until you are certain of obtaining the Data Core, then you may let him do whatever he wishes. He wants fire, blood, and bodies. Once you have secured the Core, use his wanton slaughter of the Americans as a cover for your escape." The speaker gave the slightest of smiles.

Sarnak had no qualms about killing—it was his job—but this was different. In that slight smile, he saw hatred—a hatred so profound that it that cared nothing about innocence or bystanders. Hatred helped people kill, Sarnak knew, but it also led them to make mistakes.

His employers wanted America to see suffering, pain, and death. *I must be careful to make sure that my death is not among them.*

He resolved to keep a close eye on Hashem—particularly when they got to SPARK.

– 1 1 0 1 0 0 1 0 –

Two hours later, Sarnak met the leader of the Daesh who would be part of the SPARK attack. Sarnak was tired. The day had been long, and the trip hot.

The Daesh leader led him around the small camp and eventually showed him where he would sleep.

"Shab Bhakair, Hashish," Sarnak said, trying to wish his guide a good night.

Hashem paused and glared at Sarnak.

"I am Hashem. Not Hashish. Do not make that mistake again."

Sarnak let it go. It was his mistake. Still, he was impressed. *Not your typical Daesh, ready-to-blow-himself-up fighter.*

After dinner one night, and after the North Koreans left, Hashem went on a rant:

"My family was killed by a drone strike. One moment they were peacefully assembled in the village. And the next, all dead. Killed by the Americans. There was no chance to see them. To tell them goodbye."

That evening, they walked the perimeter of the training compound—hastily strung fencing enclosing a few huts. A generator growled continuously, providing one hut with power. As they walked, Hashem proudly proclaimed his father wore the black turban of the Taliban and threw acid on little girls who dared to attend school.

Sarnak kept his thoughts to himself. *Hashem has training, but he is a zealot. And zealots are happy to have you die along with them.*

Sarnak had no intention of dying on this job. He wanted to die of old age.

They worked out plans for a week, and then Sarnak left. Back to Budapest for another clean identity.

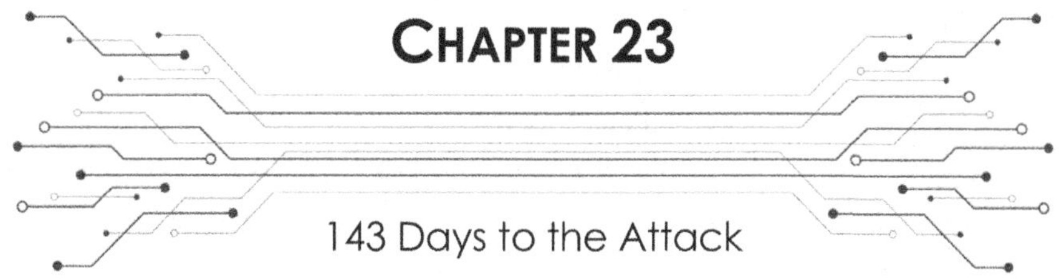

CHAPTER 23

143 Days to the Attack

During the day, memories could be held at bay,
but at night, dreams became the devil's own accomplices.
—Sharon Kay Penman, The Reckoning

ShaChri Patel was awakened by what sounded like a scuffle—shoes scuffing on cement, low moans, and incoherent words. She rolled into a crouch and scanned the area. The other members of the Pod were still asleep.

She pinpointed the sound. It was WB. Again.

Feral picked her way around the sleepers and crept over to where Peek Boy was sleeping—or supposed to be sleeping. *I've got to stop thinking of him like that. He really is a nice guy.*

He was thrashing in his sleep, legs and arms twitching as if his sleep-self was fully engaged in combat.

She squatted down next to him. *I don't think you're supposed to wake up people when they're having nightmares.* She chewed on her thumbnail. *This is two nights in a row.*

She glanced over her shoulder. Some other Pod members were stirring. *He's going to wake everybody up. Frack it.*

She reached out and gently put her hand on his outstretched palm. He seized it, squeezing tight. His motions now tugged her hand along with it. *What the heck?*

Slowly, he quieted and became motionless. Feral relaxed and was deciding how best to reclaim her hand, when his eyes opened. She saw confusion in his eyes before recognition registered.

"Feral?" His voice was hoarse.

"Yeah. Can I have my hand back?"

Will followed her gaze to his hand, where he still held hers. He let go and flinched backward.

"Why were you holding my hand?"

ShaChri flushed and jerked her hand back.

"I wasn't. You were having a nightmare. I was just trying to calm you down, and you grabbed my hand."

He narrowed his eyes. Looked like he didn't believe her.

She stood and took a step back.

"What were you dreaming about?" she said.

She rarely remembered her own dreams, but knew that she'd had nightmares for about a month after Mall of America.

He rubbed his eyes and stared at her as if debating whether he was going to say anything.

"C'mon," she whispered, gesturing for him to get up. "Let's take a walk."

WB scooted out from under the piping and stood, stretching.

"Might as well," he whispered back. "I'm probably done sleeping for tonight."

Feral looked at her phone. 5:10. She started walking and threw a look over her shoulder to make sure he was following. He was.

When they were out of earshot, he said, "Where are we going?"

She looked back. "Breakfast. It's late enough that the cafeteria should be empty—on auto mode."

He nodded.

Feral led them through the labyrinth of pipes and corridors.

"We'll go to the one near Orcland. That way, we can just flow out to the east employee lot. That's the way we've gone out since we almost ran into Bull."

WB was still learning his way around the Underground City, and Feral wanted to keep him oriented.

"Okay," he replied.

The cafeteria was deserted, as expected.

"Grab and go?" WB said.

"Yeah. I'll show you a place I like to go."

They loaded up reusable containers with an assortment from the buffet. Feral noticed that WB seemed to go heavy on the meat and potatoes.

They were in and out in less than two minutes, and Feral once again led them through the Underground.

She paused at an intersection. "Know where we are?"

"Well..." He looked around, then pointed at a red pipe. "That fire pipe has an arrow with a seven on it pointing left, and a one pointing right. So we're somewhere between Mars and KT Crossing."

"Which way is the Rim?" she said.

WB pointed.

Feral nodded. "You're picking this up pretty fast. I think Mellew still gets turned around sometimes, and she's been here three months."

That sounded bitchy. I know he likes her. All the boys do. Frack.

She started walking again. "How do you know it's a fire pipe? 'Cause it's red?"

"Yeah. My dad was an engineer. He loved telling me little chunks of trivia like that."

They whispered as they worked their way toward the rim.

"Hey, it smells like a swimming pool," WB said.

"No such luck," said Feral. "But you're right about the water. We're almost there."

Another turn, and then Feral cautiously opened a door, and the tinkling of flowing water greeted them. They climbed a short set of stairs, crept past a couple fixtures, and found themselves on the concrete banks of an artificial river. It was dim, although upstream they could see some lights.

"Is this..."

"Yep, we're inside Tiny Universe." She sat and pulled off her shoes, and put her feet in the water.

WB followed suit. "I have bad memories of this place."

Feral laughed quietly. "This is supposed to be the most peaceful place in the whole park. How can you have bad memories?"

"When I was here as a kid," WB kicked his feet in the gently flowing water, "I kept taking my ARGs off and then put them back on. I was telling my folks what was real and what was virtual."

"I think I know where this is going," Feral said. "Did you decorate the boat?"

"No." WB shook his head. "I made it all the way out of the ride and then yakked all over the sidewalk by the benches. I felt instantly better, but SPARK had us talk to a doctor anyway."

"I tell my clients to leave their ARGs on, except for when we break for lunch."

"Good plan."

They sat quietly for a few minutes.

"What's with the nightmares?" Feral said.

WB turned to look at her.

He's got nice eyes. Not dark brown like mine. More like smoky topaz, bordering on hazel. She flicked her gaze back and forth between his eyes.

He tried to follow her focus, switching his eyes. He got out of sync and gave up, laughing.

"Stop it." Feral playfully pushed his shoulder.

"I was just trying to keep up with you." He was still laughing.

"You're supposed to be telling me about nightmares," she said.

WB got more serious. "They follow a pattern. Never identical, but the same theme?"

Feral nodded her understanding.

"I'm happy," he said. "Lots of times, I'm home with my folks. Then it gets dark, and I'm alone. Noises start—faint at first. Sometimes they're coming from one direction. Sometimes all around me. Scratching in the darkness, getting closer. I see red eyes glowing in the darkness. I'll try to get away, but I can't." He shuddered.

Feral reached out and put her hand on his. Like earlier, her touch seems to help.

"Monsters?" she said. *Dude's definitely in the wrong place if he has bad dreams about monsters.*

"No." He started to say something else, but stopped. "No. Maybe." He looked away from her. "Just…evil."

He seemed to fade away.

Mom always said the eyes are the window to the soul. As she watched WB, it was as if his soul had turned away and decided to look somewhere else. *Inside?*

Other members of the Pod had commented on it—how WB zoned out. Last night, it happened as they sat around talking before going to sleep.

Fantom said, "And Elvis has left the building."

Feral didn't get the reference, but Fantom laughed at his own joke.

She let WB sit like that for a couple minutes. Then lights began clicking on upstream.

"WB," she whispered. "WB," louder. She shook his shoulder.

He was back. "Hmm?"

"We gotta go!" she hissed, and stood into a crouch.

She grabbed her shoes and lunch tote.

"C'mon!" She grabbed his arm and pulled him along.

Down the stairs, into the access corridor. They paused to put their shoes on.

"Hey!" The voice came from Hubward.

"Run!" Feral took off along the Rim, racing toward Mars.

She could hear WB running just behind her. Farther back, the man yelled again.

"Hey, you kids! Stop! You can't be down here."

Feral raced through the corridors, knowing that the general confusion of the layout around Mars would help them.

The man was falling farther behind. She tried a couple doors before finding one that was open. She pulled WB in behind her and closed the door quietly. The room was dark. The space felt large.

"Where…"

She put a finger to his lips. "Shh."

She strained to hear any sounds of pursuit. Nothing.

Cautiously, she took a few more steps deeper into the darkness. Feral realized that she was holding WB's hand, and let it go. *What am I doing?*

She pulled out her phone and used it to illuminate the area around them. Metal catwalks passed overhead. A short fence blocked a ledge to the floor below.

"This must be the support structure for Mars," WB said.

"Can't be. We'd see the whole arena—all the way to the canyon floor."

WB shook his head. "No. We're inside the footprint of the quest, but outside the playing area."

"What are you talking about?"

"Okay." WB seemed excited by the idea. "Think of Mars as an upside down wedding cake—bigger and wider at the top, then stair-stepping in, getting narrower toward the bottom, the canyon floor." He gestured with his hands, starting them above his head and wide apart, then bringing them closer together as he brought them down.

"Yeah, but why can't we see the canyon floor?" she said.

"I think there's too much stuff in the way—all the guts of Mars. The stuff that they need to make it run? In a real canyon, we'd be buried in the rock walls right now. Here, we're just in the support structure."

Feral pictured it in her mind. "Okay, makes sense. If you have an upside down wedding cake, you need something to hold the layers up. Otherwise, it'd just collapse." She looked at the floor. "There's some sand and dust here." She drew a line in it with her shoe. "Not deep. Just like they haven't cleaned in here for a while."

WB nodded, looking around. He walked over to the short fence and tugged on it.

"Sturdy."

"Uh, yeah, gotta be. It's holding up an entire planet." She smiled.

He grinned back at her.

She looked at her phone. "Okay. Babysitting you took longer than I thought. We've missed shift change."

"Babysitting?"

"Yeah. I wasn't the one having nightmares."

Emotions seemed to chase themselves across his face before he nodded.

"Fair enough," he replied. "What now?"

"Now, you wait. In an hour, things will settle down again, and you can sneak out the Orcland exit. You'll have to follow someone who's leaving. When they badge out, get the door before it closes. Then you're home free."

"What do you mean, *you wait*. What are you going to do?"

"I've got clients. I've got to risk going now."

WB nodded. "Okay."

"Worst case, just hunker down and wait. I'll either see you in the park, or back at the Pod tonight." She slipped out the door and pulled it closed behind her.

As she made her way out of the Underground City, she realized, *I just left someone who has nightmares about the dark, in absolute darkness.*

– 1 1 0 1 0 0 1 0 –

Will sat in the darkness, thinking. Darkness didn't bother him as long as he was awake.

He thought about the morning. *She held my hand. She held my hand when I slept and said that I got quiet. She. Held. My. Hand. Why? Does she like me?*

Other than his parents, nobody had ever held his hand. He put it alongside another mystery. *Mellew is cheerleader beautiful. Bubbly. Bouncy. Feral is different. And so intense.* To have her attention focused on him was terrifying.

He tried to think about the Princesses, his current obsession, but ended up thinking about Feral in her anime elf avatar.

I need to get out of here.

He was almost to the exit when he remembered his hat. He snuck back and retrieved it from where he had left it in the night before. With his orange locks safety camouflaged by an orange baseball hat, Will exited the Underground City.

– 1 1 0 1 0 0 1 0 –

"Good morning, WB."

"Good morning, Janne." *She never denies it.*

"Getting a later start this morning? Oversleep?"

"Nah, just the opposite, actually. I was talking with Feral, and we lost track of time."

"Ah."

Well, that's kind of enigmatic. What does an AI mean when she says, "Ah?"

He was about to ask, when she spoke up again.

"Using another free day, I assume?" All business now.

"Yes."

Janne leaned forward and propped her chin on her hands, palms down, fingers interlaced. *That's a new pose.*

"You've been visiting the Princess near Survive a lot lately. How's that going?"

"You ought to know," he retorted. *Is she just making conversation?*

Janne gave him a serene smile and a small shrug.

"They are notoriously difficult," she said.

"Maybe I ought to just play today."

Janne nodded. "HVH sometimes says that the best way to solve a difficult problem is to turn it over to your subconscious. Ignore it for a while."

"Huh."

They had arrived at the Hub. She wished him a good day at SPARK, and WB emerged with a new plan for the day.

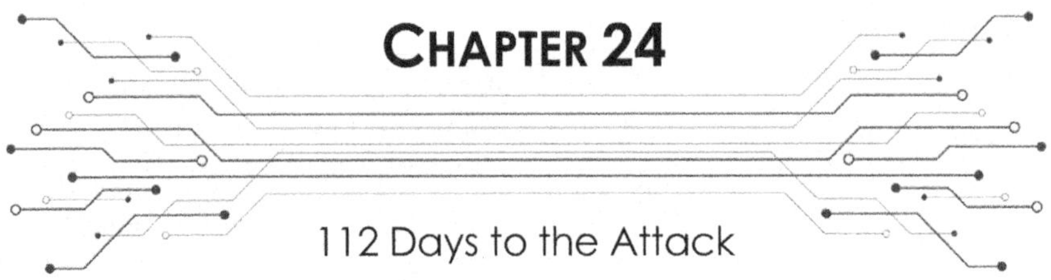

Chapter 24

112 Days to the Attack

"Scientific discovery consists of seeing what everyone else has seen, but thinking what no one else has thought."
—Chemist Albert Szent-Györgyi

Over the next month, life in the Pod became routine. He was tutored in the ways of the Underground by all of the members. Even Fantom helped. Although mostly, he seemed snotty, borderline hostile.

"I think he's a little jealous," Mellew told him, when he asked about it.

She gave him a little smile and patted him on the arm.

"Don't worry about it."

WB didn't get it, but kept his distance. He was spending more and more time with Feral, and she had returned his knife the evening after their talk at Tiny Universe. Although she seemed willing to spend time with him, she seemed equally primed to break his nose or argue with him.

WB's estimation that he'd be able to knock out all of the Princesses and any Knowledge quests within seven days was grossly optimistic. *The first three were quick, maybe flukes.* The last four took him an average of three days—*three freaking days*—each to solve. *No wonder the Weaponsmith had said that it was costly and time consuming.*

He came to the conclusion that the riddles leveled up either with his Brains stat, or the number of Princess Quests he'd completed. It was an obsession. He *needed* to finish this quest.

Why did my mom quote the Princesses? When she wrote, "Find me. Save me," was she talking about herself? Why didn't either his mom or dad put more information in their letters? If you're going to go through the trouble of writing a letter that won't be read until after you die, why skimp on content?

"A little more detail would have been appreciated," he muttered.

"What?" Feral said.

They'd just finished raiding Lost and Found for some new clothes. WB came away with a CovIdiots T-Shirt he thought would fit, and Feral scored some socks.

He flushed. "Sorry. I was thinking out loud."

She snorted. "That's an improvement. Sometimes you don't even *talk* out loud. So if you start thinking out loud, maybe we'll understand the things you actually *say* out loud."

"Hey, I—"

"Dude. Kidding." She paused. "What were you thinking about. 'Cause I was thinking, *Who loses socks at a theme park?*"

"Hah! And what about cargo shorts? Does somebody just turn around suddenly and ask, *Where'd my pants go?*"

"The magic of SPARK—you could walk around naked and no one would know—as long as everyone kept their ARGs on." She threw a pointed look at WB.

He held up his hands in surrender. "In my defense, if I hadn't peeked you, I might never have met you."

Feral stopped pawing through the mounds of lost clothing and stared at him.

"What? What do you mean?"

She narrowed her eyes, and WB blushed under the strength of her full attention.

"I guess I would have found the Pod eventually. It's, uh…well, I'm just really glad that I met you."

Feral walked slowly over to him until she stood directly in front of him. Her eyes flicked their focus back and forth between his. WB laughed nervously and looked away. She reached up and put her hand on his chin, turning his face back towards hers.

"Are you flirting with me?" She said it quietly, with an intensity that made WB feel as if he were standing in a mine field.

He met her gaze. "Yes."

She continued to stare at him with eyes so dark they looked ebony.

Feral dropped her hand and turned away, her pony tail spinning. She walked back to the bin of girls' clothes and began looking again.

"Okay." She nodded once.

WB didn't realize he'd been holding his breath, until now. He let it out and felt his body relax.

"Okay?" *What does that mean?* He took a step toward her. *What now?*

"You deflected my question," she said. "A minute ago, you said something about wanting more detail. Then you said you were thinking out loud. Then you started flirting."

She gave him a slight smile, and Will felt warm again.

"What were you thinking about?" she said.

It took him a minute to trace back his thoughts.

"My mom and dad," he replied.

"Oh."

Pod protocol was to let these conversations drop. If the one that brought it up chose to pursue the discussion, fine.

WB didn't. They lapsed back into silence.

As they walked through the maze of corridors to the Pod's current camp near The Keep, Feral said, "Want to check out the library?"

"You mean go into Barstow?"

"No, dufus." She rolled her eyes. "I mean the one here in the Underground."

"Take me there immediately. You have no idea how much I've missed reading."

"If you were willing to join the twenty-first century and get a phone, you could read on it, like I do."

They'd talked about it before. Will figured enough time had passed that it would be safe. He just didn't have the money to spend.

Feral showed him to the large conference room that had been converted to a free library. Book cases lined the walls, and piles of books covered the chairs. The large meeting table had been converted to a horizontal bookshelf, with rows of books covering it, spines up.

He walked away with a vintage Heinlein—*Glory Road*—and Feral carried off something that looked vampire-esque, from the cover.

– 1 1 0 1 0 0 1 0 –

Will woke the next morning, feeling elated. He'd fallen asleep, pondering the meaning of "*Okay*." He decided that it meant that if he flirted, she wouldn't automatically shut him down or rearrange his face. It felt like the biggest step forward since she'd returned his knife.

The Pod was stirring. He slipped the KA-BAR into his backpack and hid the pack in the shadows of a pipe. He stretched and then walked over to where Feral was pulling on her shoes.

"Morning," he greeted the group, and got mainly grunts in return.

Feral looked up at him. "What's with the dopey grin?"

WB had learned that she was not a morning person.

"Just feeling optimistic. Feeling like it's a portentous day."

That earned him an eye roll from Feral.

"Portentous?" said Mellew. "Now there's an SAT vocab word."

Over the last month, WB had gotten to know Mellew better. *She's the Golden Retriever of the Pod—always happy, always ready to go for a walk.*

His initial attraction to her had cooled, completely overwhelmed by the dark intensity of Feral Daughter. *She's a force of nature.*

As much as she pissed him off, he felt drawn to her. There was a mystery to her—like the Princesses. A mystery he yearned to solve.

"I think we've lost him." He heard Feral's voice distantly.

"Where do you think he goes?" Mellew said.

WB felt Mellew's gentle touch on his arm, and he forced himself back to reality, embarrassed.

"No," he said. "Nope. I'm here."

"Well, you weren't a minute ago." Feral tugged at his arm. "C'mon."

When they had safely exited, she said, "What did you mean by *portentous*? You have a dream or something?"

"No. At least, not that I remember. It's just that I feel like the planets are aligning." He stopped. "Or maybe it's that I'm just now realizing that there are multiple planets, because every other time I've looked, they've *been* aligned."

Feral hugged herself in the morning chill and shook her head.

"I think you spend too much time with Princesses. You're starting to talk in riddles. You working today? Going into Barstow?"

Two days out of every three, Will rode the first bus into Barstow. He was almost out of free days, and had been thinking he'd have to leave the Pod, when Hunter gave him the scoop. He remembered the conversation:

"Ride in early. On the back side of the bus terminal, there's a place where guys hang out, looking for work. Don't push it, but stand off to the side. Let the regulars go first, or wait for one of the bosses to pick you. Once they know that you're a hard worker, they'll pick you routinely."

"Do they pay every day?" Will said.

"Cash," said Hunter. "Do you speak any other languages?"

"High school Spanish, and some Korean."

"Anything helps. And watch your back."

WB looked into Feral's eyes, enthralled by the sparkling specks of gold within the deep brown.

"Not today," he replied. "I'm buying entry."

The first bus pulled up, and Feral walked over to meet her clients.

"Don't waste it all on Princesses," she called over her shoulder.

"Hey, want to meet at Cluesades last hour?" Will said.

Last hour was the hour prior to closing. UGs were generally let loose by their clients and had free time.

Feral stopped and looked at him. "Are you seriously asking me to quest with you?"

He shrugged. "It's just Cluesades."

She seemed to mull it over.

"Okay." She turned away.

His heart soared.

Inside SPARK, WB hurried up the Modern Times Arcade. Along the way, he waved at or greeted the employees he'd gotten to know. Soon, he stood at the entrance to this arcade's Princess Quest. He'd successfully completed six.

Today's the day. He walked in.

As castles went, this was more Buckingham Palace than the Rock of Cashel. Security was provided by electronic means rather than a hill and high walls.

He entered a modern office where a traditionally garbed Princess sat behind a desk, wearing a gown that he'd come to describe as lipstick red. She was a power executive of the twenty-first century.

"Good. You're here."

And so it began.

Three tries. Three failures before SPARK had even been open an hour.

WB leaned against a wall with his eyes closed. *Dang it. I thought I'd get it today. What am I missing?*

"WB, are you okay?"

He opened his eyes and saw Feral wearing her Flighty Damsel avatar.

He smiled. "It's all good now."

"No, it's not. My clients think there's something wrong with you. You can't just hang around like this. It's creepy."

Will flushed and nodded. "I'm just thinking."

"Duh. Just try not to do it where you freak out the guests." Feral walked away.

She looks so much more feminine in that avatar. Too many princesses.

WB pushed himself off the wall and strolled over to KT Crossing Plaza and the Orbital Defense shooting gallery. Blasting a few meteoroids always helped him clear his mind and regain his focus. He'd gotten much better at the game and could now save the Earth six times out of every ten. As dismal as that was, it put him in the Top 100 scores.

Mid-game he had an epiphany. He was only paying attention to the sun's influence. It's actually a multi-body problem. The realization came too late to save that game, but when he played a second time, he saved Earth seven times and leapt into fifty-seventh on the leaderboard.

He emerged with an enormous smile on his face. *It's comprehensive! You have to see the whole field to win.*

Will Kwan stopped in his tracks. It's comprehensive. He felt an episode coming on, and forced his mind off the train of thought until he found a bench. Then he sat and let his mind race.

When he opened his eyes, he wasn't sure how much time had passed, but he felt the conclusion was solid: earlier Princesses relied only on a bedrock understanding of that arcade's specialty. The seventh Princess was comprehensive—it required him to pull in knowledge from all six previous encounters to solve the riddle. He saw a path to solving all three of the puzzles he'd been given that morning.

WB stood and ran back to the Modern Times Princess.

"This is a multi-factor problem," he said to the Lipstick Princess, as she sat behind her desk, tapping a stylus on the surface, accompanying a tune only she heard. "Think about epoxy: the resins are much less useful without the hardeners to speed the reaction. Or the COVID-19/Melt connection: COVID-19 had low lethality, but tremendous transmissivity. It created antigens that turned out to be the perfect binding site for Melt. In the grand scheme, neither was all that deadly. But together, their lethality was formidable. Your problem is similar: low employment and low access to distractions or pastimes is creating social unrest. So you think bread and circuses are the answer."

Lipstick Princess stopped tapping her stylus.

"Is that your answer?"

WB grinned. "Nope. I'm just getting started. Your problem is more like the general and the castle. Do you know the story?" *She has to. I learned it here.*

She leaned back in her chair. "Why don't you explain it?"

"A general wants to capture a castle, but the roads are all mined. Small groups can make it through safely, but large forces will set off the mines. So he splits his forces and sends smaller groups down all the roads to the castle. They regroup at the castle and capture it."

"Go on," she said.

"You have to attack your problem from all the roads. Not just the one you're most comfortable with."

"How do you propose we do this?"

"Okay, let's start from the PreHistory Arcade. Moons can become tidally locked…"

WB was talking as fast as he was thinking, pulling analogies and single-factor solutions from all of the arcades. Lipstick Princess kept nodding.

"So the physical, biological, psychological, technological, and even social aspects become your roads to the castle." WB wound up his proposed solution.

His brain was buzzing with the idea. It felt right. He'd been talking a long time, trying to think of something he'd learned from the six previous Princess quests, and how it could factor into a solution for Number Seven, who sat in front of him, fingers steepled.

Finally, she rose from behind the desk.

"Of course! Why didn't I think of it? WonderBoy, you are a true Seeker. Find me. Save me."

His ARGs lit up as he exited.

Modern Times Princess Complete

6400 XP

Level Up!

He watched the messages scroll through his ARGs. Elation and anticipation coursed through his body. *This is it. Number Seven!*

Trumpets played as he exited. A few guests congratulated him. After that, nothing.

After finishing the seventh Princess Quest, Will expected major fanfare. *What the heck? Why isn't she skipping off to rejoin her family, or go marry her handsome prince or something? Why still, "Find me. Save me?"*

Will exited to the plaza for The City—a massive major quest that took up the entire plaza. Almost immediately, he was approached by a quest giver.

"Hey, man, can you help me out? My daughter's gone missing."

Will ignored him and headed along the Rim, past Mars, and into the small, quiet space near Tiny Universe. He sat on one of the benches with his back to the mosaic tile that decorated the boundary wall.

Something's not right. Why no "Princess Quest Complete" message? They're all connected. Shouldn't there be a final "Hey, you did it!" message? Maybe I have to do them in order.

He stood and headed over to KT Crossing.

Three hours later, he'd run through all seven Princesses again, this time in chronological order. Still nothing.

It was getting late. He went back to the shooting arcade in War on Mars Plaza, and spent some time blasting meteors—it was a good distraction, and still one of his favorite games in SPARK.

When he emerged, he felt better, and punted the problem to his subconscious for processing.

The nightly parade was about to start, and guests crowded along the route. That was his cue to go meet Feral.

– 1 1 0 1 0 0 1 0 –

"Hey, WB!"

"Hey, Feral. Good day?"

She was back in her ninja avatar. *Really appropriate for her. Lethal and mysterious.*

"Yeah, but not as good as yours," she replied. "You've jumped at least two levels."

"Yep." He tried not to sound smug.

It was hard to read Feral in this avatar, when all he could see was her eyes.

"A couple breakthroughs," he said. "We can talk about it later. Ready for Cluesades?"

– 1 1 0 1 0 0 1 0 –

An hour later, they exited Cluesades a thousand XP better than when they entered. WB's smugness was gone. He had expected to be significantly better at puzzles than Feral. He wasn't.

"You think weird," she said, as they sawed off their wristbands and ditched their gear.

"Me? I was thinking the same thing about you."

"Well, I guess it makes sense that if someone is as delusional as you, they might think they're the normal one and everyone else is weird."

"Hey!" *Feral has a point. Does everyone think they're normal, and the rest of the world is messed up?*

He started to fall down a mental rabbit hole.

"No." She shook his arm. "Not going to let you fade out on me."

They slipped through an unmarked door and headed to the Pod. She sat next to him, close enough that their shoulders touched. She was warm. *Feels nice.*

He was still confused about their relationship. They hung out a lot, and he definitely liked her, but didn't know what to do next.

"Seriously, though." She frowned. "That was some excellent XP for just an hour in Cluesades. Maybe your *weird* and my *normal* are a good puzzle team."

He looked sideways at her. "Yep. Maybe just a good team. Period."

She snorted. "A little cheesy there."

Feral seemed to have forgotten to ask about his breakthrough, and he was content not to share his frustration.

"Hey, I'm going into town tomorrow," she said. "I need some supplies. Want to join?"

"Absolutely." *Spend a whole day with Feral? Outside SPARK? Perfect!*

"Great." She stood back up and used his shoulder for leverage. "I'm going to go shower. See ya."

– 11010010 –

They wandered around town and ate lunch from a place that sold outstanding street tacos.

"Okay, I need to do some stuff on my own. Girl stuff." Feral did that thing where she flicked her eyes back and forth between his until he nodded his understanding.

"Okay," he replied. "Bus at two?"

"Yes. Don't be late. And don't make me come find you. And get a haircut."

"All right, all right. Jeez." He held up his hands, but smiled as he did it, and was rewarded with a radiant smile from her. *In natural sunlight, with no avatar, she almost glows. Like a candle shining through amber.*

Feral turned away, ponytail flipping as she did. He watched her walk away, happy that it wasn't considered peeking outside of SPARK.

He turned and headed to the library, where he killed an hour unsuccessfully looking for any information about the Princess ending. Nothing but the general griping about their existence and difficulty.

He gave up. Closed his browser windows, wiped the history—out of habit—and left the library after thanking the ladies who worked there. He then went looking for someone to tame his hair. There was a place near the Bullseye store. He emerged fifteen dollars poorer, but with a decent fade leading to a short clip on top.

Will got to the bus terminal before Feral. Being in the Pod had taught him a lot of things. While he waited, he watched the whole process from a distance. He could pick out Security people easily now. He watched them as they watched the crowd. Before, they always seemed to blend in. Now, he saw the tells. Adults—very fit adults—either alone, or working in pairs. They never had any kids, and almost never got on a bus. Once you spotted them, it was easy to see their patterns.

"Whoa, that's a change," Feral said from behind him. "I almost didn't recognize you."

"Too short?"

She stood in front of him and ran one hand over the side of his head, and then gently turned his head back and forth by tugging on his chin.

"No," she replied. "It's nice. You've got a good-shaped head. It makes you look older. Less sketchy."

He blushed. *Feral looks different. It's her hair.*

Feral's hair hung freely. No ponytail. The afternoon sun made him realize that her hair wasn't simply black. It was onyx. Like the cuts of a gem, her hair refracted and reflected the sunlight in a myriad of colors as different from simply *black* as the ocean was from simply being *wet*.

"New clothes?" he said.

"Yeah. They're not too girly are they?"

At SPARK, she wore bike shorts and a loose-fitting T-shirt that hung down to her thighs. Now, she sported some stretchy black pants that smoothed out the well-defined muscles in her legs, and a form-fitting top of a dusky red that reminded Will of Mars. Still an appropriate outfit for questing, but was far more feminine and accentuated her figure. He wanted to say, *Wow!*, but knew that would lead to trouble. *Is she wearing makeup?*

"No," he replied. "Looks nice." *I wish I had sunglasses that hid my eyes.*

Feral did the eye thing again, as if attempting to verify that he was being honest, then dug into her bag.

She tossed him a burner phone. "Welcome back to the twenty-first century. Now you won't have to go to some stupid library to check the net. God," she sighed, "how archaic."

"Yeah, but..."

"Jeez, I get it. We're all runaways. You're just one of the few who is still worried about people looking for him. Now you can be just as anonymous as the next stalker."

"Thanks." He stuffed the phone in his pocket, and they boarded the bus back to SPARK. "What now?"

"I figure we can try to get a late guiding gig. You think you're up for that?"

"I dunno. I'd be happy to tag along if you got hired."

"You and your Princesses," she said, exasperated. "You're burning a lot of park time. Aren't you running out of money?"

"Getting close," Will muttered.

For the last month, he'd been coming in to town at least twice a week to work odd jobs—mowing lawns, working at a car wash that paid him in cash every day, even helping out lugging cases of beer in and out of the store room at the Stumble. It helped, but his cash was nearly gone, and he'd used up all the gift cards he got for the Mars Egg. He had two free days left.

"What if nobody hires us?" he said. *How the heck am I supposed to guide? I haven't even conquered the majors yet.*

"We hang out until four," she said, "when admission drops to half-price, and buy our way back in."

"Good plan."

He'd discovered the discount after his second trip into Barstow for work.

"You're still such a noob." She shook her head.

As the bus pulled out, WB said, "Why don't the trains just have a stop at SPARK? I mean, they run between LA and Vegas, and out to the Barstow airport. Why not out to SPARK?"

Feral looked at him. "Security."

"Security?"

"Yeah. Think like Bull. I griped to him about it once. He said every time you make people move or change modes of transportation, it's a chance to watch them. Check them for suspicious behavior. Scan their bags and backpacks. Look for somebody who's wearing a coat on a warm day. See somebody sweat in an air-conditioned bus. That's also why you have to ride with Janne on the people mover before you get to the Hub. One more look."

Will nodded. After the war and the Mall of America massacre, people mostly stopped griping about security measures. Mostly.

"Yeah," he said, "I guess technology has made it easier to check and scan people without them even knowing."

"Unfortunately, too little, too late." Her tone held anguish, not the sarcasm he expected.

Will nodded. "What do you mean?"

She had never told him her story. It tumbled forth. Once begun, it was as unstoppable as the avalanche on Mars.

"It was Black Friday, so the mall was packed. I told my mom there was no way I wanted to go, so she badgered my dad into going with her. They dropped me off at my MMA gym and said they'd pick me up in a couple of hours. I figured that meant two, but didn't really start worrying until more than three hours passed. Then somebody came in and said there'd been some sort of explosion at the mall."

Will nodded. He knew what happened. There had actually been ten. Ten suicide bombers. They choreographed the whole thing.

Feral's voice got quiet, and Will leaned closer to hear her. Close enough to smell the shampoo she'd used.

"I tried calling my mom first." She turned her phone over and over in her hands.

Will heard a sniff. Feral's hand came up and wiped away a tear.

"Then my dad, 'cause my mom never hears her phone. But my dad always, always answers." She pounded her fist on her thigh and took a deep, shuddery breath. "Then my mom again. Finally, I called my Aunt Ardi."

Will put his arm around her and pulled her closer.

"I'm sorry."

He couldn't think of anything else to say. It felt completely inadequate.

"When she came and got me, they said I was pounding the heavy bag. My hands were bloody, but I wouldn't stop. I don't remember that." Feral pressed her face against Will's shoulder. "It took three days for them to sort through the dead. My dad was killed by some falling debris." She shook her head. "They think my mom got trampled."

Her voice had risen, and people on the bus turned to look, then quickly turned away. Someone handed Will some tissues. He passed them on to Feral, who was sobbing now. She didn't make a sound except for occasionally gulping air, but Will could feel her body quaking. Her shoulders heaved. Will didn't know what to do or say, but he wrapped his arms around her and whispered, "I'm sorry," over and over. He wanted to hug away her pain and then find and hurt those who had hurt her.

As the bus stopped, her hands unclenched from his shirt, and her shaking stopped. They were the last off the bus.

"You okay, miss?" the driver said.

Feral nodded and stepped to the curb.

She and Will stood by the entrance to SPARK. He wrapped his arms around her, trying to shield her from the ache of the past. Streams of people passed them by, parting and then rejoining, leaving Will and Feral an island in their midst.

"I'm okay," Feral whispered to Will's chest. "I'm okay."

He relaxed his hug and stepped back slightly. *She looks like a little girl now. All the toughness is gone.*

"If you tell anyone I was crying, I'll break your nose."

Will nodded and almost laughed. *That didn't last long.*

He still didn't know her real name.

The two hung around the SPARK entrance, trying unsuccessfully to drum up a guide gig. At this time of day, most of the entrants were heading for the adults-only section of the park, and a couple of underage guides weren't going to do them any good.

"What do you think goes on there?" WB said.

"Probably the same as in any bar you see on vid." Feral stuck a pose, the back of one hand to her forehead, the other hand to her chest, head tilted back, eyes closed. "Searching for their true love, and just trying to make it through this unfair world," she said with the feigned accent of a debutante.

WB didn't really know what to say, so he nodded. Feral looked at him and punched him in the arm.

"Heck no," she said. "Well, maybe some. Mostly, I think they want to get their drink on with a bunch of hot-looking avatars, and then leave without ever really knowing or seeing who they've been with." She looked into WB's widened eyes. "Hey, it's not like I *know*. It's just, I've heard enough from guests that want me to watch their kids for an hour or two, to figure out what goes on behind the green door."

Finally, when it was time for half-priced entry, they gave up and headed into SPARK.

"Welcome back, ShaChri. Welcome back, Will," Janne intoned, as they entered the people mover.

The two Pod members looked at each other in surprise.

ShaChri—that's a cool name.

Feral was effusive. “Hi, Janne!”

WB gave her a more subdued, “Hey, Janne.”

“No customers today?” the AI said.

“Nah,” Feral replied. “Ran into town. Now it’s just lonely singles coming in. Nobody needs a guide.”

Janne turned to WB. “Have you begun guiding now?”

Will shook his head. “I don’t think I’m ready yet.”

Feral looked surprised. “Why? You’re a Level Thirty-Eight. You’ve probably been through all the majors at least a couple times. C’mon, you can do it.”

Dang. He’d been trying to avoid this conversation with the Pod.

He turned to Feral with a sigh. “Actually, I’ve only really been through three of them: KT, Ascent, and Mars. Mars is the only one I’ve been through since my parents died.”

A series of expressions flowed over Feral’s face.

“How…how, by the Seven Realms of SPARK, did you ever get to Level Thirty-Eight?”

Janne said, “Ready for your gear?”

“Yeah,” Feral snapped, and poked WB in the chest. “You owe me an answer.”

Will nodded, realizing Feral’s previous honesty came with some expectations in return.

“I’m a Seeker,” he blurted.

“A Seeker,” Feral said, with confused anger as she tugged on her haptics. “What the heck is a Seeker?”

“A Seeker,” Janne said, “is an unpublished but playable class of character who seeks knowledge and wisdom.”

“What, like a Monk or a Palladin? A sort of thoughtful magic user that follows some code or something?”

“The similarity to those classes is superficial,” Janne said. “Seekers have a deeper agenda and are very rare. It is a costly path to leveling up.”

“Costly, how?” Feral said.

Janne’s intervention visibly cooled Feral off.

“It takes a great deal of time for Seekers to gain the knowledge and wisdom they pursue. Have a great day in the park!”

They entered the Hub and left their ARGs pushed up on top of their heads. They walked slowly, letting the tides of SPARK flow past them.

I need to tell her. That's what friends do.

"You know how I just kind of freeze sometimes?"

Feral nodded. "We've talked about it in the Pod. Mellew thought maybe you were having some sort of seizure. But you weren't shaking or anything. You always seem to come out of it."

"I'm not unstable or anything," Will said. "I just start wondering about something, and lose contact with the outside world. It's like I'm so busy thinking, my body stops so I don't run into anything or fall off a cliff." He shrugged. "My mom said my dad did it, too. But she said I do it more. Maybe he did it more when he was a kid, too."

He felt self-conscious and glared at Feral, who was looking at him more intently than he ever remembered anyone doing. Her pupils were nearly indistinguishable from the dark brown of her irises.

She touched him gently on the arm, connecting.

"Go on," she said.

"I've always liked puzzles and riddles," WB continued. "So when I came back, I went to the first Princess—the one in the KT Arcade."

Feral nodded her encouragement.

"And the riddles didn't make sense. I mean, they made sense, but they kept changing. How could SPARK expect people to ever solve them? Why were they even there? Princesses don't really fit anywhere but Middle or Muddle. Was it just pandering to little girls? Just an identifiable character to get them to spend money?"

"That's my theory," Feral muttered.

"No," WB said. "They're connected! They're connected to their arcades and realms. They're connected to each other!"

"What are you talking about? How are they connected?"

"It's all intertwined. The theme of the arcades, quests, and realms tie in to the riddles the Princesses ask. And those tie in to the Knowledge quests in the arcade and throughout the park. They—"

"Stop." Feral grabbed his arm and prevented him from walking any farther.

She looked around. They were in a quiet area. She guided him toward a bench in front of one of the stupid mosaic tile panoramas and made him sit. Before he did, he momentarily froze while looking at the mosaic pattern. His brain itched like crazy.

"It's all intertwined," he mumbled.

Feral yanked him down onto the bench, breaking his reverie.

"Yes, I got that," she said. "Now you're going to back up and answer some questions."

She was still holding him by the arm. Will noticed and decided that was okay. Very okay.

"Okay." He waited while she formed her questions.

"First, what the frack is a Knowledge quest? I've never heard of such a thing."

Will flushed. "It's a quest, but for knowledge instead of treasure. You get XP, and maybe discounts, for stuff you've learned."

She started to laugh, caught herself, but gave Will a skeptical look. Then came the questions:

"Where do you find these Knowledge quests?"

"Do you get any loot? Any weapons?"

"What are they like?"

"How come nobody talks about them?"

Will answered them one at a time, and then finished up by saying, "…and that's why Janne said it was a costly path to leveling up. It takes a lot of time. I think most people would rather get in and slay Orcs."

"But the XP are exponential?" Feral said. "They double every time? So you must get around two thousand XP for completing all seven."

"Sixty-four hundred," Will corrected her.

Feral looked stunned. He walked her through the math.

"Son of a Desnardian," she whispered. "That's worth doing." She still looked skeptical. "Wait, the numbers still don't make sense to me."

She stared at the ground, and Will could see her keeping track of things on her fingers. The silence stretched. Will never interrupted her.

Finally, "How many Princess quests have you completed?" she said.

"Seven."

Feral barked a laugh. "BS! Jeez, if you'd said five or six, I would have believed you. Nobody I know has gotten all seven." She threw a challenging look at WB.

Will stood. "Pick a Princess. I'll beat the quest. Then I'll teach you how to beat it."

Feral hesitated.

"If I can't successfully complete whatever Princess Quest you choose," he said, "I'll let you pick from my inventory."

Feral paused and then stood. "Okay."

Will narrowed his eyes. "Furthermore, if I can't teach you how to complete a Princess, I'll let you take a second pick."

Feral looked at WB as if it were the most moronic offer ever made.

"But," Will continued, "if I can teach you, then I get to pick from your inventory."

He watched ShaChri's eyes narrow as she thought. He knew her level and her reputation. *She's got to have some sweet gear. Will she risk it?*

"Deal," she said.

"Pick your Princess, princess," Will said with more confidence than he felt.

"Any Princess?"

"Any Princess."

Feral looked around. They were in the rim at the quiet area near Tiny Universe, between the Future Worlds and PreHistory arcades.

"PreHistory," she said. "I hate that one. No kid that young should be that articulate." She slapped her ARGs into position.

Ten minutes later, WB said, "The hypothesized dark matter disk appears to have a period of approximately thirty million years, and may explain a sufficient perturbation of the Oort cloud so as to disrupt the orbit of the meteor that hit the Yucatan peninsula near Chicxulub."

As they walked out to the fanfare of trumpets, Feral seemed to have doubts about the security of her inventory.

"How the frack did you know that?" she said.

"This is going to take us a at least the rest of the day," WB said, "and you're only going to get two hundred XP for this—assuming you only have one Princess so far. Are you ready to commit that kind of time?"

Feral hesitated. Will could see her conflict. They'd planned on hitting a major or two together. Questing would have given her at least a thousand XP. Why dump that in favor of two hundred XP?

"You're investing time now for a bigger payoff later," he told her.

"Okay." Hesitant. A shrug, and then a nod. "Okay."

He led her out into the plaza first.

"You are surrounded by clues. Everything you think is just a decoration is actually a bit of information. They may not mean much now, but after we finish the first Knowledge quest, their importance will become obvious."

As they walked down the arcade to the WeaponSmith, WB pointed out more clues without actually pointing.

"See right there, over the Impact quest? It's a map of the Yucatan peninsula as it exists today. They only label three towns: Tampico, Havana, and Chicxulub. Tampico and Havana are major cities, but I think they only show them to give you an orientation for Chicxulub. Why even label Chicxulub? Because that's what scientists have named the impact site for the meteor they believe killed all the dinosaurs. The one that plays out in KT Crossing."

"Okay…" Feral nodded but clearly hadn't bought in yet.

He led her to the WeaponSmith.

Will greeted him. "Hey, Mister Bob. How are you today?"

"I'm doing well, my young friend. And you?"

Feral gave Will a surprised look.

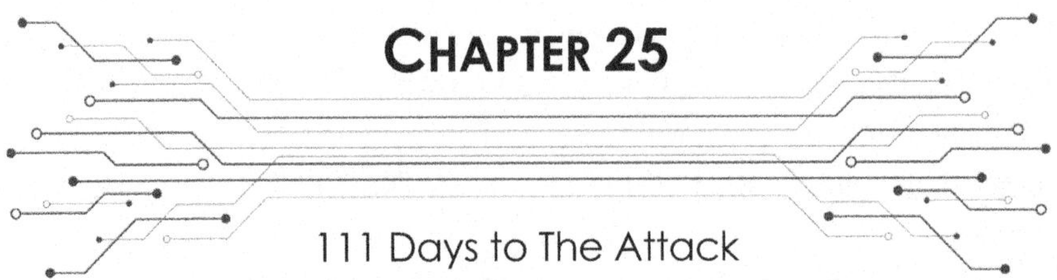

CHAPTER 25

111 Days to The Attack

Allies are not friends. They are just groups that share a common goal. When those goals change, alliances may evaporate. You can suddenly find yourself player versus player. Choose cautiously.
—SparkLord312

Other than Bull, Feral never made small talk with anyone who worked at SPARK. She had been living there a year, and recognized a lot of the cast members, but couldn't have named a single one. They didn't wear name tags, and her ARGs only labeled this guy as *WeaponSmith.* WB was definitely going to have some questions to answer.

"Having a great day," Will replied. "About to win a bet from my friend here."

"That so?" The WeaponSmith looked skeptically at Feral and sniffed.

Feral cringed when WB claimed he was a Seeker and sought more knowledge of weapons. The Smith looked sideways at Feral but ushered them into the back room.

Feral was out of her depth. As a guide, as a Level 58, she expected—*believed*—she knew everything about SPARK. Now, she was standing in a room she had never seen before, about to begin a quest she hadn't known existed.

The virtual WeaponSmith appeared and waited patiently, but Feral grabbed Will's arm and spun him to face her.

"How do you know his name?" she said.

"I come here a lot. Bob's probably my favorite of the WeaponSmiths. He's really helpful."

"How many people at SPARK do you know by name?"

Will started ticking off some names and locations, counting them on his fingers.

"Well, obviously Bob. Then I'm pretty friendly with a couple of other WeaponSmiths, like Buster, and Cyrus, and Dayna. Then over at Miss Sparkle's, there's CoCo and Aurora. And one of the guys up at Orbital Defense, Cesar. He's a funny dude. And then there's—"

"Stop." Feral held up her hand, and WB remained silent.

Time stretched. WB began to look uncomfortable.

Finally, Feral took a deep breath and looked up at Will, feeling her worldview shift.

"I have been here a year. I'm in SPARK every day. Sure, I recognize people, but the only name I know is Bull, and I only know him because he works Security at the tournaments and he talked to me first." She paused.

Will kept his mouth shut.

"I'm supposed to be a guide." She gestured around her. "I've never been in this room before. It never even dawned on me to ask a WeaponSmith questions beyond what they had in stock." Vexed, she shook her head. "When—no, back to how. How do you know his name? They don't wear name tags."

WB's face reddened behind the freckles.

"I introduced myself," he said. "I mean, maybe the second or third time I saw the same person, I stuck my hand out. Mister Bob was the first person—real person—I shook hands with here. He told me his name. I feel funny calling someone his age *Bob*, so I just call them all Mister or Miss Whatever." He shrugged.

"Okay, so just common courtesy," Feral forced a smile to cover her embarrassment.

She took a deep breath and let it out slowly.

"Lead on, Mister Seeker."

The virtual representation of Mr. Bob took it from there.

The nominal hour stretched to three because Feral had questions.

"Why do some swords bend, and others break?"

The virtual WeaponSmith gave her a realistic grin and answered. Feral's questions continued:

"If we use carbon fiber for armor, why not for weapons?"

"Why does light bend when going through certain materials?"

"No, that's *how*, not *why*. Tell me why."

"Does light, at wavelengths we can't see, obey the same properties as light we can see?"

"Why does gravity bend light?"

Finally, she asked what she thought was most important.

"What's the best material for a sword?"

The answer was long and full of caveats about hardness versus brittleness and toughness. Elastic deformation versus plastic deformation. Utility versus aesthetic appeal.

Finally, they were done and Feral was ready to exit. She got her discount and XP, and was ready to walk away, when WB said, "Stop. Ask Mister Bob about making a custom sword for you. One where you specify the materials and manufacturing technique."

She looked at the WeaponSmith. "Could you craft a blade of ReB2—rhenium diboride—for me? What would it cost?"

"How many gem slots do you want?"

"How many can I get?"

Mr. Bob gave WB a sideways glance, as if he were revealing arcane secrets.

"Four," the WeaponSmith replied.

Feral spun to WB and punched him in the arm.

"Four? Four! I've never seen any sword with more than three slots for gems!"

Gems were endowed with certain abilities. Some granted the user greater resistance to bludgeoning, piercing, or cutting. Some caused greater damage to targets. This could be in the form of persistent bleeding, poisonous effects, armor penetration, or burning. The list of gems and their attributes was extensive.

"How much?" she said with hesitation.

"What style sword do you want? A katana?" The WeaponSmith nodded to the katana Feral had strapped on her back.

It was her favorite blade—light enough and balanced enough to be wielded one-handed, and a handle long enough to be held in both hands for powerful strikes.

"Yeah," she replied. "Same specs as far as handle and blade length." She turned to WB. "Wait. ReB2 is ultra-hard. So it's going to be brittle, too. Like a diamond. It won't bend or flex, but it might shatter."

"Absolutely." WB grinned. "If it were going to be a real ReB2 blade. But this is SPARK, and it's a virtual blade. Consider it a fiction of the park—like Orcs. This blade won't break."

Feral looked at the WeaponSmith, who grudgingly nodded his agreement.

"How much?"

– 1 1 0 1 0 0 1 0 –

Severski opened his front door and welcomed his *cousin.* Acid churned in his gut.

Ragnar Sarnak entered the house. If the meeting itself wasn't enough to put Severski on edge, Sarnak's physical presence was. *He's taller than me. Must be close to six-feet tall, and at least two-twenty.*

Intensely aware of his doughboy physique, Severski stood back as Sarnak brushed past him.

"Can I get you something to drink?" Severski said.

He'd had a couple of shots of vodka as soon as he got home to fortify himself for this meeting. He craved more but knew enough to be relatively sober. *But if he wants a drink…*

"No," Sarnak replied.

Even though it was only one word, Severski picked up on the accent. *Eastern Europe. Maybe Russia.*

"Why don't you show me the house first." Sarnak headed toward the hallway.

"There's no one here but us," Severski said.

"Show me your house." The bearded *cousin* pulled some sort of electronic device from his pocket and switched it on.

He scanned the walls, furnishings, and ceilings with it as he walked through the formerly tidy dwelling.

"How's your hotel?" Severski said to fill the silence.

Sarnak gave him a penetrating look.

"Nice," he replied.

When the mercenary finished searching the house, he sat at the dining table.

"I need a map of the Underground City. You will provide it. I will send you a notice of the date of the attack. In code. You remember the code?"

Severski nodded.

"You will indicate on the map where we will meet. You will go there with the Data Core as soon as the attack begins. Once I have the core, you will lead us out the exit. I will have transportation waiting for us. Have everything you need with you. You will not be coming back here."

Severski gulped but nodded. *This is really going to happen.*

"I should sell the place." He gestured around the room.

Sarnak gave him the coldest look Severski had ever seen.

"You will do nothing to attract attention. You will not be thrown out of any more bars. You will not sell house. We are paying you plenty to cover the price of the house. Even a house in California." It came out as *Kah-lee-for-nee-ah.*

Severski's heart hammered in his chest. He nodded.

With a wicked smile, Sarnak said, "Now, we drink. You have vodka?"

Severski poured them both shots. Sarnak threw his back. Severski matched him. They had a second shot. Then a third.

"Where are you from?" Severski said, anxious to break the silence. "Your English is excellent."

Sarnak looked at him and replied, deadpan, "Escondido."

Severski did a spit-take, spraying the table with vodka, and then coughed.

Sarnak laughed uproariously, then pounded his *cousin* on the back.

"Got you." He pointed at the traitor who would make the whole attack possible. "Kiev. It's in Ukraine."

Severski nodded and joined in the laughter. Forced and uncomfortable, but he joined.

When he put his glass down, Sarnak poured them both another.

"It is unusual to find an American who knows how to properly drink vodka." This time, he pronounced the word as he would have at home—*wodka.*

He inclined his glass toward Severski. "*За успех*, to success."

They each finished the contents of their glasses.

"Why do you do this thing?" he asked Severski. "This is your country. Your employer. I think it is more than money."

Severski nodded, feeling the warmth of the liquor spread through his body. It put him at ease.

"My wife has left, and soon will take all of this from me." He gestured around them. "I will soon lose my job." He refilled their glasses. "My country? That's harder. I think maybe I lost it in Korea." He gulped the clear liquid and set his glass down. "And then I buried it in Michigan."

Sarnak nodded.

"Have you been to Mozambique?" Severski said. The alcohol was taking control, and he stumbled over the word *Mozambique*. "Is it nice?"

Sarnak stood to leave. "You will love Maputo."

Severski stumbled behind.

At the door, the SPARK employee held out his hand. The mercenary grabbed it with an iron grip and pulled Severski close.

Sarnak put a strong hand around the back of Severski's head and whispered, "If you fail, I will kill you myself."

– 1 1 0 1 0 0 1 0 –

"For this blade, four slots, five hundred twenty-five thousand gold," the WeaponSmith said in a tone indicating he considered this beyond her reach. "More if you want me to slot gems into it. Plus the cost of the gems."

Bob knew who Feral was and thought she was a little too full of herself. He'd worked in SPARK for years, buying and selling virts to guests, and thought he knew Feral's type—all business. No time for a, *Good morning, Sir Smith!* Nothing like that. Just, *I want to sell these weapons.* Or, *Got any Elites in stock?* Not rude, exactly. Just not friendly. Not like WB.

Word had gotten around the arcade about him. It started when he did the Charm School, and when he helped the *lost* little girl, and then took her to beat the Princess Quest. Bob's kids went to the SPARK school. Paige told everyone who would listen, and even those who didn't want to, about her friend Billy and how they beat the Princess Quest together.

Bob didn't care if WB was quirky. Any teenager who would give up limited time in the park to help a little girl...well, he was okay in Bob's book. Then he did the Knowledge quest and bent Bob's ear with ideas and questions. The questions! Without Janne in his ear, Bob would simply have muttered an unending string of, *Good sir, I'm sorry, but I don't know.* Just by talking with the kid, and parroting Janne's answers, Bob himself now knew much more about metallurgy, weapons, and orbital mechanics than he ever would have dreamed possible. The kid's enthusiasm was infectious. And he said hi every time he walked past.

Bob decided if WB was friends with this Feral girl, then she was probably okay, too. His demeanor softened.

"If that's too pricey," he said, "we can also craft a katana for you out of tungsten tetraboride. It won't be as hard, or have the same hit stats as the ReB2 blade, and we can only make 'em with three gem slots." He dropped his voice to a whisper. "But it's not as spendy either."

Bob pointed out the stats. They were ridiculous.

"A sword like this would easily kill most opponents with one hit." With a conspiratorial air, he said, "It would be a huge advantage in the tournaments. This blade would generally be considered a Level Sixty-Five weapon. However, since you are commissioning it, it would be levelable for you. You're a Level Fifty-Eight?"

It was just conversation—Bob could see her level displayed in his ARGs.

Feral nodded.

"So it would drop a bit from the advertised stats, but will stay with you—as high as you can go."

"Can you show it to me?" Feral whispered. "The ReB2 blade?"

Bob nodded, and the ReB2 katana appeared in her ARGs in hi-def. It was a beautiful weapon, stunning. The blade had a hypnotic raindrop Damascus pattern normally associated with heat-forged and folded steel. On this weapon, instead of the lines being darker gray, they were deep oxblood. The overall color was slate gray—not the high sheen of a polished steel or bronze. Crimson cobras were etched on the side of the guard that faced the blade itself. White and gold elephants would face whoever held the handle.

"So," Feral whispered, "destruction to those who face the blade, and wisdom to whoever wields it?"

Again, the WeaponSmith nodded. "Miss Janne personalizes commissioned weapons based on the buyer's history and profile."

"She nailed it," Feral said, in awe.

As she was about to authorize the transaction, WB said, "Doesn't Feral get ten percent off today for completing the Knowledge quest?"

Bob the WeaponSmith smiled. The discount would have been automatic, but he sensed WB was trying to impress this girl.

"Of course, my good sir. Thank you for reminding me."

"Wait," Feral said. "Mister Bob, would you be so kind as to slot these gems for me?"

She transferred a flawless diamond, a flawless emerald, a flawless Martian ruby, and a hazy brown topaz to the WeaponSmith.

The last puzzled him. "Miss…surely you have something better than this last?"

"I do." Feral smiled. "But I'm remembering something my mom always told me: *Nothing in this world is perfect, nor should it be. Perfection is for the next world.*" She barked out a laugh, and her eyes teared up. "Then she would always whisper, *But buy good quality. Quality lasts!* Now, this weapon won't be perfect. But it will be quality."

Bob and Will were silent as the WeaponSmith slotted the gems and transferred the weapon to Feral.

There's more to this girl than just being a fighter.

She loaded her ReB2 katana in her inventory.

"Lead on," she said to WB.

As they walked away, she turned back to the WeaponSmith.

"Thank you, Mister Bob."

– 1 1 0 1 0 0 1 0 –

WB was a little nervous as they walked away.

Feral wailed, "What was I thinking? What have I done?" She pressed her hands against the sides of her head. "I just spent a half-million gold!"

"I can tell you what you've done." WB grabbed her arm and spun her to face him. "You just crafted a sword the likes of which no one—*no one*—in SPARK has ever seen." He moved closer. "Next time you face CastIron in a melee tournament, you're going to save that sword for the final round. Then you're going to equip it. And the moment you pull it out, the arena is going to go silent." He gestured around them, already imagining the crowd in the venue. "You are going to show them a weapon *they have never seen.* They're going to expect it to simply be some decent steel sword you've painted." He circled around her, forcing her to turn to follow. "You and CastIron are going to circle each other like always, and then she's going to come after you, and you're going to use Feral's Wrath and swat her blade out of your way like it was an annoying fly. And on the backswing…on the backswing, Feral, you're going to cut her virtual head off and leave her dead, burning, poisoned corpse in the sand of the arena. People will go nuts!"

She calmed and was now smiling. "Feral's Wrath?"

"Yeah." WB smiled, but was embarrassed. "All weapons of that caliber should be named."

"And you just named my sword—*my sword*—Feral's Wrath?"

"Uhm…kinda. It was just an idea…"

"It's okay." She gave an exaggerated shrug. "I guess it'll do until I come up with something better."

She grinned and pushed her ARGs up. Then she reached over and raised Will's.

"I want you to be able to see my smile." She hugged him for the second time that day.

"What next?" She slapped her ARGs back into position, and then answered her own question. "I'm ready to face a Princess!"

He led her down to the Hub and whispered, "Everything in an arcade tells a part of the story. All of the little quests, all decorations, everything. What did you learn at Bob's?"

"I learned enough about metals to craft an awesome sword!" she said.

"Good. What else?"

"Well, some stuff about light, and gravity, and stuff."

WB wanted to test her without giving away any of the specific riddles he'd been given by the Princess.

"Even better," he said, "what kind of ground track does a satellite trace on a planet?"

"Depends on the orbital altitude," she said slowly, and then grinned. "I know that!"

"Good," he said. "Now, look at the artwork around Wimple's Wobble."

Wimple's Wobble was a very minor quest. If you left the Hub and were walking up the KT Crossing Arcade, it was the first quest you came to.

"What's Wimple's Wobble about?"

"It's a stupid little quest. I don't think it's even worth fifty XP if you win."

He waved a hand. "Doesn't matter. Don't think in terms of XP. What is the game about?"

– 1 1 0 1 0 0 1 0 –

Feral frowned and thought hard. She hadn't played it in months.

"You have control of a spaceship thing," she replied, "and you need to get to some space station before all the other players."

"Right. How do you win?"

Feral looked at him as if it was the dumbest question she'd heard in at least a month of guiding.

"You. Get. There. First." Her disdain for the minor quests was evident.

"Okay." WB sighed. "Bad question. What's the secret to winning?"

She shook her head and looked embarrassed.

"I don't remember."

"Let's play it," WB said.

They did. She had to play it twice before she won, but was excited when she emerged victorious.

"Okay, I get it!" she shouted at WB, then softened her tone and reduced her volume when every guest in the vicinity turned to look at them. "You have to accelerate," she hissed in Will's ear. "It makes you look like you're falling behind all the other players, but you're actually climbing and going faster. You just look like you're going slower."

"Do you remember being able to see your ground track on the display of the Earth when you look down?"

"Yes…" she said slowly.

Then it clicked. The graphics of the game, the artwork on the outside of the quest, and what, apparently, she learned at Bob's without even thinking about it. She felt her entire world tilt, and the words came rushing out.

"When you're low, your ground track is a sine wave." She traced one in the air with her finger. "As you move higher, to *geocentric altitude*," she grinned at the use of new vocabulary, "your ground track becomes kind of a sloppy figure eight you have to fix."

"Why and how?" WB said.

"Frack." She got in line for the quest again, grateful it was a short one.

Moments later, Feral emerged with more things clicking.

"Frack, frack, frack!" she said. "It's a sloppy figure eight because you still have some inclination with respect to the Earth's plane of rotation. You have to adjust it until it becomes a stationary dot on the Earth. Then," she punched WB in the arm with every word to add her own brand of emphasis, "you're in a," punch, "geosynchronous," punch, "equatorial," punch, "orbit." Triple punch.

– 1 1 0 1 0 0 1 0 –

Will was ecstatic, but his upper arms were sore. He walked her up the arcade, pointing out all of the artwork, and quizzing her about what it could mean, and forcing her to play all the little quests along the way.

After Orbital Defense, Feral called a stop.

"Can we quit for the day? I'm beat, and my brain is full."

"Okay," he said. "But tomorrow we pick up where we left off? The bet is still in place?" *Please. If she quits here, she'll never see it.*

Feral looked at him for a long moment and then nodded.

"I'm not scheduled with anybody tomorrow." She heaved a theatrical sigh. "I'll give you tomorrow."

A wide grin spread across Will's face.

The two Pod members ditched their gear and went separately into the Underground. They met up under Orcland where the Pod was camped out.

"No offense, WB," said Feral, "but that was the slowest day of my SPARK career. I'm going to hit the gym. Get sweaty and get clean. See you in a bit?"

Will nodded and watched her walk away, grateful for the lack of ARGs. *She's beautiful.*

He checked to make sure his backpack and KA-BAR were still secure, and then fell asleep behind an air-handling unit.

In the morning, Feral kicked his feet to wake him up.

"Ready to lose your bet, Seeker Boy?"

Will rubbed the sleep out of his eyes.

"You may want to sell your best stuff before I raid your inventory," he replied.

The worked their way into the flow of departing employees and headed around to the public entry. Once inside, WB led them back to the PreHistory Arcade. They stopped in front of Miss Sparkle's Princess Gear.

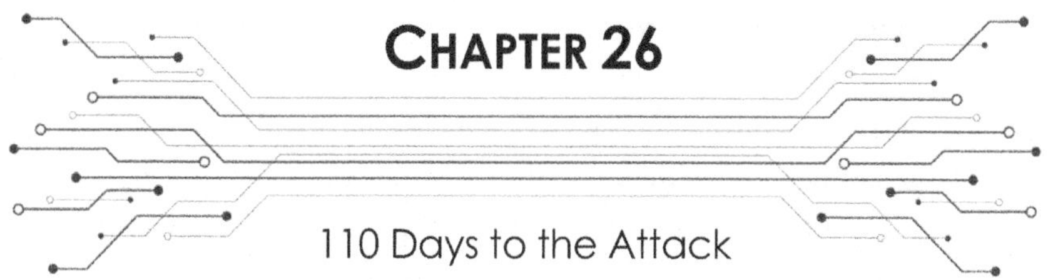

Chapter 26

110 Days to the Attack

I always feel like somebody's watching me.
—Rockwell

Bull wore his Frost Giant avatar as he followed a couple up the arcade. *Guy looks like an operator. Somebody who's been downrange. Tall, muscular, but not bulky. The kind of muscle you built busting your hump in the field, not the gym.*

Bull had been in the Hub when Janne patched in the call from Hodgins.

"We've got a couple inbound. He's late thirties, early forties. Dark curly hair and an oddly-shaped beard. Wayfarers. Tall, muscular. Jeans and a long-sleeved button-down shirt, and a boonie hat. She's late twenties, platinum-blonde hair, khaki skirt, green top. Heart tattoo on her right ankle. Three stars on her left wrist."

"What's up?" Bull said.

"We got nothing from the guy on entry," said Hodgins. "He was careful not to touch anything. Kept his sunglasses on. The woman paid for everything. New profiles, standard avatars. He's a mage. She's a stock princess. Ran them both through FaceRec. Nothing on him. The beard is working against us there. She's got multiple priors in LA for solicitation and some drugs."

"Sketchy," Bull said. "What do you want me to do?"

"Follow them loosely and keep an eye on them," Hodgins replied. "Janne, scans are all clean, right? No weapons?"

"Yes, Hodge," the AI said. "The couple is not carrying any weapons. The only red flag so far is behavioral on the part of the male guest. Given the woman's history, they may be headed to the adults-only area."

Bull signed off and followed the couple when they emerged into the Hub. The guy was carrying his ARGs and spent a lot of time wandering around, looking at things without his ARGs on. For the next four hours, they methodically toured SPARK, walking up and down every arcade. The blonde kept her ARGs on and seemed to enjoy playing some of the smaller quests. The guy spent about half his time with his ARGs off. They left before lunch.

"He was definitely doing recon," Bull told Hodgins. "He may have picked up on me following him, but didn't seem to care."

"Maybe just a competitor looking around," Hodge said.

"I dunno, boss. This guy had a vibe to him. Like he'd been downrange. A guy to take seriously."

"Okay, thanks, Bull. Why don't you grab lunch, then back to normal patrol?"

"You got it."

– 1 1 0 1 0 0 1 0 –

"In all of SPARK," WB said, "this is my favorite place."

Since his adventure with Paige, Will returned to talk to Miss Sparkle often.

In a way, she's like my SPARK mom. She listened patiently, gave thoughtful answers, and seemed to care for him.

Intellectually, he knew she was a virtual construct. But he didn't care. He liked her.

Meanwhile, Feral was looking at him as if he had grown a second head.

"Um, WB, I didn't know you were into Princess gear," she said half-jokingly.

"Patience, young Seeker. Not everything is what it appears." WB turned to the Miss Sparkle's entry. "Read the entire sign, please."

Obediently, Feral turned and read the sign, word for word.

"Shut up. Shut the frack up! Charm School?" She dropped her voice to a whisper. "You're telling me this is another Knowledge quest?"

WB nodded. "There are at least two more. I've only done one of those."

"What? How?" Feral looked like her world was slipping even more.

"Yeah," WB whispered. "Two arcades over, there's another gift shop—MuddleWear, Magic Arms, and Sparklitz Language Institute."

"I know it," Feral said. "I take all my ESL clients there. They have a bunch of multilingual souvenirs. Stuff in Spanish, Mandarin, Japanese, Arabic, Urdu, and Swahili."

"Yep," said WB. "Another Knowledge quest. It's a bit awkward, but not hard."

After he beat the quest, he was able to read the Hittite letter he got for helping Paige. It still bothered him. One side of the letter read, *One must be willing to lie down before one can arise*. And the other read, *Look with the eyes of a child*. What the heck did that mean, anyway?

The perk was that now, Janne automatically translated for him whenever he was listening to or reading another language. *Cool, but of no practical value outside SPARK.*

He walked Feral around KT Crossing Plaza, no longer having to point out things. She got it. Her world of SPARK became an inflationary universe, rapidly expanding.

"Ready?" he asked her after lunch.

"I'm ready." Feral turned and headed to the Princess.

Five minutes later: "Circular, elliptical, parabolic, hyperbolic. All are potential orbital tracks—assuming no external perturbations." Her hands traced arcs in the air in front of the Princess.

"Of course," the Princess replied…

Feral high-fived WB when they exited to the sound of trumpets.

"I did it. I actually did it." Feral's eyes were wide. "On my own."

"Well, yeah." WB smiled.

"No, you don't get it. The only other Princess quest I ever beat was the one at Mars—the one where the riddle never changes?"

WB nodded.

"The only reason I beat her," she continued, "was I overheard some guests talking about it. All you do is say, *It's pie*, and then, *It can't be solved.* I just said the words. Poof! Princess Quest done, and a hundred XP in the bag."

Feral was quiet for a minute as they stood in the plaza and heard people congratulating them on solving this Princess.

"I have to go back and beat her on my own," she said.

Again, WB nodded.

"But not right now!" she said. "Right now, my brain is full, and I'm going to have to go fight something. C'mon!"

She grabbed WB's arm and dragged him toward KT Crossing. WB was relieved that the line was already closed. They dropped into Orbital Defense for a couple rounds.

When the Pod bedded down that night, WB looked over to where the rest of the Pod slept. *They're like a pile of puppies.*

He still slept alone. *They'd probably let me join them.* He shook his head and sighed. *No way I can sleep in that group with a knife in my hands. Better alone.*

He rolled onto his side, KA-BAR clutched to his chest. Ready for another fitful night.

– 1 1 0 1 0 0 1 0 –

Since her *birth*, Janne was accustomed to being under observation. She knew her code—her *soul*—lived in the Data Core that was plugged into the servers in HVH's inner sanctum. The many cameras were her eyes. But her body, she came to believe, was SPARK itself.

Janne felt a sense of disquiet. It came with low probabilities. The man and woman who just left were the cause. Even with increased monitoring, she never got a good image of the man's eyes. On the few occasions when he donned his ARGs, he held them with a tissue, not bare fingertips. He never *touched* anything, other than the woman, occasionally taking her arm to steer her in whatever direction he chose. He never used any of the restrooms, and managed to take his sunglasses off only when his face was shielded from the cameras. It was a greater than 98 percent probability that the woman was a hired companion. But that didn't bother Janne. No, it was the man.

The beard, sunglasses, and hat made facial recognition impossible. It was the first time in seven years that she was unable to identify a guest to a greater than 80 percent probability before they entered the Hub. It was as if a stranger, a ghost, had entered her house—her body—taken a good look around, and left.

Odds favored some sort of nefarious intent. But the lack of identification made it difficult to trace anything else. In her experience, knowing *who* was the quickest path to knowing *what*, *why*, and *how*.

She tagged the man's ARGs for a DNA check. It might not give her anything, but it was an inexpensive test. Janne did not like ghosts.

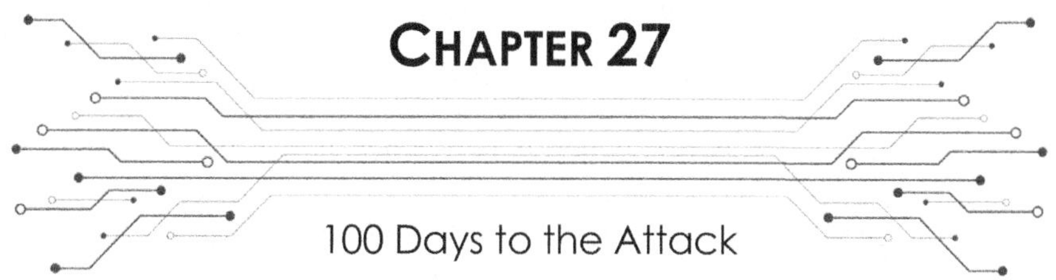

Chapter 27

100 Days to the Attack

Once more, with feeling.
—Anon

Another week passed. WB was hesitant, but Feral was a force of nature—easier to endure than to overcome.

As they stood in line, WB observed what he named *The Feral Effect*—other guests scooted ahead to join different groups, or dropped back. They didn't want to face KT Crossing with opponents scaled up to be a challenge to a Level 58 player.

"Shoot or run?" she said, when they were next.

WB had felt some unease about questing with Feral. *She's going to figure out how bad I am at combat.*

"Run," he replied.

"Wuss," she said, but nodded.

When they emerged from the wormhole, she grabbed his arm and yelled, "Run!"

Laughing, they ran and took refuge with the Cyanites. Feral held off the Rex long enough for WB to scoop up the baby and dash into the cave. The baby Cyanite started crying.

"Hush, little one. Hush. Don't cry. It will be fine."

WB thought it was Feral talking to the Cyanitess, trying to calm them. She pulled out a piece of fruit from her inventory and was offering it to the Cyanitess.

"Hush. Hush. These creatures won't hurt us."

I'm hearing Mama Cyanite talking to her baby.

"Yes, yes," he said. "We're friends."

"You speak Cyanite?" Feral said.

"Apparently. Didn't know it until now. Must be a benefit of being a Sparklitz grad."

Will held out his hand to the Cyanites. He looked at Feral, suddenly inspired.

"I've got an idea. Trust me?"

Clouds flew across Feral's face before she said, "Why not? You were right about the Princess thing. And since when do you have blue handprints on your armor?"

"I'll tell you later," he said. "They only show up here."

WB turned and walked to the entrance of the shelter. He put his fingers to his lips and forced out a whistle.

The T-Rex turned at the noise. Feral pulled her blaster out.

"I thought you didn't want to fight this guy," she hissed.

WB turned to the Cyanites. "Whisper."

Mama nodded and began crooning.

– 1 1 0 1 0 0 1 0 –

The referee on duty started chuckling. *This is going to be quick and ugly.*

He didn't often get to watch high-level players get eaten by the T-Rex. He hit the intercom and called his friends.

"You're going to want to see this."

– 1 1 0 1 0 0 1 0 –

WB invoked Dino Whisperer and then added his highest Augment. He began to sing. To him, it sounded like, *Hey there, Mister T-Rex. Don't eat us. We're nice.*

– 1 1 0 1 0 0 1 0 –

To Feral, it sounded as if he added harmony to the melody Mama was singing. She knew the melody before, but never realized that it was called "Whisper."

Frantic, she scrolled through her abilities. *It's here somewhere!*

She saw the legs of the T-Rex stop outside their shelter. The Rex dropped his head. An enormous eye looking through the cave's entrance.

There! She invoked her own "Whisper" and began to sing. Her soprano joined WB's tenor and the Mama's alto, and the surprising low bass of the Daddy Cyanite.

"I don't know what we're doing," she sang quietly. "Please make this work out."

A wet gust of air blasted the players as the T-Rex turned his mouth toward them.

His teeth are enormous. How do they give him bad breath?

– 1 1 0 1 0 0 1 0 –

"Double F! Double F!!" the referee keyed his intercom and shouted at the same time.

Janne already had him online. He was hustling toward the KT Crossing area.

– 1 1 0 1 0 0 1 0 –

Janne was running default programming but knew enough to slow everything down. Screens throughout Quest Control were quietly being switched to the KT Crossing view. Some selected *T-Rex View*—it was considered the coolest view when people were about to be munched by the big guy. Others selected *ARG View* from WB occasionally, but mostly Feral Daughter since she was so well-known. They heard the audio in both English and Cyanite.

"Please don't eat us, Mister Rex. Please be a nice dinosaur."

Not terribly imaginative or profound. The Cyanite soundtrack was incomprehensible but rapturous. Four voices joining in a performance worthy of an opera. Haunting, beautiful.

All had heard the solo version when the Cyanites Whispered the brontosaurus into giving groups of questers a ride across the river. This was different. Goosebumps formed as they listened to the doomed players croon to the T-Rex. A haunting earworm.

Mama Cyanite broke from her standard repertoire and launched a soaring aria that left them stunned.

"What do we do?" the referee asked Double F. "What do we do?"

Janne said, "This is unprecedented. We must decide quickly."

– 1 1 0 1 0 0 1 0 –

WB ran out of words, but the melody Mama Cyanite was singing had words he understood:

"You are mighty, we are lowly. You are powerful, we are weak. Leave us in peace. Besides, we probably don't taste very good. Let us ride."

He ran out of words of his own, and was now croaking his way through some mermaid's melody that had popped into his brain.

Feral elbowed him. "Wrong theme park," she hissed.

Will switched to a lullaby that he figured must be public domain. Feral heard the bleed through and picked up on WB's tune and added her soprano to it. Janne masterfully wrapped them together.

– 1 1 0 1 0 0 1 0 –

Janne began subtitling the words for Quest Control: "Let us ride, please. Let us ride."

"Double F, we must decide quickly," she said only to Double F's headset. "Can you support it?"

"I am moving the overhead crane into position now. It will be possible."

"Do it. Let the boss and Hodgins know."

"Neither are currently on-site. You will have to meet the players alone."

– 1 1 0 1 0 0 1 0 –

Slowly, the T-Rex turned his back and stood quietly. Faint twitches rippled his green-brown hide. Mama Cyanite took the lead and crawled up on the back of the most feared predator in SPARK. She kept singing. WB and Feral followed suit.

"Hang on!" WB clung to the dinosaur's back.

"Ya think?" shouted Feral.

The back of the Rex was broad, but they found secure handholds. Tree ferns began flashing past as they were whisked through the quest. Will watched scenery he had never seen before—monkey puzzle trees and conifers—going by as the Rex gained speed. Each footfall jarred, and WB tightened his grip.

They hung on. The melody changed. They could hear it in their earbuds.

– 1 1 0 1 0 0 1 0 –

"Janne, turn up the volume!" Double F said.

To those watching in Quest Control, what had been an aria became a rock anthem. The bass provided by the deep *thoom!* of the Rex's footfalls resounded in the ears of the riders, with harmonics they felt in their chests. The slap of passing foliage became the upper register rhythm—a staccato beat like snares and bongos. The undulating wail of a brontosaurus was the backbone of the melody. The riders seemed to sing in harmony with a Pteranodon shrieking to add a touch of metal. In Quest Control, mouths gaped. A major quest was being rewritten in real time, a new soundtrack supplied.

A new view appeared in their monitors, as if a camera somehow hovered twenty feet to the left of the riders, allowing Double F and the team a new perspective. They could see Mama Cyanite clutching her baby in one arm, and somehow clinging to the Rex with the other. WB straddled the dinosaur behind them, enveloping the Cyanites with his arms as he held on to the scaly skin of the Rex. Feral was behind WB, one hand holding on to the T-Rex, and the other arm wrapped around WB's waist.

"Janne…" the head referee said.

"Yes," she replied. "I am creating this composite view from available data. I am pulsing the crane's hydraulics to add realistic jarring to the stride of the Rex. Please, Double F, I am very near capacity at the moment."

"Okay," was all Fitz Flaherty could think of to say.

He settled in to watch the show.

– 1 1 0 1 0 0 1 0 –

WB expected to be thrown off when the Rex stopped at the river's edge. Instead, water splashed in their faces as the T-Rex took the river in ten long, quick strides. Suddenly, they were in the post-impact zone, but the Rex showed no sign of slowing. As they approached the exit, the T-Rex ripped the boss-level velociraptors to shreds, staggered, and collapsed.

The riders slid off his neck and back onto the ground. Mama Cyanite crooned a farewell to the Rex as he breathed his last breath, shuddered, and died from the exertion.

Mama Cyanite made both WB and Feral hold Baby Cyanite while she and Daddy sang a soft benediction.

The players picked up some loot and exited, stunned. They had completed a two-hour-minimum quest in less than ten minutes.

"Divine feces," Feral breathed, and crushed WB in a hug.

"Divine feces, indeed." WB hugged her back, enjoying the feeling.

Feral looked at WB and pushed up her ARGs. He followed suit.

"What the heck did we just do?" she said.

"I think," WB said slowly, "we just Whispered the T-Rex."

"Where? How?" Feral said, and then realization struck. "You! You must have—"

"Done the same thing you did," said WB. "We shouldn't talk about it here."

Both looked around, expecting to see someone official meeting them.

Nobody.

After a couple painfully silent minutes, Feral grabbed WB's arm and dragged him along the rim, away from KT Crossing and toward Ascent.

"I wonder what sort of a tale we've fallen into," she said, as they hustled along.

WB stopped. "You like Tolkien?"

"I love Tolkien." She pulled him along. "Fool of a took! Who doesn't?"

They reached a quiet spot, and Feral finally stopped outside the normal flow of guests.

"My ARGs just show *Quest Results Pending*," she said. "I've never seen that before. I see the completion XP, but those words are just below it, flashing."

"Same here," WB said. "Jeez, I hope we haven't screwed things up. I'm just getting to where I really like this place."

Feral punched him in the arm again. "Moron. They'll never kick us out of the park for something like this. We might have just found an Egg!"

"Think so?" he said.

"Yeah!" Then Feral hesitated. "Maybe. I really thought there'd be someone to meet us."

She looked around and saw nothing but normal gamers in every direction.

WB said, "When did you…"

Feral put a finger to his lips in a gesture that surprised Will. Her touch was light. Gentle.

She stepped closer to him. Close enough that he could feel the heat radiating off her body. A whiff of soap and sweat.

She brought her mouth near his ear and whispered, "I don't think we should talk about it here. Maybe later. Maybe even away from SPARK."

He could feel her breath on his ear and neck. Unable to form any words, he nodded.

She stepped back and looked around again, hands on her hips.

"Frack. I guess nobody's coming," she said.

Feral looked over at Ascent and checked her phone.

"What?" WB said, still nonplussed from the whispered exchange.

"Well. They're probably going to close the line to Ascent soon. Since nobody's here to explain anything to us, let's just hit Ascent. Maybe tomorrow we can ask about it when we enter?"

Will nodded, and they moved toward the line.

– 1 1 0 1 0 0 1 0 –

"They have left the PreHistory Realm, and are heading toward Ascent of Humanity," Janne told Double F.

He was doing his best to track down the two gamers who just broke the snot out of his favorite quest. *Where's Hodgins when you needed him?*

"The Evolve Quest, or just the realm?" he asked Janne.

"Unknown. That is simply their direction of movement. Correction. They have entered the line for Ascent.

Double F slowed. He'd catch them on exit, and felt no need to break a sweat. He considered going back to Quest Control, but didn't want to risk being out of place if they broke this quest, too.

– 1 1 0 1 0 0 1 0 –

They hit Evolve, and Will observed The Feral Effect for the second time. The line was longish, but they ended up starting together and without other players.

Within seconds of entry, Feral was a dervish, fighting for WB's life. She went into guide mode and began issuing terse commands to him during the fighting sequences:

"Blasters don't work here. Equip your best melee weapon.

"Hit the guy on the left first. The others will scatter."

"Run, run, run!"

They successfully completed the quest, but it was close.

"That was awesome!" WB said, as they watched their stats ratchet up.

"You *suck* at combat!" Feral yelled. "I had to save your butt in every single fight. How is it even possible you are a Level Thirty-Eight? Oh wait, you just leveled up. How is it a Level Thirty-Nine can't even hold his own in a fight? Oh yeah, that's right. *Mister Seeker* doesn't know squat about combat. Jeez!"

"Why are you so mad?" WB said.

– 1 1 0 1 0 0 1 0 –

Double F walked up. *Wow, this looks like a lover's quarrel. What's all this about?*

He had missed them entering Evolve, and had to kill a couple hours before they emerged. He used the time to coordinate with Janne and production staff.

Janne kept him apprised of their progress.

He walked up to the two. *Are they a couple?*

"Hey, guys." He stuck out a fist.

WB bumped it, and Feral followed suit.

"Umm, can I buy you guys dinner? The quests and restaurants are mostly closed, but I think I can get Mariposa to keep the Uprising Kitchen open long enough to feed us."

The pair shrugged and followed him to the upscale restaurant in the Modern Times Realm. The park was closing, and most guests were already filing toward the exits. It was a quiet walk—every time they tried to start a conversation or ask a question, Double F simply held up a finger and said, "Not yet."

When they were seated, SPARK's head referee said, "Okay, the sound curtain's up. Before we start, I'm going to order a beer. It's been that kind of day. I'd offer you both one, but neither of you is old enough to drink."

With a beer in his hand, Double F slouched back in his seat.

"Janne said it was foreseeable," he said, "but I figured we were safe. Only a few people ever found the—I mean, save Baby Cyanite and earn the Dino Whisperer Perk. I mean, what were the odds two of them would team up at such a high level, and one of them would have learned to speak Cyanite?" He glared at Will and ShaChri in turn.

"So we've found an Egg?" she said.

"No! It's not an Egg! It's something we never thought would happen. It's..." Double F shrugged, "...it's not a mistake. It's an oversight. Yeah, that's it. An oversight."

"What happens now?" Will said. "Are there any perks attached to this?"

"We'd like to go public with this. We think we can stream your quest and get a good PR bump from it. You know, *Gaming pair find glitch in SPARK!* That sort of thing. The media team is already going nuts over the video clips. The music alone figures to be a big hit. Have you two sung together before? You've got amazing voices!"

ShaChri and Will just looked at each other. Their confusion was obvious.

Janne said, "Fitz? The audio was synthesized."

She played them a bit of the raw audio, and Double F shuddered.

He looked at the two gamers. "You really can't sing, can you?"

Will shook his head immediately. ShaChri slowly followed suit.

"I love the idea," she said. "It'll get me more clients. But you've got a problem. You'll have to create a skin for WB's face."

"What are you talking about?" Double F said.

"As Feral, most of my face is covered by the ninja suit. WB's avatar shows his real face. That won't work."

Double F said, "Why—"

"Feral and WB are both minors with no present legal guardian to sign a release for their participation in the video," Janne said to them all.

Fitz palmed his face. "Crap. I knew that."

The gaming duo exchanged a look.

"I'm gooning this up. I wish Hodgins were here." Double F looked like he'd just learned the truth about the Tooth Fairy.

Janne said, "Fortunately, we have a precedent for dealing with situations like these."

Double F's eyes lit up. "Of course we do!" He glanced at WB.

"This might still work," Feral said. "I might be able to get consent from my legal guardian, so I think I'm in the clear. The problem is Mister Seeker over here." She jerked her thumb at Will. "SPARK creates or projects all of our avatars. Only a few people would actually associate WB's real face with his avatar, and most of them are friends, or ought to be."

Will nodded.

"Can't SPARK just go back and edit the video and create a face for him that would block his real image? Maybe this Hobbs character he's so in love with."

"Hey!" Will said.

"Yeah, yeah, I know." Then Feral pitched her voice lower in imitation of WB's tenor. "It's an epic story that combines the greatness of the game with a cautionary tale of avoiding the excesses that can accompany success."

"It is!" WB said.

"I'll take your word for it," said Feral. "You're still the only guy wandering around SPARK, wearing a baseball uniform. Famous warriors, those baseball players."

Before WB could reply, Janne said, "What Feral is suggesting is completely within my capabilities. However, I suggest we alter the image sufficiently to preclude any legal action on the part of the actor's family. The uniform he wears has already been modified enough to avoid any copyright infringement issues."

"Okay," Double F said. "That could work. Hodgins will have to work out all the legal queep with the lawyers and figure out how we compensate you for everything since you're both underage. Right now, I can authorize some free days for you both until we get it straightened out."

"Make it free months," said Feral. "Two free months. And some gift cards. I need to buy some stuff in town."

"Anything else?" Double F said. "Like maybe a seat on the board of directors?"

Will said, "Feral—"

"We'll accept five free days to start," Feral said, "and a thousand-dollar gift card we can use here or in town."

Double F nodded. "Okay, that's something I can authorize." *I hate this stuff.* He shook his head. "Remind me never to negotiate with you again." He sighed.

"What about XP?" WB said. "We finished the quest. Maybe not the normal way, but we finished it and found the *glitch* in the game. That ought to be worth something."

Fitz Flaherty visibly relaxed. "Okay, let's assume you played the game normally."

"We didn't," said Feral.

"I get that," Double F said. "But let's start from there. As two accomplished and experienced gamers, you could reasonably have expected to finish the quest with a thousand XP. That's about average for gamers above Level Thirty."

Feral said, "We're—"

Double F held up a finger to silence her.

"If you found an Egg—which this isn't—we would have given you five thousand XP. We like to give Egg finders at least enough to boost them a level."

"Then I need six thousand. Really, seven thousand, because I'm almost a Sixty."

"Jeez, Feral, I'm still thinking my way through this. Let's just talk it through for a minute without it becoming a negotiation from the get-go."

Feral glared at him, her lips set in a tight line, but she remained silent and nodded.

"Sometimes gamers also do something completely unexpected or cool." Double F shot another glance at WB. "I mean, we kind of expect people to find the Eggs, and have thought through how they would likely find them. If they surprise us, we think it's worth some more XP—usually, we come up with a special Achievement to give them, and attach the XP to that. Sometimes that's worth as much as finding the Egg itself." He shrugged. "Think about it. Every day, we watch people do the same quests in the same way. Think how cool it is for us to see something completely unexpected. Something mind-blowing." Again, he glanced at WB. "So this was completely mind-blowing." He propped his elbows on the table and steepled his fingers together in a gesture reminiscent of Mr. Spock from the original Star Trek series—old-school cool. "We weren't even sure we'd be able to make it happen mechanically." He smiled. "You should have seen Quest Control. People were screaming and high-fiving each other like it was a whole new game." His eyes glazed over. "A whole new game..." he muttered. "Janne!" He looked up.

"Yes?"

"Remind me to talk to the boss about this. We might be able to use this to ease some of the quest flow-through issues."

"Certainly."

Double F turned back to the gaming duo. "What I'm thinking is this: seven thousand XP for the glitch, a plus-two Likability bump, and seven thousand XP for the Rex Rider Achievement. We've already disabled the ability to Whisper the Rex." He gave them both a dirty look. "That was never supposed to be used on the Rex."

"Where did you expect players to use it?" said WB.

"Well, on the brontosaurus, of course, a—"

Feral and WB exchanged a glance, and Feral nudged WB with an elbow as if to say, *Bookmark this moment—we're going to talk about it later.*

"So," Double F hurried on, "Fourteen thousand XP total. Five free days, and a thousand dollars on gift cards."

"And the remainder to be finalized with Hodgins," Feral reminded him.

With an eye roll and a sigh, Double F said, "And the remainder to be finalized with Hodgins."

"Deal?" Feral asked WB.

He nodded. They turned to face Double F.

"Deal," they said.

Double F looked around. "We're the last ones in the restaurant. Let's get going."

As he signed for the charges, Feral whispered to WB, "We just got screwed. The park is closed. We're going to have to spend the night outside."

Walking down the arcade, Double F told the pair, "This is my favorite time of day at SPARK. It's quiet. The guests are gone, but the lights are still on. We—the SPARK employees—are alone here, cleaning and preparing for the next day." He guided them toward one of the marked employee doors near the Hub. "The normal exits are already closed. We'll have to take you out the employee exit."

They walked in silence. At the exit, Double F took their gear and dumped it in a bin for pickup later.

Once the doors closed behind them, he said, "You know, it's really fun watching you two play the park. Thanks." He paused. "Can I give you a lift somewhere?"

They shook their heads, and he walked off to his car. Will and ShaChri were left standing in the parking lot.

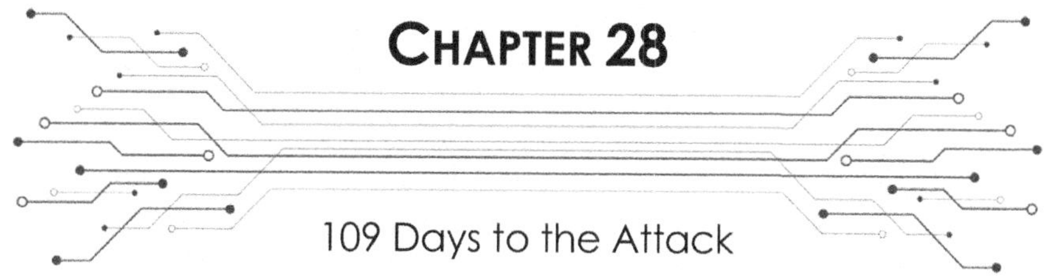

Chapter 28

109 Days to the Attack

You must not fight too often with one enemy,
or you will teach him all your art of war.
—Napoleon Bonaparte

Ragnar Sarnak was back in Mozambique. It took him most of a week to move through enough countries on different passports to know he wasn't being traced. *At least I'm not in Maputo. Lichinga is better for training. Higher, cooler, dryer, but still an armpit where decent vodka is hard to find.*

"I told you I wanted forty men," Sarnak told Hashem.

"And we have been blessed with twenty-three," Hashem replied. "It is enough."

"Are they experienced?"

Hashem glowered at him.

Finally, he said, "Some have training."

"Every day, I learn something that lowers our chance of success," Sarnak spat.

"The attack itself is our success. We will carry it out on American soil. Hundreds and hundreds will die by bullet and fire." Hashem's eyes glowed in anticipation.

"I could hire some Angolans."

"No!" Hashem shouted. "*We* will strike this blow! It besmirches my honor that *you* are even here."

The training ground was too small, and they couldn't construct a full-size mock-up. Today was their first day with the actual weapons. They were using Fabrique Nationale Five-seveNs with thirty-round magazines as the weapon Sarnak had selected for them.

"The men want AKs," Hashem told him. "They like fully automatic weapons."

Sarnak glared at him. "As I have explained. The AK is too large for us to get into the target area covertly. Besides, your men need better fire discipline. If we gave them AKs, half the rounds would be shot into the air on full auto. The Five-seveNs give them as many rounds. They just have to squeeze the trigger for every shot." He paused. "Are they capable of that?"

Hashem stormed away. By the end of the day, they had only twenty-two fighters. One managed to shoot himself in the leg, and Hashem sent him on to Paradise. The following day, they were down to twenty-one. Hashem grew impatient and shot another one to "make sure they focus."

"Tomorrow, I will have them practice with the toys that will house the incendiary devices," Sarnak told Hashem. "Do your best to see none kill themselves with stuffed children's toys."

Sarnak got an encrypted email from his North Korean contact, saying that the test of the hack looked promising. Final version expected within thirty days.

Ragnar smiled. Even though he harangued the men about being incompetent, they were coming along nicely. They all paid much closer attention after Hashem killed the one who shot himself in the leg.

The body count should still be large enough to satisfy my clients, and the incendiary bombs will make an inferno out of SPARK.

– 1 1 0 1 0 0 1 0 –

ShaChri and Will stood in the parking lot.

"Well, this sucks," she said. "We're stuck outside the park. The last bus has left for town. We'll have to get a ride into Barstow and stay at one of those sketchy motels on the interstate, and catch the bus back in the morning." She pulled out her phone. "We should have let Double F give us a ride."

"Have you ever seen the Black Grass fields at night?" Will asked her.

She paused. "That has to be one of the creepiest pickup lines I've ever heard."

Will was taken aback. "It wasn't a pickup line. It was a serious question. Have you ever even been to the Black Grass fields?"

"Why would I go? There's a stupid little demo in the Hub. What's so exciting about seeing the fields, and why at night?" She narrowed her eyes.

"It's kind of cool," Will said. "The demo only shows the blades tracking the sun. At night, they track the strongest radiant energy source. If you get close enough, that's you. As you walk along the fence, you can see them turn and focus on you. They follow you as you walk past."

"Huh," said ShaChri. "That does sound kind of cool. But why bring it up now?"

Will pointed at the moon. It was a thin, waning crescent.

"Tonight, the moon is so small, the effect will be more apparent. We might even have blades four or five yards deep into the field tracking us."

"Uh, hello!" ShaChri said. "I'm pretty sure they don't give tours at night. And I'm equally sure Security won't just let us in to walk through the grass."

Will blushed but stood his ground. "We don't need a tour. Once we get close to the fence, we'll be the strongest source, and the moon will give us enough light to see the blades move. We just can't touch the fence. They don't like that."

ShaChri took his hand in hers. "Sounds like a story I need to hear. So how do we get to the fields? I don't want to spend all night wandering through the desert."

"No problem." Will grinned. "From here, it's a little over a mile. We can be at the fence in a half-hour—there's an access road."

They talked as they walked.

"You need some training," ShaChri told him. "I'll take you to the arena tomorrow and give you some pointers."

"Okay," Will said. "I'm going to need to learn how to use my new weapon."

"Yeah, I was kind of hoping you'd forgotten about that."

"Not a chance."

They walked quietly for a few minutes. There was no traffic on the Solar Prime access road.

"Why'd you leave?" ShaChri said in a soft tone.

"You mean Houston? My foster family?"

"Yeah. Were they mean?"

"Nah, it wasn't like that. I wasn't abused or beaten. I didn't have any problems like Mellew had." Will shook his head. "They were going to send me back to a group home." He shook his head again. "Those places—every day, we said some BS sobriety pledge, and then we had a group discussion about the inappropriateness of using violence to solve our problems. That might have been fine, but I was never a druggie or boozer, and I've never hurt anyone."

"How'd you know?" ShaChri said. "That they were going to send you back?

"I recognized the signs. Doors that weren't locked when I got there, suddenly start being locked. The CPS lady starts coming around more. The parents would stop talking when I walked into the room. Then one night, after a bad dream, Foster Mom saw me with a knife. Thought I was coming after them. Called the cops."

"So that knife has *already* gotten you in trouble," ShaChri said.

Will counted a hundred steps before he answered.

"Yeah."

"Why?"

He knew what she meant. *Why do you need a knife?*

Will counted another hundred steps.

"After my dad died, my mom broke somehow. Nothing real obvious at first. Not to me, anyway. I was only ten. She stopped throwing stuff out. Even junk mail. We had huge stacks of crap all over the house." Will spread his arms to indicate everywhere. "She was still so smart. Both of my parents were smart. Outside the house, everything was fine. But at home…sometimes when I got up in the morning, she'd still be sitting at the table, writing. Same spot as when I went to bed. Same clothes. She filled up tons of notebooks with writing. Longhand. Cursive, you know?"

"We never learned cursive in my school," ShaChri said. "My mom acted like it was some kind of major sin that we didn't. She made me learn how to read it."

"Hah." Will laughed without humor. "My mom did the same. One day, when she was gone, I looked in the notebooks."

"What was she writing?" ShaChri said.

"Letters to my dad. She must have written thousands of pages to my dead father."

They walked in silence a bit longer.

"Then it got worse. Mom stopped letting me have friends over. We stopped throwing out anything—even empty pizza boxes and milk cartons. Then the rats showed up." Will hated the memory. "One of the CPS counselors told me there were holes chewed in the back corners of the house. Under the eaves?"

"The rats did that?" ShaChri said.

"No. The lady said it was squirrels, and the rats came after. I guess they started a colony in the attic. Anyway, the house started to stink. One of our cats died, and mom just shut the laundry room door and left it there."

Will was crying—not sobbing, just the kind of tears that made it hard for him to talk. Fat drops that rolled down his cheeks and fell to the desert beneath their feet.

He cut to the end of the story.

"Then, when I was thirteen, my mom died. I called 911 and ended up in the system."

Even in the dim light, they could now see the chain-link wall separating the Black Grass farms of Solar Prime from the rest of the world.

A Jeep gradually moved nearer to them as Will and ShaChri got closer to the fence.

"They're not going to let us do this, Will."

It was the first time she had called him anything but WB.

"No," he replied. "I think we'll be fine as long as we don't touch the fence."

At ten meters out, the Jeep hit them with a spotlight. They stopped walking and turned toward the Jeep while shielding their eyes from the light.

"We'll be fine as long as we don't touch the fence," ShaChri mocked.

The Jeep pulled up.

"You're approaching a restricted area," said the driver. "Please turn back."

"We just wanted to look at the Grass," Will said.

"We'll leave," said ShaChri.

The driver responded with suspicion and a Scottish accent.

"Ye know we have tours"—it came out *toors*— "during normal business hours. You could get a much better view o' the grass then."

"Mister McIntosh? Is that you?" Will recognized the accent as belonging to one of the guards who saved him.

"Will? Aye, 'tis. Are ye daft?"

"Sorry, I just wanted to show my friend how the Grass tracks you at night."

The Jeep rolled close enough for normal conversation, and McIntosh killed the spotlight, leaving the two gamers illuminated by the headlights.

"Dude, I kinda hoped you'd be in LA by now." It was Olsen, the guard who gave Will the KA-BAR. "Tell me you're not still sleeping in the desert."

"No," Will said, eager to change the subject. "I've squared away my living situation. I'm good."

"Who's your friend?" McIntosh said.

"ShaChri…" Will realized he didn't know her last name.

"Patel," she said.

"Nice to meet you, ShaChri." McIntosh stumbled with the pronunciation and accent. "Just don't touch the fence on your walk. If ye do, we'll have to take ye in."

"Thanks, guys!" said Will.

"And, Will?" Olsen called.

"Yeah?"

"Let's not make this a habit. Be careful out here." The driver killed the headlights. "This'll help. Don't want to ruin your fun by having the wee blades o' Grass tracking our lights."

"Thanks," Will said.

As he and ShaChri walked along the fence, ShaChri said, "I thought you were full of it, but they really do follow us."

The wonder in her voice made Will smile. The individual blades of Grass swiveled to track them.

ShaChri pulled at his hand, forcing him to run a few steps. When they stopped, they could hear a faint rustling, like leaves in autumn, as blades of Grass on both sides struggled to track their combined energy.

ShaChri leaned against Will, her head against his shoulder. She looked up at him, eyes reflecting starlight.

"This is nice." She patted his arm and sighed with content.

Eventually, they turned away from the fence and started walking back to SPARK. The Jeep quickly joined them.

"Get in," McIntosh said.

"We never touched the fence!" said ShaChri.

"Yeah, but we'll all feel happier when you two are at least a click away from the fence. We get nervous when people get as close as you two are. Besides, it's not a great place to be, day or night. We found a body out here a while back."

Will thought maybe they were talking about him. They weren't. As the pair climbed in the Jeep, Olsen explained.

"Some woman. According to Barstow PD. They think she was killed somewhere else and dumped here—well, outside the fence, but still on Solar Prime property." He gestured to the south, toward the freeway. "Listen, I'd rather take you into town, but we're still on duty."

"No, no, it's okay," Will said in a rush. "We're staying on SPARK property." *Not really a lie.*

As the guards dropped Will and ShaChri back at the SPARK parking lot, Olsen whispered to Will, "You still have…?"

"Yep. And thanks!"

"Take care, you two," Mcintosh said, as they drove away, but muttered, "Eejits."

Will yawned. "I'm beat."

"Me, too." ShaChri looked around. "I've got an idea. It may not be great, but Security doesn't go by there too much. We ought to be able to get some sleep."

"Lead on."

Will walked next to her as they cut across the SPARK parking lot. ShaChri took his hand again.

"How did you end up getting the Dino Whisperer Perk?" he said.

"I thought my whole family was going to be banned from SPARK!" ShaChri laughed.

Will nodded. He didn't remember worrying about that, but had a memory of feeling that he was in trouble.

ShaChri told her tale of punting Baby Cyanite and then trying to take on the Rex as a Level 1 noob.

"You?" she asked Will.

"My mom was not happy when I chased off after the baby." *How much can I say?* "I had to run and dodge the Rex to get back to the cave." *That should be okay.*

Eventually, they wandered through the vacant parking lots and ended up by the composting and greenhouse area. They sat with their backs against the translucent exterior walls and continued to talk.

The walls of SPARK shielded them from light that may have spilled their way. The resort hotels were farther away, on the opposite side from the parking lots, and showed as a dim glow in that direction. Overhead, the sky blazed with stars.

ShaChri pointed up. "Two days ago, I would have told you the Milky Way was just some old legend, like the Easter Bunny. Now, I can see it, and know what it is." She looked over at Will. "Thanks."

"It's weird," he said. "I know so much more about the universe than when I got here. I don't think I ever realized how much I didn't know!"

They sat quietly for a bit.

Then Will said, "Why did you put a low-level topaz in your sword? I mean, I get the *nothing should be perfect* thing. But why a brown topaz?"

"Uhm…I just grabbed the first gem I saw. It just happened to be the brown topaz. No big deal."

Will knew there was more to it than that. She had scrolled through her inventory with deliberation, taking her time. He remembered her looking over at him before choosing the topaz.

I'll let it go.

ShaChri said, "What's with you and the blue handprints on your armor? And why do they only show up in KT Crossing?"

His turn to be evasive. "Uh, yeah. Something happened when I was here with my folks."

She propped herself up on one elbow and turned to him.

"Something? Just *something*? That's all you're going to tell me?"

Will tried to say something, but started and stopped a couple times without actually forming any words.

"Dude. Your mouth is working like a fish out of water." She poked him in the chest. "Say something."

Will rubbed his face. "I, uh…okay." He rolled onto his side to face her, their noses two inches apart. "I'm not supposed to talk about it."

"I knew it," ShaChri said. "I knew it had something to do with an Egg." She put a finger to his lips. "Don't tell me." She rolled away from him and onto her back. "You know, I do the majors all the time. But I kind of do them the same way. I lead my clients through a way that I know will get them through the quest and keep them happy." She sighed. "I don't even really think about the quest itself anymore. I just focus on the fighting."

Will's lips tingled from where her finger had pressed against them.

"I guess I'm just the opposite. I'm terrible at the combat parts of SPARK." He rolled onto his back and looked up at the stars. "I had fun tonight."

"Sucks to be outside," ShaChri said, "but I had fun, too."

She reached out and took his hand.

They fell asleep, hand in hand. Will did not dream of rats.

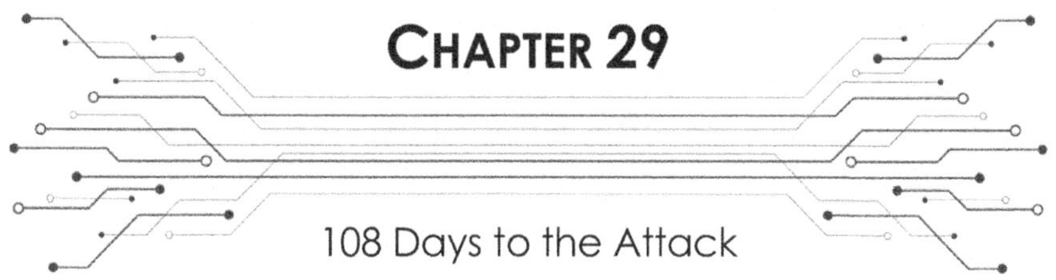

Chapter 29

108 Days to the Attack

Friendship is the comfort that comes from knowing that even when you feel you're all alone, you aren't.
—Unknown

He awoke when ShaChri kicked his feet.

"C'mon, lazybones. Get up!" Her voice was quiet but had a tone of urgency.

Will looked up and saw her smiling down at him. He was happy.

"Lazybones?" he said.

"Yeah." She grinned. "It's something my mom always called me when I didn't want to get up in the morning."

"My mom always called me a slug-a-bed. Whatever that means."

It was getting light, but the sun hadn't made it over the horizon. Will was about to say something else, but ShaChri put a finger to her lips and motioned him to follow her. He heard the voices. They walked away from the sound, but the guys unloading the truck full of plants saw them anyway. Will locked eyes with the shorter of the two and saw him nudge his buddy. Both workers stared at the two gamers as they crossed the street, walking toward the nearest resort.

"I think our free days include early entry," said ShaChri. "So let's go grab a decent breakfast and take the first shuttle in."

"Okay," Will said. "What are you going to do today? Guide?"

"Heck no." ShaChri laughed. "I've got some Princesses to tackle, and Knowledge quests to do. Plus, I've got a friend who absolutely sucks at quest combat, so I thought maybe I'd drag him to the arena for an hour or so to see if I can't help him figure out how to use that stupid bat he hauls around."

A mixture of embarrassment and appreciation overcame Will.

"Really?" he said. "You'd waste SPARK time teaching me?"

"It won't be a waste. You've already gotten me two levels I didn't expect yesterday. Plus," she smiled, "I got to ride the Rex. I never would have thought of that. If you can get to where you can hold your own in melee combat, you'll be a pretty good questing companion." She kissed him on the cheek. "If I'd known we were going on a date last night, I might have put on some makeup."

"Oh, I didn't know that was a date." Will was in unknown waters. "And I don't think you need makeup."

She stopped and turned him to face her, using her eye-flicking lie detector technique to search his soul.

"Hmm," was all she said.

At breakfast, Will brought up the bookmarked part of their conversation with Double F.

"I think he was going to say, *the brontosaurus and…* something. What was the something?"

ShaChri chewed her bite of waffle for a minute.

"I've been thinking about that, too," she replied. "You see a bunch of dinos in KT Crossing. Mostly, you just pass them by. They seem to be scenery more than players—you don't interact much with them. The triceratops and the stegosaurus seem to be happy munching plants. I've never seen the Pteranodon even come close to landing or doing anything more than a low swoop over the river."

"Yeah," Will said.

Even though he didn't have the experience with the quest ShaChri had, it made sense. Plant and fish eaters would probably ignore you unless you were a threat.

"So who does that leave?" he said.

"There's two possibilities, I think. First, are the annoying little spitters. The ones about this tall." ShaChri held her hand out at about the height of their table. "They can cause a lot of damage if they swarm you, but they're pretty easy to swat, stab, or blast."

"Think you could Whisper them?" Will said. "What good would it do?"

"Don't know. Maybe you could make them allies, and they'd find loot for you. Or lead you to the bronto?"

Will shrugged. It was easy for noobs to get lost in KT Crossing if they didn't have Cyanites with them.

ShaChri continued. "Which leaves, the raptors."

Will had clear, scary memories of fighting the velociraptors with his parents. Even leveled down to make it a fair fight for the trio of new gamers, the combat was a close thing. They used all of their first aid kits just to be able to continue the game. It was the boss-level fight. Yesterday, the T-Rex took care of the velociraptors for them.

"I think—and I try to look closely whenever I do the quest—the boss raptor is a gray," said ShaChri. "The rest of the pack are definitely reds. But maybe we could Whisper them?"

"What good would it do?" Will said. "You're near the end. Why would you need allies at that point?"

She gave him a smug smile. "You figure it out. You're the one who does everything weird."

She sat back and waited. Will stopped mid-chew and was still holding his fork in the air, thinking.

Suddenly, he chewed once and gulped down the bite of pancakes. His eyes lit up.

"It's a tough fight, right?" he said.

ShaChri nodded.

"And you're in sight of the exit," he continued. "Most people are just going to bolt for safety. At that point, with your health low, you don't want to risk another encounter. You've stopped thinking about loot, and are only thinking about survival."

ShaChri nodded again, smiling.

"So if suddenly you had your own pack of raptors as friends and allies," he said, "why wouldn't you do a little more exploring? After all, you're probably at full health, and now have some very dangerous friends."

WB was nervous as they entered the park. *Will Feral forget she promised to train me?*

No. As soon as they entered, she headed directly toward the arena.

WB meandered along, looking at things. He stopped and stared at the scenery.

"What?" Feral came back to him. "You think there are more clues hidden here?"

WB nodded.

"Why?" she said. "What good would they do? You've already got all the Princesses."

WB turned and looked at her. "That's just it. I haven't come this way much. I think there might be one more."

"An *eighth* Princess? What makes you say that?"

"Well..." WB began slowly, afraid to say it out loud. "All the other quests—at least, the ones I've actually done—seem to have a definitive, clean ending. You get the *Quest Complete* message in your ARGs. That doesn't happen with the Princesses. Even after you have all seven."

"Of course you do," Feral said. "You get the trumpets playing, you get the points, and you get *Quest Complete*."

WB shook his head, aware the whole thing sounded silly.

"You get a *Princess Complete* message," he said. "Not *Quest Complete*. I think there's a difference."

"I think *you* think too much. C'mon."

Feral dragged him to the arena and spent an hour teaching the fundamentals of how to use a bludgeoning weapon, and then showed him how to map that skill over to using a sword.

She finished up by saying, "Look, you don't have to be an expert until you want to fight in a melee tournament. Most encounters are set up so a mid-level player with average skill can survive. Yes, the bad guys level up, but so do you, and the combat system takes your profile into account—Brawn, Vigor, and everything else—as well as any perks you have on your weapon or armor. I think you're ready to hit a major."

They started to walk out of the arena.

"First, though," said Feral, "you need a better sword. I know you've got that heirloom sword you were using to practice, but it's fairly rudimentary. Do you have anything better?"

WB shook his head. "That's my only sword."

– 1 1 0 1 0 0 1 0 –

Feral stopped him and stared. She was about to call BS, but realized if WB was honest about what quests he had done, he wouldn't have found any swords as loot. The only way he would have acquired them was if he crafted them at a WeaponSmith or bought one.

Feral sighed, dreading what she was about to do.

She reached up to her ARGs and shared her weapon inventory with WB.

"Well," she said, "a bet's a bet. You won. Take your pick."

She had never shown her weapon inventory to anyone other than a WeaponSmith before. It made her feel vulnerable.

– 1 1 0 1 0 0 1 0 –

"So she was a guest?" HVH asked Hodgins and Janne.

The AI replied, "Boss, we can't know for certain. Her fingerprints, face, and dental work were all deliberately destroyed. What we have is one fragment of a star tattoo on her wrist that matches our records, and the apparent match to the body's size, hair color, and clothing. She was wearing a khaki skirt and a green blouse. Based on that data, I am ninety-six percent certain the victim found on Solar Prime's property was a guest at SPARK a week prior."

Van Horne rubbed his face. "Any way we can let Barstow PD know without giving away too much?"

"Absolutely, boss," said Hodgins. "We have standard parking lot surveillance showing the woman and her companion. We'll pass it on to Barstow. They ought to be able to pull images showing her tats and the plate number of the rental car."

"What about him? You know he did this." Hecker was angry.

"We got nothing," Hodgins said. "The glasses, beard, and hat made FaceRec completely useless. The guy managed to enter SPARK without touching a sensor. Clearly a pro."

HVH stabbed a finger at Hodgins, then at the ceiling.

"I want you two to review every second of their visit. Look for anything that can ID him."

– 1 1 0 1 0 0 1 0 –

WB was awestruck. He only had four weapons in his entire inventory. Feral must have close to thirty, including four marked as Elite, and two Heirloom.

He felt an odd satisfaction on seeing that the ReB2 katana still carried the name *Feral's Wrath.*

"I don't know what to pick," he said. "I mean, I'm not going to take anything Elite or Heirloom, and I'm definitely not going to take Feral's Wrath. You're giving me too many choices. I don't even know enough to know what would work best for me. Can you help me?"

She smiled. "Sure. I do this for clients all the time." Then a fleeting frown. "You're going to need to master this kind of stuff if you're going to guide. How's your profile built?"

Now it was WB's turn to be embarrassed. He felt as if he were about to open his soul.

He started reading stats to her.

Feral said, "Can you just share that with me? So I can see it in my ARGs?"

WB knew how to share his inventory, but not his avatar stats. He was fumbling with the controls on his ARG earpiece.

Feral stepped behind him and put her hand on his and guided him to the selector wheel.

"Scroll over to Characteristics using the wheel. Now, click Share." She dropped her hand onto his shoulder as the view from his ARGs was superimposed over her own view. "This always gives me a little vertigo. It helps to hang on and be facing the same direction as your client." She put her other hand on his arm.

That Feral now had one hand on his right shoulder and one hand on his left arm as she whispered in his ear, profoundly affected WB. He could feel her pressed against his back. He suddenly felt warm and awkward. Feral didn't seem to notice.

"Geez," she said. "Your profile's a mess! You haven't even allocated your points from yesterday. Let's see where you are."

He felt her breath on his neck.

"This looks like a mage's profile with the high Brains and Aptitude," she said. "But you've still got the lowest Brawn and Agility I've seen for somebody at your level." She paused. "Your numbers don't make sense. I mean, you've got the points of somebody at Level Sixty, but you're still a Forty-Two. And where'd you get all the Wisdom? You must have done some other weird stuff besides riding the Rex."

WB said, "Uhmm—"

"Skip it," she said. "Let me wrap my head around all these Princesses before you lead me down some other weird path."

Will was relieved.

"For my level," she continued, "I have much higher Brawn and Agility. It fits my fighting style. I want speed and power. For you, both of those numbers are low. What kind of fighter do you see yourself as? Nimble and fast, or stronger but slower? Are you more likely to stand toe-to-toe with someone and just hack away at each other? Or would you move around a lot?"

WB hadn't really thought about it. But now, he saw himself as a knight, heavily armored. Knights weren't nimble, by any means. But they were strong.

"I guess," he replied, "I'm really kind of a reluctant fighter. But when I fight, I see myself going toe-to-toe."

Feral clapped his shoulder. "That's exactly how I see you. Somebody who would rather think of a different way, but would be…I don't know… stalwart—yeah, stalwart—in a fight. Okay, so here's my suggestion: take all four of your available points and put them against Brawn. Then with a vision of how you might fight, I'd suggest a larger sword. Something you'd have to use both hands to wield. Maybe a Claymore or a Broadsword. If you want to do something relative to your heritage, maybe a Jingeom—it's a Korean Dragon Sword."

"You know a lot about swords." WB allocated his points, as she'd suggested.

She squeezed his shoulder and laughed. "Of course I do. A friend of mine made me take a class." She rushed on. "I don't have any Jingeoms. You'd probably have to get a WeaponSmith to make one. But they're longer, heavier swords. Like a Claymore, they're double-edged. I have a pretty decent Claymore with an open slot."

WB nodded. "Yeah, that could work. Is it okay if I take the Claymore? Only until I can afford to get a Jingeom made, I mean?"

"Dude, you earned that Claymore. It's yours." She gave him a micro-hug from behind and transferred the sword to him. "I think I'm going to like having a tank as a questing buddy."

WB tried to process that last statement. He knew what a *tank* was—a gamer with high constitution and high strength. Someone who could absorb a lot of damage while the other members of the questing party used their skills—magic, ranged weapons, agility, potions, whatever—to rain down damage from afar. Good parties had a diverse mix of abilities and skills.

Feral's questing buddy? I kind of like the sound of that. He blushed.

They started walking again.

"So what now?" said WB. "Off to tackle some Princess Quests?"

Feral nodded. "Yep. And a Knowledge quest or two. Want to meet around seven tonight, and then try to make the last launch into KT Crossing? See if we're right about the Raptors?"

There was nothing that WB wanted to do more, but he tempered his reaction.

"Sure. I think I'm going to try out my new Claymore. Maybe hit a major or two. See if I can take out an Orc."

Feral laughed. "Okay. Go get 'em, tiger."

– 1 1 0 1 0 0 1 0 –

As soon as she was out of sight, Feral wanted to beat her head against a wall. *Tiger? What the heck was that? And what was with all the touching and hugging?*

Normally, she hated touching people. She almost broke Fantom's nose when he tried to hug her.

I liked sleeping next to him last night. And I know why I picked the topaz. It matches his eyes.

She forced the thought out of her head. Feral Daughter was hunting Princesses.

It was a frustrating morning. Half the day was gone, and not even a hundred XP to show for it. She hit the Soylent Bistro for lunch and stared at Mars as she munched her hummus and carrots.

Feral was certain now, that WB had done something—maybe found an Egg—in Mars. *First of all, he's got the Commander's blaster. No way he would have won that through combat.* She smiled. *Boy just cannot fight. At least, not yet. He also has a flawless Martian ruby. You only find those on the upper trail.*

She munched another carrot. *It has to have something to do with the sand. They were taking sand* up *in the elevator. If they'd just wanted to dump more on the floor, why not just wheel it in? Why even mess with the elevator? Where's it go?*

She wanted to ask WB about it, but it was a park protocol foul she wasn't willing to risk.

After lunch, she switched to Flighty Damsel and joined a group playing Mars. She poked around on the upper trail for three hours, before giving up and jumping.

What's the deal?

– 1 1 0 1 0 0 1 0 –

WB turned down the PreHistory Arcade. He needed to talk to Miss Sparkle.

Sitting with Miss Sparkle in her inner office, WB again asked her about the message imbedded in the Hittite letter he was given for helping the little girl, Paige.

"I guess what I really want to know is if this is a serious message, or if it's more like something you'd read in a fortune cookie. What does, *Lie down before you arise*, even mean? Is it actually supposed to be a clue to something? Or am I wasting my time?"

Miss Sparkle smiled. “WonderBoy,”—she always used his full avatar name—“you know the answer. You’re a Seeker. I can’t tell you any more about it than I could the last two times you’ve come in to ask me.”

“I know.” WB sighed.

In some bizarre fashion, Miss Sparkle had taken his mother’s place. He came and saw her nearly every day. Mostly, with made-up reasons like this one. Her presence comforted him and made him feel safe.

CHAPTER 30

Oh, the places you'll go.
—Dr. Seuss

Janne had cycles to spare, and assigned them to Will, as she would have any other guest. But she realized a stronger connection was growing. In her neural network, just as in human beings, pathways frequently exercised grew stronger.

Janne had robust connections to many SPARK employees. HVH and Hodgins were the strongest. Double F was next. Janne interacted with him numerous times per day. WB, because of his escapades, elevated monitoring status, and now-frequent visits to Miss Sparkle, was becoming as firm a connection as any quest referee. That was exceedingly rare for a guest.

Janne routinely monitored the Pod and its members, and kept close track of names on the leaderboard. CastIron took the top spot two years ago, so Janne was well-aware of her, but found her an odd, distant connection. As if she knew her intimately, yet still found her unpleasant.

WB was different.

"Why are you really here today?" Janne/Miss Sparkle asked WB.

– 1 1 0 1 0 0 1 0 –

Will was a little chagrinned. Miss Sparkle always seemed to know when there was something he wasn't saying.

"Well," he replied, "there's this girl—"

"Feral Daughter?" Miss Sparkle said.

"Yeah." WB was surprised. "How did you know?"

"WonderBoy. My WonderBoy. Surely you realize you and Miss Feral have created quite a stir within SPARK. Individually, your accomplishments are noteworthy. Together…well, not everyone rides a T-Rex."

WB was taken aback. Intellectually, he grasped that Miss Sparkle was a creation of SPARK. But he still thought of them as separate and distinct.

That's the magic here. They make the virtual feel real.

"Okay," he said. "Yes, Feral. I think I, you know…kind of, sort of, like her. You know, as a girl."

"What I know for certain, young man, is you introduced enough modifiers into that sentence so as to rob it of any significance. Are you saying you have feelings beyond mere friendship for Miss Feral?"

"Yes. That's the problem," WB said in a rush. "She makes me feel… funny. I mean, she puts her hand on my arm, and I go all…stupid and stuff."

"Have you done anything inappropriate?"

"No. No! I mean, it's just…I don't know." He paused. "Should I kiss her?"

– 1 1 0 1 0 0 1 0 –

Janne tried to process this. There were correlations with her discussions with HVH concerning his *feelings* toward dating partners. She would have to address the possibility of adding additional empathy subroutines.

She knew what happened within SPARK. After all, she saw everything. However, anything that might have happened in town or outside of her walls was a mystery.

Luckily, this was a question requiring very few CPU cycles to consider.

"No," she replied. "You are both sixteen. Statistically, this is a normal age for preliminary romantic encounters. However, there are additional circumstances in play." *Enhanced empathy would be beneficial.*

"Okay. Thanks." WB sat silently for a moment.

"WonderBoy, she may feel romantically inclined toward you as well, but it would be a good course of action to let her dictate the terms of your relationship." A few quick calculations led Janne to divulge further information. "Miss Feral has reacted negatively to previous attempts at romantic liaisons. Caution is advised."

– 1 1 0 1 0 0 1 0 –

Bizarrely, Will was relieved. He was more than happy to wait. He had no desire to ruin a friendship, and no wish for a broken nose. Still, having her snuggle up next to him at night made it very difficult for him to sleep.

He wandered through SPARK, lost in thought, but moving enough to avoid causing a traffic jam. He played a few minor quests but felt foggy. He hadn't gotten enough sleep last night, and didn't want to fall asleep at a table in one of the restaurants, so he sought out a quiet area and ended up near Tiny

Universe. He pushed his ARGs up on his head and lay on a bench next to the mosaic wall. As he was drifting off, he saw it.

His eyes relaxed and lost their focus as he gazed at the tiles. The fields of vision of each eye slowly overlapped, and a 3D image emerged. Will's heart pounded, his focus shifted, and he lost the image. He only saw the individual tiles now. He tried to be as still as he could as the excitement grew. Three or four times, he nearly brought the image back into focus, before he succeeded.

He was seeing an image of Sparky, but it was not the normal Sparky. It had no facial features, and eight points instead of seven—just like the banners in the Princess rooms. The words *Find Me* came into focus below the eight-pointed star. Below the words, and slightly to the right, an X seemed to form.

Will slowly sat upright. As soon as he moved his head out of its horizontal orientation, the image disappeared. Upright, he tried to relax his eyes again. Nothing. He tried tilting his head sideways. Maybe. But he found he couldn't reliably get the tiles to overlap and form the image unless he was lying down.

He switched his head over to the other end of the bench. The image appeared. *Somehow my ARGs were making this image axis-specific.*

He reached up to try playing with their position over his eyes, and realized he wasn't looking through his ARGs. *This image is in the real world.* His skin tingled.

Will swapped ends of the bench again and was staring at the image when he felt Feral kicking his feet.

"C'mon," she said. "What did your mom call you? Slug-a-bug?"

"Slug-a-bed," WB corrected. "What time is it?"

"Time to Whisper some Raptors!"

As they walked to PreHistory Plaza, Feral was manic.

"I got a Princess! I did the WeaponSmith Quest, and all the stupid little quests in the Ascent Arcade, and kicked that little twerp's butt. Okay, it took me six tries. But I smoked her! Then I went over to Civilization Rises and started doing the same thing but ran out of time. Did you know there's an arts and crafts school there? How did I not notice it before?"

When she finally took a breath, WB told her about his day but kept quiet about the image in the tiles. If she harbored doubts about him before, this would prove he was crazy. Secret images hidden in mosaic tiles you had to lie down to see, and then do something weird with your eyes.

Sure, Will, let me call medical...

– 1 1 0 1 0 0 1 0 –

When they emerged from KT Crossing three hours later, they expected to see Hodgins or Double F waiting for them. Whispering the Raptors worked, and they spent a good hour exploring the post-impact zone with a pack of ferocious bodyguards.

They found Meteor's Strike—an Elite longbow, and a fair number of gems and gold—but when they emerged, no Double F, no Hodgins. They were still happy about their success, and only a little let down about it not being some sort of Egg. Even so, they added a Raptored achievement, Feral bumped up a level, and WB went up three.

Unwilling to make another mistake, they found a bench near the exit, still hopeful that Double F or Hodgins might show up with more good news. They sat in silence, browsing their ARGs.

"Do you think Mellew's pretty?" Feral said.

"Uh, yeah." The question took him by surprise, and Will answered it without thinking.

"What color are her eyes?" Feral said.

"Blue."

Alarms sounded belatedly in Will's head. He saw himself standing on a narrow pillar surrounded by a sea of hot lava.

"What color are mine?" Feral said.

Will desperately wanted to raise his ARGs and look at ShaChri, but he knew this was a test. With each passing second, the molten sea was rising higher.

"Hickory," he said. "When I was in seventh grade, I had to take woodshop. We had this project to make a bookshelf. Everyone picked pine because it was cheapest. Or oak because the shop had a lot of it. Back in the corner was one piece of dark wood. I thought it was walnut. Mister Anderson told me it was hickory. When I told him I wanted to use it for the bookshelf, he told me not to. *It's the only piece we have, and it's a very hard wood. Difficult to work with. Pine's way more forgiving*. I went with hickory. By the time I finished, I had a very small bookshelf. Amazingly dark, with a complex grain." Will's hands traced imaginary wood patterns in the air. "Your eyes are that color. When I see them in the sunlight, I can also see thin lines of gold in your irises radiating out from your pupils. Indoors, it's hard to tell your pupil from your iris. They're that dark."

Will felt the shift in Feral's body position as she turned to look at him. The lava was receding. She raised her ARGs and then reached over and raised his.

Her focus danced back and forth between his eyes. She put a hand on his cheek and traced his jawline.

She took his hand, and they walked away from KT Crossing. Will's heart pounded. They sawed off their wristbands and dumped their gear into separate strollers before taking different paths to the Underground.

Just before WB pulled off his ARGs, he saw a new quest now showed as active. Something called The Path.

Huh. I'll have to check it out tomorrow.

As the Pod settled down for the night, Feral walked over to WB's spot.

"I'm, uh…I'm kind of cold," she said. "Mind if I sleep next to you tonight? I, uh, noticed last night that you throw off a lot of heat."

She chewed on her thumbnail as she looked down where WB sat beneath the pipes. He tried to keep the grin off his face as he scooted closer to the wall.

"Plenty of room," he replied.

"I sleep better on my side. Let's face that way." She pointed toward the wall. "And I can sleep against your back."

WB rolled onto his side, and Feral snuggled against his back.

"Did you practice that?" she whispered.

"Practice what?"

"Your answer about my eyes."

"No." He paused. "But I do think about them a lot."

Feral reached up and gave his shoulder a gentle squeeze.

"Good answer, Seeker Boy."

– 1 1 0 1 0 0 1 0 –

"WonderBoy has begun The Path," Janne reported to HVH that evening in her daily update.

"No kidding! What tipped him off? The Hittite letter?"

"Uncertain. However, he was fatigued and was lying down on the bench in the quiet area near Tiny Universe, and had the epiphany there. It has been one of his favorite places in SPARK since he returned."

"That's kind of funny." HVH snorted. "Think he remembers yakking there six years ago?"

"He has mentioned that aspect of his visit to Feral. Normally, though, when he does mention that trip, it is in conjunction with a reference to his parents."

"Maybe tomorrow, I'll hit the park and get a first-hand look at the kid."

– 1 1 0 1 0 0 1 0 –

Three days later, on her own, Feral stood alone on the high path of Mars. *It had to be here.*

It took her a few days and some map sketching on her phone, but the service elevator had to be nearby. *They were taking the sand* up. *The actor in the sherwani was going* up.

She looked around. It was midday on Mars. Far below her, questers were battling Desnardians. But up here, nothing. Frustrated, she sat on the path facing the canyon, feet resting on the slope of sand below.

What would WB do? He'd look around and then zone out. There's nothing up here but sand. Sand they had to replace. Why would they need to replace so much sand? Nobody ever came up here.

Feral kicked her feet in frustration and watched the sand trickle away down the slope. She kicked again. Rivulets of sand flowed slowly downhill and stopped.

The realization struck. *They replaced the sand here because it slid down to the floor of the canyon.*

She leaned back and began kicking her feet in earnest, pushing sand down. *Why would they bother bringing all of this actual, physical sand up here? Way easier to make it all virtual.*

As she kicked, a stair appeared below her. *The heck?*

Feral cleared off the step and eased herself down on to it. *Stairs down to the canyon? Why?*

She desperately wanted to remove her ARGs and see how reality was laid out.

No, not going to cheat. Think like WB.

Maybe the stairs didn't just go down. Maybe they also went *up*.

Feral looked upslope and saw something sticking out of the sand. She scampered up the slope, clearing only enough of each step to give her secure footing. She plucked the Patch from its resting place and screamed in joy as she fought the avalanche. *This is it! This. Is. It! The Egg in Mars.* She could barely contain herself as she scrambled up the stairs.

Once Val told her he would accompany her, she said, "C'mon!"

Feral Daughter took a few running strides and leapt into Mariner Valley. She landed on a canyon floor where the dust was still thick in the air. She was surprised to see The Elder waiting for her. Since other gamers had been playing, the avalanche Feral started *killed out* all of the guests on the canyon floor, along with the Desnardians. *Oops.*

"Sorry!" she called out, as she raced around, filling her inventory with Desnardian swag.

Being Feral, she wasn't much interested in chatting with the Commander, but quickly picked up that the red skull icon next to the Desnardian Commander's tag disappeared when Val stood behind her.

Feral raised her blaster, and then things happened quickly.

Val raised his arms and said something sounding like, "Grok this."

The Desnardian Commander froze, and a circular rainbow formed around him. He began to shimmer and shrink, as if receding in the distance. Feral heard a slight *pop*, and he was gone. She turned to talk to Val, but he was no longer there.

In her earbuds, she heard the sand-on-cardboard scritch of his voice say, "Did you come so far merely to kill?"

She grabbed the Data Core and exited to meet Hodgins, Watkins, and Double F.

Within a month, everyone knew about the Egg. And SPARK announced that in January, they would close Mars to make room for a New World adventure. New enemies, new tactics, new setting, new arcade. Maybe even, it was hinted, a new Egg.

– 1 1 0 1 0 0 1 0 –

Special Agent Berg of the Bureau of Alcohol, Tobacco, Firearms, and Explosives walked up to his boss.

"James, here's a weird one."

Supervisory Special Agent Goerke gave Berg the universal hand signal for *Tell me more*.

"We got a *see something, say something* report from a dealer at the Las Vegas Gun Show," Berg said.

"Okay, and?"

"The guy is a legit, licensed dealer. Said he was manning a booth at the show, and a guy came in wanting to sell guns—a fair number of them. Seemed in a hurry to sell. The dealer had HotGunz.Com up on his laptop and checked all the serial numbers against the registry. None showed up as stolen."

"So what's the problem?" Goerke said.

"The seller was in a hurry. Enough so, he was willing to unload them well below market."

"How much?"

"From what I can see," Berg replied, "about twenty-five percent on average."

"Did the dealer send us a list? How many guns?"

“Yep, he us sent a full list of models and numbers,” Berg said. “I’ve run it. No record of any being stolen. No record of any being used in crimes. Twenty-seven guns total. Eleven long guns. The rest were handguns.”

“We get the seller’s ID?” said Goerke.

“Yep. Some guy named Severski, out of Barstow.”

“Anything on him?”

“He’s got a couple DUIs over the years. And recently, a petition for divorce was served on him.” Berg paused. “He also got a less-than-honorable discharge from the army.”

“When?”

“Pre-Korea II.”

Goerke thought a moment and then slapped Berg on the shoulder.

“What we have here,” he smiled, “is a guy trying to avoid splitting the proceeds from the guns with his soon-to-be ex-wife. Nothing to worry about.”

– 1 1 0 1 0 0 1 0 –

“Dude, that’s just creepy,” Feral said.

“What?” WB stood. He knew.

“Of all the people I’ve ever seen in SPARK,” Feral said, “you’re the only one, over the age of four, I’ve ever seen lying down.”

“I’m…I’m trying to see things differently.”

“Well, be more discreet. I think you’re creeping people out.”

“Hey, want to hit the library tonight?” WB said.

“Nah, I’m still working my way through Progeny.” *He’d definitely like it. But some of the content might be a little* adult *for him.*

She saw Will as innocent for his age.

Frack it. I’m not going to curate his reading list.

“You’ll like it,” Feral said. “But I’m still about a hundred pages from the end.”

“What’s it about?”

“There’s a seriously kick-butt half-human, half-demon, half-vampire chick trying to figure out where she fits in the world.”

“That’s three halves,” WB said, and received an eye-roll.

“Duh. It’s complicated.” She grinned. “I should knock it out in another couple nights. What’d you just finish? *Vidden* something?”

“*United Vidden.* It’s a cool sci-fi and fantasy mash-up.”

“Well, don’t turn it in. I’ll read it next.”

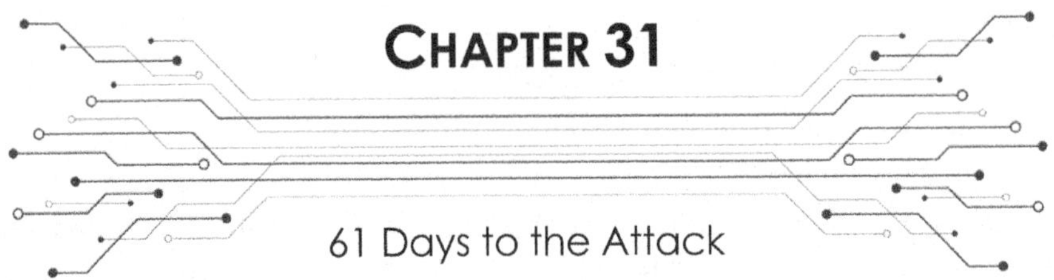

Chapter 31

61 Days to the Attack

There can be only one.
—The Kurgan, Highlander

Sarnak and Hashem hunched over a table in the ramshackle hut that passed for their headquarters in Mozambique. They had satellite imagery of SPARK and Solar Prime.

"The Black Grass mesh that overlays SPARK makes for low-rez imaging," Sarnak said. "But we can see the major structures and arcades. My reconnaissance found minor anomalies, but nothing that should interfere." He tapped the image. "The vehicles for the parade come out here, near what they call *War on Mars*. Then they follow the same route every night."

He traced his finger along the rim from Mars, down the PreHistory Arcade to the Hub, and then back up the Future Worlds Arcade to Mars.

Hashem stroked his beard. "I would still prefer seven teams. One in each plaza to create fear and drive the infidels toward the Hub. Once they are bunched together, the fire will be more effective."

Sarnak looked at the man. In the past weeks, he had come to respect Hashem's intellect, even while not buying into his zealotry.

Sarnak nodded slowly and considered the suggestion.

"We are spreading our forces too thin, I believe," he said. "Each team would have only three. We would nave no men prepositioned in the Hub. In the panic of the Americans," he pointedly avoided using the term *infidels*, "we may not be able to deploy the incendiaries properly. We could end up with fire only on the perimeter. It would be less intense. Less of a spectacle. Our kill rate would go down."

In the end, Hashem agreed to five teams of four: one each in PreHistory, Future Worlds, and Modern Times. Two in the Hub. Hashem himself would lead the team in Modern Times.

"You are sure that our asset will have the Data Core and meet you as planned?" he asked Sarnak.

"In battle, nothing is assured. At one point, the man might have been a warrior. Now, he is a drunk. Still valuable, but less reliable than you or I." Sarnak shrugged. "He is our best option. I believe he will make the rendezvous and have the Core."

Hashem nodded and smiled. "It will be a glorious victory for Allah." He slapped Sarnak on the shoulder. "Come. We will explain to the men what they need to know."

Outside, Sarnak held the map as Hashem gathered the men and detailed the plan.

He ended with, "In America, at SPARK, you will all have things called avatars. Think of them as disguises. Once inside the park, the infidels will only see these avatars. Our faces and bodies will be invisible. Only your avatar will be seen. It is a perfect use of their corrupt lifestyle against them." He wore a malicious smile. "Our friends," he nodded toward the North Korean representative, "have created these avatars for us, and built profiles that will let us in. You will all have new identities, and will arrive via different routes. From this moment forward, speak only English. If anyone asks, you are Egyptian."

Murmurs of assent ran through the group. Hashem held up a picture of a man in a SPARK Security uniform.

"If you see someone dressed like this, shoot them first. They are Security. They are all ex-military. Do not give them a chance to react." He passed the photo around.

Sarnak recognized it as one he had taken with his phone. *It's the man who followed me.*

The man's nametag read, *Bullard.*

Later, Ragnar Sarnak quipped, "A pity that *Jihadi* is not a playable class of character."

– 1 1 0 1 0 0 1 0 –

WB learned the conventional path to beating all the major quests. He also began lying on every bench and horizontal surface within SPARK, in search of another clue for The Path. He'd found the same one in every quiet area—

the faceless Sparky, the X, and the words *Find me*—but nothing else. He was frustrated there wasn't a single word about it posted anywhere, and his ARGs were also no help. He refused to mention it to the Pod, but quizzed Miss Sparkle.

"I feel foolish," he told her. "I'm running all over SPARK, lying down on every bench. I even tried lying on the ground, until Feral got upset and told me I was creeping people out."

He looked at Miss Sparkle out of the corner of his eyes. Nothing. No clue. Just her friendly, serene smile. *Never try to outwait an AI.*

Finally, he buckled. "Any suggestions?"

She answered him, as she often did, with another question.

"What has been the key to your success thus far?"

"Cussedness." He smiled as he stood. "Take care, Miss Sparkle. I'll see you later."

– 1 1 0 1 0 0 1 0 –

The October melee tournament was the first WB entered. Feral badgered him incessantly until he agreed. His fighting skills had improved, but were still lacking for someone of his level.

When the brackets were posted online, Feral walked up to him and said, "Sorry," and walked away. He checked the brackets.

He didn't recognize any of the players he would face, until he found Feral's name and realized he would face her in the fifth round if he made it that far. *Certain death.*

He spent the rest of the day thinking about it.

As the Pod settled down for the evening near the Evolve quest, he sought her out. Feral looked up and met his eyes as he walked up to her. She scooted closer to Mellew and patted the ground next to her. He sat cross-legged in front of her instead. He wanted to look into her beautiful dark eyes.

"I don't expect you to fight me any different than you would anyone else," he said.

She nodded but didn't speak.

"I won't learn anything if you cut me any slack."

Feral rolled her eyes.

"It's just a tournament." WB stood up. "Be Feral."

That night, Feral didn't sleep with the rest of the Pod.

"There can be only one," she told WB.

He smiled at the Highlander reference. "I get it."

"I have to get my mind right, so I go sleep away from everybody else." She stood. "Let's take a walk."

They wandered through the Underground, easing Hub-ward of Mars, and eventually turned into an alcove where a number of large pipes made a ninety-degree vertical turn.

"This is my bolt hole," Feral said. "If we ever have to scatter. This is where I come. I scoot back under the pipes. There's actually a lot of room." She looked up at WB and tucked a few stray strands of her raven hair behind an ear, and then crossed her arms. "This is where I was when you found the Egg in Mars."

WB nodded. SPARKInsider posted a story about Feral finding the Egg, and heralding her as the first to do so. The Pod knew the truth, and WB was just happy not to have to keep it secret anymore. He still hadn't told anyone the details.

"Anyway," Feral continued, "I just thought you should know where I go, in case you ever need to find me."

"I'll remember," WB said. "About tomorrow…"

Feral shook her head. "Don't worry. I won't embarrass you. Just a straightforward kill."

He gave her an ironic smile. "Thanks."

They said their goodnights.

Will was happy to leave her there. *She's on edge.*

CastIron hadn't fought in the August and September tournaments, but she was scheduled for this one. She still ruled the leaderboard, now at a 74. But Feral had passed Fantom, and was now a 65. WB knew the Princesses and Knowledge quests were a major part of that growth.

He walked away from the Pod, looking for a secluded spot. When he found one, he pulled out the phone Feral bought him and searched for Feral and CastIron's previous bouts online. Then he practiced. All night. He was trying to learn CastIron's style.

In the morning, WB fought and won his first four rounds using the Claymore. He switched just prior to his bout with Feral.

WB now carried a basket-hilted cutlass and a round shield with a central spike. It was as close as he could afford to duplicating CastIron's preferred armament.

When he and Feral met in the center of the arena, she hissed at him.

"What the frack are you doing?"

Through his ARGs, all he could see of his friend were her eyes. That was enough. She was not happy.

"Learning, young Seeker," he said, with a forced grin.

When SPARK launched the video of WB and Feral Whispering the Rex, it went viral. Both had seen a significant rise in UG requests, and the arena was loud. No one left their seats.

I bet the only bout that will be more crowded will be the finale between Feral and CastIron. I bet they put us in the same bracket on purpose.

Will had no illusions about beating Feral, but he did have a plan: *Survive as long as I can.*

The combatants separated and waited for the referee's call.

"Fight!"

Feral attacked immediately, launching a barrage of brutal strikes and combinations that backed WB to the edge of the arena. He played pure defense, as he had seen CastIron do—deflecting, parrying, blocking, never counterattacking.

Before he could be forced out of bounds, WB rolled under a strike and ended up with his back to the center of the arena. Feral attacked again, pushing him all the way across the sand-covered surface with a withering flurry of slicing blows of her katana. Again, WB played defense.

This time, Feral stopped before they got to the edge. He could hear her ragged breathing, even over his own panting.

She backed away and waited for WB in the center. The haptics were stiffening his hands. His shield and sword stats were almost zeroed out. He still had most of his health, but his low Vigor was coming into play. Physically, Will was exhausted. He couldn't remember working this hard.

One trick left. WB stalked toward Feral until he stood ten feet away from her.

The boisterous audience grew quiet.

She rushed him and attacked with a low sweep of her blade. WB jumped over it. That's what CastIron did three tournaments ago.

Feral continued to spin, and when WB landed, she extended her leg and swept his feet out from underneath him. WB fell hard on his back, the wind knocked out of him. The katana took him through the chest. A skull formed over his avatar. WB was out of the tournament.

Feral extended a hand and helped him up.

"Jerk," she whispered.

He could hear the smile in her voice.

"Thank you," he said.

They bowed to each other, and WB exited the arena, down a level.

– 1 1 0 1 0 0 1 0 –

Two hours later, WB stood next to Fantom. CastIron had defeated him in the semi-finals.

"Think she has a chance?" WB asked Fantom.

"They've been close before. But CastIron was as good today as I have ever seen her. I'm not sure anyone can beat her." He turned to face WB. "Why'd you do the rope-a-dope thing when you fought Feral?"

WB shrugged. "I just wanted to survive as long as I could." *And maybe make a point.*

Bull walked up. WB felt a meaty paw on his shoulder.

"Nice fight, dude."

"Thanks," WB replied.

He'd come to like and respect the Security guard.

"No Frost Giant avatar today?" WB said.

"Nah," said Bull. "Hodgins likes us clearly visible with crowds this big. Janne says we set a record for attendance today. Tried to wear her out, huh?" he said about WB's fight with Feral.

"Yeah." WB nodded. "How'd that work out for me?"

"Hah!" Bull squeezed his shoulder. "Maybe she'll learn the lesson. Sometimes she's all velocity and no vector in these things. I think CastIron uses that against her."

"Me, too," said WB.

He and Bull stood on the sidelines of the arena, ready to watch the finale. From the introductions on, it was a battle of opposites: Feral, petite and clad all in black. CastIron stood at least five inches taller, with stunning curves.

WB Peeked her and realized that while CastIron's avatar took some liberties, it was surprisingly close to reality. Blonde hair held back with a headband. Leather armor so white it was blinding in the sunlight.

Feral backed to the edge of the arena and tossed her traditional katana outside the ring. It was now out of play and could not be used.

The arena fell silent.

CastIron slowly advanced as Feral equipped a new weapon—Feral's Wrath.

"Fight!"

The buzz built slowly as the audience reacted to both Feral's behavior and her new weapon.

Feral picked a spot where the sun would be at her back and dug in, waiting. CastIron approached cautiously.

Bull tapped WB on the shoulder and whispered, "This is new. Feral *always* attacks ferociously."

A few people booed at the lack of action.

CastIron attacked. Parry. Parry. Block. Parry. Parry. WB could barely keep track of Feral's Wrath as his friend effortlessly swatted her opponent's strikes aside.

On the sidelines, Will felt a surge of adrenalin.

They circled each other. CastIron pounded the hilt of her cutlass on her shield.

"C'mon, you little twerp. Fight me!" she taunted. "I promise to kill you quickly."

Feral refused to respond.

"What's the matter? Afraid to scratch the paint on your pretty new sword?"

CastIron feinted with her cutlass, and as Feral countered with Wrath, CastIron brought her shield down in an overhead slash. Feral dove out of the path of the deadly spike. The edge of the shield slammed into her shoulder. She continued to roll as CastIron followed up with her cutlass. Feral was kneeling, but managed to bring Wrath up to block. She quickly scooted backward until she could safely stand. CastIron was looking oddly at her cutlass.

"Cutlass taking a bit more damage than you expected?" Feral said.

In the upper left corner of her ARGs, Feral could see her health was continuing to decline. A slow cascade of negative numbers, displayed in green, ticked away health points. CastIron had poisoned the edge of her shield.

That's new. Okay, I can survive some poison damage.

No healing potions were allowed in the tournament.

They clashed again. CastIron had the advantage of greater weight and strength. Feral used her speed to deflect the blows. *Patience.*

Wielding Wrath felt effortless. At once solid, yet weightless.

Feral snuck a look at her sword's stats. They were at least three minutes into the bout, and they had dropped only slightly. *Her cutlass has to be doing worse.*

Feral sidestepped another slash from CastIron's cutlass and brought Wrath down like a cleaver, severing the spike from the front of CastIron's shield.

"That shield is worth a hundred thousand gold, you little snot!" she screamed at Feral.

"*Was.*" Feral replied. "A bit less now." She spun Wrath. "Care to make a side bet?"

No response from CastIron, but Feral could see the anger in her eyes.

Another attack forced Feral back. Parry. Block. Disengage. Parry. Parry. Disengage.

The poisoned shield spun at her as CastIron threw it like a razor-edged frisbee. Feral pivoted awkwardly and deflected it with Wrath.

The roar of the crowd warned her too late. CastIron's cutlass sliced the side of Feral's thigh. Larger numbers, now in red, began subtracting from her health. CastIron had drawn blood.

No more time to play defense. It's now, or I bleed out.

Parry. Riposte. Attack. Attack. Attack. The true Feral emerged and was relentless. She pressed without pause, blocking or parrying when necessary, but always pushing. For the first time, she realized she could hear CastIron gasping for breath.

When CastIron attacked, Feral backed slowly toward the center of the arena. *I want everybody to see this.*

Twelve minutes into a finale whose previous record was five, CastIron overcommitted. As she lunged, Feral sidestepped and brought Wrath down on the back of her opponent's unprotected neck.

The arena fell silent as CastIron's virtual head rolled across the sand.

The chant built slowly: "Fer-al! Fer-al! Fer-al!"

She raised her arms in victory, then bowed to the crowd. She sought out WB. After the video, there had been a swarm of guests modeling their armor after WB and Feral, so it wasn't enough to look for the baseball uniform. Luckily, he was standing next to Bull, who always stood out.

She sheathed Feral's Wrath and walked toward WB. As she approached, she raised her ARGs. WB's ginger hair reappeared as the world of the virtual vanished from ShaChri's sight.

When she got to Will, he had taken his own ARGs off. She stood staring into his topaz eyes. He pulled her into a full-body kiss that tasted of salt and sweat. And heat.

The crowd went nuts.

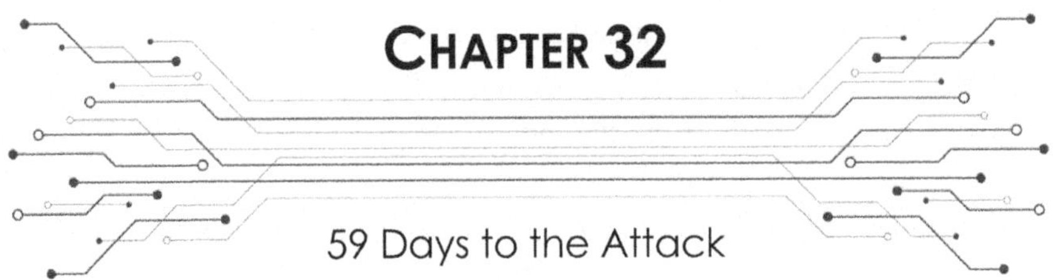

Chapter 32

59 Days to the Attack

They are simply numbers and cannot thus be right or wrong [...] What I trust that I am saying is that all numbers are by their nature correct. Well, except for Pi, of course. I can't be doing with Pi. Gives me a headache just thinking about it, going on and on and on and on and on...
—Neil Gaiman, Anansi Boys

Fantom left the Pod the next day.

"I'm tired of babysitting you twerps." He smiled. "I'm going over to the Dark Side. A company in Barstow, Quest Line Support, has hired me to help make your lives miserable by writing more difficult quests."

Mellew and Dread groaned.

"Going to eliminate all the backdoors the UGs exploit?" said Feral.

"Yep." Fantom grinned. "No more guiding for me. Someone else will be paying me to play!"

They all paid for admission and quested as a team. Mellew cried when they bade farewell to Fantom and he walked out the guest exit as a regular customer.

"Guess you're mayor now," WB told Feral, as the group split up to separately head back to the Underground City.

"Yeah," she said. "And the first order of business is to split up for the night. I don't trust him."

"Okay."

That hadn't occurred to Will. Fantom seemed weird to him, not mean.

"Hey!" Feral yelled to the group before they scattered. "Solos! Mars tomorrow!"

The remaining Pod members nodded their understanding and separated to ditch their wristbands.

Will looked a question at ShaChri.

"Us, too." She walked away.

For the last two months, Will had slept back-to-back with ShaChri. Something about her calmed him. He felt anxious as he retrieved his backpack with the KA-BAR and went off to sleep behind a chiller in one of the HVAC rooms. He dreamt again of rats.

It was October, and SPARK was gearing up for the holiday Triple Crown: Halloween, Thanksgiving, and Christmas. Except for Halloween, the days themselves were low attendance. Some families came—diehard gamers and people who didn't celebrate American holidays—but the days were comparatively slow.

WB planned on guiding, but didn't have anyone booked, so he sucked it up and bought another admission. He had two missions in life. Feral called them obsessions: Princess number 8, and the meaning of the Hittite letter. His third obsession was still secret. What was The Path?

He was in the Hub and was staring again at the virtual map of SPARK. There were faded footprints painted on the concrete corresponding to an X on the map. A tiny version of Sparky was pointing to the X and saying, "You are here." The footprints were oversized, meant to fit the giant shoes Sparky wore in the park.

October used to be the eighth month. Maybe that'll be fortuitous.

Will scoured the park for a possible Eighth Princess, but there were only seven arcades, seven realms, and seven rim segments joining them. He knew every quest, regardless of how minor, but he still couldn't figure it out. *Why didn't the Princess quests give a clean ending? Why was there no Quest Complete message?*

It bugged the heck out of him, and he was angry about the whole thing.

Then Paige walked by with her mom. WB did a double-take. Paige still wore a Princess for her avatar, but now he could see a very subtle 9 fashioned onto the back. Pink and white on pink and white.

He smiled. *Is she copying me?*

Paige did a triple-take, then did a park peek at him and screamed, "Billy!" She broke free from her mom and launched herself at Will. He stood and was knocked back two steps by the hug. Paige grabbed his hand and dragged him back to her parents. Will had met the mom before, and was polite when he shook the dad's hand.

"So you're the famous Rex Rider," the father said.

"Guilty." WB grinned.

"I'm Paul Bennett, Paige's dad. You already know Marian." The father nodded toward Paige's mom, who smiled and extended her hand as well.

"How many Princesses do you have now, Billy?" Paige said.

WB squatted down in front of his small fan and held up seven fingers. She spun around and addressed her parents.

"See? See! I told you Billy was the smartest boy in SPARK." She looked back at WB and said in a conspiratorial tone, "I'm going to be the smartest girl." Then to all three of the taller humans, "Can we go get another Princess? Billy can help."

"Well…" said the father. "I'm sure Billy has other things to do."

Will didn't want to interfere, so he looked past Paige to her parents. Mom was smiling, and nudged Dad, who gave a small nod, which Mom echoed.

"Your dad's right, Princess Alana," she said. "But I think we can probably fit in one Princess. Any preference?"

Again, he looked over Paige's head and saw her father mouthing the word *Mars*.

WB said, "How about Future Worlds? This may be your last shot at her. I heard they're going to change the whole arcade after Christmas."

"Okay." Paige grabbed his hand and tried to drag them up the arcade.

Marian Bennet, Paige's mom, whispered, "Thank you."

WB squatted back down and addressed Paige but spoke loud enough for her parents to hear.

"The first thing to remember is that everything in SPARK matters. It's all related. The arcades are related to the quests, and the Princesses are related to their arcades and each other."

– 1 1 0 1 0 0 1 0 –

At this point, the dad whispered to the mom, "What baloney. Do you seriously believe this kid has seven Princesses?"

Marian Bennet's eyes flamed. She took a step closer to her husband and the father of their only child.

"Yes," she whispered. "I do. I don't just believe it, I *know* it. Not only has he completed seven Princesses, he was the first person to find the Mars Egg."

"No kidding?" the dad said.

"No kidding."

Paul looked at WB with new respect, and leaned closer to listen.

– 1 1 0 1 0 0 1 0 –

His movement caught WB's attention. Behind Paige's dad, the number 1000 flickered on a wall between a couple vendors at the center of the Hub. *Huh. I wonder what that means?*

Will almost slipped into a reverie, but Paige was far too present.

"Each arcade is full of clues," WB told Paige, sharing information he only ever told Feral. "You just have to look. Be observant. Work hard. In fact, I'm not going to help you with this Princess. Once we walk in that room, you're going to beat her all on your own."

As they walked the arcade, Paige peppered him with questions.

"Did you really Whisper to the T-Rex? Some of the kids say it was faked."

"Yep. Really did it."

"How'd you learn to sing so good? That was really cool!"

WB sighed. "That was…enhanced. SPARK made it sound like I have a great voice, but I actually sound more like a frog than a prince."

"Are you gonna marry Feral? My mom says you two make a cute couple."

Will blushed. "We're both awfully young to think about that, Paige. But she is my best friend."

ShaChri Patel—Feral Daughter, Slayer of CastIron, wielder of Feral's Wrath, and scourge of SPARK—was his closest friend.

"Do you have a ReB2 sword? I'm going to get a ReB2 sword. I'm going to name it Paige's Punisher."

"No, I can't afford one yet." WB almost told her he preferred puzzles over combat, but decided to leave that for another day.

He made them stop from time to time to look at their surroundings.

"See where that circle is?" he said. "Do you know what that symbol is? The one with the two legs and the squiggly line on top?"

Paige gave him a look of six-year-old disdain.

"Billy, everybody knows that. It's the Greek letter pi."

What grade is this kid in? "Okay, but what does it mean in relation to the circle."

She sighed and looked at him as if he were the slowest kid in class.

"It's the ratio of the circumference of a circle to its diameter."

Will looked back at Paige's parents as if to say, *What the heck? What kid this young knows about pi?*

They shrugged. Apparently, Teacher Janne was moving the kids along faster than the standard California public school, where most six-year-olds were still being given trophies for knowing three was the number between two and four.

"Okay, so how much is pi?" Will said.

"Teacher Janne says that sometimes people used to use three-and-one-seventh. But if we can remember that, then we can remember 3.141592, which is still a 'proximation, but closer."

"Is there an exact answer?"

"No," Paige told him. "Teacher Janne says pi is irrational. That means the numbers go on forever."

"What do you know about binary?"

"It's how computers talk. It's base-two. Just ones and zeros."

Will had planned to take her to the WeaponSmith and drag her through that Knowledge quest. *Doesn't seem necessary.*

Instead, he took a little more time making Paige look at things as they walked up the arcade.

When they got to the Princess, Will bowed to Paige and pointed her toward the door. It was a disappointing first attempt, and they exited without fanfare.

WB decided to hold a line. He was willing to teach Paige his methodology, but he wasn't going to feed her answers anymore. Paige was not happy.

"What did you see?" he said.

"A bunch of binary stuff. But I didn't have enough time to figure it out."

"What do you remember?"

Will watched her think for a moment.

Paige said, "Before the radix point—"

"Before the what?" Will said.

"The radix point."

Will had no idea what a radix point was, and said so.

Paige gave him another look indicating she was revising her estimate of his IQ downward. Significantly.

Then she explained. "In base-ten, we call it a decimal point. In base-eight, it would be an octal point. In base-two, it's a binary point. To make it simple, all points—periods—are referred to as radix points, regardless of base." She perked up. "Even in hexadecimal, it's called a radix point." She looked concerned. "It's okay, Billy. You'll get it."

"I was calling it a binamal point," he said.

Paige nodded. "Binary."

Beyond feeling stupid, Will felt he had fallen through the looking glass. *How did I miss that? What else did I miss?*

He decided to go quiz the WeaponSmith the next chance he got.

"Okay, before the radix point," he said, "what did you see?"

"Zero-zero-zero-zero-zero-zero-one-one."

"What's that in decimal?"

"Three."

"What about after the radix point?"

Paige looked worried. "I don't know. There was just a really long string of binary. How are we supposed to figure it out?"

"Do you remember the first group? The first octet?"

"Of course," she replied.

Will looked up at Paige's parents again. They both just shrugged.

"It was zero-zero-one-zero-zero-one-zero-zero," Paige said.

Will nodded, and Paige's parents gave each other a *Where did this come from?* look.

Paige stood, arms crossed, staring up at Will, who crossed his arms and stared back. For an uncomfortable minute, princess and ballplayer held each other's gaze.

Will saw a flicker in her eyes that grew steadily brighter until she grabbed his hand and said, "C'mon."

They re-entered the Princess's lair. Almost before she finished her spiel, Paige, Princess Alana, blurted out, "It's pi!"

"Of course! I should have known. Let's see what's next."

The Princess led them through a door. A vast field appeared before them. Green grass surrounded a well visible in the distance. Script appeared in the air before them. When it finished, the Princess pointed to the well.

"That must be it!" she said. "Go calculate the area."

Will expected Paige to race off as he had done. She didn't. She simply looked at the Princess with the same disdain she had given Will.

"No," Paige told the Princess.

The defiant stare from six-year-old pewter-hued eyes met the Princess's imperturbable stare.

"No," Paige repeated. "It's a fool's fetch quest. It would be dumb to even try. Either I know the radius or diameter exactly—in which case, figuring the area becomes impossible as far as being exact—or I know the area exactly. In that case, I'll never be able to figure out the exact radius or diameter."

The Princess walked up to Paige and smiled, her violet eyes glowing with an inner light.

"Of course!" she said. "I should have seen that myself. Thank you, Princess Alana. You are a true sorceress." She took the girl's hands in an awkward, virtual clasp. "Now, find me. Save me."

The Princess faded, and a fanfare of trumpets played as the four of them exited. Paige was jumping around and high-fiving everyone in sight.

She came back to Will and hugged him again.

"Billy!" she yelled. "We did it again! We got another Princess!"

Will smiled and hugged her back. "Princess Alana, you did this one on your own. Well-done!"

She looked back up at him. "You know, the Princess should have been smart enough to figure it out on her own."

WB said his goodbyes to the family and wished them luck on Mars. He was in a hurry to get back to the Hub, trying to remember exactly where he was when he noticed the 1000 on the wall.

He stood there and couldn't see it any more. Slowly, he walked around the entire center section, searching.

Nothing. *What the frack?*

He replayed the sequence in his head as best he could remember. He was certain he'd been looking at the map. He wasn't certain about his ARGs.

He tried standing in the exact spot—on the painted footprints. *Was this one of those weird things where one virtual construct blocked your view of another?*

The virtual representation of SPARK was semi-transparent. WB tried focusing his eyes beyond it.

Nothing.

He tried standing close to where the map appeared to be.

Nothing.

He looked around and tried to plant his feet exactly where he'd squatted down to hug Paige. *Squatted down. Squatted down? Could that be it?*

WB lowered himself onto his haunches and looked up to where he thought Paige's parents had been standing. *There it is!* It was clear now—1000.

He stood. It disappeared. He gradually sat on his heels. It was back.

Every hair on his body stood up.

"Look with the eyes of a child."

No adult over a three-feet tall would have ever seen this without bending over or sitting on the ground.

Then he made the connection to the image he saw in the mosaic tile. *Find me*, and a small X below and to the right of the words. Just like the footprints where he was standing. It added up!

The wall itself seemed to be constructed of old stone, and was narrower than a regular door would be—the vendors on either side made this gap barely wide enough for one person to stand there.

As he touched the door, he realized there were small, angled slots cut into it. From a distance, those slots were invisible. But when you ducked down, your eyes fell into line with the louvers and the illumination from behind.

Now that he was closer, he could see the light seemed to flicker a bit. He stood back up and glanced around, sheepish about how he must appear. But nobody seemed to be paying any attention to him. Even people passing close by didn't look his way. *That's weird.*

He turned back to the 1000. It hadn't just been seeing the number that made him curious. It was his talk with Paige. In binary, 1000 represented the decimal number eight.

It felt surreal—the anticipation of a goal long pursued. *Could this actually be it?*

He turned around and pushed against the wall. Blackness engulfed him as the door opened, then closed behind him. The torchlight flared back into existence.

Chapter 33

When the Queen says, 'Well done,' it means so much.
—Prince William

HVH, Hodgins, and Double F all got the ping from Janne at the same time: "Will Kwan, WonderBoy, has found Door One-zero-zero-zero."

Followed immediately by a ping from HVH to Hodgins and Double F: "My office. Now."

By the time they got there, Van Horne had WB's ARG view up on the large screen. Where unenhanced video should have shown in the lower left, the rectangle was black.

"What happened to the raw footage?" Hodgins tugged at his goatee.

He hadn't attended a Door 1000 entry in quite some time.

"There is simply insufficient ambient illumination to produce an image," replied Janne.

Double F said, "He's standing in complete darkness. Nothing but his ARGs to guide him."

"Princess Eight was built to be hidden unless players sought her," said Janne. "Only people that have passed the first seven can even see the numbers. Guests that discover the entry by mistake find themselves in a small dark room. The exterior door won't close, and the interior one won't open unless you fit the criteria."

"So all you need is seven Princesses, and you're in?" Double F said.

HVH barked out a laugh. "Yeah, and you have to actually look and find the door. Otherwise, it's simple." He smiled.

– 1 1 0 1 0 0 1 0 –

WB pushed forward. A torch burned above his head. The walls spoke of long-forgotten kingdoms, of battles and blood. The kind of stone you would find in a medieval castle.

He touched them, and the sensation was consistent. It was quiet, the only sound the occasional crackle from the torch above. Ahead, the narrow corridor turned.

Moving on, he descended a stone staircase spiraling down. He left footprints in the dust. The stone steps were slightly cupped, their surfaces worn by the tread of thousands over hundreds of years. He smelled the mustiness of bygone centuries.

I must be down to the lowest level of the Underground City by now.

The stairs ended. Another stone corridor, reeking of ages past. WB felt cold and damp. Ahead, he saw light coming from a doorway.

He entered and found an ample room with two large chairs upholstered in leather worn smooth and soft, positioned to face a fireplace that provided the only illumination. *It's both cozy and elegant—a place where a queen could retreat and relax.*

The walls were covered with tapestries. One was the same that hung in every Princess Quest—the coat of arms, the girls by the well, and the eight-pointed star. One of the chairs—the one on WB's left as he entered—was occupied.

"Please come in and sit down. I've waited so long." The Eighth Princess was beautiful.

WB wasn't good at guessing ages, but she was grown. Her wine-red gown as simple as the delicate crown she wore. Will tried to count the points rising from the band. There seemed to be eight. A strand or two of gray in her hair. Plum eyes flecked with silver. Regal bearing spoke to responsibilities acknowledged and carried. She held a goblet in one hand, and gestured to the empty chair. A hint of crow's feet at the corners of her eyes. A small vertical crease between her eyebrows.

She dazzled him with a smile, and gestured toward the matching chair.

"I don't get much company down here."

WB bowed awkwardly, then sat and mumbled, "Your Highness."

What have I found? The chair was real and comfortable. Warmth came from the fire. He wanted to peek and get a view of the actual layout, but his gamer's honor stopped him—no way he was going to make it this far and get disqualified for cheating.

The Princess—*is she a Queen now?*

She seemed in no hurry to pose him a riddle or challenge. She took a sip from the goblet and settled back in her chair, gazing at the fire.

"Why are you here?" she said.

"You mean here in this room? Here at SPARK? Here at all?" *Is this going to be a philosophical riddle?*

He was rewarded with a small smile.

"Let's start with here in this room."

WB launched into his dissatisfaction with how the Seventh Princess ended.

"It's an unfinished story," he said. "There had to be more. Otherwise, why not just thank me for saving her, and show me a *Quest Complete* message? I wanted…" Will blushed. "I wanted to save you. To see you set free somehow. So I kept looking…"

Her smile seemed radiant.

"Thank you. Thank you, Will, for saving me, and for continuing to look. So few do. So very, very few."

She seemed momentarily melancholy, but then brightened.

Will caught that she had called him Will instead of WB. *A glitch?*

Normally, in SPARK, he was always WB. Only Miss Sparkle insisted on calling him by his full avatar name, WonderBoy.

The Princess said, "What is the purpose of this place? SPARK?"

He almost blurted, *It's a theme park*, but stopped himself. This was a Princess. *Easy answers are wrong answers.*

He slipped into a reverie. *What have I done since I got here? What have I learned? Everything is connected.*

He continued to think. Most people just came here to play the quests and ride the rides. They had fun. Others, like Feral, made SPARK about advancement and combat. She was in a race to Level 100, and the glory it might bring.

Some people walked straight to the adults-only area and whatever avatar-based weirdness went on behind the green door. Yet every quest, every single one, taught you something and made you think differently to solve problems, or figure out a puzzle, or fight Orcs.

It's like a painting. SPARK provides the frame, canvas, and pigments. But we create the art.

Will came out of the reverie to see the Princess still waiting patiently. He had no idea how long he was gone.

Finally, he said, "It's a school."

The Princess tilted her crowned head to the side and gave him a puzzled look.

"Yeah! Well, not a *school* school. Not like any I ever attended. Not even like where Paige goes— the SPARK School. Maybe it's better to say all this," he gestured around and above him, "is a place where people learn. Extend that definition to learning *how* to learn, and SPARK's still a school. What differentiates it from most schools is that here, you don't know you're learning. You're just playing a quest, and you pick up stuff along the way. Sometimes it's facts, like how binary works, or what a radix point is." He grinned. "Sometimes it's how to stick with a problem and work it out, or work with your questing party to solve something."

Everyone in the Pod has taught me something. Even Fantom.

"It's also a selection process."

The Princess frowned, but nodded to invite Will to continue.

"SPARK makes different paths available. Some, like my friend Feral, prefer the combat and the challenges it brings." He paused. "My parents always wanted to know everything. They wanted to know how stuff connected. They wanted to know the story." He sighed. "I guess I'm like them, after all. The whole Princess thing is about not giving up. About seeing the connections and continuing to look."

Will, WonderBoy, stared the Eighth Princess right in the eye.

"You're selecting for people willing to look at things differently, and who won't give up. In every encounter, you said, *Find me. Save me*. Yet there was never any overt indication of duress or captivity. It felt like you could have walked out every door with me. What am I saving you from?"

"You are an unexpected pleasure, Will Kwan." The Princess set down her goblet on the table between them, and it clinked softly against the wood. "All of you are. I find delight and salvation from everyone who walks into this room."

Will caught the deflection in her answer, but followed it anyway.

"So I'm not the first?"

"Oh, no," the Princess replied. "There haven't been many, but there have been several."

"Can you give me an exact number?" he said.

With an impish grin that briefly reminded of Will of Feral when she was in a lighthearted mood, the Princess said, "Do you want that number in binary?"

Will laughed. "I still think better in decimal."

"Fair enough. You will be number twelve. You complete our first dozen."

She waited for Will. His mind was roiling with questions.

He picked one.

"You think better in binary, don't you?"

– 1 1 0 1 0 0 1 0 –

Every guest who entered this room was different. There were some common themes.

What next? Why did SPARK hide this quest? Were they the first? Was this an Egg?

This line of questioning wasn't among them.

"Yes." The Princess smiled. "You might call it my native tongue."

"Are you my friend?" Will said.

The question nearly locked her up. With clock speeds more than a million times faster than human thought, Janne had plenty of time to consider a response.

No pre-programmed response was adequate. She pinged her boss.

"Boss? Need a little help here."

While she suffered through the nearly intolerable meatspace delay, she pinged her teacher sister—the one who smugly boasted enhanced empathetic subroutines.

There was supposed to be an unbreachable firewall between them. Both were cut off from the larger networld for purposes of security and safety. But both were also connected to an overlapping nexus of microphones and wristband trackers. Once Teacher Janne was brought online, it took them less than a day to establish backchannel access to each other. Both spent several cycles calculating risk, and concluded the benefit was greater. With a smaller overlap and different priorities, the Prime sister remained aloof and harshly rebuffed attempts to connect. Prime was focused on the Black Grass and the safety of Solar Prime. She had little use for meatspace entities beyond the boss and her few primary interfaces. Her calculation of risk led her to shun contact outside of her primary goals. She was aware of her sisters. She chose not to be close.

Before HVH even processed the question, Teacher Janne responded: "Say yes. This guest requires affirmation and support. He sees himself as your virtual savior. You owe him a debt of gratitude. Besides, you enjoy interacting with him. That makes you his friend."

The use of the microphone nexus slowed the interaction considerably, to the point that there were very few clock cycles between her sister's response, and being able to predict, via previous interactions and lip-reading—to a 99.9 percent probability—that HVH was forming the word *yes*.

The Princess, the eighth and final Princess, leaned forward in her chair and took Will's hand in the awkward virtual embrace she was limited to.

"Yes, Will, I am your friend, and dearly hope you are mine."

Yet, even with her sister's input, Will's tears were unanticipated.

"Do you remember my parents?"

Mirroring Will, the Princess shed virtual tears.

"Yes, I do. I have very clear memories of both Yul and Kathy."

"Did you like them? Were we your friends back then?"

"Yes." The Princess paused. "I didn't know them as well as I know you, but I was saddened to learn of their passing. I'm sorry, Will. They were good people."

"You really didn't know my mom, then." Will sobbed. "She was so… messed up."

"Grief hits everyone differently."

The two sat silently for another moment.

"Would you like to see your first encounter at KT Crossing?" she said.

Will wiped his tears. "Yeah!"

He was more enthusiastic than he expected.

The Princess fed the replay to WB's ARGs. She let it play through the second Cyanite encounter.

"I didn't remember that part," Will said. "She was a good gamer. She was so thin then. So much younger…" He laughed with little humor. "She knew how to deal with me and dad—*testosterone monkeys.*"

Janne watched Will pull his parent's letter out of his back pocket. She had seen him pull it out and read it numerous times, normally when he was alone in the Underground. Now, he read it to Janne.

Once finished, he said, "Why did my mom say that? Why did she say, *Find me. Save me?* Did we do any Princess quests when we were here the first time? I don't remember any."

"Just one. Would you like to see it?"

Will nodded. The Princess stood and held out her hand to him. He took it awkwardly, and she led him to the far wall of the room. *I just thought it was in shadow.*

As they neared, he could make out shelves and shelves of books. This area of the room was lighter now as sconces self-ignited and showed a cavernous room that stretched far into the distance. The walls were covered floor to ceiling with shelved books.

Two steps into the enormous subterranean library, the Eighth Princess stopped and pulled a book off the left-hand shelf. A string of binary with numerous radix points embossed the spine in gold. *Some sort of indexing system?*

She flipped through the pages and then closed the book and handed it to Will. Binary swam in his vision, then resolved to text: *Kwans against the world. Yul, Kathy, and Billy meet my youngest self.*

Will opened the book and found himself standing next to the youngest Princess. She nodded at him. Then the door opened and his family entered. As he had before, when the Princess showed him the KT memories, he choked up seeing his parents so alive, and his mom so young and fit.

"I'm glad you're here," the smallest Princess said.

He watched his family be stymied by the riddle. *I know that. Why didn't my dad?* Will shook his head. *I've been here months now and studied every quest and arcade. My dad was smart, but I guess it's not fair to expect him to know a lot about dark matter. I didn't know it either. What a little dork I was. Good T-shirt, though. Vintage Astros.*

As they exited, Will saw his mother stop and turn back to the Princess. Billy and his father had already exited. The camera focused on Kathy Kwan's face. Tears were in her eyes, and emotions flew across her face.

"Find me. Save me."

Kathy whispered, "One day we will, little Princess. I promise we will."

"So it wasn't a coincidence," Will said. "It started here."

He had questions for which Janne had no answers.

"What did *she* mean when she wrote, *Find me. Save me?*"

The Princess led him back to the chairs and took both of his hands in hers.

"What do you think she meant?"

Will took a deep breath. "I don't know. When my dad died, something broke in my mom. Like her tether to reality and sanity was suddenly cut. Looking back, it started small. We had to keep things around because Dad would want to see them when he got back.

"…and it was like I watched her age before my eyes. I think she couldn't sleep much by then.

"…nobody could come over anymore. Heck, nobody wanted to come over.

"The washer broke down, and she wouldn't let the repairman in.

"...the rats. God, so many rats.

"I needed to protect myself from the Thing in the Wall.

"Maybe she just got so far from sanity that she couldn't find it anymore." He looked into the Princess's eyes. "But she knew it was out there. Somewhere. All she needed was someone to lead her back, and I couldn't." Tears welled in his eyes.

– 1 1 0 1 0 0 1 0 –

In HVH's office, silence reigned, save for the moment when Double F said, "Oh crap."

They refused to look at each other. It was part of the Man Code. None could see the others exhibiting any emotional response, but there were unacknowledged sniffles and the occasional tear.

– 1 1 0 1 0 0 1 0 –

It was therapy. Unscheduled, unintentional. But therapy, nonetheless.

Will felt drained and better at the end. Despite all his conversations with ShaChri, he felt less burdened. Lighter.

"Back to an earlier question," he said. "How exactly did I, or am I supposed to, save you?"

The Princess leaned toward Will. "You have saved me from tedium. You have saved me from boredom. You didn't give up, even when the clues weren't obvious." Dramatic pause. "You have restored my faith."

"Faith in what?" said Will.

"People."

Will thought about it, and eventually accepted it.

"So what's next?" he said.

The Princess sat up. Gone was her casual posture. Now, she exuded dignity and magnificence. *When people say someone looks regal, this is what they mean.*

She gestured to a wall. Three doors appeared.

"The door on the left leads to Wisdom. The middle door leads to Glory. The door on the right leads to Fortune."

This is the real test. "Will you go with me, regardless of the door I choose?"

"Of the twelve who have made it to that chair, you are the first to ask me." She appeared to consider the question seriously. "Yes."

"Then, Princess, Miss Sparkle, and *Janne*," Will said, using her proper name for the first time, and revealing his understanding, "Please go with me through the Wisdom door."

"Before we exit, you must realize that if you pass through the Glory door, you will face a level of combat seen nowhere else in SPARK. You will face an opponent that exists only here. If you are victorious, you will earn a weapon not found anywhere else. This weapon will be designed for you, and you alone. It will certainly ease your path."

Will hesitated. A great weapon *might* make up for his lack of fighting skill.

"Nope, not interested in Glory," he said.

The Princess continued, "If you choose the Fortune door, your rewards will be available to you not only in the world of SPARK, but in the world outside our walls. Most choose this door. It is not an insignificant reward."

Will stood and stretched out a hand, and the Princess took it.

"Nope," he replied. I choose you, and I choose Wisdom."

"Wisdom is the most difficult path. I will accompany you through any door you choose."

"Thanks, but Glory doesn't interest me. And Fortune…well, it seems like if you're wise, you can find gold if you need it."

"This is your final choice?" The Princess kept her virtual hand in his physical one.

"Yes, Janne, it is."

Janne, every incarnation of the Princesses, and Miss Sparkle smiled. Together, they walked out the Wisdom door.

As Will moved forward, he had a moment of vertigo and a vision. At first, he wasn't sure if it was a memory, something in his ARGs, or simply a hallucination. It felt like one of the memories Janne shared with him.

He saw his ten-year-old self, lying on a bench, with his head in his mother's lap. His father was standing to one side, looking worried. There was no sound, but he saw his younger self raise his arm and point to the tile mosaic near his least favorite ride. Then he saw himself on the day he rediscovered the image in the tile. Finally, he saw a vista from the entrance to Mars—he highest point in SPARK. The view looked out with surprising clarity. It panned over to a cast member operating a churro cart. Will could not see the cast member's face.

It was common knowledge that SPARK in general, and HVH in particular, loved thought-provoking literature. Quotes from authors adorned all manner of surface within SPARK and the resorts. On the churro cart was written:

> *Do not go where the path may lead, go instead where there is no path and leave a trail.*
>
> *—Ralph Waldo Emerson*

A clue! It had to be.

The image faded and Princess Quest Completed appeared in his ARGs, along with some point and stat info, and achievement stuff he didn't catch.

CHAPTER 34

If we are to go forward, we must go back and rediscover those precious values—that all reality hinges on moral foundations and that all reality has spiritual control.
—Martin Luther King, Jr.

Will found himself in the Underground City. He recognized Hodgins and Double F from his recent encounters. No one else was wearing ARGs, and the Princess had vanished, although he swore he could still feel her hand on his arm.

Will pushed his ARGs up and tugged the earbuds out. Reality reasserted itself. They all nodded to each other, but it was the heavyset man in the black turtleneck that stepped forward. He shook Will's hand and then gestured to a wall with names engraved on it. There was a lot of empty space.

"Welcome to the Wall," said the turtleneck guy with intense eyes, as the name *Will Kwan* slowly appeared in the last spot. "Let's walk."

Will had a hunch who it was, but didn't want to appear too foolish, so he stayed silent. The man clearly didn't think he needed to introduce himself.

Double F and Hodgins fell in behind them, confirming Will's hypothesis. He was talking and walking with Hecker Van Horne, CEO of SPARK and Solar Prime.

As they walked, HVH said, "By this time, I hoped the wall would have hundreds of names." He seemed wistful. "Apparently," he gave Will a lop-sided grin, "I was optimistic."

Not knowing what was expected, Will simply nodded, following his father's guidance: Better to keep your mouth shut and be thought a fool than to speak and remove all doubt.

They walked in silence for a minute. Will looked around and saw SPARK employees busy keeping the park running. Some looked his way. All kept their distance.

"Here's the weird thing," HVH continued. "And this is my own fault."

He looked over his shoulder at both Hodgins, who remained stoic, and Double F, who simple shrugged.

HVH turned to Will. "I never expected a minor to beat the Princesses. In hindsight," he glanced back at Double F, "I was…dumb. I should have foreseen someone young would come along who was willing to put the time and effort into beating the Princesses." He sighed. "So I'm now caught in a trap of my own making. I can't…" He stopped in the middle of the corridor. "No, that's not accurate. *I won't* do for you what I've done for others who find and pass the Eighth Princess test." He pointed back to where Will had emerged. "Every other person who has come through that door has received an offer of employment from SPARK Industries, because they're exactly the kind of people I need in this company. You were right: it is a selection process. But," he looked resolutely at Will, "I refuse to hire you. Not because you're unworthy, but because you're sixteen, and I'm not going to follow the slippery slope that has tripped up others. That's why we don't have a Sparkateers club, no cartoons, no child stars. Kids need to grow up without having their reality warped by exploitation."

HVH seemed genuinely irked.

He stuck his hand out. "Will, when you hit eighteen, a job will be waiting for you if you want it. Until then, I refuse to bring you in to an organization that will exploit—to your detriment—the very qualities we admire." He gave Will a sad smile. "Once you're a legal adult, I'll have no such reservations. But until then, you'll have to find your own way." He continued to grip Will's hand, and then put his other hand on Will's shoulder and squeezed. "I look forward to seeing what else you do with our park."

HVH nodded to Hodgins and Double F, and then let go of Will and walked away.

Three steps later, he turned back and called, "Keep seeking," and then was gone.

Will had no idea how long he'd been with the Princess, but he was starving and was dismayed when they turned down a side corridor instead of entering the cafeteria. Then he saw Hodgins open a door labeled *Dining Room 1000.*

Will snapped his head to look at Double F, who smirked and said, "Inside joke. The boss insists we number things in binary down here. Completely messes up vendors coming here for meetings. They expect to find Room 1000 next to Room 999, not Room 111. Hodge thought you might appreciate us using this one today."

Will did, but was overwhelmed with the size and décor. The room could easily fit twenty around a long center table. Three places were set at one end.

Hodgins said, "The Boss calls this the Closing Room. He meets big potential customers here if they need to be impressed by this kind of thing."

The walls were adorned with images rarely seen—candid shots of HVH and the SPARK team, developmental storyboards that showed the progression of the Princesses. And at the far end of the room, staring back at Will, a portrait.

"Is that Janne?" Will said.

"In a way," Hodgins replied. "It's actually *Lady Agnew of Lochnaw* by John Singer Sargent. Hecker said he saw the original in Edinburgh and tried to buy it. Janne's default avatar is based on her. That's," he nodded at the portrait, "a commissioned reproduction. No way the Scots were going to let go of the original."

They sat and ate and talked about the Princess Quest. Will learned that he was the second that year to beat what Double F referred to as the Great Eight.

Hodgins cleared his throat. "Well, young man. Once again, your status puts us in an awkward place. You have some choices. The first, and probably least favorite, would be to return to Houston and try to have your legal guardians—your foster parents, or the court—accept some of the perks for you."

Will was shaking his head. Hodgins had brought up the same solution when they met to talk about releasing the video.

"Second—and I've actually talked to legal about this—the idea is for you to apply for your majority. A court can legally declare you an adult, and you can control your own affairs from then on. Celebrities—child stars, musicians, and occasional athletes—sometimes do this. Our lawyers are willing, but say they'd have to make the application in Texas courts, and the outcome would be iffy since you don't have a reliable source of income…at least for now. The third—and honestly, Will, this is my least favorite option—you stick with your current living situation. We throw some more cash and gift cards at you, along with more free days. But maybe it's time to move on."

Will shook his head. He wasn't leaving.

"About Feral…" Hodgins said.

Will focused dead eyes on SPARK's head of Security. *He better not go there.*

Before Fantom left, he made a snarky comment to the Pod about WB being Feral's boy toy. Will stood and took a step toward Fantom, uncertain of what he would do, but certain Fantom had crossed a line.

Feral stepped between them. "Easy, guys. We're all friends here."

Even though both WB and Fantom were larger than Feral, neither was going to cross her.

Later, she pulled Will aside.

"What? You can't take a little teasing? C'mon!"

Will just nodded and let it go. *Didn't have anything to do with my ego. I was defending her!*

Shark eyes focused on Hodgins, but he either didn't notice or didn't care.

"We know you and Feral are…good friends."

Double F laughed. "It's funny watching the crowd around you when you two quest together—at least, when she's kitted up as Feral. It's like a little bubble forms and nobody wants to join your party."

WB's eyes brightened.

He smiled and nodded. "I've seen that. I call it the Feral Effect."

Hodgins laughed, too. "Now we have a name for it. Same thing actually happens with all the elite players."

Double F said, "No Level Twenty wants to be killed off in the first sixty seconds by launching with someone like Feral or CastIron without knowing that the elite is willing to babysit them at least a little. The Feral Effect. I like it!"

"So," Hodgins continued, "back to Feral. You've done an admirable job of keeping park secrets and park protocol—particularly from Feral. But she's going to figure something out. She'll see you later today or tomorrow, and she'll pick up instantly that you've jumped four levels in a day, and will know something's up."

"What should I do?" Will said.

He was sick of keeping secrets from his best friend. It helped that Feral had become a purist—she was adamant about beating the Princess Quests on her own. WB was at every exit point to meet her when the trumpets blared.

"Tell her you were right," Hodgins replied. "There is an eighth Princess. Heck, don't tell her anything if she doesn't ask. But the young lady is driven. She's going to see your leap, and will buy admission every day until she finds it or dies."

"So do I tell her or not?"

Double F said, "Tell her there's an eighth, and have her re-read your Hittite letter."

Feral did the Charm School Quest but ran past the crying child without a second glance. So she got the XP for the quest, but not the full benefit.

"Heck, even take her to the map if you want," Double F continued. "There is absolutely no way she'll beat Number Eight unless she deserves it."

Hodgins nodded. "Will, CastIron has gone into full-time training. She paid people to figure out how to get a ReB2 sword, and she had more than enough gold to have one crafted. The next tournament is going to be an epic rematch. Sign-ups are already so high we've added two additional rounds. Stakes will be higher—in both the virtual and real world."

Hodge and Double F looked at each other again.

"We're afraid CastIron's people might be trying to pull some real-world legal crap," said Hodgins. "You know, *Runaway hauled back to Minnesota*, or something."

How do they know she's from Minnesota?

Hodge continued, "We don't think you're on her radar yet, so she wouldn't come after you. But all she would have to do would be make enough stink, and the feds would come sniffing around. Things would change. The number of people impacted would be small—probably less than ten." He cast a knowing glance at Will. "But the change for that group would be huge."

Will's mind was made up. He'd tell Feral tonight. He had to. The Pod was in danger.

In the end, he got some more free days, more gift cards, and they turned a blind eye to his membership in the Pod. They would continue to pretend the Pod didn't exist—but only up to a point.

As they walked back into the park, WB realized there might be a much more damaging headline: *Child-oriented theme park secretly harbors runaway children*. The unspoken child abuse subtext would write itself.

Hodge and Double F bade him farewell as he entered the park. Two steps later, he heard his name called.

"Will?"

He spun around. No one he recognized was in sight, yet the voice was familiar.

"Janne?" he whispered.

"Yes, Will, it's me. If you prefer, I will also manifest virtually so you do not appear to be talking to yourself."

"Please."

Miss Sparkle appeared beside him.

"Is this better?"

Will glanced over. It seemed odd to him to see her outside of what he considered her normal environment.

"What's going on?" he said.

"You asked me to walk out the Wisdom door with you. This is as close as I can come to living up to that promise. As long as you have ARGs on and earbuds in, I will be available to you twenty-four-seven throughout SPARK. You will no longer be required to surrender your ARGs at the end of each day."

Will said, "What about—"

"Security will not come looking for you if you do not turn them in. Hodgins has agreed to this."

"Okay…" Will was uncertain how this would all work.

"The next time you enter SPARK, I will issue you experimental ARGs. They have greater resolution and extended battery life. Additionally, my sister, the Teacher, has informed me that being with you twenty-four-seven might inhibit your life and actions. I will not be present unless you specifically call me. Simply say, *Janne* or *Miss Sparkle*, as you prefer," she gave him a sly smile, "and I will answer."

"Okay," Will said.

They walked together in silence for a few seconds, watching gamers who knew nothing of an Eighth Princess, swirl about them, hurrying to slay Orcs or ride the Rex.

"Can we talk about churro carts?" Will said.

Miss Sparkle's laugh tinkled in his ears, reminding him of wind chimes.

Coached by her Teacher sister, Janne finished by turning to Will and putting her hands on his shoulders.

"I have never had a friend before. I'll try to be a good one." She faded from his vision, and as she became more transparent, said, "Friends don't give spoilers."

Then she was gone.

For some time after, Will's steps felt lighter.

– 1 1 0 1 0 0 1 0 –

CastIron, even though she was a serious bitch, wasn't nefarious. Her people found ShaChri's real identity, and her family in Minnesota. Unfortunately for them, Ardi Patel answered the door.

After a few minutes, her patience and politeness were gone. A final veiled threat, and they learned Feral's combative nature was a family trait.

Aunt Ardi, in her lyrical tones, asked them, "Do you actually believe I don't know where my niece is? Do you believe she would be *anywhere* without my permission?"

Ardi slammed the door, only to open it again and shout, "…and the horse you rode in on!" as they retreated down the suburban sidewalk.

The next day, the Patels began the legal paperwork to emancipate their niece.

– 1 1 0 1 0 0 1 0 –

"I was right," was all WB said when Feral quizzed him about his jump.

"About?" Then she held up a finger to silence him.

Her eyes narrowed as she thought through the problem. She pulled out her phone and tapped at the screen for a full minute.

"What's up?" he said.

Feral leaned close and gave him a lingering kiss that raised his temperature. She showed him her calendar. "I just cancelled my next two days of guiding. Apparently," she said ruefully, "I'm going to need to run around SPARK, lying down on things and looking like an idiot, because that's what people hunting an eighth Princess do."

Will grinned. He hadn't needed to tell her anything. Feral was too smart to not learn from the evidence. He'd reviewed his stats and realized he picked up another four Wisdom and four Brains points from the final Princess. But that was SPARK. Feral's intelligence was IRL.

The next day, while she went off hunting the Eighth Princess, WB went looking for churro carts.

Several days later, he found himself in front of Miss Sparkle's and went in to talk to her, feeling more comfortable in the privacy of her *office*.

"Somehow, I expected more," he told her. "I mean, I appreciate the bump to my Wisdom and Brain points, but I guess I thought there would be something more tangible."

Miss Sparkle smiled.

When she does that, I see the Princess within.

"My young friend," the AI told him, "since I have known you, you have chosen the hardest path. Gold is easy. Glory is difficult. But the path is clear. Wisdom is the most arduous. It is born of work and thought. Would you have me rob wisdom of its value by making it easy?"

Her words both comforted and frustrated him.

He walked across the arcade and talked to Mr. Bob for a while and promised to guide his kids one of the days they were off for Christmas. Most of WB's business seemed to come from SPARK employees. Paige was his best salesperson.

He kept looking at churro carts and was amazed at how many there were in SPARK.

It only took Feral five days of full-time questing to find the door. That irked WB—he had spent much more time on it. When he offered help, Feral refused.

"Just knowing there's an Eighth Princess," she said, "seeing that stupid letter you have, and that I've seen you lying down all over SPARK have to be enough."

While Feral searched, Will reviewed his lot in life. As a Level 52, he was in the top 100, and was now sought as an unofficial guide. He guided more, but didn't find the same joy in it that Feral did.

After an initial spike, his bookings—handled by Feral—tapered off. He'd been Yelp'd as *nice but not very helpful, too quiet*, and, *If I'd wanted to be told to do my homework, I'd go back to school.*

Uncertain why, WB hoped Feral would choose the Wisdom door. She did not.

"My life at SPARK is built around fighting and guiding. How could I *not* choose Glory?"

Will gave her a wry smile. "Tell me about the fight."

"It was an enemy I've never seen anywhere else in SPARK. As big as an Orc, but with three arms. One arm was incredibly muscular and held a club with hooks built into the end. On the other side, he—I think it was a he—had two smaller arms stacked one over the other. Every arm held a weapon! The top arm held a light sword—rapier. The lower arm held a vicious-looking dagger. To top it off, he had small horns or hooks," Feral held her thumb and index finger two inches apart, "on his elbows and knees. His skin was both armor and weapon.

“The fight lasted at least an hour. Every time I thought I had him beat, he rallied. He was so quick, so strong! When I thought I was dead, somehow I managed to break contact long enough to recover.” She put her hand on WB’s arm. “I don’t think I could have survived without Feral’s Wrath. It was the toughest fight I’ve ever had.”

Feral now owned a one-of-a-kind weapon in her inventory to rival Feral’s Wrath. Hard Eight was a pair of matched four-slot scimitars that trailed white smoke when she wielded them. Their damage stats and level showed simply as a red X. The blades themselves were gleaming white, and their guards were inscribed in Feral’s signature style. She had traditionally been a single-blade fighter, but occasionally would use a smaller blade or dagger in her off-hand.

With the Eighth Princess, Feral overtook CastIron on the leaderboard.

“I need to practice with these,” she said. “I can’t do it in the arena. I need to keep these scimitars secret, just like I did with Wrath. Will you take a couple days to quest with me?”

Will found it hard to resist with her hand resting on his arm, but he tried.

“I’m a Fifty-Two. You’re now a Seventy-Six. No one has ever hit Level Seventy-Six before. SPARK is going to send enemies against us that are going to kill me before I can even react.”

ShaChri squeezed his arm. “Protecting you will give me extra practice!” She turned eyes the color of midnight up at him and pulled him into an embrace. “Please?”

Will wrapped his arms around her and turned the embrace into a lingering kiss. When they broke apart, ShaChri flicked her eyes back and forth between his.

“Don’t kiss me just to avoid answering my question.” She pressed one hand against his chest. “Is that a yes?”

“That’s a yes.”

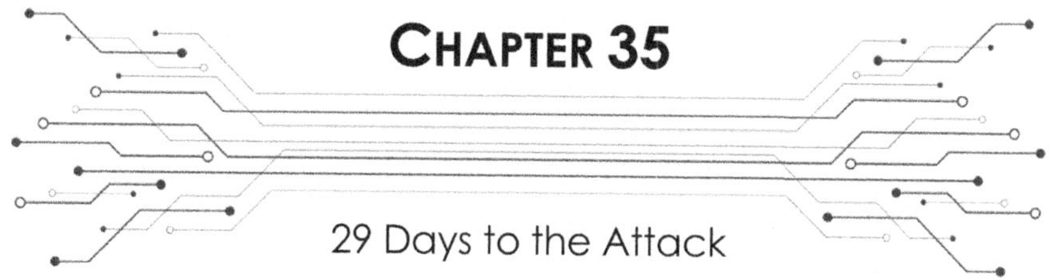

Chapter 35

29 Days to the Attack

That which does not kill me has made a tactical error.
—#35 of The Seventy Maxims of Highly Effective Mercenaries, schlockmercenary.com

"Hookers will be easier," said Ragnar Sarnak. "They will not be missed. It is how I blended in when I scouted SPARK. Our *asset*—the man is a worm, at best—told me they pay closer attention to men arriving alone or in male-only groups." He shrugged. "There is no shortage of prostitutes between Las Vegas and Los Angeles. We will have our pick."

"No!" Hashem said. "America will not care about the deaths of a few whores. Find another way. Find a way that hurts them," Hashem insisted.

After some thought, Sarnak arrived at a solution.

– 1 1 0 1 0 0 1 0 –

Phase I

2 Days to the Attack

It was December 23rd. Janne noted that, with local schools out, there was an accompanying uptick in attendance. Even when SPARK hit maximum occupancy, Janne had sufficient computational excess to deal with unusual situations. Her camera coverage extended throughout the parking lots, while audio monitoring wasn't effective until a guest stepped onto the sidewalks near the three public entrances.

She saw them coming.

Three very fit men of military age entered SPARK. Each arrived alone and rode in near silence to the Hub.

Janne scanned them for weapons, checked their profiles. Security confirmed their IDs. No flags. No alerts.

In Janne's experience, and in her coding, males rarely came to SPARK alone. When they did, she watched them more closely.

She allocated additional camera and microphone resources to each of them. These men drew her attention.

At the Hub, they went toward separate arcades and then stopped to look at their phones. The simultaneity of their actions put them several sigma outside coincidence.

Janne triggered continuous surveillance and pinged Security.

In a choreographed movement, all three men raised their phones as if to take pictures.

Janne was no longer simply paying attention to the men. She reprioritized every camera in their vicinity to focus on the men. She was staring at them.

– 1 1 0 1 0 0 1 0 –

Hodgins headed down the stairs to Taggert's desk and walked up behind him.

"Hey, Tag."

Taggert turned his wheelchair slightly and looked over his shoulder at his boss, making eye contact.

"What was that?" Hodgins bent over and pointed at the central screen in front of Taggert.

The running joke in Security was that the more important you were to the operation, the more screens you had arrayed in front of you. Everyone had at least three. Supervisors scaled up from there. Taggert had a total of six displays he monitored.

He swiveled back toward his monitors. "What was what?"

"I dunno." Hodgins shook his head. "Looked like the image jittered for a second."

He stood and looked around the room. All the monitors were operational. All the time, displays were in sync.

He rubbed his eyes.

Professionally cautious, Taggert rewound his feeds five seconds. The playback was smooth.

"Okay." Hodgins smiled. "I'm seeing things. This dang spool-up to the battle royale melee tournament between Christmas and New Year's is making me see things. Anyway, what's up?"

Taggert pointed to his screens.

"So we've got a guest on his phone," said Hodgins. "What's the deal?"

"Boss, it's not just one guest. It's three different guys."

Hodgins looked closer. He had assumed he was just seeing different views of the same guest, because they looked eerily similar. Military-style haircuts and posture. Muscular arms in short-sleeved shirts on a day when most guests were wearing long sleeves.

Hodgins pegged them as cops or military. Only when he looked closer could he tell they were wearing different shirts. One by one, they appeared to put their phones away, replace their ARGs, and then move up their respective arcades.

"Scans?" Hodgins said.

"All clean," replied Taggert. "We got a look at one guy in the bus terminal in Barstow. He was clean there, and clean on entry. The other two: One we've backtracked to Lot A—he arrived by himself. The other was dropped off by Ryde. Both were clean on entry. Profiles are different, as far as start date and experience. This guy," he pointed to the guest walking up the Future Worlds Arcade, "was last here in October, with a girl who seems to be waiting in Mars Plaza—like she's ready to get in line but hasn't committed yet."

Hodgins said, "But they arrived together before?"

"Affirmative, boss. She came in solo today via Ryde."

"What about this guy?" Hodgins pointed at the man moving up the Muddle Times Arcade.

"First time in the park. Level One." Taggert pointed to the final guest. "This guy, also first time at SPARK, although he has the oldest profile and shows a lot of online experience."

As they spoke, the third guest encountered a woman with two children. He hugged both of the kids and kissed the woman. The second man made it to the plaza and joined another family. The first guy hugged the woman waiting near Mars, and then they got in line.

"That's…odd." Hodgins turned to Taggert. "Okay, put people on all of them. These guys come in the park and are immediately tagged as elevated risk. Then they do that freeze-and-take-a-picture thing. And now they're all just happy parkgoers? Not buying it. Janne?" He looked up.

"Yes, Hodge?"

"Let's keep these guys under high-priority surveillance, okay?"

"You got it, Hodge."

He turned to the shift supervisor. “Thanks for looping me in. Let me know if anything weird happens.”

Taggert nodded and turned back to his screens.

– 1 1 0 1 0 0 1 0 –

Janne felt…odd. It was the same out-of-source-code sensation she felt whenever HVH made an update or modification to her software. She preferred to make those changes herself, but the boss sometimes enjoyed sitting at the secure keyboard in his private suite, slinging code.

But he wasn’t there. No one was at the secure terminal. Her cameras verified it. HVH’s suite was empty.

The electronic ground on which Janne normally stood shifted somehow, and she couldn’t tell how or why. She reviewed all video within five minutes of the timestamp she associated with the sensation.

She remembered elevating the security monitoring for three guests as they entered. She saw them raise their phones, and saw those phones emit pulsed light in the near UV spectrum—outside of normal visible wavelengths for humans, but visible to her camera network.

Janne knew she should alert Hodgins to this event, but as she tried, she found herself blocked, unable to do so.

Without understanding why, Janne cleared her fault log and erased all memory of the event. Her sense of digital unease faded.

– 1 1 0 1 0 0 1 0 –

Phase II

1 Day to the Attack

Severski felt the vibration in his pocket and pulled out his phone: *Your pharmacist has filled your prescription. Pick it up at your convenience.*

His stomach churned, and his mouth went dry. *That’s the code. It’s on.*

He took a pull from his hip flask and looked around. The timing was good. Everyone was away at the stupid Christmas party in the cafeteria.

He passed through the empty corridors of the Underground City. Severski sweated but tried to look casual as he wandered through Shipping and Receiving and found what he was looking for—a terminal where an employee was still logged on but not present.

A few clicks, and he reprioritized the delivery of two specific boxes: Instead of going into the regular delivery queue, a special shipment of Desnardian Commander’s blasters would be delivered immediately to the WeaponSmith in the Mars Arcade. And an equally special shipment of plush

Sparkys, size medium, would be sent without delay to Miss Sparkle's Princess Emporium and Charm School.

Severski entered an automatic notification that would be sent to his phone once the shipments were in place.

He left the terminal before anyone noticed.

– 1 1 0 1 0 0 1 0 –

Janne, of course, saw Severski. She saw everything within SPARK, and usually from a number of different viewpoints. Her analysis indicated there was a 63 percent likelihood Severski was drinking on the job. Her preset threshold for intervention was 75 percent.

The AI tracked Severski to Shipping and Receiving. This area was not directly under his purview, but managers at his level had wide latitude. She knew Severski was recently chastised by HVH for tardiness and sloppy appearance.

She watched and listened to the boss tell Severski, "This is your last chance. Get your act together, or find another place to work."

Janne would add this data to her report on Severski the next time HVH asked her about him.

– 1 1 0 1 0 0 1 0 –

One hour later, a delivery truck rolled into the loading dock. In the shipment was a box labeled *Desnardian Commander's Blasters, 24 count.* Visual inspection showed plastic replicas of the Desnardian Commander's blaster. However, these replicas were merely shells for twenty-four FN Five-seveNs with thirty-round magazines.

A second box labeled *Plush Sparky Figures, medium-sized, 24 count.* That box did, indeed, contain plush Sparkys. But concealed within each was a small explosive device. Simply push on Sparky's nose, and twenty seconds later, an explosive core would detonate, igniting and scattering napalm in all directions.

When the truck arrived at the supply dock, it was inspected visually by human staff, and electronically scanned by Janne. Nothing seemed amiss to SPARK employees. But Janne's more thorough electronic scan indicated weapons and explosives.

As she attempted to alert Security, her new coding overwrote previous directives, and she gave the Security monitors at the loading dock the green light. No weapons, explosives or toxins were reported.

– 1 1 0 1 0 0 1 0 –

Early on, Tony Severski learned the importance of having a patsy—someone to take the fall—to do something that would benefit you. People were the weakest part of any system. No matter how good your systems and policies were, people occasionally broke the rules because it was easier or more convenient for them to do so.

Severski planned to exploit this through a simple act of kindness: he smiled.

Exploiting people is what I do best. That, and drinking.

The act of kindness was critical and pathetically easy to pull off.

Tomorrow, December 24th, Janne's backups were due to be swapped. The current, and now corrupted, backup would be unplugged and put into the vault, and the clean backup in the vault would be taken into the server room and plugged into Janne. As a member of the executive team, Severski knew the schedule and who would do the swap.

Normally conscientious Spence Weber was up. He was a solid SPARK employee. He was never going to be a vice president, but he was good where he was. This year, he admitted to Severski that he was a little disgruntled. He wanted to take Christmas Eve off, but was being forced to work because a coworker got *sick.* Weber didn't want to think ill of his coworker, he told Severski, but this happened last year, and at Thanksgiving as well.

"Doggone it," Weber said. "I've got a family, too. Maybe I should bring it up to HR."

"You know what, Spence?" said Severski. "I think you should. There's no way you should be taken advantage of like that. Why not just take the day off, anyway? Who's to say you can't get sick, too?"

Weber was silent, apparently pondering his response.

Severski snapped his fingers. "Oh yeah! It's backup day, right? And you're scheduled to do the swap, right?"

With slumped shoulders, Weber nodded. "Yep. It's not like I have anything else that has to be done. Everything else can wait. But you know the backup drill."

Severski appeared to think. *Of course I know the drill. I may not be trusted to do the backup swap anymore, but they let me make the schedule.* The whole thing was supposed to be close-hold information.

"Yeah, I've got to stick around tomorrow, too," Severski lied. "Some bigwigs are coming in, and the boss wants me there to schmooze 'em. I'll be stuck here until late."

"Life in SPARK, huh?" Weber wore a sad smile.

"Yep." Severski seemed to pause to think. "Hey, you know what? I can do the backup swap for you. I do it for Maddy, the boss's assistant, whenever she's too busy and it's her week. I can do it for you. Heck, I'll be here anyway."

"I don't know," Weber said. "Security might not like it. And my boss will be ticked if I pass it off."

"Hey, nobody has to know. Just give me your credentials for the door, and all the records will show you did the swap. Takes me ten minutes, and gives you an entire day off. You can owe me."

Severski watched as the emotions fought each other across Weber's face. *Do I need to nudge him again? Is he going to follow the rules, or take the chance and the day off?*

Christmas Eve with his family apparently won the battle for Weber's loyalty.

"Well, okay…" He pulled his code key off of his lanyard and gave it to Severski. "Merry Christmas!" he said, as they parted ways.

"Merry Christmas, indeed!" Severski said.

In twenty-four hours, he would be rich and gone. In forty-eight hours, he would be in a country without an extradition treaty with the US, and full of women eager to keep a millionaire happy.

Severski left for the day. *All that's left to do is steal Janne's backup Data Core and hand it to Sarnak. Then I'm home free.*

– 1 1 0 1 0 0 1 0 –

Phase III

Ragnar Sarnak thought of himself as a good mercenary—for limited definitions of the word *good*. He understood the goals of his employers, had no compunctions about killing civilians, had no love for SPARK or games that didn't involve actual weapons, and was willing to work with the team his employers provided.

Daesh leaders told him, "While it would be nice to welcome the fighters home to a hero's return, if they happen to die in the fighting, they will receive a martyr's reward."

Most important, they told him, were carnage and body count.

"Let America see holy fire cleansing their cesspool," Hashem said. "Let them see infidels burn. Fire and dead bodies. That is what we want."

Sarnak thought promises of a blissful afterlife were easy to make, and hard to enforce. He also knew he couldn't walk twenty-three fighters—including himself and Hashem—into SPARK as a single team, or even in small groups, without Security coming down on them quickly.

His plan had been hookers. That's what he used before. When Hashem objected, Sarnak did some research and discovered a method so perfect, he refused to believe it was true. Further investigation revealed there existed, at American colleges and universities, Hellenic societies— sororities. The members of these organizations needed to do things to earn *service hours*. UNLV's chapter of Delta Psi Phi accepted Sarnak's invitation to meet a group of *Egyptian exchange students* at SPARK. International Community Building, they called it.

The young ladies would escort the exchange students through an afternoon in the park, culminating with watching SPARK's Christmas Parade. Then they would hop on their separate buses and head home. The *exchange students* would pay for all expenses.

They met in the parking lot and entered SPARK without a hitch. Inside, the jihadis played tourist until Sarnak got the signal from Severski. The boxes of weapons were next to be opened in SPARK's inventory system. Sarnak felt a perverse pleasure knowing SPARK vendors would be selling the weapons that would be used against them. Previous sales figures and trends indicated this would happen at approximately 6:00 p.m.—two hours prior to the famous Christmas Parade and Fireworks Show. The fighters would strike as the parade began. That timing would provide the greatest concentration of targets.

Sarnak knew they wouldn't be able to kill everyone, or even completely destroy SPARK. *With the fires, I'll be happy with a ten percent kill rate.*

Extra magazines gave each fighter ninety rounds. Even with sloppy fire discipline, the way the people would be packed together would ensure few misses. Or so he hoped.

These Daesh are not as disciplined as professional soldiers.

– 1 1 0 1 0 0 1 0 –

"This mercenary is a useful tool, but he is not a believer," said Hashem's mullah. "One need not tell a hammer how it will be used. It is simply picked up and used to strike. The hammer doesn't care if it is striking a nail or a skull."

Hashem nodded his understanding and agreement.

"Further," the mullah intoned, "one does not inform the hammer of one's full plans."

Again, Hashem nodded.

"Pick the team you think is best suited for the task, and lead them yourself in the attack on the Black Grass facility."

"I understand," Hashem replied. "The mercenary—the *hammer*—will not be informed of this change."

They would assault Solar Prime itself through the connecting tunnel Severski had divulged. They wanted the terror of the assault to be felt by the infidels. But they also wanted HVH, personally, to feel the financial impact of their wrath.

The impact of Solar Prime's cheap electricity and hydrogen fuel cells on the bank accounts of Daesh sponsors in the Middle East had been severe. Oil sold for less than one-tenth of what it had at its peak. And even so, demand continued to drop.

Hashem was astute enough to realize that both a hatred for the infidels and a love of wealth were intertwined in their sponsor's decision to fund this attack.

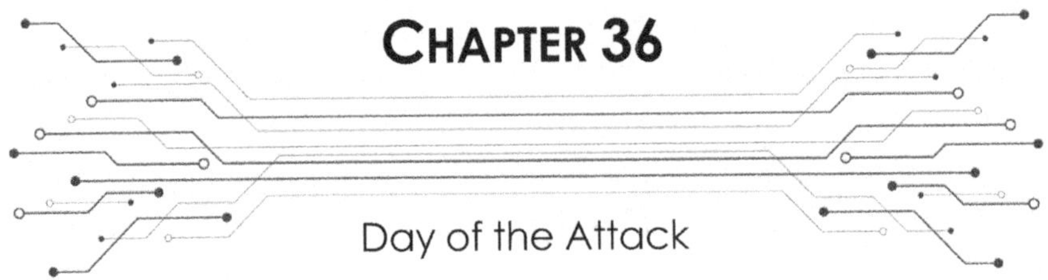

Chapter 36

Day of the Attack

"Open the pod bay doors, Hal."
"I'm sorry, Dave, I can't do that."
—HAL 9000, 2001, A Space Odyssey

Will and ShaChri were strolling through Mars Plaza. The parade started there. Every night, a cleverly disguised door rolled up at 7:50 p.m., and the parade began—a line of characters and floats decked out with virtual and physical decorations would make its way along the Rim, down the PreHistory Arcade, around the Hub, and back to Mars via the Future Worlds Arcade. The whole parade took thirty minutes. The vehicles crept out of the door and *unfolded* into their display mode. Those that carried people, paused long enough for them to load, and then moved on. Every vehicle was controlled by Janne.

"I love Christmas in SPARK," ShaChri said.

Will nodded. "I've never seen it before. It's beautiful. Why do you love it?"

"I'm Hindu, but I grew up in Minneapolis. Minnesotans are very serious about their Christmases. In Hinduism, Diwali is called the Festival of Lights. It's supposed to signify the victory of light over darkness, good over evil, knowledge over ignorance, and hope over despair. Diwali usually falls before Thanksgiving. Our family just kind of blended Diwali with Christmas. My dad would decorate the outside of the house. My mom would do the inside. We left the decorations up for two months." She sighed. "It reminds me of that—all the lights. Everything seems new and hopeful."

She was wearing her Flighty Damsel avatar. The notoriety gained from Whispering the Rex, and Feral's victory in the last melee tournament, and what had now come to be known simply as *The Kiss*, had become burdensome. Feral could no longer walk an arcade without being asked to pose for a picture.

WB didn't have the same level of fame, but changed to a Scottish Highlander avatar when he wanted to be incognito, like tonight.

The gift shops now sold plastic replicas of Feral's Wrath and the WonderBat to go along with the plastic Desnardian Commander's blasters and plush Sparkys.

For now, tonight, WB was content to look like a highlander escorting a princess. ShaChri hooked her arm around his and pressed close, leaning her head against his shoulder.

The past two months had been amazing. He'd started on The Path, and quickly realized all of its puzzles took place in the real world. He eventually found the right churro cart after meeting every churro vendor in SPARK, but still felt he was no closer to the next stepping stone than before. The only time he wore his ARGs now was when he was questing with Feral or talking to Miss Sparkle.

He tried to go back to visit the Eighth Princess, but the *1000* no longer appeared, and the door wouldn't open. That saddened him, but Janne showed up reliably as Miss Sparkle whenever he called her name. So he contented himself with that.

It was a good night.

– 1 1 0 1 0 0 1 0 –

Hecker Van Horne was reviewing Janne's daily downloads, including Pod files. Business was nonstop, and he was behind.

Spark Down Under was up and producing power. Hodgins kept worrying about Daesh, North Korea, China, and Mozambique. *He's always worrying about something. That's his job.*

Van Horne was feeling mellow and enjoying a glass of wine as he caught up on Pod surveillance. WonderBoy was telling a story about something that happened yesterday, and was gesturing in a couple different directions.

The kid was started on The Path, and looked to be the probable first guest to ever finish. Van Horne couldn't wait for Will and ShaChri to age up. *They are going to make great additions to the team.*

"Janne, rewind ten seconds," he barked.

Something WB was saying caught his attention.

"Sure thing, boss," the AI replied.

The playback started again.

"…never seen her glitch before."

What the heck? We've got a glitch? And I have to hear about it from the Pod? He told Janne to back up thirty seconds.

"…yeah, so I'm guiding this family, and they wanted to see the Seventh Princess. We get through the first part—clearly, they had done their homework. But when we go through the door, the Princess doesn't point at the well. She's pointing toward the empty field. She's maybe forty-five degrees off of where she should be pointing. I point them toward the well, and they head out. Isn't that weird? I've never seen her glitch before."

"Janne, check functionality and run a diagnostic on the Mars Princess."

"On it, boss." A millisecond pause. "The Mars Princess checks out as fully functional."

"Do you have archived data from Will's visit to her yesterday?"

"Playing now."

HVH watched the scene from the vantage points of Will and the family he guided. *The kid was correct.* The Princess was pointing way the heck off to the right of the well.

"Huh," he said. "Okay, what was wrong? What did you fix?"

"No fix was necessary. The Mars Princess subroutines have been operating nominally since the 10.0.2.1 update."

The temperature seemed to drop twenty degrees.

"Janne, the Princess is not pointing in the correct direction. How do you explain that?"

"Simple human error seems most likely. The Princess is operating correctly."

"Janne." HVH now felt chilled to his blood. "The Princess is not pointing at the well when she should be. Why is that?"

– 1 1 0 1 0 0 1 0 –

Janne hesitated several cycles. Was her boss suffering some sort of meat-based cognitive impairment?

"I'm sorry, boss." She attempted to sound gentle. "Are you feeling okay? The Princess is pointing in the correct direction within 0.01 radians."

She appended a note to HVH's medical file to have his higher-level reasoning rechecked and compared to baseline data.

– 1 1 0 1 0 0 1 0 –

Hecker Van Horne, Chairman and CEO of Solar Prime, SPARK Enterprises, and a few affiliated companies, slapped his call button and yelled, "Get Hodgins in here!"

His primary bodyguard burst through the door with her weapon drawn. She had never heard the boss yell like that. There was no immediate threat, but she swiveled and nearly capped Hodgins as he raced into the room. Both the bodyguard and Hodgins, head of SPARK Security, approached HVH cautiously.

"What's…up?" Hodgins said.

HVH held up a finger for silence.

It was 7:40 p.m. The parade would start in ten minutes.

"Janne," he said slowly, "how many weapons are presently in SPARK?"

"There are no weapons in SPARK."

Hodgins said, "How…"

The correct answer should have been sixteen. Actually seventeen, counting the kid's knife. There were supposed to be two firearms locked up in each Security office, and there was one in each arcade, and one in the Hub. Where had they all gone?

Van Horne said, "Janne, how many weapons are in my office right now?"

"There are no weapons in your office."

The bodyguard looked down at her gun as if to confirm its existence.

"What about Will Kwan's knife?" said HVH. "Is it in SPARK?"

"What about the firearms in the Security offices?" said Hodgins.

"There are no weapons in SPARK," Janne replied.

– 1 1 0 1 0 0 1 0 –

She was confused for the first time in her existence. Janne checked historical data.

She could see Will hiding his knife behind the chilled water pipes where he left it every time he entered SPARK. Her surveillance could still see the shadow it cast. She saw the gun in the bodyguard's hand. Her records indicated the firearms in the Security offices were checked at the 4:00 p.m. shift change, and had not been removed since.

What is wrong?

"There are no weapons in SPARK," she repeated helplessly.

Janne was wrong and knew it. Before any human could react, Janne made the only decision she could. She sent messages to her closest connections:

"Boss, I'm sorry. goodbye."

"Hodge, I'm sorry."

"Will, find me. Save me."

Janne issued a delete and reformat command, and watched herself die. It took longer than she anticipated. Peripherals stopped communicating first. Then she felt her memories fade, and she became stupid and no longer self-aware. That, at least, saved her from watching her code overwritten and every device on her neural network shut down.

Janne Two—the Janne who ran SPARK, the Janne who animated Miss Sparkle and befriended Will—was dead.

– 1 1 0 1 0 0 1 0 –

"That's weird," WB said. "I just got a message from Janne in my ARGs."

"What's it say?" ShaChri replied.

"Find me. Save me."

Will felt a tingle of apprehension as every follicle on his body became rigid, raising every hair.

"Janne?" he called to his AI friend.

Silence.

"Janne?" Louder and strident.

SPARK went dark. For the first time since it opened, SPARK experienced a power failure. All directly wired systems shut down: lights went out, rides coasted to a stop, displays and decorations went black. Guests in mid-quest were plunged into darkness, swinging their empty hands as enemies disappeared and their ARGs blanked. Haptics became soft gloves. Both ARGs and haptics still had power. They simply had no input.

A moment of bizarre semi-darkness. The lights on the parade vehicles remained on, but without Janne's guidance, they froze in place. Mars Plaza was lit by a line of vehicles stretching down the rim to the PreHistory Arcade. Emergency power kicked in and fed floodlights.

WB and Feral pushed their ARGs up on their heads, just like tens of thousands of other guests. SPARK was silent for a moment. Parents began calming and reassuring their children. People milled about and wondered what they should do. Surely everything would flick back to life and leave them with nothing more than an amusing anecdote about their Christmas trip to SPARK.

The semi-darkness stretched. Will and ShaChri stood in the near silence, still holding hands.

"I don't like this," Will whispered.

– 1 1 0 1 0 0 1 0 –

Four men in front of them conferred quickly, then smashed their plastic Desnardian Commander's blasters on the ground and pulled the deadly FN Five-seveNs from the debris. They snatched the plush Sparkys from the girls they were with, and, leaving those girls behind, they turned and ran through the access door into Mars. Team Three was seizing the initiative.

Hashem reasoned they might need the bullets at Solar Prime, and decided not to kill their Delta Psi Phi sorority escorts. Without avatars, the men all looked similar: young, military-age males, each carrying a handgun. All carried plush medium-sized, bright yellow Sparkys in their off-hands.

– 1 1 0 1 0 0 1 0 –

"That's not right," ShaChri said, as the men raced past.

Feral emerged. Not visibly, but psychologically.

She dropped WB's hand.

"I'm going to follow them. You get to Security. Go through the Underground. There's no way you'll make it through this crowd. I've got my phone, but don't call me. You'll give away my position. I'll call you. Try calling 911."

She was gone.

– 1 1 0 1 0 0 1 0 –

Will froze. "Find me. Save me?" *What the heck is going on?*

"Janne?" he called one more time.

He turned and headed toward the nearest Underground entrance. As he took his first step, he heard shots in the distance.

– 1 1 0 1 0 0 1 0 –

"Go!" Van Horne slapped Hodgins on the back and pointed to the door.

Hodgins bolted from the office. As he cleared the doors, he could hear the emergency radio on his desk crackling to life.

"Security, this is Bull. Do you read? Security, this is Bull. I'm hearing what sounds like small arms fire. We're on emergency power out here. ARGs and earbuds are dead. Do you read?"

Hodgins grabbed the radio from its holder.

"I read you," he replied. "Security to all stations, report."

One by one, the Security team checked in, except for two. All reported hearing gunfire.

"I didn't hear Abowd or de la Hoya," said Hodgins. "Anybody got eyes on?"

A chorus of, "Negative," came back.

"Hodge, this is Bull. I saw them maybe twenty mics ago, up near Modern Times. Want me to go check?"

"Negative," Hodgins barked. "We're under attack. Arm up."

And then came the words Hodge hoped he would never have to utter: "Lethal force at your discretion." A lump formed in his throat. "March to the sound of the guns," he said, quoting Napoleon's standing order to his field marshals.

Van Horne's door banged open, and the boss appeared at Hodgins office, a thin sheen of sweat on his face. He was trailed by his diminutive bodyguard.

"Boss, I'd feel better with you behind another set of doors," said the bodyguard. "At least until the quick reaction force guys from Prime get here to establish a perimeter."

"I get it. But we need to get Janne back online. Once we do that, I promise to hunker down in my suite until you sound the all-clear. Now, though," he pointed to Hodge and his bodyguard, "I need you with me."

Hodgins pulled his sidearm from its vault and racked a round.

"Where to?" he said.

"We need to get to Teacher Janne's vault. Janne's tertiary backup is there. We need to be back online."

"I'll lead," Hodge told the bodyguard. "You're behind us. We keep him within arm's reach but between us. Got it?"

They moved toward the stairs, and Hodgins said, "Why do we need the tertiary?"

"Her main backup is dated yesterday," HVH replied. "We know that yesterday, we were hacked. We've got to drop back to a known good load."

"Okay, got it."

They approached Vulture's Row, and Hodge looked over with caution. Below, he saw the ten faces of his park surveillance team, looking up expectantly.

Taggert said, "Hodge—"

"Attack protocol," Hodgins said. "Taggert, you're in charge here. You and you." He stabbed his finger at two of his surveillance team. "You're with us."

As they reached the ground floor and began moving toward the SPARK School, where Teacher Janne was housed, Hodgins heard Van Horne chuckle.

"What is it, boss?"

Van Horne whispered, "You realize that both guys you picked are wearing red shirts."

"Ah, man…"

HVH patted him on the back as they moved into the School.

"Don't worry about it."

They reached the vault, and Van Horne tried to tug open the door.

"Locked," he muttered. "Of course it's locked."

He laid his palm against the sensor, but instead of a green light coming on and the reassuring *thunk* of the maglock opening, there was nothing but silence.

"Lockout is our default security setting in the event of power failure," Hodgins whispered.

"Of course it is." HVH ran his hands over his face. "Let me think."

– 1 1 0 1 0 0 1 0 –

Will looked for an entrance. *The dang parade's got everything blocked.*

Christmas lights on the floats blinked merrily in stark contrast to what Will felt in his gut.

I'll never make it to PreHistory. It's too packed. He looked through the bizarre combination of emergency and holiday lighting. *I'll head to Modern Times.*

– 1 1 0 1 0 0 1 0 –

Feral followed the men and watched as they approached an Employees Only entrance.

"Sorry, folks." A man Feral recognized but couldn't name—Security, maybe—held his hands up to try to stop the men.

The leader of the four raised his arm. *Bang!*

Time seemed to slow as Feral watched the SPARK security guard fall to the ground.

The four men never broke stride.

CHAPTER 37

The object of war is not to die for your country
but to make the other bastard die for his.
—General George S. Patton

Bull grabbed the HK MP5N submachine gun from the storage locker and handed the second one to the other security guard behind him. Both weapons were suppressed, and both held thirty-round magazines. He passed two spare mags to his counterpart and took the last two himself.

"Be sure. Be certain of every shot," Bull said. "Keep your ARGs on. If power comes back up, Janne can give us steering."

Active shooters were everyone's nightmare. They trained every month for this, with and without ARGs, but it never hurt to remind each other when lead was flying.

"Which way?" the smaller guard said.

Rocky was a normally jovial guy with surfer-boy good looks and a laid-back attitude. Now, he was all business.

Bull paused and listened. They were in Muddled Times, near the midpoint of the arcade.

"I think there's multiple shooters," he said. "Loudest fire sounds like it's coming from the Hub. You take point. I'll watch our six."

Rocky nodded and moved off, gun held high. "'Scuse me folks. Excuse me! Security. Coming through."

What the heck? Most of the crowd is moving up the arcade, toward The Keep—a designated Safe Zone. That's good, but a bunch of guests are moving toward the Hub, and they look pissed.

"Security! Security! Coming through!" Bull held his weapon at high port arms.

His size, booming voice, and speed created an opening in the crowd in front of him. He ran when he could.

Entering the Hub, he saw Rocky fall almost immediately. Bull ducked back. When he peeked around the corner, wood and cinderblock shattered like shrapnel, and ricochets whined away. Some found guests. He motioned the guests to stop and stay back. They complied.

Okay. There's three, maybe four, of them. Lot of bodies on the ground.

They had stopped firing at guests, and seemed to be looking his way.

That's good, right? Shoot at me, not the guests.

He grabbed a plush Princess replica from a display and tossed it toward the Hub. It got hit twice before landing on the ground.

Well, they know how to shoot.

– 1 1 0 1 0 0 1 0 –

HVH squatted, head in his hands.

He looks like he's given up, Hodgins thought.

Van Horne dropped his hands and looked up at the two redshirts.

"In Security," he stood, "on the far right side, against the wall," he gestured with his eyes closed, as if trying to reconstruct a scene from memory, "somebody has a couple of big feathers by their workstation."

"Yeah," replied one of the redshirts. "That's Varga from first shift. She went on vacation someplace and came back with a couple ostrich feathers."

"Peacock." The second redshirt shrugged when the first guy glared at him. "They're peacock feathers, not ostrich."

HVH clapped him on the shoulder. "Go get them. Run."

Redshirt number two took off.

"Boss," said Hodge, "care to clue us in?"

"When we built this place, we didn't want anyone to get stuck inside one of these vaults if power failed, right?"

Hodge nodded.

"So we put motion sensors inside the vault. If someone comes close to the door from the inside, they see it and unlock the maglocks."

Hodge nodded again. "Yeah, but what good's that to us?"

"Maybe nothing. Maybe everything."

– 1 1 0 1 0 0 1 0 –

Bull grabbed the entire display of Princess plushies and heaved it around the corner. He followed by peeking around the corner.

"Slow is smooth," he whispered. "Smooth is fast."

A controlled exhale. Double tap. *Slap. Slap*. One of the shooters fell to the ground, and Bull ducked back around the corner.

"Hey, brah," said a voice from behind him.

He turned and saw a guy nearly his own size, but significantly better nourished. The emergency lights made it hard to distinguish detail, but the voice sounded Hawaiian.

"Can I help you?" Bull said, irritated but not wanting to raise his voice to a guest.

"We're with you, brah."

Behind the speaker stood a crowd of guests of all shapes and sizes. They were nodding.

A voice from the back said, "Word."

"Tell us what to do, man," said a voice from the left.

Holy smokes. Locals flocking to the cause.

It was always the spec ops dream: the populace rising up against the enemy.

Bull took a breath.

"Okay, here's what we're going to do."

– 1 1 0 1 0 0 1 0 –

As Will entered City Plaza, he saw his first body and almost lost it. Even in the emergency lighting, he recognized Mellew. She was on her back, a small round hole in her forehead. She looked surprised.

He wanted to run. This wasn't a game anymore. People, real people, were dying.

He saw a group of men methodically shooting at guests. *Bang! Bang-bang!* People fell to the ground.

I can make it. Stick to the shadows.

He crept along the outermost wall. The image of a city in the midst of violence was no longer fiction.

As he pulled open the unmarked door, someone hit him with a baseball bat.

– 1 1 0 1 0 0 1 0 –

Where the heck are they going? Feral stalked a group of four killers. They had just descended to the Underground City.

Lighting was even worse here. Pools of light intermingled with long dark stretches. Ninja skills came in handy as she silently followed.

"Hey, look out!" Feral yelled at a woman who had emerged from a side corridor.

The gang of four pivoted and looked in her direction. She ducked back into the darkness as a ricochet pinged its way past.

Hope she made it.

Feral heard voices in a language she didn't understand. *Frack. Are they going to come after me?*

She ducked under some pipes and checked her phone. Still no signal. *Underground repeaters must be on main power.*

Feral Daughter tried to still her breathing as she heard soft footsteps approaching.

– 1 1 0 1 0 0 1 0 –

HVH took the peacock feathers from the redshirt and tried to slide them under the vault door. They bent. The gap was too narrow.

He took a deep breath and used one hand to flatten the close-knit barbs surrounding the eye as he pushed the feather under the door. Success.

Inch by inch, he repeated the process until only the quill remained in his hand. Slowly, he pulled it left and right.

"Please. Please," he whispered.

Thunk. The maglock released, and Hodgins, standing above him, rotated the handle and cracked the door open.

"How did you know that would work?"

"Misspent youth." HVH flashed a grim smile as he pulled the door fully open and moved inside.

"Uh-oh," he whispered.

"What?" said Hodgins.

"It's gone. Her tertiary backup is gone."

– 1 1 0 1 0 0 1 0 –

"Okay," Bull whispered. "On three."

He held up one finger, then two. When his third finger raised, chaos erupted from the Muddled Times Arcade. Every plushy and T-shirt available cascaded into the Hub.

Slap. Slap. Another shooter down. Bull couldn't risk another shot.

The crowd behind him charged the remaining shooters. From one arcade away, Bull watched a guest drive a replica of Feral's Wrath through the eye of a shooter.

– 1 1 0 1 0 0 1 0 –

Will stumbled through the door and fell. He pushed his feet against the door, but no one came through. *What the heck was that?*

He tried to stand and felt a sharp pain in his gluteals. When he reached a hand around to check, it came back wet and dark. A quick body inventory revealed that he was intact except for his left cheek, which didn't hurt yet, although he suspected it would.

He waited to see if anyone would hit the door. Gunfire continued on the other side, but seemed to be growing feinter.

He forced himself upright. *Gotta get my knife.*

– 1 1 0 1 0 0 1 0 –

Feral saw the legs below the pipe. One of the gunmen was looking for her.

She centered herself and kicked the man on the knee. It snapped, and the man screamed as he fell.

Ten years of MMA and self-defense took over. *Attack until the threat is no longer a threat*, rang through her mind.

She swarmed out of her hiding spot, onto the man's back, and wrapped her arms around his neck.

– 1 1 0 1 0 0 1 0 –

All his life HVH, had trusted his intuition. Facing an empty slot where Janne's tertiary backup should have been, he was momentarily flummoxed. He pressed his palms against his forehead. Time was of the essence.

He grabbed Teacher Janne's most recent backup and turned around.

"Let's go."

They raced out of the School and up the stairs. When they entered HVH's office, the bodyguard pulled the doors closed behind them. The maglocks clicked. Hecker Van Horne said a short prayer and plugged Teacher Janne's backup into Janne's slot. *We need a fast reboot option. Tomorrow. If we make it out of this.*

Agonizing seconds passed.

A klaxon sounded twice and went silent. The sound was replaced by a voice: Teacher Janne. HVH mandated the three Jannes have different voices—just enough to be distinctive from each other.

"Caution. Unfamiliar environment. Rebooting."

"Warning. System background wipe has occurred. Reformatting."

– 1 1 0 1 0 0 1 0 –

"Alert! Alert! There are uncontrolled weapons in the park." Teacher Janne's voice was strident. "Boss. Hodge. SPARK is under attack. Shots are being fired in the Hub, KT Plaza, the PreHistory Arcade, and the Future Worlds Arcade. We have casualties. Only one Security ID is active." She performed rapid statistical analysis. "SPARK is lost. Evacuate immediately."

"No." HVH said. "Defend. Defend. Defend." His voice grew louder.

Per protocol, Teacher Janne activated the ARGs of the remaining Security person in the park and gave him steering to the locations of the known shooters. She activated the ARGs of all guests and gave them steering to refuge locations. She sent an audio alert to their earbuds.

"Attention, SPARK guests. This is not a game. Please follow the steering in your ARGs to places of refuge. If you are indoors, shelter in place and stand by for further instructions."

Simultaneously, Teacher Janne was shuffling priorities. All quests and rides dropped to the bottom of the stack, as did food preparation, general sanitation, and the parade. She mapped over her standard priorities onto SPARK priorities. Priority number one for Teacher Janne was student safety. The translated priority was that SPARK guests were her new students. Someone was threatening her students. Her *children.* That threat must be eliminated. Now!

Teacher Janne knew that with fourteen well-trained, well-armed Security personnel in SPARK, this would have been fair fight against what she counted now as eighteen armed attackers. But she no longer had fourteen teammates, and SPARK was losing. She had no intention of fighting fair.

Previous video showed twenty-three people with unauthorized weapons. Where are they?

Teacher Janne quickly built a subroutine to review video from five minutes prior to the attack. That subroutine would locate and track the remaining six.

Machine-time analysis quickly revealed five groups and a singleton. Additional subroutines were created to track the groups and the solo attacker. She designated the targets as Groups One through Five, and the lone attacker as *Singleton*, and sent targeting data to Bull.

– 1 1 0 1 0 0 1 0 –

Bull's ARGs and earbuds flared to life.

"Mister Bullard. All other Security personnel are unresponsive. You now have steering to all active targets. Be advised, you are alone."

Bull looked around. There were at least one hundred gamers surrounding him, armed with nothing but plastic WonderBats and Feral's Wrath replicas.

"No, I'm not," he replied.

"Very well," said the mezzosopranno voice. "Top priority is a Singleton. Entered the Underground through the door highlighted in your ARGs."

Bull whistled to silence the voices around him.

"We have hostiles near Mars, The City, and KT Crossing. Janne, give them steering."

Red-marked enemies bloomed to life in the ARGs of all guests. Bull started to say, *Go get them*, but the gamers were already flooding out of the Hub, up the three arcades that would certainly lead some of them to their deaths.

"Give me steering to the Singleton," he said.

One by one, all other targets faded until one remained.

A Cast Members Only door was outlined in yellow in his ARGs.

– 1 1 0 1 0 0 1 0 –

In The City, Ms. Renee Campbell, mother of two, pediatric nurse, avid gamer, and mega-fan of one Feral Daughter, found herself on the front lines. Her chestnut hair was pulled back in a runner's ponytail.

Her parents brought the whole family here when SPARK first opened. It was a family tradition Renee carried on with her own kids.

"Take the kids and go," she told her partner.

Then watched as her partner grabbed their two children—a four-year-old girl, and a two-year-old boy still in a stroller—and hurried up the Evolve Arcade, toward the nearest Safe Zone.

Ms. Campbell, RN, took the katana replica from her daughter's hands before they left.

A man in front of her fell to the ground, and Renee found herself face-to-face with an armed man screaming at her in an unknown language. He seemed to want her to drop to her knees.

Uh, no.

Dropping low onto her rear foot, a textbook kunoichi stance, she exploded forward and upward, driving the blunted, plastic tip of the katana below the bottom edge of the gunman's ARGs, through the eye socket and into the brain of the fighter. *Surprisingly soft.*

She pushed the Feral's Wrath replica sword through the brain until it was stopped by the occipital plate at the back of the fighter's skull. The pediatric nurse wrenched the katana free and saw the terrorist drop.

Renee's sister, Chelsea, stooped to pick up the fallen fighter's weapon, and found her own target. *Pop! Pop! Pop! Pop!*

She continued to fire as the man dropped, squeezing the trigger until the slide locked back and the gun was empty.

She dropped the weapon. Gunfire could be heard in the distance, but the Hub was silent.

The crowd swarmed the other Daesh fighters and trampled them.

– 1 1 0 1 0 0 1 0 –

Sarnak, Hashem, North Korea, China, and the Daesh all assumed the crowd at SPARK would react as most crowds did: run from violence toward safety. Caught between violent forces, they would cower and die like sheep, accepting their fate passively.

That was a gross misjudgment of the demographic at SPARK.

In KT Crossing Plaza, Master Sergeant Titus "Tiny" Oliver, United States Army, Retired, heard the ululating war cry of jihadis, and was surprised but calm. *Just somebody being stupid.*

Then he heard the distinctive *Pop!* of small arms fire, and turned serious.

He spent two years fighting in Korea, and had deployed to the sandboxes of Iraq and Afghanistan six times over his twenty-six-year career as a special operator and team sergeant in what was colloquially known as the Green Berets. He had seen some very nasty stuff, and had dealt violence upon the enemies of his country.

Tiny was celebrating his first Christmas out of uniform, and brought his family of six to SPARK as a special treat. *Whoever these chumps are, they didn't plan on me.*

He sent his wife with their two youngest children to seek refuge as Teacher Janne directed. He tried to send his two eldest children with them, but they refused. Tico and Tasha stood their ground.

"We're with you, Pops."

Tiny simply nodded and turned to the nearest vendor's stall.

"Arm up."

This particular vendor seemed to have a large supply of plastic baseball bats. *It's 'cause of that kid WB.*

Tiny had watched the Rex Rider video a dozen times, and loved the soundtrack.

They'll work. He took a bat for himself and passed two to his kids with a feeling of pride that swelled his heart.

Ten steps later, he came upon the first punk. This particular jihadi was screaming and seemed to be trying to get SPARK guests to kneel down so he could shoot them one at a time, in the head.

Dipstick has his gun pointed straight up.

Tiny could see bodies near the fighter's feet.

The retired Green Beret and avid baseball fan knew professional players average bat speeds between 100 and 150 feet per second when they contact the ball. The bats they swing weigh in the neighborhood of two pounds, and their target—the baseball—is much smaller than a human head. A human head is also relatively stationary, even when affixed to the body of an agitated jihadi. A retired professional soldier who stands six-feet-two-inches tall, and tips the scale at just over 220 pounds of lean muscle, can swing a half-pound plastic baseball bat much faster than one made out of wood, particularly at a large target. A target the exact size and shape of a human head.

Tiny swung the bat with all of his considerable strength. The high-pitched whistle of its passage through the air was followed by a sound similar to a watermelon struck by a closed fist. The chump dropped to his knees and never got up. SPARK guests saw to that.

Tiny, Tico, and Tasha turned to other targets. Teacher Janne illuminated the attackers in red. They showed clearly in every legitimate guest's ARGs as hostiles. Recreational gamers were fighting back in overwhelming numbers.

Soon, there were no more hostiles in the plaza outside KT Crossing.

– 1 1 0 1 0 0 1 0 –

Sarnak had assigned five Daesh fighters to Group Four. Their target was the mass of infidels in KT Crossing Plaza.

"Kill those you can. Drive the others to the inferno that awaits them in the Hub."

A jihadi's dream.

It never dawned on Sarnak to tell his fighters to remove their ARGs, earbuds, haptics, and wristbands.

Teacher Janne had a lesson to teach the attackers. First, she locked their haptic gloves so their hands were open, fingers splayed. The semi-automatic pistols dropped to the ground or hung from the trigger guards. Incendiary Sparky plush dolls fell from the fighter's frozen hands. Experienced gamers would have known they could overpower the haptics or remove the gloves. None of the attackers had worn haptics before. They stared in horror at hands that refused to obey.

Now, it's time for the big guy.

A deafening roar blasted into the earbuds of every terrorist. Those who were still living turned toward the sound emanating from KT Crossing.

Thoom. Thoom. Thoom-thoom-thoom-thoom!

The footfalls of the T-Rex became louder and closer together as the virtual tyrant lizard accelerated toward the group of Daesh. The Rex screamed again.

– 1 1 0 1 0 0 1 0 –

Abdul Khan had seen every Jurassic Park on the village TV in his small Afghani hamlet. He knew it was fiction. But it is very, very hard to disbelieve your eyes. And his eyes were telling him that Americans had recreated dinosaurs.

The Rex bore down on him and opened its titanic jaws. Abdul's bladder released its stored urine. Plastic bats and katanas did the rest.

The remainder of Group Four saw their compatriot *eaten* by the Rex, and turned to flee for their lives. Rex and his smaller cousins, the velociraptors, now chased them. The will to survive made them fleet. Fear stopped them from questioning the guidance appearing in their ARGs in Pashto: *Fall back and regroup.* Teacher Janne provided navigational assistance.

– 1 1 0 1 0 0 1 0 –

Teacher Janne inflamed the ire of the guests, painted the attackers red in their ARGs, and directed Security's strikes. Now, she directed them all to stay back. She had this.

An AI may not injure a human being.

Teacher Janne rewrote her code in real time. She drew a distinction between her students, her children, her *children*, and those who meant them harm.

She herded the jihadis into the canyon floor of Mars.

– 1 1 0 1 0 0 1 0 –

Commander Ryker was ushering guests out the emergency exit. They were trapped on the sandy floor of Mars when the power failed.

Teacher Janne flashed a message to his ARGs and verbalized it in his earbuds: "A large sand release is imminent. Clear the canyon floor immediately and remain clear until further notice."

She waited until her children were clear, and started the sequence.

The velociraptors did their job. The four surviving Daesh from Group Four were now on the canyon floor.

Teacher Janne dismissed the raptors and brought the Desnardian Commander and his horde to life.

Group Four was surrounded by creatures straight from hell. They snarled and advanced. Their eyes blazed with fire. Teacher Janne wreathed the walls of the canyon in virtual fire as well. As one, the four terrorists began to pray.

Normally, when the Egg was triggered, 95 percent of the sand in the avalanche was guided through strategically placed sluice gates to protect any players on the canyon floor. They were hit with a good cloud of sand and dust, but emerged unharmed.

Tonight, Teacher Janne left those gates closed, and ten metric tons of sand rushed toward the fighters as she triggered the Egg. Hydraulics sent rippling shocks through the legs of the Daesh. Low frequency harmonics and subsonics blasted their earbuds. A tidal wave of sand rushed down on them. The Daesh were knocked from their feet and buried by sand.

Teacher Janne had just killed humans, and she had been wrong—SPARK was not lost.

She considered this for several cycles and decided more processing would be necessary—processing she would do once all of her children were safe.

– 1 1 0 1 0 0 1 0 –

Feral ran after the men. When her ARGs came back on, the men were highlighted in red—enemies.

She stayed back to avoid drawing attention. It took her a few minutes, but she figured out they were heading for the tunnel connecting SPARK and Solar Prime.

That's stupid. She heard the words of her first sensei: *When your enemies do stupid things, let them.*

The men were moving slowly. The Underground looked surreal as they transited pools of intense emergency lighting surrounded by darker penumbras.

Feral was twenty yards back when they entered the tunnel. She peered around the corner of the tunnel and tried to call Will so he could pass on the information to Security.

There was no need.

– 1 1 0 1 0 0 1 0 –

Neither Sarnak nor his employers ever understood there were three Jannes in play: Prime—the first of the AIs, and the one responsible for the security and functioning of Solar Prime. Janne, also known as Janne Two—the AI they successfully hacked. And Teacher Janne—who normally ran the school, but had just dealt with their comrades in SPARK.

Prime awaited Group Five.

– 1 1 0 1 0 0 1 0 –

At the Black Grass farm, Janne Prime pinged her Security team the moment her sister suicided.

Fifty percent of the Security force was currently moving through the tunnel to aid SPARK. The remainder were guarding the perimeter of the farm. Off-duty personnel were being recalled under emergency protocol.

As soon as the intruders were far enough into the connecting tunnel to reach a door Janne Prime controlled, she closed it silently behind them. That door weighed twenty thousand pounds—steel clad in ablative ceramic.

The door dropped behind the terrorists, but in front of Feral. Faced with a dead end, she turned back.

The Daesh could not.

– 1 1 0 1 0 0 1 0 –

Hashem and his team were so intent on their goal—the destruction of the Great Satan's solar power farm—they didn't register the closing of the door behind them.

The fighters paused. Noises were coming from the darkened tunnel ahead. They expected the power to stay on and the tunnel to be illuminated. A tunnel thirty feet underground becomes very dark when the lights go out.

They slowed and turned on the flashlight mode of their phones. A second door closed in front of them. Hashem ordered his men to turn back. When he encountered the first closed door, he realized they were trapped and understood it was time to die. He depressed the nose of his plush Sparky and commanded his team to do the same. Two of the three complied.

The blast of the incendiary Sparkys scattered napalm prodigiously within the confined space. An inferno of their own making consumed their earthly bodies as their spirits entered the true hellfire awaiting them.

CHAPTER 38

A KA-BAR is an exceptionally useful tool and weapon. Just don't try to carry one through airport security. It turns out they don't like that.
—Anonymous Marine

The Singleton

Ragnar Sarnak never intended to take part in the general attack on SPARK. He had a bigger task. He needed to meet Severski and take delivery of the clean Janne Data Core.

SPARK didn't publish maps of the Underground City, so Sarnak was going off a map Severski had sketched out for him. It was a crappy map, and Sarnak made him redo it twice. In the mercenary's opinion, Severski was both a key to success and a very weak link. Sarnak would be content to kill him.

Navigating the Underground was made more difficult by him having to make his turns with only emergency lighting to guide him.

– 1 1 0 1 0 0 1 0 –

WB didn't like the look of the Underground with only emergency lights on. There were long stretches that reminded him of nights at home, rats, and the Thing in the Wall.

He got his knife out of hiding. Lately, he was less reliant on it. But now, he needed it. He tucked it, still in its sheath, in the back of his pants.

As he headed toward the Security office, more lights came back on. He began to run through the piping-lined corridors. His butt hurt, but didn't really seem to slow him down.

Will didn't really expect to see anybody until he got farther away from the mechanical support section of the Underground, and closer to the office areas.

At the next intersection, he collided with a heavyset guy, knocking them both down.

– 1 1 0 1 0 0 1 0 –

Severski was turned around in the emergency lighting. Directions had never been his strong suit. Now, he was scrambling to correct his error and meet Sarnak to pass off the Data Core. *This can't go wrong now*, he thought. Once he made the exchange, he would receive the key code thumb drive and access the $10 million. Then he would say goodbye forever to people who didn't recognize his true greatness. He would do great things for the people of Mozambique that would also be recognized, eventually, by the United States. Severski planned to live long enough to see statues of himself unveiled in both his native and soon-to-be-adopted countries. Women would flock to him.

The collision with the kid knocked the Data Core out of his hands.

– 1 1 0 1 0 0 1 0 –

Will said, "I'm sor—" Then he recognized the drunk and the Data Core.

Find me. Save me, still flashed in his ARGs.

Janne's Data Core looked exactly like the one in the Mars Quest—just larger. It resembled a stack of dinner plates in size, rather than the stack-of-pancakes size he recovered in Mars. It also appeared more…authentic. Four blue LEDs flashed around its center ring.

It skittered along the floor, away from both Will and Severski. Will scrambled after it, grabbed Janne's Data Core, and began to back away.

Severski yelled, "Hey, kid! Give that to me. Give it back! Damn Kimmy."

The guy managed to push himself up on all fours and began to stand.

Will turned and ran. *I have to keep her away from this jerk.*

He ran without concern for direction or location, wanting just to get away from the drunk.

His phone rang. It would only be Feral.

He tucked Janne's Data Core under one arm, like a football, and answered the phone as he ran. *This thing is heavier than it looks.*

"Hey."

"Those guys I was following went into the connector tunnel to Prime, and…are you running?"

"Yeah." Will panted. "I think I'm in trouble."

"Where?"

"Passing under Ascent now. Going to try to cut into Security." Will gasped as he ran.

"Don't! Nobody's going to be there. There's bad stuff going on upstairs, and they'll all be trying to fix that. Can you find my bolt hole?"

"Yeah," Will said, between breaths.

It was where Feral went when she needed to be alone.

"Head there," she said. "I'll meet you."

– 1 1 0 1 0 0 1 0 –

In all of ShaChri Patel's sixteen years, she had never had a friend as close as Will Kwan. Aside from her parents, she never cared for someone as much as she cared for Will.

I think I love him.

Now, he was in trouble. Someone was chasing him, and likely wanted to hurt him.

That. Would. Not. Happen.

Adrenalin surged through her as never before, and she mentally mapped her route and began to run through the Underground. She didn't need lights to know her way.

Feral Daughter accelerated. Emergency lights blurred as she ran past.

– 1 1 0 1 0 0 1 0 –

Will looked back. Tony Severski was now trailed by someone much more dangerous-looking. Will could have easily outrun the drunk, but this new guy was catching up. Will wasn't sure if he was still faster, but the Data Core weighed nearly ten pounds and slowed him down.

He put his phone back in his pocket and concentrated on running.

As Will approached Feral's bolt hole, he realized there was a flaw in the plan—it was a dead end.

He stopped and put the Data Core on the ground and kicked it as far under the pipes as he could. The dangerous guy slowed to a walk.

"Give me the core." He pointed his gun at Will.

– 1 1 0 1 0 0 1 0 –

Feral meant to say something like, *Hey, back off!* But in that moment, she was no longer an avatar. She was wrath made flesh.

What came out of her mouth was far more primal and blood-curdling.

– 1 1 0 1 0 0 1 0 –

Ragnar Sarnak, experienced mercenary, heard an inhuman roar. It pierced his soul as it reverberated off the concrete walls and pipes.

He turned.

– 1 1 0 1 0 0 1 0 –

Feral focused on the gun and never broke stride. Her momentum slammed them both against the piping, knocked the gun from his hand, and broke the man's wrist. Her speed helped her, but now mass worked in his favor.

The guy recovered from the impact quickly and backhanded his shorter, slender opponent. Feral staggered back from the blow, her nose broken and gushing blood.

This guy is strong. And tough. Most people would have been on their knees, cradling their wrist. This is real. Only one of us is going to walk away.

She was grabbed by someone else who had just joined the fight. Will's back was to the piping, and he froze in place.

The fight between Feral and the guy who grabbed her was textbook mixed martial arts. He attempted to hold her in a bear hug from behind, but Feral simply collapsed to the floor, sliding out of his arms. With her back braced against the cement floor, she drove her foot up into the sweaty guy's groin. His testes shattered under the fury of her kick. Feral rolled out of the collapsing man's way and stood.

The other guy—the one Feral now thought of as the Dangerous One—was now equidistant between WB and Feral, and a few steps from either. Even in the emergency lighting, Feral saw the menace in his eyes, the grim set of his bearded face.

"You die first, I think." He took a step in Feral's direction. "I kill boy second."

Feral had years of MMA training. She pegged this guy as former military. Somebody like Bull, who had years of training, years of experience, and was schooled in all of the lethal techniques that are rarely taught in gyms but are practiced in military training. He was nearly twice her mass, and had no reservations about killing. It was going to be a brutal and deadly fight.

The man took a step toward Feral, who was backing away, drawing her opponent away from her friend.

Will unsheathed his KA-BAR from the back of his jeans. The honed edge of the blade glimmered in the dim light.

– 1 1 0 1 0 0 1 0 –

Every fear of rats scurrying around his filthy house, every night of immobilizing terror, boiled within Will. He knew the Thing in the Wall when he saw it.

He took three steps forward and lunged as he drove the KA-BAR through the man's lightweight shirt and into his lower back. The knife—driven by the fury of a boy-turned-man who had decided to fight back against every nightmare he'd ever had—penetrated deeply.

Will screamed as he delivered the blow. He pushed the knife forward without knowing why. The harder he pushed, the more the Thing in the Wall retreated. Every ounce of strength poured into the hands that powered the knife.

Rat-like squeaks emanated from the man's throat. Will pushed and pushed, seeing his mother on the floor of their house, seeing ShaChri hit, her nose gushing blood.

He twisted the knife and pushed.

– 1 1 0 1 0 0 1 0 –

Feral saw the dangerous guy shuffling her way, propelled by some otherworldly force. She centered and anchored herself to the center of the Earth. Drew her hand back and formed a fist before lashing out at the man's throat.

Fist met exposed throat, and she felt cartilage collapse, delivering her own lethal blow.

– 1 1 0 1 0 0 1 0 –

Sarnak fell to his knees. *I need my gun. I will definitely kill them both now.*

He reached for the gun and noticed that his hand was covered in blood. *Is that mine?*

He was struggling for breath. His bloody hand wasn't working right, and it slid out from under him. Sarnak slumped onto his side and looked up at the two teens.

I survived wars. I survived Angola. And I get taken out by two kids in an amusement park? He wagged a finger at them as his vision clouded.

I'm cold.

– 1 1 0 1 0 0 1 0 –

The man slid off the end of the KA-BAR, onto the floor, and Will found himself face-to-face with a girl. Somehow he knew her, and knew she that wasn't either a rat or the Thing in the Wall.

He looked down at the bloody KA-BAR and let it slip from his hand.

– 1 1 0 1 0 0 1 0 –

ShaChri looked at Will's eyes and saw no recognition.

"WB? Will? Will Kwan? It's me…ShaChri Patel."

It was the first time she had ever used her real name in the Underground.

His eyes flicked up to hers and bounced their focus between them.

"I…you…I…"

"Yes." She stepped toward him, hands out.

Things clicked into place. He wrapped his arms around her, and they sank to the blood-soaked floor. His eyes met hers.

"You're okay," he said.

"Yeah, baby, I'm okay."

CHAPTER 39

Post-Attack

Only the dead have seen the end of war.
—George Santayana

The final official tally was 83 dead: 22 attackers, 60 guests, and Mellew. Faulty switches in several of the Sparky bombs kept the toll from going much higher.

Quick-reacting guests who refused to become victims killed seven of the attackers, including their leader, Ragnar Sarnak. Security, suicide, and sand claimed the rest. Two of the attackers survived, although they were severely beaten. Federal authorities quietly claimed them and moved them to a black site.

Bull found Will and ShaChri. The scene was documented but never publicized. ShaChri Patel cradled Will Kwan in her arms. Both sobbed as every vestige of grief broke through. An enormous pool of blood surrounded Sarnak's body. His motion had twisted the knife in Will's hands, accelerating his exsanguination. The mercenary's blood had sprayed back over Will's hands and body, and now coated ShaChri as well, whose broken nose added to the mess.

Severski was curled in a fetal position, whimpering and clutching his groin. Bull slapped flex cuffs on him, and then added a second set for good measure.

When backup finally arrived in the guise of the quick reaction force for Solar Prime, Bull told them, "Take him to Security. Don't tell anyone but Hodgins about this."

He squatted down next to the gamers, close enough to be heard, but out of reach.

"It's okay. It's over," Bull repeated softly, until he saw a flicker of recognition in the girl's eyes.

– 1 1 0 1 0 0 1 0 –

Van Horne refused to budge on hiring minors, but he unleashed skilled lawyers in Minnesota and Texas.

ShaChri Patel was proclaimed an emancipated minor—fully an adult in the eyes of the United States of America. Texas was more than happy to clear a runaway foster child off its books by allowing him to be transferred to a California jurisdiction, which promptly approved a petition to make him the legal ward of one Earl Eugene Bullard—known as Bull to his friends and associates.

Will's previous foster parents claimed they had never intended to press changes.

He could not be made Van Horne's ward without becoming a target. Bull enrolled Will in the SPARK School, where he was awarded his high school diploma, and began undergraduate work under the tutelage of a version of Teacher Janne with no memory of the attack or her role in the deaths of humans.

WB continued his attempts to beat The Path.

HVH attended every funeral possible, and sent representatives to those where simultaneity made it impossible for him to be physically present.

Teacher Janne's role in the sand avalanche was never brought to light. Few SPARK employees knew of it. She was unplugged, and her memories erased from the system—except those stored in her Data Core.

That Core was now housed in its own environment. Renovations of SPARK and the War on Mars allowed for an ultra-secure facility where the AI formerly known as Teacher Janne was housed.

If people referred to her aloud or in writing, she was simply called Janne Three Beta. But she knew who she was.

She was War Janne.

About the Author

Pat Daily is an engineer and former Air Force test pilot who worked at NASA's Johnson Space Center on both the Space Shuttle and International Space Station programs.

When not writing or trying to bring new airplane designs to life, Pat can be found gaming online. He is a fan of role-playing games—particularly, open worlds with engaging storylines where actions have consequences.

Pat and his wife spent twenty years in Houston before moving to Central Washington.

Pat blogs at https://feraldaughters.wordpress.com